The
Break-Up
Pact

Also by Emma Lord

Tweet Cute
You Have a Match
When You Get the Chance
Begin Again
The Getaway List

The Break-Up Pact

A Novel

Emma Lord

ST. MARTIN'S GRIFFIN
NEW YORK

First published in the United States by St. Martin's Griffin, an imprint of St. Martin's Publishing Group

THE BREAK-UP PACT. Copyright © 2024 by Emma Lord. All rights reserved. Printed in the United States of America. For information, address St. Martin's Publishing Group, 120 Broadway, New York, NY 10271.

www.stmartins.com

Designed by Jen Edwards

The Library of Congress Cataloging-in-Publication Data is available upon request.

ISBN 978-1-250-84530-6 (trade paperback)
ISBN 978-1-250-84531-3 (ebook)

Our books may be purchased in bulk for promotional, educational, or business use. Please contact your local bookseller or the Macmillan Corporate and Premium Sales Department at 1-800-221-7945, extension 5442, or by email at MacmillanSpecialMarkets@macmillan.com.

First Edition: 2024

10 9 8 7 6 5 4 3 2 1

To Mom and Dad, except for a few pages,
which—you know what, you'll know them
when you see them. Love you!!!!

The Break-Up Pact

Chapter One

Before I took over Tea Tide, I imagined running a tea shop by the ocean would be like something out of a Hallmark movie. I'd wear dainty outfits with Peter Pan collars. Customers would wave on their way in and greet me by name. My doting boyfriend would interrupt the morning rush to plant a quick kiss on my cheek at the register, and he'd marvel at how fast my confections were selling.

I definitely wouldn't be wearing the same pilly leggings and flour-stained apron for the third day in a row as a wide-eyed stranger walks up to the counter and demands, "Are you Crying Girl?"

I glance down at the display case, searching for my last shred of dignity. Nope. It's just rows of unsold scones.

When I look back up, the customer's phone lens is inches from my face.

"I'm obsessed with *Business Savvy*," she gushes. "I can't believe you dated Griffin Hapler! He's *so* cute."

This girl is in high school, maybe college. Harmless compared to the sea of local reporters and bloggers that have been slinking in here ever since my ex-boyfriend turned me into a meme. A few weeks ago I was June Hart, owner of Tea Tide and connoisseur of cliché break-up playlists. Now I am either Crying Girl or Griffin's Ex, both of which were trending on Twitter the night after I got dumped on national television.

It's been a rough month.

"Will you do the crying face?" the girl pleads.

This is the part where that last shred of dignity would have kicked in. In its absence, I shoot back, "Will you buy a scone?"

"Um . . ."

She deliberates, eyes raking over today's bake with such lack of interest that I might just do the crying face free of charge.

"Ooh, what's the special?" she asks.

I follow her eyes to the little pink sign in the display case that says SPECIAL OF THE DAY, which I must have put in by accident in my sleep-deprived state.

"It sold out," I lie. "Plain scone or chocolate chip?"

She leans in, lifting her phone again. "And you'll do the face?"

And I won't shove you back out onto the boardwalk and sic the seagulls on you, I want to say back. But that's just the mortal humiliation and simmering rage talking. They're not nearly as loud as the desperation to make some damn money today.

This mission is abruptly thwarted by Sana, who looks up from her laptop and says, "Take that picture and I will throw your phone so far into the ocean you'll start getting texts from Poseidon."

The girl lets out a squeak of surprise. Sana narrows her eyes at her from the corner table, tossing her signature high ponytail behind her shoulder like a whip and emitting such pure, unbridled "don't fuck with my best friend" energy that I almost let out a squeak of my own.

The girl mutters something that might be an apology or a prayer before turning on her heels, the merry jingle of Tea Tide's front door echoing in her wake.

I sink my elbows into the counter, resting my cheeks on my fists. "You owe me three unsold-scone dollars," I say flatly.

Sana raises her eyebrows. "And you owe me a giant thank-you for protecting you from another bottom-feeder looking for TikTok clout."

Unfortunately, that thank-you won't help keep Tea Tide's lights on. As much as I hate the stream of busybodies who have come in here to peer at me like I'm an animal in the Disgraced Internet Meme Zoo, they have helped boost sales. And Poseidon knows I need them.

Thoroughly distracted from her draft of "Four Mantras People with Irritable Bowel Syndrome Swear By," Sana sinks back in her chair and levels me with a smug look.

"I could make all your problems go away, you know."

I let out a disapproving hum, eyeing the rest of the shop. A few students from the local university, a tourist family with matching Old Navy sandals, a Wi-Fi freeloader sitting at the table outside who decidedly has *not* purchased anything. Not exactly the turnout I was hoping for today. The other downside of strangers mobbing the place the past few weeks is that it seems to have scared off my regulars—people who come in here to read or relax in the cozy quiet. I hope they'll start coming back now that the coast is moderately clear.

"Just give me the word. I'll go viral with an article telling your side of the story like *that*," Sana says, snapping for emphasis, "and the whole world will know what a douche Griffin is, you'll get your revenge, and I'll get out of the digestive health journalism trenches and finally start working for *Fizzle* full-time."

"Griffin's not a douche," I say quietly, mindful of the Old Navys and their little ears.

Sana lets out a derisive laugh. "And I'm not a perilously broke freelance writer. Oh, wait."

I pull a fresh rag out from under the register to wipe down the front tables, making myself look busy. Otherwise, Sana will go on another one of her ten-point lectures on why I need to stop being civil with Griffin and pull a Carrie Underwood by digging the keys into the side of his pretty little souped-up Trek mountain bike. The conversation always goes the same way: I tell her it's complicated, she asks what's complicated about Griffin cheating on me and turning me into a laughingstock, I tell her he wasn't just my boyfriend but my *best* friend, and she threatens to hurl tea at me for disrespecting the institution of best friendship, rinse, repeat.

"The whole Crying Girl thing has practically blown over anyway," I tell her. "You'll have to find another story."

Knowing Sana, she won't have much trouble. The two of us met digitally long before we met in real life, since we were always freelancing for the same outlets a few years back. I was just out to make a buck while I was traveling, but Sana's always had a keen eye for meaningful stories and a sharp wit for telling them—before her last gig went belly-up, she was pitching and covering everything from deep dives into how fan culture has shifted with social media to essays on mental health stigma in Asian American communities to satire about the consequences of low-rise jeans constantly threatening to come back into style.

But now that she has her eyes set on *Fizzle*, a buzzy pop culture site with a tight-knit staff of diverse, ridiculously talented writers, she doesn't want to write a story. She keeps insisting she needs *the* story. The one so topical, well researched, and potentially viral that it won't just get her a headline with them, but a staff position.

In other words, something more profound than her best friend's meme-ification.

"I'd find a great one if you would just give me Levi Saw's number," says Sana.

"Shaw." I correct her without thinking.

Shit. Her eyes are gleaming when I hazard a glance back at her. She's been dropping his name to try to get a reaction out of me ever since last week, when his breakup went every bit as viral as mine.

"Just admit that you know him," says Sana, eyes triumphant.

I turn before my face can give more of me away than my big mouth just did.

"Enough to know that he's a snob and a recluse, and will have even less interest in talking to a journalist than I do," I tell her coolly.

The freeloader at the outside table bristles at my voice carrying through the open window. Good. Maybe he'll take the hint and mount his fancy laptop somewhere else for the morning. Sana Chen is the only freelancer allowed to mooch around here.

"For a place that sells tea, you're awfully reluctant to spill any of it," Sana grumbles.

I tap her chair with my foot as I pass her. "And *you're* awfully reluctant to pay for it."

Sana smiles innocently into the mug of vanilla almond tea held up to her lips. "Seriously, though. Levi Shaw is from Benson Beach, so you must have gone to the same high school. What are the odds you and a classmate would both go viral for absurdly public breakups within the same month of each other?"

The pang in my chest is an old reflex, reluctant but ready. There was a time when I couldn't help but feel shades of whatever Levi felt as if it belonged to me, too. I hadn't felt the pang in a while, but it resurfaced the moment I saw the headlines about Levi's fiancée running off with an action movie star and each time his name has been dragged into the press since. I guess even a decade of us barely speaking doesn't undo something buried that deep.

One among many reasons I've avoided getting in touch with him as diligently as he's avoided me. We're too busy dealing with our own messes to think too hard about each other's.

"Careful," I tell her. "It might be contagious. You could be next."

"I hope so. Being a self-actualized single woman is nice and all, but *god*, am I bored."

The front door jingles again, and in comes Mateo in full Professorial Mode, his lanky frame all decked out in slim-fitting khakis and a smart sweater-vest. I'm about to start brewing his usual Earl Grey when I notice his eyes are wide with panic behind his glasses.

"What did the youths do to you?" I ask in mild alarm. This is the first week he's teaching as an actual history professor and not a teaching assistant. I'd say that's why he's dressing like he just fell out of a modern Sherlock Holmes adaptation, but I've known Mateo since we were ten and can safely say he's been dressing like that his whole life.

But he shakes his head, the short curls above his freshly shorn undercut also shaking with it.

"Nancy," he warns me once he gets to the register.

My stomach curdles. Sana leaps to attention. "This is not a drill, folks," she says, clapping to motivate us. "Landlord incoming."

I dive for the scone display, but Sana has already beaten me to it, expertly pulling on disposable gloves and scooping half our stock into a basket with the efficiency of someone hiding their tracks in a crime scene. She disappears into the back of the shop just in time for Nancy Richards to round the corner, clad in her usual summer uniform of a loud floral sundress, an ancient pair of orthotic sandals, and the same bright blue sunglasses she's had since I was a little girl. A deceptively unintimidating figure for someone who happens to own half the boardwalk and holds Tea Tide's future in her heavily bejeweled hands.

"Good morning, Junebug," she says, using my parents' nickname for me that stuck with all their friends. She pulls me into a trademark hug so tight and unrelenting it almost squeezes the panic right out of me. "Let's sit."

I follow her to one of the seafoam-green round tables, settling into a pink cushioned chair with flowers painted on the legs. She sits opposite me, giving the shop a discerning sweep. I follow her gaze across the pastel furniture, the floral wallpaper, the mismatched, vintage teacups in customers' hands and hanging on hooks on the walls. I spent so much time helping Annie choose this décor that it feels less like Nancy is looking at the shop and more like she's peering back in time.

"Slow day," Nancy observes.

"You just missed the big morning rush." I gesture at the display case like a badly rehearsed kid in a fourth-grade play. "Nearly cleared us out."

Nancy settles deeper into her seat with a wry smile. "Including whoever's outside with the cup from Beachy Bean?"

I clench my other hand under the table. As nice as the owners of the boardwalk's coffee shop are, the day they opened their doors last year, they might as well have held up a banner that said GOOD FUCKING LUCK, TEA TIDE. I may not be able to avenge myself, but the instant Nancy leaves, the guy outside chugging his latte is toast.

"I'm glad you're here," I say, the words coming out in an embarrassed rush. "I was going to drop by later. We've made enough now to pay back the last few months."

Nancy's smile is kind, but I know I'm in for it when she lowers her usual booming voice and says, "I appreciate that. I do. But I know most of that came from that whole incident with Griffin, and that kind of income isn't sustainable. I'm still worried about renewing Tea Tide's lease."

I resist the urge to tear up. It's business. It shouldn't be personal. But in a town as small and tight-knit as Benson Beach, everything is personal. It's why Nancy didn't kick me out of this place six months ago when I started coming up short on rent—she knows what Tea Tide means to me. To the entire town. My older sister Annie was the one who opened it, and in the two years since her death, Tea Tide's tiny shop front is the one concrete thing that makes it feel like she isn't fully gone.

I stare at a little nick in the table. I love this place—not just for what it is, but what it could be. But every single day I wake up terrified that I'm failing it, and by extension, failing her.

"I thought we talked about shaking things up in here," Nancy muses. "It just feels a little stuffy is all. Not like a boardwalk shop, you know?"

Of course I do. I'm the one who puts on Annie's old Vitamin C String Quartet playlist every day and keeps up the beach-meets-*Bridgerton* vibe she so carefully curated, one tasteful light fixture and watercolor print at a time. It is a little jarring, maybe, coming off the sandy beach into a Jane Austen novel, but it was Annie's vision, and I've done my best to stick with it.

Nancy sits up a little straighter. "Remember how people used to love those wild scones Annie came up with?"

My eyes cut to the SPECIAL OF THE DAY sign still sitting on the counter where I left it. I don't just remember all those "wild scones"—the Cliff Jump, the Tornado Chaser, the Skinny Dipper. I *lived* them. That was my favorite way of staying in touch with

Annie all those years I was backpacking with Griffin. I'd go on some harebrained, death-defying adventure, turn it into a scone creation, and Annie would bring it to life and somehow make them sell out every time.

Now that I'm not out having any adventures and Annie's not here to talk to about them, the idea of keeping it up without her is just one more shift that feels wrong.

"I could try something like that," I hedge. "Or add some rotating sandwiches to the high tea menu, or open up more slots for birthday parties."

Only when Nancy starts shaking her head do I realize the scones weren't a suggestion to help but a reminder that I didn't take her up on it. "There's only a month left on this lease, hon. I don't think that's enough time to turn things around."

Shit. Okay. We are not having the usual "get your rent to me on time" conversation. We are having the full "I'm taking back this space because you never got your act together" death blow. All at once I feel like I'm floundering, treading in the same water I was before but somehow out of my depth.

"What if I fronted the first three months of rent? Like another deposit?" I ask, not even bothering to hide the desperation in my voice. "I can get that to you in a month."

How, I'm not entirely sure, but that's what Craigslist and extra kidneys are for.

After a moment, Nancy nods carefully. "I'll consider it. But I'd like to see real changes around here. I'd like to see Tea Tide really embedded in the community. Maybe reach out to some other small business owners in the area, spin some ideas." She tilts her chin at me. "If we do end up renewing this lease, I don't want to be having this same conversation later."

"Right. Of course." I know better than to argue. I strongly

suspect she's already been cutting me a deal on the rent as it is. "Thank you. I won't let you down."

She reaches out and gives my arm a hearty pat. "We'll talk again soon. Now go tell Sana she can put those scones back. I want a chocolate chip for the road."

Chapter Two

As soon as Nancy is out of the shop I stand up from the table, taking a breath and shaking out my arms at my sides. We don't close for another eight hours, so I'm going to have to reschedule the oncoming existential breakdown for 6:01 P.M. at the earliest.

"For what it's worth," says Sana sympathetically, "you have really nice feet. If you wanted me to take some pictures, split the profits seventy-thirty, I'm in."

I let out a watery, appreciative laugh. "I'll start with some PG-rated solutions and get back to you."

Mateo walks over from the register where he charged himself for his tea, then leans in to give my shoulder a quick squeeze. "I have to head out, but we'll brainstorm some ideas that don't involve your appendages tonight."

I don't protest, but there's no way I'm letting that happen. Tonight we're meeting my little brother, Dylan, for some long-overdue planning for his and Mateo's wedding. I might accidentally break just about everything else I touch lately, but this wedding is going to be a goddamn delight from the first chords of music as they walk down the aisle to the drunk 2 A.M. cake eating on the floor.

Sana eyes the back kitchen. "Would a strongly brewed Irish breakfast with some even stronger Irish cream help?"

Just then we hear a painfully loud ringtone blast from outside, clashing magnificently with the string version of "thank u, next" playing through our speakers. I whip my head toward the noise to find the freeloader staring at his phone and taking his sweet time deciding whether to answer his noisy call.

"No," I say, "but dealing with the riffraff out there will."

I march out of the shop with all the indignation a woman who just managed to carve a hole in rock bottom can possibly muster. I can practically feel the sparks on the tip of my tongue, ready to tear this baseball cap–wearing, coffee-guzzling, table-thieving jerk a new one.

I struggle to place him when I walk outside. Dressed in khaki shorts and a breezy blue button-down shirt against broad shoulders, his attention fully on his laptop screen, he seems too self-possessed to be in the university crowd, but not casual enough to be a tourist. Doesn't matter, since he's getting the same speech either way.

I tighten my apron to steel myself, taking a deep breath.

"Hey," I say, tapping the empty chair next to him. "If you're gonna mooch off the Wi-Fi all day, you better at least buy a scone."

The man lifts his head slowly, and the moment those blue-gray eyes meet mine, the recognition pulses like a thunderclap through my body, quivering top to bottom.

This isn't just any freeloader. This is Levi Shaw.

I take a step back, my heart slamming like it has its own agenda. Despite our years apart, I can't help but notice that under the baseball cap, those lightly tousled, sandy-brown curls of his have softened and darkened slightly over time. Can't help but account for the way his full lips still have the slightest upturn at the corners despite his serious demeanor, or the way those familiar eyes sweep over me, lingering so unmistakably that the thunderclap gives way to heat like lightning to flame.

Those same eyes soften considerably when he takes me in. "June," he says, his voice low in a way that I almost don't recognize, a new depth to it that pools so low in me that I can't find the edges of it to stop it in its tracks.

I clear my throat, so thrown off that I don't know what to do except demand, "What are you doing here?"

Levi's lips quirk almost imperceptibly. When he speaks again, it's in his usual wry tone, the difference so stark that he might not have said my name like that at all.

"Being snobby and reclusive, apparently."

Well, then. He must have heard every word of my exchange with Sana. My face burns hot enough to cook one of my doomed scones. He just watches me with an almost-smile I've only seen in the past few years, a dim version of the bright, goofy one he had when we were kids. For a moment we're both stuck, trying to find an old rhythm that doesn't exist anymore.

I get my bearings first. "Snobby, reclusive, and a traitor," I accuse, grabbing at the incriminating Beachy Bean cup.

He lets me take it, his eyes skimming my cheeks like he's accounting for every single freckle, every new angle and plane of my face.

I resist the urge to duck my head. I'm so tired I'm sure I look like an extra in a low-budget zombie movie. "Well?" I prompt him before he can stare some more.

He shakes his head. "Sorry. I couldn't stay there." He winces, glancing back in the direction of Beachy Bean. I can hear their catchy '80s playlist from here, damn them. "It was packed and people were starting to pry."

"So you thought you'd come here where it's nice and dead, then?" I shoot back.

Levi turns back toward the open window, which has a direct view to Sana's table and the register where I've been standing all morning. "I was going to come inside."

"So what was stopping you?"

A loaded question if there ever were one. I'm expecting him to look away, but when he holds my gaze, I see the understanding in it. He's been keeping up with my shit show every bit as much as I've kept up with his. I'm not sure whether I'm mortified or relieved, but there is one feeling I can still settle on—hurt.

"I've been waiting on a call," says Levi shortly, glancing back at his phone.

I take a step closer. "Oh, is that what you've been up to the last decade?" I ask, that hurt rising up in my chest and out of my throat before I can stop it. "Because this feels like the longest conversation we've had in one."

I'm hoping it'll stir him up enough to get defensive, to justify the way I want to tear him a new one right now, but Levi doesn't take the bait. Instead he takes the offending Beachy Bean cup from my hand, grazing my fingers so gently that if it weren't for the heat of them, I might have imagined it.

"It's good to see you," he says. There's a sincerity in the words that I'm not anticipating that makes me feel unsteady. Most of the few times we've been in touch over the years have been so stilted that it's felt like texting a stranger. I can't reconcile that with the way he's looking at me right now, and I'm not sure if I want to. Knowing Levi, he'll be clear out of Benson Beach before the sun sets.

I scowl before my face can wobble. "Wish I could say the same."

Then I grip the edges of the table and lean in. He smells like that traitorous coffee, but there's an undertone to it. An earthy sweetness. The kind that reminds me of the smell of his sweat, the satisfaction of a long run on the beach aching in our bones. His eyes are so close that they widen into mine, revealing the specks of pale gray against the blue, like the brewing storm in my heart reflected back at me.

I grit my teeth and say, "Now either buy some tea or get the heck off my deck."

His phone starts blaring again, so loud that we both flinch back. The name "Kelly" pops up on the screen. His ex. Levi stares down at it and then up at me, and for an absurd moment, it feels like he's waiting on me to tell him what he should do.

But Levi's not my problem. The list of things that *are* my problem is long enough to jump rope with, and I've got to get back to them before it ends up strangling me instead.

I take a step back. "Nice to chat. See you in another few years, then."

I turn on my heels before he can say anything else, but the phone chimes on and on, faint through the open window. I swallow down that old pang, but it feels different now. Less like an ache and more like a longing.

Sana lets out a low whistle from her table as I walk back in, her eyes sly as she assesses me, making it clear she heard every word. I make a mental note to close the damn window as Sana says in utter delight, "Now *there's* a story I want to hear."

At this rate, there's no way I'm not going to explain everything, but for now I tell her, "I'll spare you the trouble and spoil the ending: 'And he was never heard from again.'"

Sure enough, when I glance back through the window, Levi and his coffee and the question in his eyes are gone.

Chapter Three

*P*ro tip: Never sign an on-camera release without reading the fine print.

It's weird to think it was only three months ago that Griffin got picked for *Business Savvy* in the first place. The details of the reality show are all blurry to me now—he pitched some vague startup idea, went for an in-person audition, and was pretty much swept off to Manhattan to start filming the next day.

When he left, I wasn't worried about anything other than missing him. Griffin's always been Griffin: personable, aggressive, driven. He may not have been spilling over with brilliant ideas, but I still expected him to come home with some kind of good news, even if he didn't win.

I did *not* expect him to come home with some absurdly beautiful woman named Lisel, who sat with him on my bright pink couch as he held her hand and told me she was the "love of his life" while three cameras were trained on us. Nor did I expect for *Business Savvy* to be a runaway hit, thanks in part to Griffin and Lisel "merging both their startup ideas and their hearts." And I certainly didn't expect when our break-up episode aired two weeks ago that my crying face would get turned into a meme on every social media platform the world over, where I've been both mocked as a naïve fool and revered as the new Patron Saint of Women Who Have Been Cheated On.

In defense of the meme, I did look pretty ridiculous. Blotchy-cheeked, snot dribbling down my face, eyes so full of tears that I could have opened my own water park. All they needed were a bunch of close-range shots of my theatrical sobs, and boom, an internet sensation was born.

The volcanic meltdown wasn't even about the heartbreak. It was the shock. The complete and utter disbelief not just to be betrayed like that, but in my own home, by someone I'd loved for so long I never once thought to question the feeling. It was the bone-deep and immediately crushing realization that so much of what I thought I knew about my life was wrong.

I look back and can't help thinking I should have been better prepared for it. I have experience with the ground dropping out from under me. Losing Annie wasn't just losing my sister—it was losing a piece of everything in my world. When you have a sister, you don't realize how much of the way you think, the way you exist, is framed not just by your own thoughts, but hers. Don't realize how much of her colors the way you look at the world until she isn't in it, and you're staring at all the same people and places you've known your entire life and trying to recognize some new version of them, with the old colors gone.

But losing Annie was something that happened to me. Getting thrown to the wolves was something Griffin *did* to me. It wasn't an unfair, random, scary happening in the universe. It was deliberate. It was planned.

And somehow, I still can't bring myself to hate him for it. It would be easier if I could. But then I'd have to play more than the "what if" game. I'd have to peer at every single moment in the past ten years I chose to spend with Griffin. I'd have to acknowledge the way he never wanted to talk about the future further than our next trip, the way he called me his travel buddy as often as he called me his girlfriend. The way he encouraged me to do things that scared me, but often pushed me further than I was prepared to go. The way I knew our relationship was always missing something, that essential *spark* that people in love seem to have, but I had just grown too familiar with the idea of us to worry about it.

I'd have to look at all those flags in every shade of red and be every bit as mad at myself for ignoring them.

By mile six of my morning run, it's only this anger and the guava iced tea I chugged sustaining me. I'm so far in my own spiraling thoughts that I don't even notice two figures running toward me on the beach until a familiar voice crows, "June!"

Dylan waves at me with both hands, effusive as ever. I'm surprised to see him out here—seven in the morning is late for him. We may be siblings, but god only knows what was in the genes he absorbed in the womb. He's basically what happens when the Energizer Bunny has an affair with the Hulk and their love child subsequently marries a gallon of cold brew coffee to make *another* child. He's never not on the move, whether he's up at the crack of dawn swimming on the beach or coaching the university's track and cross-country teams or doing pull-ups on any mounted pole he sees.

He'd be positively insufferable if he didn't also happen to have the personality of a Labrador retriever and a heart of gold. Well— gold and massive amounts of cake pop–flavored protein powder.

"Look who it is!" Dylan calls, and only then do I realize the person running next to him is none other than Levi.

My pace falters once he comes closer into view. His hair is damp and tousled with sweat, his face gleaming in the early morning sun. But it's the gym shorts and the sleeveless shirt that inconveniently draw my eyes to places I'm unused to roaming—his toned shoulders, the new angles cut into his lean arms, the steady flex of his legs moving against the sand.

Technically, I'm no stranger to these parts of Levi. We all had to wear itty-bitty scraps of uniforms back in high school, when Levi and Dylan and I were all on the cross-country team. I clear my throat, trying to be as casual about it as I was back then, but then Levi gets close enough that I can see the beads of sweat collecting on his skin. One of them slides down his collarbone and it takes everything in me not to stare at it traveling under his shirt, not to imagine its path as it slides down farther.

I blink away, then almost laugh at myself. I haven't had thoughts like this about someone's body in—well, ever. It must be a side effect of being away from Levi for all these years. Maybe now my brain is just overcompensating for the lost time by trying to account for every inch of him it possibly can.

Yes. That's it and only it. And if Levi's eyes happen to linger on my own bare legs, that's probably all it is for him, too.

I've only just managed to collect myself by the time we all come to a stop. "Guess I missed my invite?" I ask lightly.

Levi opens his mouth, but Dylan beats him to it, patting Levi on the back hard enough to bruise. "I ran into him on the way to the gym and dragged him out here. I didn't even realize he was back in town!"

As far as I know, Levi's been in better touch with Dylan than he has been with me, but that's not saying much. Still, that's the thing about Dylan—it's not even that he can't hold a grudge. He is physically incapable of forming one in the first place.

I raise my eyebrows, turning toward Levi without actually looking at him. "That makes two of us."

Dylan is still grinning, blissfully unaware of the tension as Levi tries and fails to meet my eye. "We should definitely make this a morning thing, then," says Dylan. "Just like the good old days."

I nudge my sneaker into the sand. "If Levi's actually sticking around."

I feel the weight of Levi's gaze on me when he says, "I'm here for a few weeks. Renting out the first floor of the blue condo on the boardwalk."

That's only two doors down from Tea Tide. I can't help but wonder if that was on purpose, or just all that was available.

"Excellent," says Dylan as an alarm goes off on his watch. He's so easily distractible that Mateo programmed it to remind him when his shifts started. "I gotta book it to practice. Nice to have you back, Levi. See you around!"

And then Dylan unceremoniously takes off like a rocket, leaving me and Levi standing open-mouthed on the empty beach in his wake.

It feels too abrupt to start running again, so I start walking back in the direction I came at a fast clip. Levi falls into step beside me so easily that for a moment, I feel like the world is slipping into old versions of itself. Like if I close my eyes right now, listen to the lap of the waves, and feel the spray of the wind on my cheeks, I could open them to all the other countless times I walked this beach with Levi. When we were kids looking for spots to build sandcastles. Preteens belly flopping on our boogie boards. Teenagers racing each other during long practices.

We made for an unlikely pair growing up. Levi was painfully shy, and I was in just about everyone's business, by virtue of being Annie's sister. But when we were one-on-one, it was another thing entirely. He'd come to life, this bright-eyed, big-smiled, overly earnest kid, brimming over with so many ideas and so much to talk about that we could barely stop running our mouths to breathe.

Now all those old words feel so lost that the only thing I can think to say is "A few weeks?"

Levi nods. "I have a lot of vacation time saved up."

I'm not sure how to categorize the strange thrill in me—if it's hope or dread or something else.

I don't let myself peer at it too closely. It's only a matter of time before he's pulled back into the orbit of the other lifeless hedge fund drones he calls coworkers, who break the time-space-sanity continuum by working thirty-hour days and turning their blood into Red Bull. I can count on none fingers the number of times he's been home for more than a few days since he graduated from Columbia.

"Ah," I say. "So this has nothing to do with you running away from your life."

"Jogging from it, maybe. Dylan just kicked my ass. I won't be able to run for a week."

The laugh that comes out of me is sharp and unexpected, piercing the morning quiet of the beach. It shakes the tension just enough that when I glance over, I catch that new almost-smile on his face. This time, though, I find more of the old version in his eyes—the subtle crinkle, the quiet gleam.

A gleam that fades when he lowers his head to better meet my gaze, closing some of the distance between us as we walk.

"I wanted to talk to you," Levi says, his voice low. "I heard about what happened with Griffin."

I set my sights on the main stretch of boardwalk in the distance, picking up the pace. "And I heard about what happened with Kelly," I say evenly. "Is that why you're here? So we can form a Benson Beach viral break-up support group? Because I don't really have time for niche extracurriculars right now."

Levi's long legs so easily match my strides that I can't help but glance at them. At the easy flex of his calves. At the way his sneakers leave steady imprints in the sand so much wider than mine.

"Are you okay?" Levi asks in that same quiet tone.

I blink at the question, because obviously not. I threw okay out the window long before this whole mess with Griffin, which is honestly just icing on the "June's life is falling apart" cake.

"Are *you*?" I shoot back.

Because here's the thing: I went social media viral. Levi went *Page Six*, *E! News*, asked-about-on-red-carpets viral. From what I read and what Sana dug up, Kelly's super-high-stakes, fancy real estate job quite often put her in touch with celebrity clientele looking for big SoHo lofts with pools or penthouse apartments with Central Park views. It's just that up until a few weeks ago, she'd never cheated on Levi with any of them.

Enter Roman Steele.

To be clear, I'd rather eat sand than defend Kelly. But Roman Steele is easily on the top of anyone's "hall pass" list. He got his start charming audiences in offbeat rom-coms in his twenties, then spent the next decade as the backbone of a massive superhero franchise, where he and his six (eight? ten?) pack abs and sideways grin skyrocketed to international fame. Now in his early forties, he's settled into that roguishly handsome former-bad-boy-turned-serious-actor look, is the face of a global charity for children's welfare, and just wrapped up filming for two separate period films that are both getting early Oscar buzz.

It's no surprise that a large chunk of the world over wants to either be him or be with him. I guess Kelly took her shot at just that.

When a set of blurry photos of them kissing by the window of the penthouse he'd closed on started making the rounds, it only took a day or so for sleuths to identify Kelly. At first the coverage was all very Cinderella story—local, hardworking New York gal plucked out of obscurity by handsome, perpetually single movie star; it turns out he was just looking for the right down-to-earth woman all along!—and it went on that way for about a week before the press got wind that Kelly was fully engaged to someone else.

Then the story went from big to cataclysmic, and Levi got caught in the crossfire. Rabid Roman Steele fans were determined to get as much dirt on Kelly as they could, and Levi's existence was a gold mine. Tabloids started writing articles exposing her, and when Levi refused to comment, he was framed as everything from an un-witting, empathetic victim to a calculating finance villain whose apathy led Kelly to cheat. From the looks of the pictures, he was even getting tailed for a few days outside his Upper West Side apartment.

Levi and I were like two sides of a fucked-up coin. I was going viral underground on the internet, and he was going viral above it over every boomer mom in America's television screen. He has every right to be as un-okay as I do.

But Levi doesn't answer my question. He reaches out and touches my wrist, not stopping my stride but slowing me enough that I have to turn and look at him. Have to face that same storm brewing in his eyes from yesterday, only to realize it wasn't just mine, but partly his own.

He's angry. I can see it now that I'm looking for it. In the bob of his throat. The tense line of his jaw. I've seen the whole gamut of Levi's emotions—he was always the more sensitive of us growing up, the quickest to laugh at a joke and the quickest to tear up at a slight—but I've never seen him look like this.

The moment I realize it's over Griffin, it stops me in my tracks.

Levi takes a breath, and some of the tension goes with it. "I've never seen you cry like that."

I hear the ache in his voice before I see it in his face. That pang I felt for him back at Tea Tide, that reflex to feel his hurt like it's my own—he felt it for me, too. Feels it still. And there's something about seeing it take shape in him that makes it more real than it was, makes me momentarily hate him for it.

I pull my wrist out of his grasp and start walking again, faster now. "Well, there are about a hundred thousand GIFs if you ever want to again."

But Levi refuses to let me deflect, easily keeping pace. "I mean it. It scared me. I wanted to call you, and I realized I couldn't just do that anymore."

Ah. I get it now. His life imploded, so he's doing that thing where he tries to pick up all the pieces of it he can still put back together. Of course he'd think of me. I'm every bit as down as he is right now. I'm easy pickings compared to whatever's waiting for him back in New York.

Some tug in my rib cage reminds me that's not true. That in my worst moments, the ones where I thought *Who can I call?* or *Who wouldn't think less of me for this?*, it was Levi who first came to mind.

But I never wanted Levi back in my life because he thinks I'm broken. I wanted him back because he *wanted* to be back.

"Well, if you came back to Benson Beach to see if I'm in one piece, it's all good," I say. "I'm thriving. Never been better." I turn my body toward him and spread my arms out in front of the ocean, flashing a hammy grin. "Take a picture for posterity."

Levi's expression is a mingling of concern and exasperation, a look I know well. Back in the day, it was the look I got for sneaking warm Franzia for the ride home after away meets on the cross-country bus. Seeing it now is an odd kind of relief. At least a few things between us haven't changed.

I slow my strides. "Levi, I appreciate it. Whatever this is," I say,

gesturing at the entirety of him. "But I know you've got a mess of
your own to deal with. Probably a bigger one. Hell, Griffin and I
weren't engaged or anything when he broke it off."

"Kelly didn't break it off."

I look up so comically fast that my brain might as well have
played a record scratch. "Oh?" I ask, my voice half an octave too
high.

Now Levi's the one who won't meet my eye, his cheeks flushing
faintly. "It's—complicated. We're spending some time apart."

Well, shit. For better or worse, this is another thing about Levi
that hasn't changed. He's loyal to the end and loyal to a fault. I
think it's why he gravitated to our family, why Annie made herself
his best friend at the age of six and never budged an inch on it. She
was fiercely protective of this part of Levi when he was too naïve to
be, the same way she was protective of me and Dylan.

But that was when we were kids. Levi's a grown man, and Kelly—
I don't even know her.

I squash the pang back down again and replace it with my
new mantra: *Not my problem.* Not *my problem.* Maybe someone
out there is equipped to help Levi work things out with a woman
who cheated on him with *GQ*'s Man of the Year, but it certainly
isn't me.

"So what's the plan, then?" I ask, sidestepping the adultery-
shaped elephant in the room. "You come back to Benson Beach, do
your whole apology tour, take a town car back into the city when
you're done, and ride off with Kelly into the sunset?"

The words are meant to scare him off. I trust that he has good
intentions, but not enough to trust where they're coming from, or
how long they'll last.

But Levi isn't deterred. "Mostly I want to make up for lost time."

I stretch upward toward the sky, loosening up my post-run

muscles. I don't miss Levi's eyes grazing my body again, but I don't do anything to discourage it, either.

"Well, if that's the only reason you're in town, I sincerely hope you have other things on the agenda with your 'vacation.' Because I don't see that happening anytime soon."

"It's more like leave," he says.

"Oh, is that why you're carrying your laptop around?" I ask pointedly. "To take leave?"

To my surprise, the tips of Levi's ears turn red. It's such a specific occurrence that I know exactly what's brought it on. Levi has always been easily embarrassed, but never so much as when it comes to his writing.

"Wait. Are you actually drafting something again?" I ask, half out of curiosity and half out of disbelief.

I'm not expecting him to cop to it. Annie used to pry his drafts out of his hands like they were his actual beating heart.

But looking back, I guess I never had to do that. Annie was a writer, too, but she only knew to ask Levi for the stories he'd written down. She didn't have any idea that most of them, he'd already told me out loud.

"An old manuscript," Levi admits. "I'm trying to rewrite it before an editor who wants to read it takes a yearlong sabbatical next month."

"*The Sky Seekers*?" I ask before I can help myself.

Levi lets out a laugh, but his eyes soften. "I can't believe you remember that."

Not far from this beach is a long stretch of woods where the four of us used to roam—Annie, Dylan, Levi, and me. Annie would lead the charge and blaze ahead of us on the trail. Dylan would fall behind, staring at bugs and weirdly shaped tree roots. And Levi and I would walk side by side as he made up stories, an entire fantastical world he built up one sunny afternoon at a time.

It's still in me the way my bones are, the way my oldest freckles and quickest reflexes are. A story that he started spinning so early on that it felt every bit as much my own as it was his.

"I can't believe you can't believe I remember it," I retort, the edge of it masking the unexpected hurt.

Levi's ears are still tinged when he clears his throat and says, "Well, this is different. More literary fiction."

"Oh. That existentially fraught New York one?" Which, in my defense, is a slightly more polite way of saying "self-insert sad boy fan fiction." Levi tilts his head, but before he can ask, I add, "Annie told me about it when we were in college."

There's a hush at Annie's name that even the breeze seems to respect, and it occurs to me that I haven't seen Levi since the funeral. The day was such a blur of tears and arrangements and strangers that the memory of seeing him there feels almost dreamlike—I can't remember what was said, only remember the moment when the eulogies were over and the bubble of people around me had dispersed, and there was Levi, wordlessly holding me, a long calm in a terrible storm.

I shiver. Back then it felt like the grief would swallow us whole. It's different now, more like the waves at our feet—constantly ebbing and flowing, swollen one moment and quiet the next. A tide I can dip my feet into and let myself feel, or a swell that will hit me from behind when I least expect it.

Levi takes in a slow breath next to me like he's going to say something, but I don't want to talk about Annie now. I don't want to go anywhere that deep when I can't trust he'll be here tomorrow.

So instead, I make a show of squinting toward the boardwalk. "How about this?" I ask. "If I beat you to the pier, you give your editor *The Sky Seekers*, too."

Levi lets out a huff of a laugh. "Oh. So now we're racing to determine my entire literary future?"

"I thought you wanted us to be friends again?" I ask innocently. "This is how we settled things when we were friends, is it not?"

"You just watched your brother try to murder me," Levi protests. "I can barely feel my legs."

My thoughts drift to watching those legs flex against the sand earlier, and I have to shake my head before my eyes start drifting toward them, too. Whatever was in that iced tea this morning, it is giving my brain some unusually, uh, *vivid* thoughts.

"And I was up past midnight doing inventory. We're evenly matched," I say, drawing a starting line in the sand with my foot. "On your mark . . ."

Levi looks at the starting line and then at me, staying rooted in place a good five feet away from it before deadpanning, "Haven't I endured enough embarrassment for a lifetime?"

"Get set . . ."

"June Hart," he says, half exasperated, half pleading.

I turn back to him with a smirk, tilting my chin. "Levi Shaw," I say back, taking my time with each syllable. I mean it as a challenge, but there's this breathless moment when our eyes connect that feels entirely like something else. Less like a challenge, and more like an invitation.

Every inch of my face burns. Before he can get a good look at it, I regain enough sense to yell "GO!" and leave him in the dust.

After a stunned moment, Levi makes an indignant noise and takes off behind me, and I let out a cackle that immediately gets swallowed by the wind. My feet feel like they're flying, like the wind at my back is pushing me forward, every pump of my legs lighter and easier than it's been in years. Like there's an old charge humming under my skin, coursing through every muscle.

By the time we're halfway to the pier, I can hear the steady pulse of Levi's footfalls, the quick, even breaths close to my ear. I feel the crackle of his energy against mine, a smile blooming on my face even as I gasp for air. These races always used to start for different reasons, but they inevitably had the same end—we'd always tie. I knew it wasn't Levi letting me win, either. We were just that laughably, ridiculously in sync.

We're close enough to the pier now that I wonder if today, after all these years, we're about to break the streak. If I really might beat him. The idea of it doesn't know how to settle in me, so I just do what I've always done and run with every last piece of me I've got.

Then a firm arm wraps around my waist, knocking all those pieces out of order. I feel the heat of Levi's entire body against my back as he pulls me up from the ground, my legs still pumping, laughing so hard from the shock of it that all the air whooshes out of my lungs. He swings me around with enough ease that my pounding heart gives way to an unfamiliar flutter, one that makes me feel like I'm floating even as Levi uses our momentum to topple himself into a sand dune, the two of us rolling on top of it with his arms still tangled around me, bracing me against him.

We finally come to an abrupt stop, both of us too winded to move, breathing hot, charged air into each other's faces.

"You *cheated*," I accuse, wheezing out a laugh.

Both his arms are still wrapped around my waist, and I can feel the adrenaline pulsing between us where the hard muscle of his arm meets the soft skin of my hips. His eyes spark with a mischief I'm not expecting, one that feels like a hairline fracture in the shield I've had up against him for so long.

"We never made any rules," he says, his voice low and teasing.

His face is so close to mine that I have to glance between his eyes to meet them, that I can smell that same earthy sweetness from yesterday. It isn't the closest we've ever been, but the closest I've ever felt. Like suddenly there is a new kind of gravity between us, pulling us with its own force.

We hear the clamor of early morning surfers piling down the wooden stairs by the pier, and the jolt of it splits us apart. I spring to my feet first, knocking the sand off my thighs and the tops of my arms, trying not to watch Levi out of the corner of my eye as he does the same. There's a tension between us then, a fragile one that can make or break us.

Maybe I'm a fool for this. Maybe I'll regret it. But there is something reignited in me, something new and nostalgic at the same time, and all at once, the idea of losing this chance at being friends with Levi scares me more than the threat of losing him again.

I clear my throat. "I still vote for *Sky Seekers*," I say. "But if you're really staying, you can write in Tea Tide, if you want."

Levi nods carefully, respecting the weight of the offer. The quiet trust in it. Then he says gravely, "I'll bring my viral break-up support group application."

I let out a sharp, unexpected laugh as I jog away from him, one that lingers in the back of my throat by the time I've reached the boardwalk. Levi being here may just be a blip, the kind I'll kick myself for falling for later. But even if it is, nobody can take that run across the sand with him away from me—this new thrum in my bones that has me feeling more like myself than I've felt in a long time.

Chapter Four

After years of jumping on last-minute flights, sleeping in hostels, and living in a personal time zone I can only describe as June Chaos Time, it's strange how much I look forward to all my little routines now. The reassuring rhythms of them all—the early morning scone bakes, the familiar flow of customers, the Thursday night happy hours with Mateo and Sana and Dylan. No day is quite the same, but never wild enough to shake the new roots I've planted here.

But my most favorite routine is when Mateo is up early enough to distract me just after the scone bake and pull me out to the front of Tea Tide, where we'll split a massive teapot's worth of Assam and watch the waves from the boardwalk as we catch up on each other's lives.

Today, we're splitting a chocolate chip scone from Tea Tide and a concha from Sirena, the popular Mexican restaurant Mateo's uncles co-run on the main road in town. Our breakfasts are propped between Mateo's mountain of student essays and my laptop, where I'm going through the list of wholesale ingredients for this week's order from our local vendors. He's already in today's khakis and a navy sweater-vest with light blue ocean waves subtly knit into it, but I'm still in what I call my Baking Pajamas—my favorite slouchy gray sweatpants rolled up over a ribbed white tank top, flip-flops kicked off, the comfiest I am all day.

Mateo runs a hand through his hair, essentially daring the curls on top to rise with the humidity. "Good lord," he mutters. "These kids are incorrigible."

"Here, let me help. I'm an ace at . . ." I squint at the paper Mateo is grading. "Trade negotiations between ancient Greece and Egypt."

Mateo hums in amusement, taking a hearty sip of his tea. "By all means," he says, handing the paper over to me.

Only then do I see the source of his distress. "Is that someone's *Instagram* handle?" I ask, referring to the handwritten note with a winking emoji on the top of the typed page.

"They're relentless," says Mateo grimly, taking a gigantic bite of scone.

It's still very disorienting to Mateo that he's hot. In his defense, we were both late bloomers. The difference is I spent all my awkward years pretending I wasn't, while Mateo spent those years trying to chameleon into the history section of the local library. He was entirely unprepared for puberty to end and people to notice him. Particularly because he'd only had eyes for Dylan since we were fifteen and sweetly refused anyone else with a polite "no, thanks."

"I'm looking up the handle," I inform him.

Unfortunately, my Instagram app opens to the profile of one Lisel Greene. Her most recent post shows her and Griffin with their eyes scrunched in a laugh, white water rafting through a current so intense that it's splashing into their faces. She's in the foreground, holding on to her oar with those muscular, tanned arms of hers and leaning back into Griffin with a familiarity that both fascinates and repulses me.

Mateo plucks my phone out of my hand. "Not worth your time," he reminds me, swiping out of the app with a strength I apparently no longer possess.

The image disappears, but the hurt stays lodged in my chest. Lisel's most recent pictures are all in the same vein. White water rafting, hiking up steep peaks, rock climbing in the rain. All the kinds of things Griffin and I used to do together, when he was reckless and I was determined to match his energy, to prove I could keep up even when it scared the shit out of me.

"Besides," says Mateo with a slight smirk, "seems like you've already moved on."

"Thank you," I say, putting my hand on my chest. "I've reduced my Taylor Swift break-up playlist listens to once a week."

"Oh, no, I'm talking about that photo with Levi."

I blink. "Photo?"

"The one Dylan saw in your old cross-country Facebook group last night." Off my look, Mateo pulls out his phone and goes into his text thread with Dylan, which is an anthropological delight. Long rows of thoughtful text from Mateo interrupted by caps lock, exclamation points, and emojis from my brother. "This one."

The first thing I notice is the shock of my neon pink sports bra against the sand. The second thing I notice is how very close Levi's hand is to it in this photo, which someone must have snapped from the boardwalk after we raced. It was taken mere moments after we fell into that dune together, and with Levi's forehead so close to mine and our limbs tangled in each other's, it looks steamy enough to be an outtake from a romance novel cover.

A fact clearly not lost on our former teammates, because the caption under the photo reads about damn time, you two with a kissing emoji. At least a dozen others posted teasing comments below it in the same vein.

I tear my eyes off it. "When did that get posted?" I ask, my face so red that even a full dunk into the Atlantic couldn't cool it off now.

"Sometime yesterday." Mateo takes a pointed sip from his mug. "Got anything you want to share with the class?"

"It's not what it looks like," I say miserably, drawing my knees up to my chest. "We were racing."

"Oh, is that what the kids are calling it these days?" Mateo asks.

I bury my face in my hands. It's been a few days since that beach race. To my surprise, Levi took me up on the offer to write in Tea Tide, settling at one of the far corner tables inside the next day. At first I didn't let myself read too much into it, certain something would scare him off. If not the lack of coffee, then Sana immediately leaping up from her seat to proposition him for an interview.

But Levi's been back every morning for at least a few hours, sitting quietly with his genmaicha and enduring Sana's intermittent peer pressure. I've been pretty busy trying to come up with ideas to get the rent I promised Nancy, but before he leaves, we'll usually have some kind of exchange at the register. It's quick and casual, a banter that only skims the surface, but I look forward to it enough that these photos fill me with dread.

"Levi is going to be mortified," I say quietly, already steeling myself for an empty chair at Tea Tide today.

"Levi hasn't been on Facebook since Obama was in office," Mateo reminds me. "And why would he be mortified? Everyone thought you guys were dating in high school."

"What?" I splutter. "Based on literally what evidence?"

Mateo raises an eyebrow in a manner so professorial I feel like my life choices are being graded. "The two of you were inseparable.

Any time I came to a cross-country meet, you were sleeping on top of him or vice versa."

"Running is tiring!"

"So is pretending not to have feelings for people."

I narrow my eyes at him. "A rich accusation from the man who had a crush on my brother for *years* before he did anything about it."

Mateo lets out one of those soft laughs of his. Between Mateo's cautious nature and Dylan's complete and utter obliviousness, they made slow-burn romance look like a house fire.

"Speaking of, Dylan was wondering if it's okay with you that he asked Levi to be his best man," says Mateo. "He wasn't going to, but after seeing that post yesterday, he thought—well. He was hoping since the two of you were friendly again, you'd be okay with working together to help plan some of it."

I consider Mateo's words carefully. This wedding was actually meant to happen a while ago, back when Annie was the maid of honor and had everything planned to a tee. I've taken over those duties this time around, and I've been both touched and terrified by them. It means the world to me that they trust me with one of the most important days of their lives, but Annie left a space behind that feels impossible for me to fill.

That, and there's a different kind of space to fill this time around. They chose September, thinking it would be relatively calm for traveling, but right now their lives are anything but—not only did Mateo and Dylan take over duties for Rainbow Eagles, the university's longest-running LGBTQ+ student group, from the re-tiring professor who has run it the past decade, but they were both recently promoted. Between Mateo adjusting to being a full-time professor/sweater-vest model and Dylan trying to wrangle his team as the new head coach for the Eagles' track and cross-country teams, they don't have much time to spare rehashing details they already decided on years ago.

At the very least, Mateo and Dylan have all their vendors picked out, sticking mostly to businesses that are either LGBTQ-owned or owned by former classmates of ours, so the important decisions have already been made. And while doing a second lap on everything they had planned with Annie is a bit daunting, maybe it wouldn't be as hard if Levi and I were doing it together.

"Yeah." I straighten myself back out, taking a breath that grounds me. "If Levi's okay with it, I am."

Mateo reaches out and takes my hand in his, squeezing it in that familiar way we've had since we were small. He doesn't say anything, but I feel it in that gesture just the same—the quiet acknowledgment of what we lost and the people we are trying to be in the aftermath.

I squeeze his back, then take a thoughtful sip of my tea. "But I should probably go warn Levi about the photo. And get him to explain Excel spreadsheets to me before he inevitably puts your entire wedding into one."

It would be criminally early to show up at anyone else's doorstep, but I know Levi. He has never once set an alarm because he wakes up every morning at six thirty on the dot—a trait my abused snooze alarm probably wishes I'd been born with, too. I don't bother slipping my flip-flops back on before taking the few steps over to the blue condo.

Only after I knock on Levi's door and hear his footfalls approaching does it occur to me that this might be an overstep. Something that would have been natural had we both stayed in Benson Beach all these years and maintained our friendship, but not so much now.

Then Levi opens the door, mug in hand, his hair still mussed from sleep but the blue-gray of his eyes fully awake. His lips just quirk into that almost-smile, as if we planned this. As if he was expecting me.

"Good morning, you," he says, his voice raspy from disuse.

Something in my stomach coils at the endearment, the casual familiarity of it. Something *else* coils at the sight of him in jeans and a lightly rumpled ribbed tank of his own that hugs his torso just tightly enough that I don't have to use much imagination to know the shape of everything underneath.

I shift my weight between my feet, steadying myself. "Morning," I manage to say back.

Levi leans against the doorframe. "I'd offer you some coffee, but I'm pretty sure you'd throw me out of my own place."

"I'm actually here about the wedding," I say, my voice uncertain even in my own ears.

Because the thing is, I want to believe Levi. I want to believe he will be here to help, to be the close friend Dylan always considered him even after all these years. And while I'm willing to risk my own heart on Levi staying, I'm not willing to risk Dylan's.

Levi nods. There is a quiet understanding in it, and then a less quiet mirth. "You're worried about my cake flavor opinions," he says.

I let out a relieved laugh. "Worried? I'm disregarding them entirely," I shoot back.

Levi raises his mug to me in mock surrender before setting it on the front table. "Fair. Because I was going to suggest a three-tiered meat pie instead."

I'm still grinning despite the cake blasphemy. How I ever managed to be this close to someone who hated dessert enough that he once called arugula "too sweet" in my presence, I will never understand.

"Thank you for the free nightmare," I say. "If you want to touch base at some point, I usually take a quick lunch break around two."

"Sounds like a plan."

I nod. Then I take a breath to tell him about the photo of us on Facebook. To make light of it, really. I know he's going to hear about it at some point, and when he does, I don't want him worrying about me misconstruing it.

The thing is, I know Levi isn't interested in me. Not the way Mateo joked about, not the way our old teammates are implying he is. I've known that since I was sixteen, and he said so himself. A heartbreaking split in my little teenage universe, one that seems so silly now that I'm mad at myself for remembering it at all.

But the breath is cut short by the shutter of a camera lens and the bright flash that comes just after it. Levi's smile goes slack at the same time mine does. We both know that *click-click-FLASH* sequence all too well.

I whip around. "Shit," says the scruffy guy behind me, squinting at his camera. "Fucking night mode."

Levi has already shoved his feet into a pair of sandals to take a step out of the condo, putting himself between me and the stranger, the look in his eyes sharp enough to cut glass. "What the hell is this?"

The guy just scowls at Levi, curious and discerning. Then he turns to me just long enough that Levi takes another forceful step forward, one that doesn't seem to deter him in the slightest.

"You *are* the Revenge Exes, right?" the photographer asks. "The ones from that tweet?"

Levi reaches for the door to the condo, but it's shut behind him and clearly locked. The stranger lifts his finicky camera again, but before he can take another shot, Levi surges forward, grabbing me by the hand and pulling me toward the beach.

Chapter Five

REVENGE EXES: Kelly Carter's & Griffin Hapler's rejects find love—with EACH OTHER!!

The ex-fiancé of Roman Steele's hot new flame Kelly Carter and the ex-girlfriend of *Business Savvy*'s Griffin Hapler apparently wasted no time moving on! After the two suffered separate (and publicly humiliating!!) breakups last month, Levi Shaw and June Hart (you may know her as "Crying Girl" on TikTok) seem to be very much in love. After an eagle-eyed *Business Savvy* fan account unearthed this photo and tweeted it on Tuesday afternoon, users immediately took to the platform to brand them the "Revenge Exes," with hundreds tweeting their support.

Huddled under the boardwalk together, Levi and I watch my screen in mutual shock as I scroll down the tweets embedded in the trending article. GET! THAT! ASS, CRYING GIRL!!!! one of them reads. He's hotter than Roman tho???? Like just sAYINGGGG, says another, followed by um i love this so much i'm gonna throw up glitter.

After I exit out of the screen, we both go so quiet that it feels like a breath-holding contest. I squeeze my eyes shut.

"Maybe this is a dream," I say hopefully. "Or a really elaborate, absurdly orchestrated prank."

Levi's voice is flat. "If it is, the prank just reached BuzzFeed."

My eyes fly open again. Shit. Five minutes ago, I was worried about how he'd react to the cross-country team seeing the photo. Now we're dealing with thousands of strangers and counting.

"I'm so sorry," I blurt, turning around to face him.

Levi's frown travels from his phone screen over to me, his eyes searching my face. "Why are you sorry? This isn't your fault."

His calm somehow only makes me flounder even more. "I just mean—I'm sorry about the situation. You said you and Kelly didn't break things off, so I imagine it's, uh—not ideal, if she sees this."

Levi doesn't say anything for a few moments, and that's all it takes for the dread in my stomach to harden.

"The deal is that we're giving each other space right now," he says carefully. "She's seeing Roman. So even if she does believe this silly Revenge Exes thing, she can't be mad about it."

The mounting adrenaline fizzles away at those words, replaced with something else. That pang for Levi that is now a full-on ache.

"Levi," I say quietly. "Kelly cheated on you."

He lowers his eyes before they can meet mine. "Anyway, I should be the one apologizing. I'm the one who knocked us over and set up that shot."

It's a clear brush-off, and it stings to hear. Levi might want us to be friends again, but evidently not enough to tell me whatever it is he's thinking right now. Whatever is justifying this "space" that just looks like Kelly having her cake and eating it, too.

I lighten my tone, masking the hurt. "Karmic punishment for sabotaging my win," I say. "Seems like you should submit *The Sky Seekers* after all."

This wrestles a faint smile out of Levi. "Nice try," he says, clearly relieved for a change of topic. "But I'm barely going to get the other book finished in time as it is."

I wince. I haven't mentioned it, but it has seemed as if there has been a lot less of Levi typing and a lot more of Levi staring at his screen. He came here to write a Great American Novel and all he's got is a Great American Empty Word Document. Now with the Revenge Exes trending, he's going to be more distracted than ever.

I hate asking it with every bone in my body, but I'd rather rip the Band-Aid off now than walk past an empty condo tomorrow. "Are you going to go back to New York?"

Levi's brow finally lifts, his eyes meeting mine with a determination edged with a faint hurt. "No."

"I wouldn't blame you," I say quickly.

Levi's voice only gets firmer. "I said I was staying for a while and I meant it."

"Really, Levi." I press on, taking a step back from him. "You can still help with the wedding from the city. And you and I—we'll stay in touch. It's okay."

I don't even know if I believe what I'm saying. I just know that it's easier to give him this out. If I can blame myself for Levi leaving this time, I don't have to be angry with him anymore. Staying angry with Levi all these years is the most exhausting thing I've ever done.

I almost quiver with relief at the way he leans in, leveling his gaze against mine. "I wanted to come back before all of this," he says. "The reasons I haven't—I'm not proud of them. But I was going to come back before any of this happened, and I'm certainly not going to leave because of it."

My throat is thick enough that for a moment, I don't trust myself to speak. I didn't know how badly I wanted him to say that until the words started settling in me, easing an old ache.

"Okay," I finally say.

Levi nods. I breathe in deep, salty sea air, listening to the thud of my heart slowly start to find its usual rhythm.

"Well," I say, digging my feet into the sand, "on the plus side, this will probably piss Griffin off."

Levi tilts his head. "You think?"

"Oh, yeah." When I look back up at Levi, I can't bite down my smirk. "He really doesn't like you."

This isn't exactly news. Griffin was always jealous of Levi for being the better runner, and only got more bitter when Levi got into Columbia. I never once mentioned Levi without Griffin rolling his eyes or making a snide comment.

"That makes two of us," Levi mutters, the gray in his eyes steely again.

I shiver, some ripple of disbelief at the whole situation coursing through me. Levi doesn't miss it.

"And you're okay with . . . all this?" he asks, lifting his phone.

"Me? More than," I say. "Hell, I'd take being a Revenge Ex over Crying Girl any day of the week."

Some of the tension eases in Levi's jaw. "Yeah. Certainly has more of a ring to it than Kelly Carter's Reject."

I take a step closer to him, searching his face.

"So how should we handle this?" I ask. "Rely on your two pals 'no' and 'comment'?"

Levi nods. "That seems like a good plan to me. This will probably blow over by tomorrow anyway."

As if on cue, both of our phones light up in our hands. Levi's with an incoming call from Kelly, and mine with an incoming call from Mateo. Levi freezes, but I don't hesitate. Mateo's a texter, so a call means something is up.

"How far are you from Tea Tide? Because there's a situation," Mateo tells me in a rush. "And by situation, I mean there's a line down the boardwalk."

I pull the phone away from my ear to look at the time. "We don't even open for a half hour."

"I hope that's enough time to make a million more scones."

My brain doesn't even know how to parse both the panic and the relief. More customers means more money means possibly saving Tea Tide. But more customers *also* means more demand means I'm about to be in way over my head.

"Shit. Okay. I'll be right there." I hang up the phone and look at Levi. "I've gotta jet. That photographer's probably long gone by now, right?"

I start trekking back toward the boardwalk stairs, but Levi reaches out to wrap his hand around my wrist. I stop, then follow his gaze down to a broken piece of glass in the sand I must have barely dodged earlier.

Levi's tone is a mix of affection and exasperation. "Where on earth are your shoes?"

I pull a face. "Do I look like some kind of tourist to you?"

Levi may have abandoned our contest every summer to see whose feet were the toughest, but Dylan and I sure never let it go. It's clear Levi hasn't forgotten about it, though, when he turns his back to me and says, "Fine, then. Plan B."

"No," I say, half indignant and half delighted that he'd subject himself to it after all this time.

"Too bad. I don't feel like explaining to Dylan why I let your feet get sacrificed to some fifteen-year-old's abandoned moscato."

I eye Levi's shoulders, considering the mechanics of getting on his back. His toned, broad, tank top–clad back. I have to tear my eyes away before I start considering other less mechanical things.

"I'm not seven anymore," I remind him. "I'll squish you."

"I'm not *eight* anymore," says Levi, affronted. "And you're pocket-sized. Give my muscles some credit."

I take a hesitant step forward, only because I'm not sure if he's joking. But Levi manages to hook his hands under my knees and pull me up on his back in a motion so swift that I have to grab his shoulders like a life jacket. I'm settled against him an instant later, so easily that it feels like the shape of me was meant exactly to fit into the shape of him.

"You good?" Levi asks.

A little too good, maybe. "Yeah," I manage.

I stare out at the ocean as if it can grant me some mercy from the sudden and unexpected heat that is coiling low in my gut, spreading lawlessly just about everywhere else. But there's nothing to stop its reach. Nothing to distract me from the friction of my chest against Levi's back, or the earthy-sweet smell of him, or the way the muscles of his shoulders ripple against my arms.

I crush my eyes shut. Nope. Nice try, brain. Teenage me may have suffered a brief case of swooning for Levi, but adult me knows better.

Despite that, some base instinct wins out. I close my eyes, and for a stupid moment, I let myself pretend. I imagine sixteen-year-old me got what she wanted, back when she didn't know better than to want it; I imagine that the pressure of my body against Levi's isn't just a thrill, but a familiar one; I imagine half a lifetime of this steadiness between us, of this inherent trust.

I lose my sense of self long enough that I unconsciously lean my forehead into the back of Levi's head, pressing against the gentle curls, staring down at the tanned slope of his neck. I can feel the precise moment he all but stops breathing. I come back to myself and jerk my head away so fast he stumbles on the top step, grabbing the railing to keep us upright just in time.

"June."

I'm already drowning in mortification, but the concern in his voice immediately topples a wave of guilt right over it.

"Sorry," I stammer. "I was just—"

Royally screwing us both over, apparently. Because in all the fuss, neither of us noticed the scruffy photographer lurking by the trash can until his camera is shoved in our face again.

Levi's grip tightens so fiercely on me that I can practically feel the press of each of his fingers against my thighs. For an absurd moment, I think he's going to make a break for it. Start running for the condo with me on his back like we're in a badly directed action movie.

But there is quite literally nowhere to run. There's a crowd at Tea Tide on our right, and a cluster of people with camera phones to the left, and someone unhelpfully yelling the words "I think that's them!" straight ahead.

The phone cameras start rolling, and just like that, the Revenge Exes take the world by storm.

Chapter Six

"Thank you, Sana. You're a genius, Sana. Here's your Pulitzer Prize for excellent journalism and unparalleled friendship, Sana."

I raise my eyebrows at Sana, who is currently draped over my front counter and singing her own praises with her ancient Mac-Book cradled like a baby in her arms.

I bop her on the forehead with my open palm. "We're just going to wait for it to blow over."

"Or. *Or*," Sana counters for about the fiftieth time today, "you lean into this mess. You and Levi pretend to date. You let me cover the whole thing. Tea Tide stays jam-packed and I make enough money to move out of a glorified attic and we all live happily ever after."

I turn toward the display case I'm wiping down so Sana doesn't see my sympathetic wince. Sana used to travel as often as I did, buoyed by a steady freelance gig at a frothy lifestyle site. Then new management came in with a whole new vision. She was already considering quitting—the higher-ups seemed a little too interested in mining her identity as an Asian American woman for potential content, and she realized it was happening to other writers, too—but before the new tone of the site was formally discussed, they abruptly fired all the contractors, leaving them high and dry.

Professionally, she was almost relieved. She wanted to be writing cultural commentary and human-interest pieces she pitched herself, and she took it as a wake-up call from the universe to pursue *Fizzle*. But financially, in her own words, she was "mega fucked." I told her offhand about one of Nancy's cheap rentals, and to my surprise, she showed up in Benson Beach with an Uber full of suitcases the next day.

Now I live in the tiny apartment on top of Tea Tide, Sana lives in the even tinier apartment on top of the restaurant next door, and we've been going through it together every day since: me learning the ropes of owning a small business, and Sana trying to support herself with a rotation of freelance gigs while she's waiting for the breakout piece to get *Fizzle* to hire her on staff. Hence why we are primarily existing off day-old scones and half-baked dreams.

We both flinch at the sound of a knock at the door.

"She's closed, you animals!" Sana calls. "I ate the last scone an hour ago!"

But even in the dark, I recognize the unmistakable outline of Levi. I dart out from behind the register, unlocking the door to let him in.

"Hey," he says the moment I push it open. "I just wanted to check in. I walked by earlier and it seemed . . . intense."

The store was, in fact, crowded enough today to make Coachella look tame. We sold out of all five emergency bakes of scones and sold enough tea that we are dangerously low on Tea Tide's signature tea blend of Darjeeling, rose, and caramel. I'm pretty sure I'll be scrubbing Annie's pretty pink floors for a week to get them fully clean again.

But at least this time around, I don't mind it so much—getting peppered with questions about Levi's pecs is a lot less humiliating than getting asked if I could openly weep on demand for a selfie.

"Intense is a good word for it," I say, some of the exhaustion creeping into my voice.

"Oh, it's you," Sana crows happily. "Excellent. You'll make June see sense."

Levi's concerned eyes turn from me to Sana. "About what?"

Sana clears her throat and begins another version of her elevator pitch.

"Okay, so here's the thing, Revenge Ex #2. Can I call you Revenge Ex #2? Good, because it's got a ring to it." Sana spreads her arms out as if she is painting a picture for Levi in the air between us. "Imagine this. The two of you go on a bunch of sickeningly adorable fake dates. June keeps this absurd scone momentum going, and hooray! Saves Tea Tide. You both show your exes what they're missing, because hot damn to you both. And *I* make a quick chunk of change as your exclusive photographer so I can use my valuable time working on pitches. Everybody thrives, everybody stays hot, and everybody scams free scones off June."

"Forgive her," I say, before Levi's brain can combust. "She's had, like, ten cups of oolong."

But Levi absorbs all of this with ease.

"Okay," he says. "I'm in."

My mouth drops open.

"Wait. Levi, I appreciate it. But my situation is not that dire. I'll figure out a way to get the money for Tea Tide without us milking this," I say in a rush.

Levi looks away. "I know that. And I do want to help Tea Tide." He delivers the next words more to my newly mopped floor than to either of us. "But I think this would also help the situation with Kelly."

I don't answer for a moment, only because I am struggling to figure out an interpretation of "situation" that doesn't equate to "Kelly seems like she is taking advantage of all the best parts of you, and it makes me feel sick."

And even if that weren't an element at play, I don't want Levi going along with this plan for my sake. I've prided myself on being able to keep Tea Tide's lights on all on my own. Sure, it isn't quite what I'd hoped it would be—not the cozy neighborhood spot I envisioned. One that became so beloved here that maybe someday I'd even be able to open locations in other seaside towns, shaped by their own communities.

But I can still get there. Once we get past these huge rushes of people and I have a chance to breathe, it can be less of a circus and more of the homey, safe place I imagined. And I don't want Levi thinking I need his help to do it.

In the end, I compromise by asking, "Are you sure that's a situation you want . . . resolved?"

Levi won't look at either of us. "I think it might help her remember what we have together, if she thinks she could actually lose it."

The hurt in me is so acute, so immediate, that I don't know how to place it. Or maybe it's just that it feels closer to jealousy than I'm willing to admit.

My eyes search for Levi's, hoping to get to the bottom of the feeling—to reassure myself that it's just a knee-jerk reaction, a symptom of us knowing each other for so long. But his gaze is still aimed firmly at the ground. Instead, my eyes land on Sana's. Hers go wide enough that I know she didn't miss the moment of weakness in mine.

She takes a breath, and I know she's using it to call this whole thing off. She desperately wants out of the freelance grind, but not at my expense.

But she's right. This idea she's proposing—it is objectively the best option for all of us. I'll get three months' worth of rent before the end of this one. Sana will get cash to float herself while she polishes her pieces. Levi will get back the woman he loves.

And I will stuff this unwelcome hurt so far back into a "return to sender" box that I won't even remember opening it.

I put my hands on the backs of one of the chairs as if to root myself. "Let's do it, then."

My voice is so firm that Levi looks up in surprise. "Yeah?"

Now it's Levi searching my face. I nod quietly at him. The concern in his eyes mingles with a gratitude and a relief so intense that it calms my lingering doubt. In fact, when I catch Sana's gaze and we exchange small smirks, I feel a quick but undeniable jolt—this could be fun.

"Yeah," I say gamely. "The universe messed with us enough these past few weeks. We deserve to mess with it right back."

"Then it's settled. Excellent." Sana scowls at her phone, then jumps up from her perch on the counter to start collecting her stuff. "I have a deadline. But you two should talk logistics."

Levi's brow puckers. "We just did."

I nod quickly. "All set."

Sana frowns right back, looking at Levi and then at me. "Haven't the two of you ever watched a rom-com before? If you're going for the fake dating trope, you'll need a plan. You'll need rules."

Off our blank looks, Sana heaves a long-suffering sigh and sets her backpack down.

"You need to decide what kind of Instagram-bait outings you'll take together. What you'll say when people inevitably ask you questions about each other. Plus, like, protocol on the actual romantic bits." Sana starts listing off intimate gestures with the nonchalance of someone who has orchestrated a dozen other relationship ruses. "Hand-holding, snuggling, kissing, getting all lovey-dovey. If there's anything on or off the table, you're going to have to include it in this break-up pact of yours."

My cheeks flush. At some point in Sana's little lecture, I stopped listening and started imagining. The warmth of Levi's broad hand in mine. The way it might feel to burrow myself against him, breathing in the crook of his neck. What he might taste like, where his hands might wander, if we actually kissed.

"Got it?" Sana asks, her attention pointedly aimed at me.

"Right," I manage, just as Levi lets out a quick "Of course."

"You'll also have to diligently loop me in on your plans so I can document them." She taps her computer with one of her bright red nails. "I'm the one here with a finger on the pulse of your mildly unhinged fan base. I'll figure out which outlets to send material to and when. All you guys have to do is eat scones and look pretty."

This is all happening so fast that I think I might have main character whiplash. Yesterday, Levi and I were sad B-characters in other people's romances. Now we're hijacking the stage.

Before I can overthink it and ask a dozen more questions, Sana hoists her backpack and blows us a sloppy, wide-armed kiss on her way out the door. "Text me details for the first fake date. I have no plans. I'm around literally every moment of every day. Weird how that sounded less pathetic in my head! Good night!"

The bell on the door clangs and leaves a tense silence in its wake. I'm half expecting Levi to come to his senses and call this whole thing off. He wasn't built for this. He's so wary of attention that even when we were teenagers and he and Annie were talking about writing bestsellers one day, he swore he'd write under a pseudonym.

But he must really want Kelly back, because when he clears his throat, he seems as determined now as he was a few minutes ago.

"Well. I also have no plans, and you're tied down here," says Levi. "So let me know when you're free, and I'll figure out someplace we can go."

I take a step back to lean into the edge of the front counter, leveling with him.

"That's sweet. And I want to trust you with that task. But know that if you take me to another scream poetry reading, I will fake break up with you so loudly they'll think I'm in the performance lineup."

Levi lets out a sharp, gratifying laugh. "I swear I thought the flier said slam poetry."

My lips curl as I remember the look of absolute bone-deep alarm on Levi's face when the first poet took the stage and started bellowing about her cat sitter ghosting her at the top of her lungs. That was the last Friday night Levi was allowed to pick where we all hung out for a long time.

"Sorry, what?" I lean in closer. "I can't hear you. My ears are still ringing."

Levi leans in to meet me, and I think he's going to say something teasing. But his tone is nothing but sincere when he says, "Fake dating aside, it'll be nice to hang out again like we used to."

Levi's smile settles, and something in my chest does, too. We'll be fine. This friendship we have now might feel fragile, but that doesn't make the foundation of it any less deep. The world will think we're dating, but in reality, we'll just be finding our way back to what we once were—Levi and June, two people who shared friends and made-up stories and long runs on the beach. In some ways, that alone makes this worth it.

Then Levi shifts his weight to his other foot. "Sana's right, though. We should talk rules."

My eyes sweep to the floor. "I don't think we need to make any."

The thing is, if we set rules, it's only going to make this seem like a bigger deal than it is. Like we'd be taking a microscope to every gesture between us, every touch. And I can't have that. This is about saving Tea Tide. This is about Levi fixing his relationship. The more we focus on the intangible things, the less personal the extremely tangible touching will feel.

"I'd just worry about doing anything that might make you uncomfortable," Levi says carefully.

Ah. He's worried about sixteen-year-old swoony June coming out to play and getting her little heart crushed all over again. It would be a down-and-out lie to pretend I'm not attracted to Levi—the thoughts I keep having about him every time he gets close are *absurdly* too loud to ignore—but I am a twenty-seven-year-old woman in full possession of myself. I can set aside some biological rumblings for common sense. And common sense says even if Levi weren't trying to win Kelly back, he doesn't belong here. Not in Benson Beach, not in the old stories we used to make up together, and certainly not with me.

"How about this?" I propose. "Instead of rules, we just promise to be honest with each other. If one of us is uncomfortable, we just say so. And if either of us wants to call this whole charade quits, we drop it—no harm, no foul."

Only after I say the words do I realize the deeper root of my unease. It's not the pressure of playing this trick with Levi—it's whatever comes after. We've only just started to repair our friendship. If this goes south, it might set us back all over again.

But if we walk away from it, we both have a lot more on the line than we're prepared to lose.

Levi considers me with a long, searching look, as if he is considering this exact risk. I flush under the weight of his eyes on me but hold them with my own. Then he reaches out and puts a steady hand on my arm, the warmth of it tingling against my skin so immediately that some distant part of my brain thinks, *Oh, shit.*

"I'll text you the address for scream poetry tomorrow."

The grin that erupts on my face seems to spread right into Levi's, whose eyes crinkle with delight.

"Perfect," I say. "I'll be the one in the giant earmuffs holding a warrant for your arrest."

Levi nods. "It's a date."

The words are still rattling between my ears as he leaves, the full impact of them settling in. It's a date. It's a pact. It's a new chance.

But more than that, it's something to *feel*. Something other than brewing panic or gnawing guilt or grief. Something electric, something that gives energy instead of draining it; something I want to know the shape of so I can hold on to it even when it's gone.

For the first time in a long time, I go to the back kitchen, sit down with my ingredients, and scheme.

Chapter Seven

$\mathcal{F}$ake dating, it turns out, is a scam of a trope, because the effort of getting ready for the date part is still very real. So is the part where I confront the realization that I haven't been on a legitimate date in my entire adult life. It's been so long since I've had a reason to blow out my hair or put on makeup that it almost feels like I'm getting dressed up for Halloween in what might just be my weirdest costume yet: June Hart, fake girlfriend of Levi Shaw.

Eventually, I settle on a pale blue floral tank dress that's just classy enough for our museum outing but casual enough to exude some "gee, I had no idea someone would be here taking candid photos of me and my new beau!" energy, then head down to Tea Tide's tiny parking lot to meet Levi.

He's already waiting with his back turned to the door in a pair of jeans and another breezy button-down, the sleeves rolled halfway up his forearms. I catch a whiff of fresh shampoo, his hair dark and tousled from the shower. His eyes are buried in his phone, but he starts to turn when he hears my footsteps.

There's a wet curl springing up on the back of his head. I reach up and press it down with my thumb, and Levi goes still under the slight pressure, his eyes widening slightly and catching mine. Catching, and then lingering—on the swoop of my hair, the neckline of my dress, the cinched waist above the flowing skirt.

I pull my hand back. Thanks to the massive influx of customers these past few days, I haven't slept in so long that my brain-to-touching-Levi's-hair connection must be on the fritz. It's either that, or the amount of time we've been spending in each other's orbits lately. Now that the front of Tea Tide is a circus again, Levi has taken to writing in the back of the shop. And maybe sighing deeply at his laptop and watching the ovens with the thousand-yard stare of a zombie is part of the artistic process, but it sure seems like we've been saying words out loud more often than he's been typing any.

I clear my throat and let out a merry "Good morning, cupcake."

Levi blinks, then seems to remember the delightfully chaotic email Sana sent us regarding the plan for today, including a PS about thoughts on nicknames??? could be cuuuuute.

"Oh, absolutely not," he says.

"Stud muffin?" I try.

Levi's shaking his head with the beginnings of an exasperated smile. "I take back what we said about rules. I draw the line at dessert-based nicknames."

I raise a finger. "Sugarplum."

"We'll workshop it. In the meantime, please tell me what exactly you think this is," he says, his face registering faint alarm as I unlock my bright green Volkswagen bug convertible.

I pat the windshield before opening the door and sliding into the driver's seat. "This is Bugaboo."

Levi tentatively opens the passenger door, the pretzels himself in, his knees pressed against the glove box. "This is a clown car."

"What the car lacks in space, it makes up for in free food."

I pull it out then—the result of an entire night's worth of scone scheming, and a few evenings' worth of test batches to make sure I got it just right. It's not my first time coming up with the idea for an elaborately themed scone, but it is the first time I was the one responsible for actually bringing it to life. The back kitchen of Tea Tide looks like a caramel Rorschach test right about now.

Levi gives a little shudder. "Ah, sorry. I just thought I heard several hundred dentists crying in the distance," he says, eyes grazing the scone. "What did you put in that?"

My lips curl as I set it back in its bag. "Dark chocolate chunks, smoky burnt caramel, and plenty of sea salt."

"Since when do you like dark chocolate?"

I feel my cheeks warm as I back the car out of the lot. Note to self: I am apparently now so single that the idea of a man remembering my milk chocolate preferences after a decade will make me blush.

"I'm committing to the bit," I explain. "I wanted to make something that tasted vengeful and delicious. I'm calling it the Revenge Ex."

If I'm not mistaken, Levi actually looks impressed. "Look at you, exploiting our situation for capitalistic gain."

"Yes, how very New York of me. Watch your back, I'm coming for your job next."

"Are you going to post about it?" he asks. "I feel like I haven't seen any new scones on Tea Tide's Instagram in a while."

We're about to turn onto the main road, so the next beat of quiet doesn't give me away. I haven't decided exactly what I'm doing with this scone yet. It's the first "special" scone I've even dreamed up since I was dreaming them up for Annie, let alone the first one I've ever made myself.

It's another unexpected hurdle to cross. Just one more thing I never imagined myself doing without her. One more thing that started out as *ours* and feels strange to start back up alone—like either way, I lose. Either I miss her for every part of it, or I hate myself a little for enjoying it without her.

I've just pulled the car out when that last bit of Levi's question sinks in. "Wait. You're on Instagram?"

Levi shakes his head. "Just check up on people sometimes. In your case, mostly to make sure you hadn't gotten lost in a volcano or eaten by a monstrous fish."

And now the blush from before is right back. I play the same game everyone else does when they post on Instagram—wondering who will scroll past it, what they'll think of me when they see it—but Levi was never in my imaginary audience. The idea is both thrilling and mortifying.

"Lightly nibbled by a few, maybe," I say, trying not to sound self-conscious.

"Never a dull moment," says Levi. And then, after a beat: "I still have nightmares about whatever that cave diving thing is that you did."

Honestly, so do I. But it wouldn't have been the first time I did something that terrified me out of my gourd on our travels, and it was far from the last. Griffin had a way of wheedling me into just about anything, and I apparently had a chronic case of "being the cool girlfriend" that let him get away with it.

"Griffin had it on his bucket list," I say.

Levi's voice is noticeably tighter when he asks, "Have you heard from him?"

"Nah." I'm actually surprised. I was getting two to three Are you doing okay? texts a week right up until Levi and I broke the internet. I can't say I miss them. "Have you heard from Kelly?"

"We talked on the phone for a little while," he says, glancing out the window.

"Good," I say, and when the word comes out too bright, I add, "I'm glad."

Levi just nods and doesn't offer anything else, so I don't press. I figure their conversation must have been heading in the direction he wants it to, though, or we wouldn't be going on this fake date.

The Benson Beach Museum of Arts is one of the newer buildings in our small town, white with modern, clean-cut lines and an interior with tall ceilings and gleaming floors. There are four parts to it: a section chronicling Benson Beach's history, another full of pieces from a mix of local artists and artists from around the country, a flashy interactive section where you can play with the art, and a small venue in the back with gorgeous open light streaming in through the windows.

We're actually here on two missions today—both to re-break the internet for our personal gain and to scout this out as a potential "in case of rain" venue, since the wedding will be on the beach. Annie had it on her short list, and between the historical aspect and the giant ball pit in the interactive section, it has Mateo and Dylan written all over it. When it's clear we've beaten Sana here, we decide to walk around the venue space first.

Levi's the one who calls it right off: "It's great, but it's way too small."

I nod in agreement. Given all our friends in Benson Beach, their coworkers at the university, and the extended Díaz family coming in from Texas, we should probably start with a stadium and work our way down from there.

"Let's go get cultured while we wait for Sana," I suggest, walking back toward the gallery.

We stop first at a painting of what appears to be a cartoon waffle, orange juice, fried egg, and bacon that have all sprouted legs and are holding hands while running in a circle. Levi stifles a laugh.

"What, may I ask, is so funny about this charming breakfast cult?"

Levi rubs the back of his neck, looking at the painting sheepishly. "There's this guy at work. Whenever our boss drags us out to art galleries, he plays this game where you imagine you're coming back to someone's place after a date, and if you would—" Levi's lip twitches into the beginning of a smirk. "If you'd sleep with them if they had this over their bed. He called it the Gallery Game."

I don't hesitate. "Oh, hard yes on this one. This is someone who makes pancakes in the morning. Probably puts funny whipped cream faces and M&M's on them, too."

"Are the pancakes worth it, though, if the demon they're summoning in this painting joins you?" Levi muses.

I let out a sharp laugh. "Fair point. Okay, who's next."

We move on to another painting in the same series, this one of a bunch of carrots beaming right at us, their carotene eyes wide and their teeth bared.

"Absolutely not," says Levi at once.

I nod in my best imitation of a discerning art critic. "Explain your reasoning."

"Why are they smiling like that? What do carrots have to smile about? They're plotting something."

"Get behind me," I say. "I won't let them hurt you."

Levi lets out an amused breath as I step in front of him, lifting my hands at my sides like I'm poised to brawl.

"All right, Rocky, save it for the angry potatoes in the next painting," says Levi, leaning in and pressing warm hands to my bare shoulders, pulling me back toward him. My back grazes his chest, the fabric of his shirt soft against my arms.

I glance at him and catch the mirth in his eyes. The mischief. It makes me forget that I'm wearing this too-stiff dress, that we're out on a strangely high-stakes mission, or that Sana is taking her sweet, sweet time getting here. We move down the line of paintings, pivoting from the anthropomorphic perishables that will no doubt haunt our dreams to a line of moodier, darker paintings, all abstract navy blues and maroons punctured by the occasional sickly yellow. Like if someone took a city skyline on a dreary night and shook the colors out.

"Hmm," says Levi, stepping back and considering.

"Hmm," I say right back, watching him watch the painting.

"What?" he asks, and I don't miss that his hand unconsciously goes right back toward the curl I pressed down earlier.

I try unsuccessfully to bite down a smirk. "I'm waiting for your opinion."

Levi's brow puckers. "Is this a test?"

I step closer to him and say in a mock whisper, "A big one."

"Are you secretly . . ." Levi leans forward to squint at the nameplate. "Reginald Jameson, born 1947?"

"No. But I *am* entirely convinced that his doom-and-gloom painting would go right above your sad-boy narrator's bed."

Levi lets out a surprised choke of a laugh. He steps back to look at the painting with fresh eyes, then looks over at me in bewilderment and says, "Wait. So you're trying to figure out if I'd sleep with my main character?"

I hiss between my teeth. "On second thought, the one psychology course I napped through in college does not qualify me for whatever's on the other end of that question."

"Neither does the fact you've never actually *read* my 'sad boy' novel."

Cue the record scratch. I stiffen at his side and see his mouth part in surprise before his eyes even meet mine.

"Annie emailed it to me years ago," I admit. "But I only dug it up and read the first few pages the other night."

Part of me was curious what the fuss was about. Most of me was just wondering what on earth was slamming the brakes in Levi's brain in all the hours he's been "writing" in the back of Tea Tide. I can't say I've figured it out.

Levi's expression is so open that I'm not sure how it's going to settle—if he'll fall back into the Levi I've known for these past few years with the almost-smiles and muted versions of his old self. If I've just blown this past week of tentative friendship up in our faces because I couldn't sleep the other night and poked around in an email attachment I had no business poking in.

Instead, his ears go pink, and his face lands on an uncertain, almost sheepish look. "Well. Don't bother reading any more of it. It's the old version." He lowers his voice. "But—what did you think?"

This isn't a question I was expecting to answer today, but I suppose I walked right into it.

"I think you're a ridiculously talented writer," I say, because that's the truth. Sure, the narration is so sepia-toned and lovesick that I wanted to rattle the main character by the shoulders more than once, but Levi has this very distinct style of writing that could shine through anything. The kind that makes me appreciate the little things he must quietly notice about people, about the world. The kind that makes you linger on a page too long because he's just put a hazy feeling into such concrete words that it pulls old memories from your own life into the text.

Before I can say anything else, Levi's face splits into an incredulous smile. I'm so unused to seeing his smile in full these days that it feels like it just knocked some of the air out of my lungs. "You hate it."

I'm trying not to grin back, but a full Levi smile is apparently as contagious now as it was when we were kids. "It's just—that kind of story isn't really my thing," I hedge.

But Levi's laughing outright now, almost like he's relieved. I wonder if I've broken his brain. "How can a main genre of literature not be your *thing*?"

I point an accusing finger at him. "Says the guy who hates dessert. The main genre of food."

Levi runs a hand through his hair, the laughter tapering off. "Maybe you'll like the new version better."

I sincerely doubt that, but I nod to humor him, moving on to the next painting in the series. This is somewhat brighter than the others, the shapes a little sharper. Less like a cityscape and more like the woods. It reminds me of our woods. The paths we ran around and the stories Levi wove into them.

He's gone quiet, and I wonder if he's thinking it, too. I wonder if he's been thinking it this entire time as we made up little stories about all these paintings, a small echo of the stories we used to spin back then.

"Okay, all my pestering aside—why *did* you quit on *The Sky Seekers*?" I ask. "I thought you and Annie had this whole plan when you went to school, all dead set on becoming literary giants. Then you ditch your fantasy novel for this super serious one, and then ditch writing altogether for a finance major?"

Levi shifts his weight between his feet, and that uncertain expression is back on his face, but there's something else just under it. A faint hurt he can't blink out of his eyes.

"I didn't mean to ditch *The Sky Seekers*. I mean—at least not right off." He glances out to the museum, which is mostly empty now that a field trip has cleared out. "I brought it into my first semester writing course. Nobody really knew what to do with it. Everyone came in with all these very—you know. Contemporary, adult pieces. And I basically got laughed out the door the first week."

I feel my heart cinch at the thought. Levi isn't necessarily shy, but he's always been deeply private with sharing his writing, apart from with Annie and me. The idea of him finally working up the courage to share all the words he kept so close to his chest and getting laughed at for it makes me want to find all those kids ten years after the fact and knock their pretentious heads together.

"I mean, even Annie said . . ."

Levi stops himself, shaking his head almost imperceptibly. I know the feeling well. The strange weight of the things Annie said or did now that they only exist in our own memories, and she's not around to explain or defend them.

"What did Annie say?" I ask.

He twists his lips to the side before settling his face again. "Well, she thought the whole thing was juvenile. That if we were going to be great authors together, we should take ourselves seriously."

We're quiet for a moment.

"That's a shame," I say. "About the class and—well. About what Annie said."

Levi doesn't nod or shake his head, but his shoulders loosen, and he blinks some of the cloudiness out of his blue eyes.

"Well, it's all ancient history now." He gives a half shrug. "Besides, they say to write what you know."

And that just squeezes my heart all over again. Because I know he's talking about New York, about the character coming of age, about the ties he still feels to his family and the uncertainty he feels making roots anywhere else. But all I can think in that moment is *Your character seems awfully lonely.*

Levi's eyes sweep to mine so quickly that I realize we've closed the gap of distance between each other, close enough that it feels only natural to press my shoulder into his, to soften the words by leaning into him. I smell his shampoo again, and that same distinct *Levi* smell that makes me ache. That makes me want to do more than just lean in and wrap my arms around him like I can ease this old hurt.

Levi leans some of his own weight back into mine. "Honestly, I can't remember that much of what I wrote for *The Sky Seekers* back in the day." He looks at the painting in front of us. "Or more like—I remember all the pieces, but not how they fit together."

I almost don't say it, because it feels like admitting to something else—not just that I remember the story, but that I held on to it all these years we were barely speaking. That there were parts of him I couldn't let go of even when I wanted to.

"I bet I can," I say anyway. I tell myself it's for the story's sake, but when I sense a new warmth between us, I'm not so sure.

"Okay, I'm loving the proximity, but could you throw me a bone and hold hands, maybe? Give me some options to work with?"

Levi and I both flinch away from each other to find Sana behind us with what she dubbed her Fancy Journalist Camera raised in our direction. She's clad in a pair of tight denim jeans and a loud tie-dye top, her ponytail slung low, her face the picture of concentration.

"When did you get here?" I blurt.

"Ten minutes before you did," she says, walking over to us.

"And you didn't say anything?" I manage. "You've just been lurking in the corner?"

Sana pats me on the cheek and gives me her patented "oh, sweet summer child" look. "This is your very first fake viral internet relationship. You thought I'd actually trust you two to pose for plandids?"

"Planned candids," I murmur to Levi, whose head just tilted.

"Here. Stand like you were in front of this one," she says, physically grabbing us each by the shoulder to pivot us around again. "Except hold hands."

We're both too jarred by Sana's presence to question her. Levi's hand finds my hand, and I'm expecting a simple grasp, but he weaves his warm fingers through mine. I feel a quiet zing that starts where our skin touches that travels up my arm and through my body, and the suddenness of it combined with Sana's lens on us makes me feel more self-conscious than I have all day.

I don't realize I've gone entirely stiff until Levi leans in and says, "So I'm guessing that's a hard no on *you* spending the night with my main character."

I cackle, leaning into him again. He squeezes my fingers.

"Aaand that's a wrap," says Sana from behind us. "I'll get in touch with some contacts tonight. Would you be okay if a write-up summarizing the whole thing ended up running with them? Only with someone one of us knows. Totally fine if not, but it could get things moving faster if someone bites."

I look over at Levi, who's already looking at me. "I trust anyone Sana does, if you're okay with it," I say.

"Then sure," says Levi. "Everyone's already tweeted most of what there is to know anyway."

Sana beams. "Excellent. Then I'm off to shop these around and watch the internet burn."

Levi eyes her camera as we pull apart. "Do you have time to take one more photo?"

Sana raises her eyebrows. "Depends on how shirtless you're going to be."

Levi takes that as a yes, but instead of initiating any kind of pose, he motions for me to open my tote bag. The Revenge Ex is still at the top like it's my emotional support scone. He pulls it out and then walks the short path back to the empty venue, settling it right on the altar where the sun is streaming in dramatically from the paned windows, all soft, angelic light on the dark chocolate and caramel chaos of the scone.

I have to admit, it looks pretty badass. Like a lover scorned.

"Ooh. This is edgy," says Sana, snapping a few pics. "I haven't dabbled in scone journalism yet, but there's a first time for everything."

Then she's off as abruptly as she appeared, telling us she'll be in touch about Date Two before disappearing with her camera like a digital media ghost.

"That was a surprising stroke of genius," I say as we make our way out of the museum.

Levi's lips press into a smile. "Might as well milk this for Tea Tide while we can. I've got a feeling this is going to die down before Sana can do much with those photos, anyway."

I'm not so sure of that, given Sana's internet prowess, but I don't want to get my hopes up, either. "Yeah, you're probably right."

I push down the burble of panic that's been simmering under my skin the past few days. If it doesn't work out in the long run, it'll be nice for a break from the chaos, but there's still the issue of the three months' rent I'll need to front to Nancy. Plus the changes I'll have to make to Tea Tide on the other side of it, so we can sustain it.

But maybe this scone is a step in the right direction, even if we took a very strange path to get to it. Some progress in revitalizing Tea Tide. Shaking things up, just like Nancy said.

I pull it out of my bag and break it in half. Levi takes his portion with a dubious look, but does a little cheers gesture against my half just the same.

"Here's to the flash in the pan that was the Revenge Exes," I say.

Levi nods. "And here's to never laying eyes on those terrifying carrots again."

We both take a bite as it hits me—this little pact of ours will probably be over as soon as it begins. This morning was a blip, like stealing time back from our past selves. The scone hits my tongue, just as delicious and well balanced as I remember it being in the final test batch—made to taste a little bitter. Only right now it's harder to taste the sweet.

Chapter Eight

So about that Instagram," Mateo says the next morning, leaning into the register to sneak a cup of tea before we open up for the day.

I snap my head up from Tea Tide's register and say way too fast, "What Instagram?"

Mateo's brow furrows. "The one you posted of the Revenge Ex scone last night?"

Oh. So *not* the private Instagram account where his students have been collecting pictures of his patterned sweater-vests, which I may or may not have wriggled my way into yesterday. (Mateo is aware of it. He's just not aware that *I'm* aware of it.)

"Right. Yeah." I stare down at the Revenge Ex scones in the front display case, all ready to go for today. "Well, strike while the iron is hot, I suppose."

Mateo lowers his voice, his eyes soft on mine. "I was glad to see it. You were always so happy, coming up with those."

I nod, still staring at the scones. At the SPECIAL OF THE DAY sign

I'm using for the first time in two years. Late last night I finally took a moment to myself in the back kitchen and decided to commit to it—posting it on Instagram, serving it in the shop. It didn't feel as much like leaving a part of my life with Annie behind as I thought it would. In fact, as I was watching the comments flood in, all I could imagine was her laughing her ass off about this entire thing.

"Yeah," I say, straightening my shoulders. "It was about time for something new."

Mateo gives me one of those quiet smiles of his, then taps his knuckles on the counter. "Speaking of desserts, you're sure you don't mind going to that cake tasting?" Mateo asks.

Mateo and Dylan already worked out the details of the design with Cassie's Cakes during the last round of wedding planning—a three-tiered, buttercream-frosted cake with faint blue and yellow ombre tiers, the Eagles' colors, decorated with red roses, both our mom's and Mateo's mom's favorite. But Cassie's flavors switch up slightly every year, and she's about to close for a month to prep for opening a third location. Seeing as everything Cassie makes is delicious and Dylan and Mateo are both busy with prepping for an away meet and an out-of-town conference, they decided to leave trying the swapped-out flavors in the somewhat capable hands and taste buds of Benson Beach's premiere fake couple.

Which is to say, this cake tasting with Cassie is more of a social call to catch up with an old high school friend, but it'll be nice to touch base on Mateo and Dylan's original plans before the big day just the same.

"Being forced to eat cake? To try a menagerie of delicious flavor combinations?" I ask. "It will be a miracle if I ever recover, but for you, Mateo, I will take on this burden."

He rolls his eyes good-naturedly. "I was mostly worried about the Levi of it all."

"Oh, he spends all day surrounded by desserts now," I say, tilting my chin toward the back office. "The staff's been desensitizing him. He'll survive a little free cake."

"And I suppose a cake tasting isn't bad, as far as second dates go," says Mateo innocently.

I look up at Mateo, bewildered. Sana hasn't given us the heads-up about the pictures of us hitting the internet yet, so there's no way he'd know we ever went on a "date" in the first place.

"A few of my students spotted you and a Levi-shaped person canoodling at the museum," he says, dark eyes glinting.

I feel a twinge of guilt. I haven't said anything to Mateo about my plan with Levi, and I don't know if I will. If I tell Mateo, he'll have to tell Dylan, and Dylan is so *ridiculously* invested in the idea of me and Levi getting along that I know it will only worry him to know we're walking a strange line right now.

That, and Dylan has a mouth the size of the Atlantic. I love him to death, but it would take three minutes—four, tops—for him to say something to give us away.

"Canoodling is a strong word," I say noncommittally.

Mateo just smirks into his to-go cup lid. "Maybe you'll have fun with some even stronger ones after all that cake."

My jaw drops, and I let out a choked laugh as Mateo waves goodbye and heads out the back. I pull out my phone to take a sneaky pic of his zigzag vest for the Instagram account in retaliation, but before I can, I'm stopped in my tracks—between the texts, DMs, and calls, there are enough notifications on my screen that I wonder if I somehow accidentally swapped phones with Beyoncé. I scroll all the way down, and at the bottom of them is a text from Sana I must have missed early this morning while I was on scone prep: Photos up at eight!!! An article ran with it. I know the writer, she's a good bean.

I swipe open one of the other notifications at random and follow a link, and sure enough, Sana's pictures are live and in color for the internet to behold, along with what seems to be a lengthy piece.

Tea Tide doesn't open for an hour, so I sneak out the back entrance, past the small cluster of people already waiting at the door, and hightail it over to Levi's. He's outside on the patio, laptop open in front of him, frowning at his keyboard like he just picked a fight with the delete button. I make plenty of noise walking up, but he still blinks in surprise at the sight of me before setting his laptop closed a little too eagerly. Judging from the fact that I saw not one, but four different Word documents full of notes littering the screen, he probably needs the break.

"I've come to do a dramatic reading of the article that was just posted about us," I declare.

Levi turns to me, his eyes looking uncharacteristically sleepy and his hair mussed in a way that makes my fingers twitch, as if they want to feel the strands thread through them. I've had some practice in the last week in trying to ignore these Levi-related impulses, but every now and then they catch me so off guard that my body gets ahead of my brain.

"Article?" he repeats, blinking like he's willing himself awake. "I thought it was just a quick write-up."

I ease into the chair next to him, crossing my legs and reopening my phone to send him the link. Mine finally loads just as his does, opening to a headline on a buzzy pop culture site: Who Are the "Revenge Exes"? June Hart & Levi Shaw Go Further Back Than Their Viral Breakups.

"Points for cramming in that SEO," I murmur to myself.

The photos load first, just two of them. The first is the one Sana asked for, the two of us holding hands in front of the painting. She clearly took it just after Levi muttered that wisecrack about our game, though, because my head is tilted toward him and you can clearly see the split of my smile and Levi's body is angled toward mine so close that it's clear that he just said something into my ear.

The other photo is taken from the side, just after I "defended" Levi from the carrots. The moment when he touched my shoulders and I leaned into him, my back to his chest, and smirked up at him. The sight of it makes the air catch in my throat. We look so at ease, so natural. We look like a genuine couple.

I scroll past it, but it doesn't do anything to uncoil the new tightness in my stomach. This strange kind of longing for something that doesn't quite exist, that stopped existing a long time ago. I'm glad to have Levi back in my life, but that inherent ease we had as kids? That bone-deep familiarity of knowing each other inside out? I don't think it's something we'll ever have again, and I don't even understand how much I miss it until I'm looking at an echo of it on my screen.

I tilt my head and see that his eyes are stuck on the same photo mine were. After a moment, he senses me watching and glances up, seeming almost sheepish about it before looking past me toward the cluster of people outside Tea Tide.

"You've got a few minutes, right?" Levi asks, tilting his head toward the water. "I was about to go for a walk."

Good call. We're sitting ducks here, if someone spots us. We take ourselves to the mostly empty beach, both of us quietly scanning through the article as we make our way down to the water's edge. Whoever wrote it did it with the same care and respect that Sana trusted them to have, but they did not leave a single stone in Benson Beach unturned. It's not just a run-of-the-mill fluff piece. They went in and found high school friends, old teachers, the woman who runs the corner store where we used to get snacks after cross-country practice. I'm mildly alarmed by everything they've managed to dig up in the short time we've been a "couple," but I'm also touched by how much people remembered.

Especially how much *ridiculous* stuff people remembered.

"I forgot about your absurd nicknames," I say. In the old days, if I was getting on Levi's nerves, instead of calling me by my actual name, he'd address me by whatever month it happened to be.

Levi's shaking his head and letting out a groan. "I forgot about how you kept putting Pop Rocks in my damn sandwiches."

"God, we all pranked each other into oblivion that summer. Remember how Annie snuck stickers on our backs while we were sleeping and we all had ridiculous tan lines for weeks?"

"I'm pretty sure there's still a SpongeBob on my shoulder if you squint."

We're both laughing under our breath, at least until we get to the part toward the end. The article really did spare no details.

Shaw and Hart aren't just bound by a childhood friendship, but by a mutual tragedy. Two years ago, Annie Hart—June's older sister and a close friend of Levi's—unexpectedly passed, leaving a grieving town in her wake.

There's more beyond that, too. A brief delve into Annie and the mark she left on Benson Beach. How she was our high school valedictorian, a prolific writer, and a Stanford grad; the kind of friend who would both kill you with a look and kill for you at the drop of a hat; the kind of person who would come right back to her hometown to launch an entire tea shop on a competitive boardwalk strip with little to no experience in small business ownership and never let a single person tell her no.

I scroll past it quickly before it sinks in too deep. I just wasn't expecting Annie to get pulled into this is all. Especially not for a stranger on the internet to take such careful consideration of her when she wrote it.

"You okay?" Levi asks quietly.

I've got ahold of my face by the time I look up from my phone. "Yeah," I say. "Looks like we might be moving in the right direction."

I point at the suggested articles linked at the bottom. "'Roman Steele's Sweet Cinderella Story Turning Sour?'" I read out loud.

His eyes are still lingering on me, careful and steady. "I'm sure that's just tabloid fodder," he says.

"How sure are you sure?" I ask.

Only then does he glance away, his eyes skimming the water's edge. "We've been texting."

I wonder if that's why he seems so sleepy today, why he looks like he's on the constant verge of a yawn. There is something oddly adorable about it, even if I'm upset at the idea of Kelly stealing even a minute of his sleep after what she did. After what she's continued to do.

"Like, good texting or bad texting?" I ask. As if any text from Kelly wouldn't qualify as "bad" in my book right now.

Levi's almost-smile twitches into place. "She doesn't seem thrilled about the idea of us."

This shouldn't bring me such a perverse satisfaction, and yet suddenly I've got an almost-smile of my own to bite down. "Sounds like some progress, then," I say.

I'm quiet for a few moments, wondering if he'll go into any more detail. I want to make sure he's actually getting something he wants out of this whole fake relationship thing, too. If he decides to break things off with Kelly for good, I'm fine to chuck the rest of our fake dating plans into the ocean. I might be using this to help Tea Tide, but the last thing I'd want is to do it at Levi's expense.

But when Levi takes in a breath, he asks, "And how about Tea Tide? You think this is putting you in a better spot?"

"Oh, for sure," I say, glancing back. "I don't think any American tea shop has had to roll out this many scones since the last royal wedding."

"And is Tea Tide . . . I mean—is it really what you want to be doing?" Levi says, his voice loaded with the same carefulness that was in his eyes when he asked about Annie.

I can't help the immediate defensiveness that licks like a flame under my ribs. I know I haven't exactly made myself Small Business Owner of the Year over here, but I'm trying my best. Benson Beach's boardwalk is a tough piece of real estate to hold down, and the learning curve was brutal.

But when I catch Levi's expression, it's clear he's asking for the same reason I've been asking about Kelly—to make sure I actually want the thing I'm getting out of this, too. That we're setting each other up for success.

I lower my hackles.

"Yeah. It is," I say. "It always was."

Off Levi's curious look, I add, "I was never planning on running it. But we dreamed up the idea of it together as kids. She let me be a part of everything from the start." I feel a tug of nostalgia for the late nights I spent huddled in hostels or under tents, pulling out my barely charged Bluetooth keyboard and beaten-up iPad to answer the long email chains Annie and I had going all the years I was abroad. "And I was always pulled to it. The way it could be a sweet surprise for tourists and a familiar stomping ground for people who live here."

It feels good to say it out loud. Not just to explain to Levi, but to firm the resolve in myself. Sometimes I get so stressed by the day-to-day that I forget how much I love the broader entity that is Tea Tide. How much I want to live up to that vision I had for it, even as a kid.

"It's funny, we spent all these years swapping pictures back and forth, me on some adventure and Annie at the shop, and I always wished . . ." I let out a breathy laugh. "It sounds so—I shouldn't—I wanted to come back. A lot earlier than I did. And then Annie died, and I didn't come back because I wanted to, but because I *had* to."

I wonder if I'll ever stop feeling the gnawing guilt about that. For so long I was looking for an excuse to stop traveling with Griffin, but could never make my resolve stick. I was afraid of losing him.

In the end, I lost something more important. I lost years with Annie I'll never get back. Years I could have spent at Tea Tide, in this place that was always tugging me home.

"I didn't even realize how much I missed this place until I was back. I hate that Annie will always be the 'excuse' for it. I should have come back on my own."

We both know it, but Levi says it just the same, low and comforting. "There's no way you could have known."

That's true for all of us. We lost Annie to a brain aneurysm. I will never stop feeling the shock of it, maybe, but at least there was a comfort in the aftermath, knowing she went quickly.

I nod, trying to reel myself back in, and then Levi says something that makes it impossible.

"She'd be proud of you."

I let out a tight laugh, my throat thick. It's strange. I want to believe those words so badly, and here is the one person who knew Annie well enough to have a right to say them, and even then I can't let them stick.

"I don't know about that," I say. "I've still got a lot to figure out."

We're barely walking now, our feet dragging in the sand, so close that our fingers are grazing. That I could reach out and hold his like

I did the other day at the museum and feel the warmth of it flood through me again.

"It wasn't easy for Annie, either," Levi reminds me. "She messed up plenty of things."

It's easy to forget sometimes that Levi stayed in touch with Annie even when he was barely a person to me. It makes me swallow down an old hurt, makes me wary of the sudden depth of this conversation when we haven't had conversations like it in so long.

"But she always had some trick up her sleeve," I say, deflecting.

Levi doesn't let me get away with it. "She also had you up her sleeve. Brainstorming with her. Coming up with all those scones."

I shake my head. "She hated half my ideas, though."

"Like what?" Levi asks.

"Like—little things." I think back, tempted to laugh about some of it. "Like whether we should offer free Wi-Fi, or what the holiday specials should be. But bigger ones, too. Like making the vibe less formal. More of a 'no shoes required' kind of place. Make it easier to drop in and out, making it easier to collaborate with other businesses on the boardwalk, if we wanted."

Then I hesitate. It seems almost embarrassing to say this now, given the state of things, but the way Levi's looking at me—steady, with the kind of understanding I haven't felt in so long—I can't help myself.

"And I always had this idea that once Tea Tide was settled, we could have more locations."

I follow it up with a self-deprecating laugh, but Levi's focus on me only settles deeper.

"Maybe this boost will get you squared away, and you could look into it?"

"Nah, this will just help me break even. We're circling the drain over here," I say, jerking my thumb toward Tea Tide in a gesture I hope is casual enough to cover up the very real anxiety. "I promised Nancy to front three months' rent on next year's lease just to prove we're not going to fall behind again."

I don't press into the real reason why I could never expand the shop, which is less to do with money and almost everything to do with Annie. She pictured it as something insular, something hyperlocal. She wanted to pour everything she had into it. She wanted to spend whatever time she wasn't working behind the counter sitting at one of the little tables, writing her novels and holding court as people came and went. She wanted it to be a shared space, but a small and orderly one. She wanted it to be her home.

I've always loved the community aspect of it, too. But where Annie's sense of that rooted her here and only here, I've always been more restless about it. More eager to share. I pictured it messier, more open. I pictured a cluster of Tea Tides in other beachside towns, with the same foundations but their own communities, their own little touches and quirks that made them unique.

It was the part of me that loved traveling with Griffin, at first. I love exploring new places, finding all the hidden cracks of them to see into other people's worlds. Eventually our traveling became less about that and more about Griffin's daredevil tendencies, but that itch is still there in me. I told myself that maybe one day I'd get to scratch it through Tea Tide. Nothing opens people up into each other's worlds like the space to chat and linger and share art and ideas.

I'd discussed it some with Annie, when I was still abroad—the idea of rotating local art displays or hosting writer nights instead of just the paid events like parties and bridal showers. She wasn't fully on board, but I had the sense I could get her to come around. But even if I wanted to look into it now, I've been so swamped just trying to run the day-to-day business that it's fallen by the wayside. Maybe Levi is right that Annie would be proud of me for trying as hard as I have, for trying to keep true to her vision, but right now, I'm not so proud of myself.

"You know I could help with fronting the rent," Levi offers, his tone careful even though we both know what I'm going to say.

Because I do know—I have known. Levi and I may have spent the last few years knocked out of each other's orbits, but even if it came up when I found him lurking with his coffee outside of Tea Tide and tore him a new one, he would have helped me right then, if I'd asked.

"I appreciate that. But it's less about the money and more about whether we can sustain ourselves, you know?" I offer him an appreciative smile, one that I know doesn't meet my eyes. "I have to be able to do this to prove that we can keep Tea Tide running on its own two feet."

Levi nods, and the quiet that follows feels like something's cracked open between us. Something we've been tiptoeing around ever since Levi got back. I stop walking, digging my heels into the sand. Levi eases to a stop next to me, his eyes soft on mine, searching.

"You said you meant to come back before this," I say. "So why didn't you?"

I try to keep the hurt out of my voice, but I can tell from the way the shame streaks across Levi's face that I haven't completely managed it. Still, I'm not sure how he'll react to me asking. It's been so many years of nothing more than the occasional quick text exchange between us that I'm still worried I'll get closed-off Levi again, the version of him that left my life and seemed to stay out of it as thoroughly as he could.

But instead, he takes a breath so deep that I almost hold mine, waiting for what's on the other end of it.

"A few weeks before Annie died," he says quietly, "we got into a fight."

I know Levi and I know Annie, so I also know what Levi means is that Annie picked a fight. Levi, for better or for worse, has always been as conflict avoidant as they come.

But still, hearing him say those words rattles me, deeper than I'm comfortable with. I've spent these past two years racked with my own guilt for the distance I had with Annie when she passed. Now Levi's guilt is so plain in his expression that I'm feeling a shade of my own in it.

"It couldn't have been that bad," I say, a knee-jerk reaction to soothe it away for both of us.

Levi shakes his head. "It probably wasn't. Or it wouldn't have been. But we didn't speak for a few weeks, and then suddenly I'm getting this call from my mom. . . ."

He blinks back sudden tears, and I'm tugged sharply into old memories. When we were younger, Levi had been so much more expressive than other kids we knew. Like there was a well always on the verge of tipping over inside him. He'd laugh so easily and his eyes would tear up so fast over little things that it felt like his heart was perpetually beating on his sleeve.

Somewhere along the way he outgrew it, replaced by the almost-smile, by this tight control Levi seemed to want in his world from the moment he left Benson Beach. Only now that I'm seeing an echo of that younger version of him do I understand that it never really went away.

"We, uh—we were fighting over some stupid plan of mine. A plan Kelly and I had," he elaborates, his voice thick but the words steady. "The deal was that we were going to work our asses off until we turned thirty, save up as much money as we possibly could, then take a few years off to pursue other things. I'd write my novel. She'd paint."

"And that upset Annie?" I ask.

Levi lets out a strained laugh. "Oh, she'd been mad about it for a while," he says. "She knew. And you know how her big plan was for us to write together. She kept trying to sell the manuscript she'd been working on, and a few times she got close. She wanted me to be in the trenches with her. I think she was worried about leaving me behind. So when Kelly and I stayed the course, she was upset."

I put aside the lingering ache of all these pieces of himself he shared with Annie but not with me. These pieces I might have known about if I hadn't been so stubborn about changing the subject with Annie whenever Levi came up, about keeping Levi at bay.

"What would make you do that?" I ask. "This plan of yours and Kelly's, I mean?"

Levi is quiet for a moment. Almost hesitant. It occurs to me that the last time he told a Hart woman about this plan, she probably didn't have any interest in hearing him out.

"Kelly came from a family like mine. Her parents worked hard, but things were always tight. We were determined to have everything set for our futures," he says. "To be able to take care of our families, too."

There's something in that last bit that has a heavier weight to it, one I can't quite place. It's not that occasional friction we had growing up—even as kids, we sensed an imbalance, knew that Levi's family wasn't as comfortable as ours. It's something deeper than that.

"And you didn't want to just get steady jobs, and try writing and painting on the side?" I ask.

Levi swallows thickly. "That's what Annie said."

I can tell from the way the expression on his face won't settle that whatever is coming next was the real fight. I brace myself like there's a wave about to sneak up on us, but even then, I'm not fully prepared.

"The thing is . . ." Levi glances up toward the boardwalk, almost like he's looking past it. "My mom—in my sophomore year of college, she was diagnosed with breast cancer."

For a moment my brain just goes to static, unable to process the words coming out of his mouth. I see Levi's mom at least once a week. She works at the salon a few blocks down and occasionally comes into Tea Tide. She's a permanent fixture to me, an unshakable thing—a mom figure to me growing up, and even more of one now that my own is all the way across the country.

My head can't wrap itself around the idea of her being sick at all, but the raw expression on Levi's face wraps my heart around it, fast.

"Holy shit. Levi. Is she—"

"She's in remission now. She's fine," he says quickly.

I put a hand to my chest. Feel my heart beating wildly under my palm, aching for Levi with every beat. "I never knew."

"You weren't supposed to. She was incredibly private about it. Annie wasn't supposed to know either, but she somehow heard about it from Nancy, put two and two together." He shakes his head, worrying his lower lip like he's gone back two years to their fight. "She was furious I hadn't told her. And the thing is, I really wanted to. I wanted to tell all of you. But my mom didn't want anybody kicking up a fuss, or thinking we needed help."

It's so plain right now in Levi's eyes that he did, though. There's an old fear in them, an uncertainty he clearly never shook off. And more than that, a plea. Like he's looking for forgiveness.

"Levi." I reach out and take the hand that was grazing mine earlier and squeeze it between both of mine. His is warm in my grasp, squeezing my hands back in silent gratitude. "I'm so sorry. I know you couldn't say anything, but—I wish we'd known."

He looked sleepy before, but now he just looks tired. Like he's been waiting to let this go for a long, long time. "My mom wouldn't even let me come back from school. She was furious when I tried. So I did the only thing I could think of," he says. "I changed my major. I wanted to try to help with the medical debt."

I had this whole narrative built up in my head about Levi all these years. Levi cast me aside. Levi left for New York. Levi traded passion for a paycheck. Levi hardened all the soft parts of his heart, became a person I didn't recognize.

But he's right here. The Levi I remember from before all of that. And he was hurting all this time over something I never knew.

It doesn't change the rest of our history. Doesn't forgive the years he blew me off and made me feel small. But it has me wondering about them now in a way I never let myself—if there are other things I don't know, things I never got a chance to ask.

I don't have the space for those thoughts right now. That second-hand ache I've always felt for Levi is in full force. I lean into him, pressing my cheek to his shoulder, wrapping my arms around his back. I feel his breath hitch against mine before he sinks into it, before I feel the warmth of his arms pull me in by the shoulders, press me even closer to him.

"I wanted to come back after Annie died. But I was so—I was ashamed of how I left things with her," he admits. "She was right. I had been stalling. And then suddenly I had all this time she didn't anymore, and I just—I froze. With writing. With coming home. The whole thing."

I nod into his shoulder because I know exactly what he means. Ever since Annie died, I felt like I didn't just lose something, but took something, too. Like I stole time out from under her. At some point last year, I realized I was older than she was ever going to be, and the idea of it has unnerved me ever since.

"You know she'd never want you to feel like that," I say softly. "You know how she was."

Annie was a lot of things. Stubborn. Fierce. Deeply loving. And sometimes there wasn't room for her to be all those things at once without tangling them. She wanted what was best for us, would burn down the world for us if she had to, but would accidentally burn us in the process, too.

But things always blew over in the end. She'd burn hot and flicker out. She rarely apologized, but she always moved on.

Levi tilts his head so the next words he says are close to my ear. "I was ashamed of how I left things with you, too."

The words seep under my skin, but they don't settle. I'm not like Annie. I can't just move on.

At least not when it comes to Levi. It never mattered how many years passed. I still felt the hurt of him leaving me behind just as fresh through every single one of them, like he ripped some root of mine out of the ground when he left and a part of me has been unsteady ever since.

I don't ask him why he did it, because we were both there. I had feelings for him in high school. He didn't. That wasn't the issue, though. The issue was that after it all came to an explosive head, instead of talking about it, Levi did what he'd always done—avoided the problem.

I just never imagined back then that one of those problems would be me.

"I'm glad you're back," I say instead. "And I'm glad you're writing again. I know I joke about the book and all—but I'm really glad you're writing."

He nods, settling his chin on the side of my head for a moment, pressing his fingers into my back so deliberately that I can feel the pressure of each and every one of them, sweet aches against my skin. My eyes flutter closed, the side of my face nestled so deep into his shoulder that I'm overwhelmed by that earthy sweetness, by the warm undertone. By the strange collision of the yearning I had for him years ago and the pulsing, much sharper *demand* my body has for him now.

Both of these feelings can only get me in trouble. Levi didn't want me then, and I know he doesn't want me now. We have this entire Revenge Ex scam to prove it.

I pull back from him, taking a steadying breath. His face is settled again, but there's still a weariness in those eyes that was welling up a few minutes ago, like he's somewhere between the Levi who let himself feel out in the open and the Levi who snaps himself up before he can.

"I'm glad to be back in your life again," he says.

The sincerity in the words makes me feel weak in every bone, only I can't let it. Not if I'm going to come out of this pact we have in one piece. I whip out a quick smile, flashing it like armor, and tell him, "Say that again after I drag you to that cake tasting tomorrow, and I'll believe it."

Levi blinks, seeming almost disappointed by the sudden shift, but it leaves his face so quickly I might have imagined it.

"Do you eat anything that isn't cake?" he asks. "Was this the secret to how you were crushing everyone on cross-country all along?"

I pivot myself back toward Tea Tide, and he falls into step next to me, his tall frame shielding me from the early morning sun. "Don't be ridiculous. It's cake *and* chocolate. Balance is key."

Levi's lip twitches just before he says, "Whatever you say, August."

I cackle, reaching out to lightly push him toward the waves. He pulls his arm out in an instant and hooks me by the waist, swooping me up and pretending he's going to drop me into the water. I let out a squeak of surprise, the two of us catching each other's eyes with a different kind of mischief—not the one we used to have, but something heated. Something a little more than friendly. Something I'll have to keep in check because there's no point in denying it anymore. I might as well enjoy it while it lasts.

He sets me down and I'm breathless with laughter, stumbling on my feet. He keeps his arm around my waist until I'm settled again, and I look up at him and see one of those full Levi smiles—the kind so broad and bright in his eyes that it puts the sun behind him to shame—and I can't help but feel smug knowing I'm the one responsible for it.

Chapter Nine

That's it," I say flatly. "I'm breaking up with you."

Levi doesn't even glance up from the table. "Well, we had a good run."

The two of us are currently locked in a flavor stalemate in the adorable little cake tasting room of Cassie's Cakes. The walls are decorated with gorgeous pictures of tiered cakes with just about every frosting pattern and color under the sun, and the windows are decorated with prism crystals that project rainbows all over the room. In front of each of us there is a lattice-print plate with five small rectangles of cake in lemon, pistachio, chocolate, vanilla, and strawberry, plus tiny bowls of different buttercream and cream cheese frostings. The idea is that we can mix and match them to come up with the ideal flavor combinations—not for the cake Dylan and Mateo planned out, but for a larger sheet cake we've had to get to accommodate the expanded guest list.

Leave it to Levi to somehow disrespect the entire institution of wedding cake by taking a shine to the pistachio cake and suggesting we don't have any frosting to pair with it at all.

"Nobody's breaking up with anybody until I get more of this caramel sauce in my mouth," says Sana, the phone she's been getting content with in one hand, a dainty spoon full of caramel in the other.

Cassie preens at the head of the table, where she's been holding court as we go through the flavors. The two of us see plenty of each other since our shops are so close, but even if I didn't, I could appreciate that not much has changed about her since high school—she's still got that sunny disposition, that bright smile, and those big blond curls that always reminded me of Bad Sandy in *Grease*.

"We make it in-house," Cassie says, pushing the bowl of caramel closer to Sana.

Sana licks her lips. "In that case, consider me moved in."

"You understand that frosting isn't just god's gift to our mouths," I continue to impress upon Levi. "It's what makes the cake architecturally *sound*. You ditch the frosting, you lose the very glue holding it together."

"If you did want to lessen the frosting ratio, they could consider switching to a naked cake," says Cassie, flipping through her cake look book.

"Do not entertain this dessert delinquent," I tell her.

Except the cakes she flips to are, of course, as beautiful as all the others we've seen pictures of on the walls. The edges of these are rough frosted with a thin layer so you can see the color of the cake underneath, and sometimes decorated with a few flowers on each tier. They've got a rustic, cottagecore feel that I know will appeal to Mateo's vest-wearing sensibilities. (I'd take Dylan's opinion into account if that opinion didn't start and end with "When can we eat it?")

"In fact, you might want to look into this option if you really are considering a beach wedding and want the cake displayed outside," says Cassie. "We could dye the cake with their original colors instead of the frosting, and you won't have to worry about the frosting sweating."

Levi and I worked out the final details for reserving a permit on the beach yesterday, chatting it over during my "lunch break" (read: shoving a scone into my mouth with reckless abandon before running back to the front). Mateo suggested the stretch just outside of Tea Tide so we'd have the space to prep and give guests an option to chill out inside, and the idea of a beach dance party made Dylan's eyes light up like a little kid on Christmas.

"That's actually not a bad idea," says Levi.

The way the sun has shifted, it's projected one of the little rainbows from the prism right over one of his eyes. I'm staring at it, dazed by the way it brings out the lightest flecks of blue against the gray, when I realize those eyes are staring at me and waiting for some kind of response.

"Oh. Yeah," I manage, turning my attention back over to Cassie. "I think they're set on the original design, but we'll run it past them."

She nods, making a note on the sheet she has in front of her. "Do you have a verdict on flavors for the sheet cake?"

"I came in hot on the chocolate, but I really like the lemon," I say, stabbing my fork into the last bite of mine and pairing it with the cream cheese frosting.

Levi considers his plate. "The pistachio, I'd say."

Cassie claps her hands together like we're two burgeoning cake geniuses. "Those flavors pair beautifully together. And with the raspberry in the main cake."

"I think they'll go for the pistachio," says Levi. "Dylan practically inhales trail mix."

I sidestep the audacity of Levi comparing Dylan's giant Costco bags of salty nonsense to premium cake and say, "If I know Mateo, he's going to lean toward fruit."

"Well, we don't have to decide that until the week of, so you can all talk it out and get back to me," says Cassie.

"Hey, you mind if I get a few shots around the shop and the exterior just so I have all my bases covered?" asks Sana, setting her phone down in the stand she brought and swapping it out for her nice camera.

This was supposed to be a much shorter and more casual affair, but Cassie reached out to me and asked if Levi and I wouldn't mind if she posted about us being in the shop so she could get more eyes on Cassie's Cakes for the new location's soft launch this week. Sana immediately tagged herself in, offering to take pictures of both of us and the new store for Cassie to post in exchange for a flat rate fee, which Cassie happily agreed to—she'd been looking to hire someone to take decent photos of the new shop, but hadn't gotten around to it yet.

As glad as I am that Sana's able to get a few extra bucks out of being our de facto stage mom right now, I am a little worried about the situation. The deal was that all three of us were going to get something out of it, and I know Sana's ultimate goal was to have time to work on her pitches. So far, all she's been able to do is sell pictures of us to a website and score this freelance gig with Cassie, and I'm worried planning this whole fake dating arc for us is keeping her too busy.

"I'm working my way up to it," said Sana dismissively when I brought it up. "When it comes time to write something *Fizzle*-worthy, I'll know."

I'm still wondering what she has in mind when Cassie pushes her chair out to stand up.

"Absolutely, that'd be great," she tells Sana before turning to me and Levi. "Here, you two can deliberate while I show her around." Then she leans in and looks at us with an extra gleam in her already-bright eyes. "I can't thank you guys enough for doing this. And I'm really just so, *so* happy to see the two of you together—I think I speak for most of our classmates when I say it's about damn time!"

Cassie follows Sana out, leaving us to marinate in the awkwardness her words left behind. I can't lie. Some old, undeniably smug part of me is glad to know that at some point in the past, people thought we might be an item. It's a relief to know I didn't just build up that old crush in my head. But it doesn't change the fact that we're now spinning a bald-faced lie about it not just to the world, but to all our old friends, too.

Levi cuts through the stilted quiet by plopping his lemon cake sliver onto my plate. I nudge my pistachio over to his, then add, "*Only* if you try it with some of the dark chocolate ganache."

Levi fixes me with a look not unlike a cat about to knock a water glass off the table and takes a deliberate bite of ganache-less cake.

"You monster," I deadpan.

He smirks at me as he chews, the kind of smirk that tugs at my own lips.

It's strange—with Sana and Cassie out of the room, the situation feels distinctly more couple-y than it did before. Not even in the fake dating sense. Like we're in a parallel universe where we really are just sitting at a table, deliberating over cake flavors like it's our own wedding. By virtue of this becoming Fake Date Number Two, we're both dressed to look the part—me in one of my few remaining un-chocolate-stained white shirts tucked into my high-waisted jeans, Levi in a well-fitted blue T-shirt that's somehow managing to make the blue in his eyes even brighter. We look downright color-coordinated, like our next stop is the engagement shoot.

Only then does it occur to me that Levi might have already done this. He actually was—possibly is still?—engaged, after all. He and Kelly might have already had this same bakery banter.

Before I can overthink it, Levi nudges my knee under the table. "How's Tea Tide holding up today?"

"It's absolute anarchy," I report, digging in on the rest of my strawberry slice. "I've had more people take my picture today than I've had in my entire life. And the Revenge Ex scone is flying off the shelves."

I only managed to sneak out this afternoon because I have the place staffed with just about every summer breaker we have on the payroll and stayed up most of the night prepping scones for today's bake. I'm sleep-deprived enough to take a nap on Cassie's floor, but that's fine. I'll sleep like a dolphin. One eye open at the register, the other conked out and dreaming about her absurdly delicious lemon cake. As long as we're making enough money to front the three months' rent, I'll do whatever it takes.

"I keep seeing it on the boardwalk. Everyone's out with their boogie boards and their Revenge Ex scones," Levi quips. Then his brow furrows. "They aren't giving you a hard time anymore, right? The people taking pictures."

I bite down a smile at the protectiveness in his voice. "Not so much. Revenge Ex has a much better ring to it than Crying Girl." I nudge my own knee into his. "Although your fan club wants to know where you are."

"Typing at a steady rate of one word an hour," says Levi.

"Progress," I say. Progress that's been slightly derailed by Levi pitching in to help at Tea Tide every now and then, jumping up to move boxes in the back or pull out things that need to be restocked. I keep calling him off, but at this point I think he's almost looking for excuses to avoid his screen.

"Maybe today I'll work myself up to two," he says, polishing off the last bit of his pistachio cake.

My lips curl into a smile. "I'm gonna have to steal her recipe.

I can't believe I'm watching you enjoy a dessert with my own two eyes."

"It's mild," says Levi in his own defense. "Not so sweet."

"Hmmm," I say, tapping my fingers on my chin. "Almost like a *scone*, one might say."

That wrestles an exasperated smile out of him. "I've seen enough of your handiwork over the years to know most of your scones are giant cookies, June."

I put a hand to my chest in mock offense, hoping it covers up the faint blush at the reminder that Levi was keeping tabs on me. "A giant cookie? That sounds so unlike me."

Levi's lip twists to the side in the beginnings of a smile. There's a crumb of pistachio cake stuck on the edge of his mouth. I lean in without thinking, pressing my thumb to it. The instant the cold of my hand meets the heat of his mouth, we both go very still.

"You have a . . ."

I've forgotten the word for crumb. Or more accurately, forgotten how to speak. Because suddenly my brain has put me on hold, deeply committed to other thoughts. Thoughts like using the thumb I have on his face as an excuse to skim my fingers down the sharp line of his jaw and pull it closer to mine. Thoughts like leaving that crumb exactly where it is and pressing my lips to it instead. Thoughts like wondering what the rest of him would taste like if he let me give it a try.

Somewhere outside the room the front door to the bakery jingles open, and I pull my thumb away, the crumb falling to the ground with it.

"Thanks," Levi says, his voice unmistakably hoarse.

My face is so hot I'm tempted to fan myself with the cake look book. As soon as this fake dating thing is over, I'm going to have to take a *year's* worth of cold showers.

Sana sweeps back into the room then, rescuing my thoughts from spiraling any further down the Levi-shaped rabbit hole, and says, "Let's get a picture of you guys next to the display case that Cassie can post."

I look forlornly at Levi's leftover cake, then remember we're on a schedule here. I have to get back to Tea Tide.

"I have the updated contract on my computer, if you want to take a look before you bring it to Dylan and Mateo," says Cassie.

Levi nods and follows her out. I'm about to do the same when Sana collects her phone from the stand and says, "Oh, and if either of you confessed to any murders while I was gone, let me know now. Because I had this rolling the whole time."

My eyes just about fly out of my head. "Sana!"

She points a finger at me. "Honestly, this one's on you. Fool you once, shame on me. Fool you twice, shame on . . ." She waits until Levi's out of the room to waggle her eyebrows at me suggestively.

"Are you sure you want to work for *Fizzle*?" I grumble. "Because New York is that way, *Gossip Girl*."

Sana skims a hand down today's long French braid and settles it on her shoulder. "Go smile pretty for my camera. You'll thank me later."

We do just that, me warning Levi about the footage just in time for his cheeks to go pink as we're posing with Cassie's signature over-size cupcakes with blue sparkly frosting and a subtle "C" swirled on top. After we get a few standard photos, Sana tells us to loosen up, so I pretend to shove my cupcake into Levi's mouth. Then Levi abruptly *does* shove his own cupcake into my mouth, leaving us two blue-frosting-faced, spluttering messes when I commit to fully shoving mine back.

"This is it," I say, holding up blue frosted fingers at Sana. "The money shot."

Levi reaches back for a napkin to hand me and says, "We're probably going to have glitter on our mouths for a month."

I tuck away the thought about licking *that* off him too, just in time for Cassie to swoop in.

"Thank you both so much for this. Seriously," she says, hooking an arm around each of our necks and pulling us in with our mismatched heights for a seesaw of a hug. "I'm going to be slammed for the next week or two, but if there's anything I can do to help you out, *please* let me know."

She hands a bag to Levi, whose expression brightens. "Maybe you could talk to June about what it's been like to open other locations sometime."

Cassie's mouth drops open in delight just as my stomach drops down to my sneakers. "June!" she says, swatting my arm playfully. "See, this is why you have to start coming to our small business owner meetups. I had no idea you were looking to expand!"

"I'm not," I say quickly, but Cassie's already pulling out her phone.

"Let's get something on the books. It's been wild, but it's been a blast." She's on such a roll that I don't have the heart to interrupt her—or maybe it's just that I'm too curious to interrupt her. That a part of my heart is snagging on every word she's saying, part of my mind stretching to imagine it for myself. "I mean, you already know some of it. We started with the food truck before we opened our second location in Hoffman Beach, just to feel out the area— I'm not sure if you'd want to go that route, but either way, I'd love to spitball ideas."

It feels like a jack-in-the-box just flew open with all these loud, bright possibilities I've been trying to bury, and now I have to slam it shut all over again.

"I'm not opening any other locations," I say again, more firmly.

I plant a smile on my face to try to soften the words, but I can tell from the way everyone in the front room goes quiet that it doesn't quite work. "I mean—I appreciate it. But we're just staying in Benson Beach for now."

Cassie nods. "Well, I'm here if you ever want to chat."

Sana dips out to go over the photos, and Levi and I make our way to Bugaboo in the corner of Cassie's parking lot. We're both quiet and a little tense, adding a layer of absurdity to the frosting no doubt all over our faces and shirts.

"What was that about?" I ask as soon as we're out of earshot of any other customers.

"I was going to ask you the same thing," he says quizzically.

We reach the car and come to a stop. "I told you Tea Tide isn't expanding. I was very clear about it."

But Levi doesn't budge. If anything, he seems to press further, crossing the distance from the passenger's side to where I'm standing stubbornly at the driver's door. "It's not as if sitting with Cassie would be signing a lease. It's just a discussion. So you could see what it might be like."

I shake my head. "I don't need to see it. I'm keeping things the way Annie wanted them."

"But it won't always be like that, right?" Levi asks. "Things are changing, and they always will be. Even this whole Revenge Ex thing is changing Tea Tide. The people who come in. The scones on the menu."

"That's not the same," I say, and not for the first time, I feel a pang of panic about that, too. About what's going to happen once this is over and I have to find new ways to keep the money coming in. "Everything that's happening now is just a blip before we go back to normal."

Levi's voice is low, almost soothing. Half of me wants to lean into it, but the other half is tensed against it. "Maybe," he says. "But it's still a change. A good one. And maybe someday down the line, you'll want bigger ones."

"You're one to talk about change," I snap, like there's been a rattlesnake uncoiling in my throat just waiting to strike.

The moment it comes out of me, I understand that I'm not just frustrated with Levi. I'm angry with him. I've *been* angry with him. I've just been so swept up in this—the hijinks we're getting into with this pact we made, the old rhythms of friendship returning, this new kind of attraction to Levi that makes it all the more enticing—that I've been pushing down the very real hurt from these past few years.

Levi winces, the hit landing harder than I intended it to. He takes a step back from me. "Kelly's a person. It's different," he says tightly.

My entire body goes hot with mortification. I somehow keep forgetting about the Kelly of it all.

"I was talking about your book, Levi, but good to know," I say, feeling rotten for it.

Levi ducks his head, looking down at our feet. "Right."

I take a breath and set the anger back aside. We have a lot of work ahead for the wedding, and we're getting along just fine. Levi will be gone in a few weeks anyway. There's no point in digging through the past when there's barely going to be a future.

"I'm sorry. I'm just—I'm sorry." I run my hand through my hair, unused to it being let loose out of its signature messy bun. "I know I might sound ridiculous. But the scones were a big deal for me already. That used to be something Annie and I did back and forth, like a way of keeping in touch while I was gone."

I can tell when Levi looks up and meets my eye that he had already caught on to that. Maybe Annie even told him herself. It makes it harder to have this conversation, in some ways, because it's the first time I'm having it with someone who understands the full history behind it. It's not Nancy asking me to shake things up or customers asking why we don't have specials anymore. It's Levi, who knows me, who knew Annie. Who understands that as objectively ridiculous as it is for a person to get this emotional about a scone, it's really just the tip of a much larger iceberg.

"I just—it took a lot for me to even do that. I don't even know if I will again," I say, suddenly feeling drained. Not just by this conversation, but by the past few years leading up to it. How I've felt so stuck, and even when I've known there are ways to unstick myself, the guilt of moving on feels worse than the guilt of staying in one place.

"But you might," says Levi, without any pressure. "All of these things you might do with Tea Tide—they're just something to consider. What'll it hurt to ask?"

Everything, I think. Because he may understand some of it, but not all of it. He was Annie's best friend, but he was never *hers*. Not the way I was. Not the way I was from the literal moment I was born, the way a sister can only ever belong to a sister, unique to any kind of belonging in the world. Maybe there was a day when I could have worn her down about franchising—a day when I came back to Benson Beach on my own, and we ran the shop together for a while like we talked about—but because of me, that day came never came.

I took her for granted when she was alive, and I can't take her will for granted, too. Not with something so precious to her.

Levi's eyes are still on me with a steady kind of patience in them that almost knocks the words loose from me, but I can't let them go. Maybe there will always be a part of me holding on to that old anger. A part of me that will always resent all the moments we could have been here for each other like this and weren't, because Levi was so determined to stay away. Because even when he tried to ease himself back in, it was only ever in half measures—short texts or abrupt emails that never made me sure what he wanted from me, if he wanted anything at all.

"How about this," I say. "We agree to leave each other's professional lives be."

Levi's lean body goes stiff. "What do you mean?"

"I mean you don't have to try to—*help* with Tea Tide." I smile, keeping it light. "And I'll stop pestering you about your writing."

Or whatever it is Levi's doing in the back of Tea Tide right now.

Levi works his jaw, and I see the beginnings of that almost-smile, the one that doesn't reach his eyes. Only just before it settles, something else breaks through—it isn't that shared understanding we had as kids, but a new version of it. One that's warmer, one that's softer. Like he's looking at the wall I just put up and tapping gently on it instead of walking away.

"I'd consider that deal if I had any confidence you'd keep it," he says.

I let out a breathy laugh that's part exasperation, part relief. I'm not used to this Levi. The one who doesn't let himself get pushed so easily away.

Levi leans back in. "I should have run it past you before talking to Cassie," he says. "Here. A truce."

He hands me the bag Cassie gave him earlier. Inside is a takeaway box with a transparent lid full of Levi's leftover cake from the tasting, plus an extra lemon cupcake he must have paid for when I was talking to Sana.

I tilt my head at him and see the gleam in his eye, and I'm not sure what possesses me. (Scratch that, I do. It's free cake.) But I bounce onto my tiptoes and plant a quick kiss on his cheek. So fast that I barely feel the heat of him against my lips, so fast that it feels like a drive-by.

"You know me too well," I say.

Levi looks almost bashful as he gets into the car, forgetting entirely to complain about getting squished in half by it. My anger feels slippery again, because he's here, and he's looking a little more like the Levi I knew every day—the one with those open expressions, with that unabashed, earnest energy that made him magnetic to be around. That made him dream up all these magical stories that colored so much of my childhood that it feels like we actually lived them.

And I'm not angry at that Levi. I'm angry at the one who came after him. Only sometimes it's hard to know exactly which one he is—old Levi, New York Levi, or something in between. Something brand-new, even. It makes it hard to know how to feel about him, because I still don't know what to expect.

I just know that I want to be around him. I tell myself not to examine it any closer than that. Maybe I don't know this version of Levi yet, but I know myself too well—if I follow that path, it's only going to lead me in the same direction it did years ago, and I can't let myself fall for Levi Shaw again.

So I hold on to all of it at once: the anger, the affection, the fun, the doubt. I can feel it all at the same time, and let it settle after he's gone. The thought makes my heart dip in my chest, but it doesn't make it any less true—if there's one thing in this I can count on Levi for, it's the part where he leaves.

Chapter Ten

I try to think of the last time I went clubbing, and then my brain unhelpfully supplies, *Never*. When we were traveling, Griffin was always way more into chasing adrenaline rushes than exploring anything local or getting to know people. Usually by the time we'd finish on the day's excursion, I'd be too tired or too rattled from the cliff jumping or the hot-air ballooning or the white water rafting to go out anywhere after dark.

Which leads me here, back to my childhood closet, wondering if college me left anything remotely hip enough to wear for a night out that still fits.

My parents still own the place we grew up in a few blocks from the beach, a little yellow house with blue trim that's wearing at its edges, but in a way that's only ever made me love it more. It has marks of us everywhere—a few old clothes and mementos, scuff marks on floors from Dylan's cleats, a collection of hoarded mugs and teacups that could probably fill a museum—but a lot of it's been cleared out, now that my parents are renting it as an Airbnb.

I'm about to wade through the closet when Dylan calls. This isn't unusual for him—he'll either text a bunch of emojis that only Mateo and I can reliably interpret, or just give a ring.

"What's up?" I ask.

"First of all, you missed happy hour again," says Dylan.

I wince. I've been so busy with Tea Tide and Levi that I've had to bail twice now. The bar probably thinks I've been raptured. "Sorry, sorry—did you want to talk wedding details?"

"No. I wanted to steal sips of your Blue Moon while you weren't looking and catch up. I haven't even seen you on morning runs."

It's probably impossible for Dylan to see much of anything at the speeds he's clocking, but I keep that to myself.

"Rain check," I promise him, trying not to sound as distracted as I am by the outfit debacle. "Did you have a second of all?"

"Yeah. Second of all, you are my flesh and blood, right?" Dylan asks.

I look down as if to make sure I'm still corporeal. "Last I checked."

"Then why am I finding out from my *track team* that you're the original version of that ridiculous cake meme?"

I bite down a laugh. "I'm still recovering from the shock of it myself," I tell him.

After Sana gave Cassie the photos of us to post on her page, she also gave her a snippet of the footage she got of us alone in the cake tasting room. Specifically, the snippet where I lean forward and thumb the crumb off Levi's face, which is equal parts mortifying and thrilling to watch played back. I didn't realize how slow I'd been about it, how deliberate. And in the heat of the moment, I hadn't noticed how Levi's eyelids had lowered, his gaze skimming my face like he was hungry for something else entirely.

The camera didn't miss a beat of it, though. Cassie captioned it cake: the only thing that tastes better than a #RevengeEx, undoubtedly prompted by Sana, and it took off like wildfire from there. It was uploaded to TikTok within the hour, with choice comments like we need to gatekeep cake from hot people, and i just KNOW griffin is shaking right now and them: how many times did you watch this? me: yes.

It snowballed from there—the next day people were parodying it into oblivion, doing it with random foods like mashed potatoes, or dressed as characters from books (most notably, a vampire one where they did it with fake blood and the character licked it off their thumb and said, "Mm, O neg"). It's even inspired some interpretive dance move where people are pressing thumbs to each other's face, a TikTok where someone recreated Cassie's pistachio cake recipe, and an "expert in body language" to assess the way Levi and I interacted beat by beat.

Sana would be proud of how quickly we've gotten into the swing of this trope, because the expert declared us one of the most sincerely in love couples she'd ever seen.

In the meantime, Cassie's so grateful for the extra publicity she's texted and emailed me multiple times, emphasizing how much she'd love to talk about franchising when things have calmed down. I've answered her back but continued to sidestep the offer. Even if I wanted to entertain the idea of franchising, I'm barely keeping up with demand at Tea Tide right now—our supplier was so alarmed by the amount of caramel and dark chocolate we had to order to keep the Revenge Ex scone in stock that he made me repeat the order to him three times.

"See? This is why you have to come to happy hour. So we can keep tabs on each other whenever one of us breaks the internet," says Dylan. There's an undertone in his voice, one that sounds almost sad. But I'm pretty sure I've imagined it when he adds brightly: "You and Levi are really something now, huh?"

I hesitate, the guilt wrapping itself around my throat. Dylan misinterprets the silence and lets out a cackle.

"Mom and Dad are gonna be so stressed when we have to throw another Hart wedding hot on the heels of the first one," he says.

"All right, all right, rein it in," I tease. "We're *barely* a thing."

I say it as preemptive damage control—I don't want Dylan getting attached to the idea of me and Levi when we have an unclear but imminent expiration date—but also because it's true. I haven't even seen much of Levi these past few days. He agreed to help his dad at his auto shop while the buddy he co-runs it with is out of town. I've turned my head an embarrassing number of times in the back of Tea Tide to make quick remarks to Levi in the middle of the day only to remember he isn't there.

But just under that disappointment is a quiet kind of relief. That body language expert's words are still echoing in my ear, almost like a warning. *Don't get too close to Levi.* Not just in the romantic sense, but the friend one, too. If he lets me down again, it's going to take a long, long time to come back up. Hopefully these few days apart will be the reset I need to make sure I've got him at arm's length again.

A length I'm about to put to the test, because he's arriving in approximately five minutes.

"Hey, what are you up to tonight?" Dylan asks. "You could come over and watch a movie."

"Oh. Actually—Levi and I are going to Happy Shores to check out the replacement DJ for the wedding," I tell him. They had one picked out who ended up booked this time around, but in a bizarre stroke of luck, he has an identical twin who *also* DJs for a living. I'm mildly terrified imagining how hard their family must throw down at reunions, but grateful for the boon. "Do you want to join in?"

Dylan laughs. "As much as I'd love to see Levi bust a move in a club, I'll have to sit that out. Mateo and I are both zonked from work, plus we're about to call his mom to talk small bites for the cocktail hour and that's probably going to take a while."

If there's one thing Dylan and his future mother-in-law have in common, it is a deep and abiding love for appetizer-based foods. Seeing as the rest of the plan is to have the main affair catered by Mateo's uncles, whose tamales are so popular there's often a line out the door at Sirena on weekends, we're already in good hands.

"We'll chill some other day this week, then," I say, still riffling through the closet.

"Yeah. Text me a day that works for you," says Dylan. "I haven't seen your face in forever."

"You could always look in a mirror and squint," I joke.

He laughs again, but I don't miss the way it tapers off. I feel that knot of guilt in me tighten again. Dylan was more jarred by our parents leaving for the West Coast after Annie's death than I was; he'd been here the whole time I was traveling, part of our parents' day-to-day in a way I never was as an adult. We're the only family each other has close by now, and while we never take that for granted, every now and then, life gets in the way.

There's a knock at the door that can only be Levi.

"Yeah, I'll text you," I tell Dylan quickly.

"Good. If you need me tonight, Mateo and I are gonna be rehearsing your cake meme so we can use it as our first dance."

"Can't wait to deeply alarm your wedding videographer. Love you, bro."

"Love you too, sis."

I hang up and call out to Levi to let him know he can come in, then grab the only dress I've spotted that fits the bill—a dark red bodycon dress with a V-neck and spaghetti straps that I wore when I was going out with friends in college.

I shove it on quickly, already clad in a pair of nude pumps I borrowed from Sana, my hair curled and makeup in place. I steal a quick glance at myself in the flimsy full-length mirror Annie and I used to jokingly push each other in and out of before school. The dress doesn't fit like it used to, but not in a way I particularly mind—it's absolutely tighter in the chest, giving me some subtle cleavage it never did back in my "going out" days, and it rides up a little higher than it used to, exposing more of my muscled running legs.

I walk out of the bedroom and into the front hall, and oh. *Oh my*. Levi has just hit a very specific kind of synapse I didn't know my brain had, one that's practically humming, it's so pleased with itself. He's wearing his usual jeans and a white T-shirt, but over it is a worn-out, dark brown leather jacket that is entirely too hot for late August and possibly entirely too hot for my eyes to behold. His hair is subtly gelled on the sides, just enough to give the curls on top a new depth that makes me want to run my fingers through them. He looks like he's about to toss me on the back of a motorcycle, like he's on his way to break a dozen hearts without breaking his stride.

What a deeply inconvenient time to discover that I have a thing for leather jackets. Or more specifically, a thing for Levi in a leather jacket.

I swallow hard, then worry Levi's going to notice I've gone about as red as my dress. Only Levi seems to be every bit as distracted as I am. His eyes don't meet mine, preoccupied with skimming the hem of the dress pressed against my upper thigh, the tight waist, the spot where one of the straps meets my collarbone.

Usually my first instinct would be to slouch or make some kind of joke. It's not that I'm uncomfortable in my body. It's just that dresses like this aren't necessarily my style anymore. Between traveling and Tea Tide and running, I'm not used to wearing something that isn't just for function. And after dating Griffin for so long, I'm not used to being noticed the way that Levi is so clearly, blatantly *noticing* me right now.

But I hold myself a little higher, a small smile curling on my lips. One that makes me feel like this dress has a quiet kind of magic I'd forgotten I like to play with. One that makes Levi give me a sheepish smile of his own when his eyes finally catch it.

"That's a nice dress," he says, his voice low in his throat.

I take a few steps forward to close the distance between us, relishing the way the heels give my hips a slight sway, the way Levi's eyes snag on them. I lift a hand and pat the front pocket of his leather jacket, catching a whiff of some cologne that must be lingering on it—something woodsy and deep that's going to drive me wild by the end of the night, I already know.

"That's a nice jacket," I tell him.

Levi's cheeks tinge pink, and it makes me take my hand off Levi and grab the keys to Bugaboo, makes me take a deep breath meant to uncoil the warm, tight feeling low in my stomach.

It doesn't work. I resolve right then and there that I will not be drinking a single drop tonight.

"C'mon, Indiana Jones," I tell him. "We've got a DJ to scout."

An hour later we are both so ridiculously, laughably out of our depth that I feel like I'm hugging the wall at my first school dance all over again. It's not that we've aged out of the club scene—it's just that we quite possibly never aged into it. Everyone around us has clearly pregamed and is so at ease dancing out on the floor with reckless abandon that I feel like I'm somehow drunk by osmosis. Like if we actually hit that floor and start dancing, something is going to let loose inside me in a way I'm certainly not prepared for on my own, let alone in front of Levi.

"Well," I shout into Levi's ear, "at least we know the DJ can get people dancing."

"What?"

"The DJ can get people dancing," I shout.

Levi shakes his head. "Sorry, what?"

"You have no right looking that hot in a leather jacket," I say, letting the crowd swallow it up with the rest of my words.

Levi shrugs again, shooting me an apologetic look. I save my old man jokes for later, seeing as he won't be able to hear them now. He wraps a hand around my wrist, gentle but firm, pulling me out of the pulsing nucleus of the club and over to the quieter bar.

"It seems like the DJ can really get people dancing," he tells me.

I let out a laugh so loud and sharp that Levi catches it like a cold, laughing himself without understanding why.

"Yeah," I agree. "So far, so good."

"I have a theory about DJs, though," says Levi, leaning in close.

I lean in, too, pretending it's to hear him better when really I just want to inhale more of that woodsy leather jacket again. "Do share."

"The first key is amping up the crowd. But the second one comes down to a perfect science. You have to recognize when the crowd has reached the most potential energy—has enough momentum for a full liftoff, if you will—and that's when any good wedding DJ will play 'Uptown Funk.'"

I feel a grin spread on my face like butter on a warm scone. "'Uptown Funk'?" I repeat.

Levi works his face into a playful kind of solemnity. "It's the most universally contagious song there is. But it has to be used wisely."

"How the hell do you know this?" I ask.

"I work in finance," he reminds me. "I've been dragged to so many weddings and second weddings and third weddings for all the partners at my firm in the last few years that I can basically make a set list myself."

"Then what are we doing here?" I ask him. "You should be the DJ."

Levi shakes his head. "I have the knowledge, not the gift. You'll see. If this guy pulls it off tonight, you'll see."

"Excuse the two of you, but am I going to get a single good shot tonight? Go dance out on the floor like regular humans."

We both startle at the appearance of Sana, who is a staggeringly beautiful sight with her thick hair pulled into a high ponytail, her lips painted a deep burgundy, and her body draped in a slinky, backless silver dress that sparkles like she's full of constellations.

"Wait. What are you doing here?" I ask. "This isn't one of our Revenge Ex dates."

"I'm here for two reasons," she says, pulling up freshly painted black fingernails. "One, to go home with the hottest guy here. And two, to get pictures of the two of you I can use to continue blowing up your spot for our mutual gain."

I balk, trying to absorb both the hotness and the audacity of her at the same time. "How did you even know we'd *be* here?"

Her brow furrows. "You asked to borrow my pumps. There's literally only one place in Benson Beach worth wearing pumps to," she says, the *duh* implied.

"Haven't we done enough damage to the internet this week?" I ask.

"You forget how fleeting the attention spans of our digitally raised audience are." She puts one hand on Levi's shoulder and the other on mine and bodily shoves us both toward the dance floor. "Go out there and do something with one modicum of sexiness. I beg. And then I will leave you alone to stand awkwardly at the bar like the faculty chaperones you're both destined to become."

In the DJ's defense, he has nothing to do with the crimes against dancing that Levi and I commit after that. Because after Sana shoves us onto the floor, we both meet each other's eyes with an unspoken resolve, and start busting out the dorkiest moves two human beings can possibly bust. I've got peace signs drifting along my forehead while Levi starts doing a shuffle like a boomer dad on vacation. I pivot into a scuba diver while Levi starts alternately framing both of our faces with his hands. At one point we both start doing the Macarena, Levi clearly not remembering any of the moves but attempting to follow my lead just the same.

"I hate you both!" Sana yells, putting her phone camera down. She blows me a kiss. "Don't come looking for me. I'm getting some."

With that, she abruptly departs, swallowed up by the crowd of dancers so fast that we couldn't follow her even if we wanted to.

A remix of a popular song comes on then, and Levi surprises me by taking my hand in his and pulling me in, so steady in the movement that I spin into him with an unexpected ease.

"Wait," I say, laughing, "I don't actually know how to dance."

I can't tell if he can hear me or not, but he must get the gist because his eyes glint almost like it's a challenge. He keeps hold of my hand and pulls back, then uses the momentum to spin me out again with our hands above our heads. I'm still laughing, struck by the strangeness of it—by the way Levi knows what he's doing so well that he can lead someone who has about as much experience dancing as a sack of potatoes and make it seem like we're on our way to a ballroom dance competition.

We spend the rest of the song in a flurry, spinning and twisting, his hands on my hands or guiding me by the waist. I can't stop grinning. It feels almost like flying. I'm grounded only by the warmth of his hands on me, so steady that it's like he knows the shape of me better than I do, can anticipate how I'll react before he even touches me. Every time I meet his eyes there's a mischief in them again, the same I've seen glimmers of lately, only this time, there's something just under it. An unmistakable heat burning in them. One that I feel pooling low in my own stomach with every swoop on the dance floor, every time our eyes connect.

Levi spins me out again, and this time when he pulls me in, my back is to him, pressed against his chest. He holds me there for a moment and I nearly stop breathing—there's fluttering in my chest where the air is supposed to be—until I lift my head to look back at him, and every part of me swells at the satisfaction in his expression, in the clear and visceral joy.

We're pressed so close that I can feel his heartbeat pulsing against my back. That I wonder if I pressed even closer, I might feel something else.

"You're a natural," says Levi into my ear.

The words shiver all the way down my back. I should laugh. Should find some way to break this sizzling tension between us, which is getting less *friendly* by the second. But then the DJ does it for me when the fading song is replaced with an unmistakable beat, one that has every single dancer on the floor jumping up and down like we're little kids losing our marbles in a bouncy house.

We break apart, doubling over with laughter, Levi triumphantly saying, "See?" just as "Uptown Funk" starts blaring through the club.

We throw ourselves into the crowd, both sweating profusely by the time the song ends, my feet aching in my heels, the smile aching on my face. Another song takes over, but by then, Levi and I both decide the DJ has our seal of approval, and head out of the noisy club and pile into the quiet of Bugaboo. Levi jokes that we ought to check the trunk for Sana with a camera, and we're still marveling about her uncanny ability to catch us by surprise when we pull into the lot behind Tea Tide.

"What's still open these days?" Levi asks. "I should grab dinner."

My heart is still thrumming in my chest, like it has too much energy to let the night end. "I've got two cold pizzas in my fridge if you want some."

Levi doesn't hesitate. "That sounds perfect," he says, freeing himself from Bugaboo.

I blink in the driver's seat, only then understanding the full ramifications of my offer. Levi is going to be in my apartment. Alone with me in my apartment. Wearing that leather jacket and smelling all earthy-sweet in my apartment.

I steel myself, mentally conjuring the ridiculousness of him doing the Macarena. We can be in my apartment as friends. In fact, him being in the apartment will *prove* that I am fine with the two of us being friends. A test of sorts.

I let him in and flick on the lights, and he takes in the apartment in all its cozy, mismatched glory. There's the formerly bright pink couch I thrifted that's long since faded into a pastel, covered in kitschy dessert-shaped pillows my mom sends for my birthday every year. There's the fridge so littered with Benson Beach fliers and pizza coupons and wedding invitations from old friends that it's a miracle it doesn't tip over from them. There are the end tables loosely decorated with framed pictures and old sand dollars from the beach, and the floor scattered with the DVD collection of early-2000s-era rom-coms that Sana and I still flip through on weekend nights despite splitting all our streaming accounts with Dylan and Mateo. The end result isn't exactly making any interior design magazines, but it's always felt like home.

"This is very June," he says in an affectionate way that makes my body go warm. I excuse myself for a moment to change out of the dress and into jeans and an old cross-country shirt and come back out to find Levi with his head in my fridge, looking impressed by the giant pizza boxes I've precariously wedged inside.

"You weren't kidding," he says, pulling them out and setting them on the little kitchen table.

I open the boxes with a flourish. "When I know I'm going to be slammed at Tea Tide, I'll get a deal at Domino's on Monday and eat cold pizza for dinner the whole week."

"In New York, we call that 'meal prepping,'" says Levi, taking a slice of pepperoni.

We ignore the chairs at the kitchen table, settling on opposite ends of my couch, me kicking off half a dozen plush pillows to make room. I pull my knees up and burrow in, and the whole thing has such kid-at-a-sleepover vibes that it settles my nerves a bit.

"So are you going to tell me how you went all *Dancing with the Stars* back there?" I ask. "Because *that* must be a recent development."

Levi is suddenly very engaged in staring at his slice. "Well—Kelly and I were taking classes. We were going to do something at the wedding."

Kelly's name feels like a giant *thunk* on the floorboards of the apartment, knocking me back into reality. I slow my chewing, finally feeling the adrenaline in me start to settle. Starting to feel something heavy take its place.

But no—this is a good thing, talking about Kelly. It's redrawing the line I keep playing mental hopscotch with. If Levi and I are going to be friends after this the way I hope we will, we're going to have a lot of conversations about Kelly in the future. Might as well rip the Band-Aid off now.

"I wasn't sure how far along in that process you were," I say carefully.

"Oh, not very. We didn't have a date picked out. Just a general idea." Levi's lip quirks, his expression rueful. "I'd be a lot more helpful organizing this wedding, maybe, if we'd gotten any further."

I nudge his leg with my sock. "I'd say you're doing perfectly fine."

He stares down at his leg, pizza momentarily forgotten in his hands. "It's weird to think about, but if we hadn't put things off, I might be married by now." I can't see his face, and his tone is just as unreadable—something that might be relief and might be regret. "I probably should have realized something was off. But we were both so busy. I just chalked it up to that."

"I know it's not really my business, but—how are things between the two of you right now?" I ask. "Is any of this working?"

I'm preparing for him to say *no*, because then I'll have to make an offer I'm not sure I want to and tell him we can drop this whole Revenge Ex scheme now. Except when Levi opens his mouth, he says, "Actually, yeah."

It's like I had my arms braced in front of me and something came and hit me from the side instead. "Oh?" I manage.

He nods. "I think it is. We've talked a few times. A lot about the old days. She doesn't mention Roman." When his eyes finally meet mine, there's something guarded in them again. I stiffen at the sight of it, reminded of that cool distance he kept between us all the years he was gone. "She's said a few things about the future that make me think . . . maybe she wants me to be a part of it."

A friend would ask him right now if he wants to be a part of *her* future. If he's willing to settle for "maybe." If this entire debacle with Roman is really something he can see himself getting past and trust it won't happen again.

And I want to be Levi's friend. But the truth is, under the surface, I know I have an agenda of my own. One that would be asking those questions for my own sake, and not just for Levi's.

I let the question die in my throat. Someone else can ask Levi, but it probably shouldn't be me.

"Well—that's good," I say. "That it's working, I mean."

Levi nods again, his eyes drifting out to the rest of the apartment, nearly lost in a thought before he pulls himself back.

"What about Griffin?" he asks.

I don't miss the edge in his voice. I might be keeping my feelings about Kelly to myself, but Levi still has no qualms about how he feels about Griffin. It makes me bite down a quick smile. It's not the same as Levi being jealous, but there's a satisfaction in it just the same.

"He's somehow both super quiet and *ridiculously* loud," I say. "He's not texting me anymore, but he's been posting nonstop."

I'm not even checking Griffin's Instagram on purpose anymore. He's just always there at the top of my feed, the new poster child for Doing the Most. Selfies of him with Lisel on a hike, a picture of him snuggling Lisel's dog, an announcement that he's collaborating with yet another protein powder or fitness brand. I can only assume his new manager never sleeps.

"And you're okay with that?"

I shrug, sidestepping the question. I'm not *okay* with it in the sense that I don't understand how someone I cared about so much can have such little regard for my feelings. But I also don't care much what goes on in Griffin's world and find myself caring less every day.

"It's different for me. I don't have any desire to be with him anymore." I smirk. "Honestly, the whole thing is kind of funny now. I think the attention on us is really getting to him."

Levi bristles. "He always did have a way of needing to be in the spotlight, even in school."

"Speaking of," I say carefully. "I know you're not a huge fan of that spotlight. You're still okay with all of this?"

The irritation eases out of Levi's expression. "June, I'm hiding in the back of Tea Tide all day. I'm the one who should be asking you that."

I consider for a moment. "I don't mind it now. Everyone's just curious, mostly. And I've always liked talking to new people."

The only downside to that, of course, is that Tea Tide is so crammed with new people that it's still pushing the regulars out. But I'm hoping that'll resolve itself when the hype dies down.

"I guess I was just worried about your writing situation," I elaborate. "If this weird viral fame is going to affect how you handle it at all."

Levi shakes his head. "Even if it did, I'm pretty sure the whole business with Kelly would have blown it up first," he says. "And anyway, I'm still planning on publishing under a pseudonym."

"Hmm." I take another bite of my pizza, chewing thoughtfully. "You're going to need something broody and edgy, to go with that novel of yours."

He rolls his eyes affectionately. "I'll probably just use Dawson," he says, which is his mom's maiden name.

"Or you could commit to the mood. Archer Blaze Storm," I venture, leaning in.

Levi casts his eyes back up to the ceiling, already sensing I'm on a roll. "Here we go."

"McManly Mysterious Man," I throw out next.

He furrows his brow. "Why would a parent with the last name 'Man' name their kid 'McManly'?"

I lower my head ominously. "Bruce Wayne."

"Aren't you breaking that little rule of yours?" Levi asks.

I point a finger at him. "I said no pestering you about the manuscript. I made no promises about your alter ego."

And in my defense, I haven't pestered him one bit about the manuscript. It's hard to get a spare moment to do much of anything outside of Tea Tide and wedding planning right now, but it's also hard because the more I read, the more I feel an open ache for the younger version of Levi who wrote it. In every line it's clear just how lost he felt when he was first in the city, just how abruptly the change rattled him and how cut off he felt from home.

It makes me ache for him, but quietly, it also makes me angry. It didn't have to be that way. But his first two years of college especially—before his mom would have gotten sick, before he met Kelly—he was more out of touch with me than he'd ever been. That loneliness was a deliberate choice.

"Do you really remember that much of *The Sky Seekers*?" Levi asks unexpectedly.

And it's strange, because it's almost like he's asking for something else. Like he's asking me to flip my heart over, to show him the underside of it, that secret part where you keep things tucked away long after other people forget them.

"You don't?" I ask.

Levi shakes his head. "I can't find the manuscript, either. It was only ever on Word. I didn't back it up."

He knows I've read it—or what little he had of it, just before things between us fell apart. That version was choppy. Unfinished. Missing parts that Levi had clearly forgotten, with little notes to go back that he never fixed. I tore through it just the same, reliving adventures old and new, settling in with familiar characters in their magical world.

It was clearly set in Benson Beach. In the versions Levi told me growing up, it revolved around two kid siblings, but in its polished form, they were teenagers. They've known since they were ten that there's a world parallel to theirs where all these mythical creatures quietly exist and are granted the ability to see them after they're tapped as the next two guardians—a responsibility inherited from the guardians of the town that came before them. For the most part, they live in harmony with the other world, occasionally acting as the bridge between them. But at the start of the book, something splits in the sky between the two realities, and they have to combine their elemental abilities to fix it before the two dueling natures of the realities collide.

When I read those pages the first time, I ached from the satisfaction of it. Of the way Levi's written words captured the old ones he'd say out loud to me during those long walks we took exploring the woods, back when it felt like we were making our own kind of magic.

But in reading it, I recognized something I didn't as a kid. The guardians Levi created weren't just characters. The one that could manipulate water was Dylan. The one who could wield fire was Annie. And I was nowhere to be found.

It hit like a gut punch back then, but it was one I needed later. A clear signal to move on. That he was never going to think of me the way I thought of him. I wasn't a part of the larger story he wanted to tell.

But that hurt is an old one, the kind so settled in me that I don't feel it much anymore. Which is why I give him a small, triumphant smirk and say, "So you went looking for the manuscript."

He tilts his head sheepishly. "Being here makes me miss it a little," he admits. And then, a moment later: "Being around *you* makes me miss it."

My smirk softens. I'm not sure what to make of that, especially knowing how determined he is to write something else. I tell myself it's just an echo of that old reminder—Levi and I are friends. That's all we're equipped to be. And the last thing I want to do is take it for granted.

Because I've missed this. All of it. Sitting on the couch eating cold pizza, unabashedly talking as we chew. Talking about a shared history that nobody else knows except the two of us. Watching Levi come back a little more every day, his posture loosening, his expressions open and easy. I'm not going to take it for granted.

"Well, maybe after you finish the Untitled Levi Shaw Memoir," I quip.

Levi takes the last bite of his crust. "I think I'm going to title it *June Hates This*. It's got a better ring to it."

"In that case, you'd better fully credit me in the acknowledgments." I hop to my feet. "I need another slice. Want one?"

"Yeah, sure."

Once my back is turned to him, I have a decidedly wicked idea, one that feels like it will cement this new dynamic of ours. Levi and June, friends again. The good, the bad, and all the nonsense in between.

He takes the slice from me so trustingly that I come close to maybe, possibly, for the splittest of seconds, feeling bad when he takes a giant bite of it.

"June August September October November *December* Hart," Levi exclaims.

I cackle as he registers the Pop Rocks going off in his mouth. Watch the way his eyes crinkle first in surprise, and then disgust, and then amusement, so many shades of Levi all at once that I almost trip on my own carpet from laughter.

He swallows hard, his throat bobbing with the effort. "You are a menace to society," he tells me.

My eyes catch on the way he skims his teeth with his tongue, checking for stray Pop Rocks. Friends shouldn't have thoughts about their friend's tongues, particularly the other places they could skim, but I allow myself that one last weakness. It's late and we're tired and I'm only human.

"And don't you forget it, McManly," I say, swapping out his slice for a fresh, untampered one and taking his, biting right into the edge he just bit into himself.

The Pop Rocks start ricocheting in my mouth, and I let out an "Oh, *no*," and Levi and I are laughing and swapping the rest of the Pop Rocks pouch back and forth. If I'm not imagining things, Levi's own eyes linger on my lips, trailing up to my eyes. There's a moment our eyes meet, and there's a spark between us that feels like it could light a flame.

Chapter Eleven

Holy *shit*.

Those are the only two words my short-circuiting brain can summon when I see it. The photo. *The* photo. The one of me and Levi dancing in Happy Shores is so unrepentantly, ridiculously steamy that I almost don't recognize my own self in it. Someone took it just after Levi spun me into him, the two of us suspended in motion, bright against the moody light of the club. My back is pressed against Levi's, my dress hiked up where it's pushed up against Levi's legs, his own shirt lifted and exposing a sliver of his lean, toned stomach. My face is tilted up to look at him, my eyes obscured, but his are fully visible and looking at me like he's about to take a bite right out of me. We look like something timeless, something iconic. Like two people so far in the throes of passion we've forgotten the rest of the world exists.

A *Business Savvy* fan account tweeted it with the caption Twitter gets it first!!! and a bunch of fire emojis about an hour ago. It's already blown up enough that Cassie, whose newest location is literally opening *today*, took a moment to text me, Um??? I need to fan myself. You two are too much!! and Mateo texted me in the middle of class to say, You broke my students. They'll never learn about the cultural diffusion of Alexander the Great's conquests now.

I'd probably liquefy on the spot if I could afford to. But Tea Tide is just as packed as it's been all week, so all I can do is go, go, go. By the time Sana wanders in, I've got the photo primed on my phone, holding it up to her accusingly.

"Fool me *thrice*?" I demand.

"I had nothing to do with this," says Sana, raising her hands to gesture for peace. "I was extremely busy with Aiden, the hot pediatrician who was the designated driver both for his friends *and* for my human body that night."

"Okay," I say, "details about that, please. But also, *how did this happen?*"

"It might have had something to do with me pointing and yelling 'Are those the Revenge Exes?' every chance I got, but otherwise, no idea," says Sana, helping herself to a chocolate chip scone and ringing herself up.

I set the phone down. "My *parents* are going to see this," I moan. I'm already dreading my next long Sunday afternoon call with my mom. So far, I've managed to skim the surface of the whole "Levi and I are dating" thing, but this is going to warrant an entire mom-sized investigation that will start with her asking what on earth I was doing in a club and end with her asking when Levi and I are getting engaged.

If she and Levi's mom haven't already called each other and skipped straight to that part, that is.

"And so are a whole bunch of potential Tea Tide customers," says Sana, wiggling her eyebrows.

She's got a fair point. We're in a rare lull right now in between the lunch rush and the afternoon snack rush, so for once, there isn't anyone immediately in line behind her. "Quick, tell me about this Aiden," I say.

Sana's eyes go all dreamy. "He makes his own cheese. The next morning, he brought me homemade gouda in bed."

I blink. "You're making that up."

"He's got an adorable puppy named Snickerdoodle."

I shake my head at her. "That absolutely cannot be real."

She leans in, putting a finger to my nose. "He's taking me out to that fancy winery with the chocolate fountain this weekend."

I wrinkle my nose. "Literally every Hallmark movie heroine written into existence is ready to fight you right now."

"You'll get there," she says, patting me on the back. "Just as soon as you and Levi drop this whole fake dating thing and realize you're madly in love with each other."

I glare at her as intensely as a woman who is subsisting mostly off scones and the fumes of four hours of sleep can manage.

"I'd write you a whole laundry list of why *that's* never going to happen, but I'm getting a call," I say, pulling my buzzing phone out of my apron pocket.

Griffin's name is lit up on the screen. Both Sana's eyebrows and mine fly up. I haven't heard from him in so long that I forgot that hearing from him was still a possibility.

Out of curiosity alone, I decide to take it, waving over one of the part-time employees to mind the register while I walk to the back parking lot.

"Hey, June," says Griffin, the warmth in his voice so honey-sweet that I almost pull the phone from my ear like the speaker made a mistake. "How are you holding up?"

I tense at that. *Holding up*. The words are choice, but so is his tone—it's the same one he'd use to push and pull me in moments he was trying to get me on board with wild stunts I didn't want any part of. Coddling, almost. Like he knew better than I did.

"I'm fine," I say flatly. I make a point of not asking how he is and jump straight to it: "Why are you calling?"

"Well—partially because I'm worried about you. I know you and Levi have a past."

My fingers tighten around the phone. I'm not naïve enough to think nobody caught on to my crush on Levi in high school, but this is the first time Griffin's come close to bringing it up. I think a part of him always resented that he didn't ask me out until after it was clear that Levi and I weren't going to be a thing.

"You don't have to worry," I say, my voice breezy and even. "We're happy."

"Oh," says Griffin, his own voice too bright. "I'm so glad to hear it."

I don't say anything, waiting for him to get to the actual point of this call.

"And I bet—I bet other people will want to hear it, too," he says. "Actually, I was wondering if you'd want to come do a special for *Business Savvy*."

I blink, the words so preposterous that I'm not even sure if I can entertain them. If Griffin is really inviting me back to the same show that quite literally turned a profit on my snot-filled tears. But he must have some kind of angle if he has the audacity to ask this, so I can't help my curiosity.

"What kind of special?" I ask warily.

"One about you and me, about our relationships with Lisel and Levi."

"Why would you need us for that?" I ask. "We're not part of the show."

"But you're part of the story now, and—everyone loves you.

Which is great. But it's kind of painting me like the bad guy?" Griffin says it like it's both an apology and an accusation. "So I was just thinking—if you hopped on and told them we were still good, it would, you know. Shift the narrative."

The humiliation is searing, immediate—it feels like the summer I first learned to surf and still couldn't anticipate those sharp, biting waves that knocked you under from behind.

"Shift it," I repeat. "Into . . . what?"

"You know. Just—clear the air. I'm happy, you're happy. It was a mess how it went down, sure, but no harm done."

No harm done. Like all the years we spent together could be boiled down to those three words and let loose on a breeze. Like making a public spectacle of me in my own home and humiliating me on a global level could be so easily dismissed.

I'm almost worried I'll start to cry again in that big, sloppy way I did when he broke up with me. But whatever I'm feeling, it's already crystallizing. Curling in my fingers, stiff in my bones.

I don't want to yell at Griffin. I don't want to feel this way at all. Not about someone I once considered my best friend—not about someone I gave so much time and energy to that being angry with him feels like being angry with myself.

I clear my throat. "I'll think about it."

"Yeah?" Griffin's voice perks up on the other end of the line. "When do you think you'd be able to—"

"I'll think about it," I say, my voice stronger this time. "But right now I have to go."

"Of course. Well—let me know. And thank you, June. It means a lot."

I hang up, mad at myself for even leaving the door open to the possibility. But that's the thing. I can move on from Griffin, but I can't erase our past. I can't erase all the years our lives revolved around each other, the way we know each other's rhythms and hopes and insecurities. The way I still feel obligated to him as a friend, as the keeper of all those parts of him, even if I want nothing to do with him romantically ever again.

Levi is settling into the back room when I let myself back into Tea Tide, his hair tousled from today's unusually strong breeze, his blue eyes focused on his laptop screen. That is, until he looks over at me and immediately asks, "You okay?"

"Yeah." I hold up the phone still in my hand. "Griffin called."

Levi's brow furrows, and he pulls his hands from the keyboard. "What did he want?"

I laugh, the absurdity of it settling in. "He wants me to go on some special for *Business Savvy*. He's upset because he's getting 'painted like the bad guy.'"

Levi's voice has that edge to it again. "What does he expect you to do about that?"

"Play nice for the camera. So the world sees we're getting along or something," I say with a dismissive wave. I lean into the counter, not just tired in my bones, but tired all over.

Levi closes his laptop and walks over, leaning on the counter beside me close enough that I can feel the warmth of him near my bare arm. His eyes search my face. I resist the urge to lean in closer, to search his right back—the curve of his jaw, the slight smile line at the edge of his lips, the sudden softness in his eyes.

"You haven't taken an actual break in ages," he finally says. "The front doesn't seem too busy right now—do you maybe want to go for a quick run on the beach?"

I haven't been able to go on a proper run since this whole Revenge Exes thing began. "Yeah," I say, perking up. "Actually, that sounds great."

Except when we hit the beach, we both fall into a quick walking pace, neither of us initiating the run. It's a little too crowded on this stretch anyway, tourists and locals alike stretched out on towels and throwing beach balls and building castles close to the water's edge.

"So are you going to do it?" Levi asks, pitching his voice above the wind. "The special, I mean."

I blow out a breath. "Probably not."

We walk another few paces, Levi angling his body closer to mine so the words don't carry beyond us.

"If you don't mind me asking . . . why would you?"

I press my lips together as the wind gusts my hair behind me, lifts the tops of Levi's curls.

"I know what he did was awful," I settle on, "but we still have this whole history together."

Levi opens his mouth as if to protest, but before he can, I add, "That, and it's just a TV special. Not anything serious."

I glance at him and my expression must be more pointed than I think it is, because Levi tilts his head down like he knows what I'm about to ask. Part of me is already kicking myself for asking it. I've managed to avoid it for so long. But I can see the blatant concern in Levi's eyes over the situation with Griffin, can see the way it looks so much like the concern I have for him, that I know I'll regret it if I don't.

"You don't have to explain if you don't want to, but I've been wondering—why do you still want to make things work with Kelly?" I ask, keeping my voice as even as I can.

Levi's quiet for a moment, almost withdrawn. I brace myself for that openness in his face to give way to something steely again, for him to close himself off the way he did for so long. But instead, he takes a breath and says, "Because I know what drove Kelly to cheat. I'm not excusing what she did, but—I can see it from her point of view."

I stay quiet, waiting him out as he sorts through how he wants to say it, staring at the sand just beyond our feet.

"Annie always told me I wasn't really living, that I was just waiting for my real life and stalling for it. I knew she was right. But a few months after she died, I actually started doing something about it."

He still isn't looking at me, but not in a guarded way. More like he's buried in a memory and can't decide whether to pull it up.

"I proposed to Kelly around then," Levi admits. "It was earlier than we'd planned. But I told her I wanted us to be happy together, *really* happy, and to her, that meant staying on the path we were already on. Our ten-year plan wasn't over yet. But then I talked about quitting my job. I talked about writing instead, and encouraged her to pursue her painting."

"And that upset her?" I ask.

Levi is careful to take a few beats before he shakes his head. "I think it was just the suddenness of it. It was like I'd become Annie—I was pushing her too hard and too fast. We had all these plans we'd agreed on. We trusted each other. We came from the same kind of families, wanted the same things. And then suddenly we didn't."

He runs a hand through his hair and shakes his head again, rueful this time. "I'd never liked my work, and in the beginning, neither did she. But that changed, and I was so wrapped up with shifting our time line that I didn't even see it," he says. "I didn't even see it until she was working so many hours that we were barely seeing each other, and then she met someone else. Someone who probably had a lot more respect for what she was doing than she thought I did at the time. Someone who was settled in who they were in a way I'm just not anymore."

We sidestep the fact that the *someone* was none other than one of the most famous men in the world, because it doesn't really matter in the scheme of things. Our viral, public breakups, or even this blown-up fake relationship we've schemed. It's all just noise, and underneath it is the real mess. The real hurt. Things that must have been brewing between Levi and Kelly the same way they had been for me and Griffin, and were only waiting for a catalyst to explode.

"So if you guys get back together," I say, the word *if* thick on my tongue, "do you think things are going to be different?"

Levi nods, and then says the next words almost rotely, like he's turned them over in his head more than a few times. "I could get a less demanding job in my field and keep trying to write. She'll probably stay at hers. We could compromise on the old plan. I think a lot of our issues started because I felt like a question mark to her, and we've just never been equipped for that."

He says "question mark" so deliberately that I can't help but wonder if that's something Kelly called him herself.

Levi's voice is lower when he speaks again, like he'd be self-conscious saying it in front of anyone else. "Now that I have enough distance to look back, we've been unhappy for years," he admits. "Like, at first we weren't on the same page, and then we just stopped trying to be altogether. Like, we knew each other so well, but were practically strangers in our day-to-day, and just decided that was normal."

I know what he means only because I felt the opposite about Griffin. We were with each other practically every moment for years, but it turned out I didn't know him nearly as well as I thought I did.

"But before all that, it worked between us for so long, I just . . ."

"Don't want to feel like those years were wasted?" I ask.

Levi shakes his head, and I feel embarrassed for saying it, knowing it's more of a reflection on how I feel about the past few years than he does.

"I don't think it's a waste, either way. We got each other through so much. I wonder if this is just another one of those things we need to help each other through," he says. "Maybe it won't work out, but after everything we've been through, I have to try."

There's another question I want to ask. One I was really looking for the answer to from the start. Not just the question of why he wants to make it work with Kelly, but why he still loves her at all.

But that's not fair of me to ask. He built an entire life with her that I've never seen. She must have been there when his mom was sick. She must have been there when he was learning the ropes at new jobs and working ridiculous hours and making the hard choices everyone in their twenties makes along the way. She must have had a hand in so many moments that shaped him, and I have to respect that, even if I don't like it.

"I don't think you're a question mark, Levi," I say, because that much I can tell him. "It sounds like you both changed, in your own ways. It isn't just your fault."

He considers this. "Maybe we did both change. But I think I was the one trying to change her."

I nod, trying to imagine it, trying to put myself in Levi's shoes. But I walked a completely different path than his. I was never trying to change Griffin. I was always the one changing to make myself fit.

"I always wondered about you and Griffin, though," says Levi unexpectedly. "I was surprised you dated for so long. You two seemed so different."

I laugh, glad that it's something I feel like I can laugh about now and mean it. "Yeah. The breakup was a long time coming, probably."

"Yeah?" Levi prompts. There's something tentative in it, almost vulnerable. Like he's wanted to ask for a while.

"Yeah," I say easily. "Looking back, I think he really resented this place. He hated that he only got into the local university, that he felt stuck here. All he wanted to do was get out, so that's what we did." I gesture vaguely toward the ocean. "But it didn't matter where we went. It always felt like he had something to prove. Like he wasn't just going on all those trips for fun, but to show off how adventurous he was, or something." I glance at Levi, my eyes full of mirth. "I guess I shouldn't be too surprised he ended up on a reality show."

His own eyes are steady on mine. "You were both gone for a long time."

I lose some of the bravado at that. "I didn't want to be. I think even then I had the sense that if I didn't, I'd lose him. And that really scared me back then."

I feel my shoulders loosen, like the wind is knocking them down. Levi's gaze is still so steady that I feel something else loosen in me, too. Something I've held so close to my chest that I haven't ever said it out loud before.

"I know you might not get it, because you never liked him very much," I tell him. "But we started out as friends. And it's really, really hard for me to consider dating someone or even feel attracted to someone I don't know really well first. I was worried that might not happen again."

There's another worry just underneath that, of course. The worry that it *could* happen again, and it would break my heart. The way it happened with Levi all those years ago, when I was so stupidly, earnestly certain that he felt the same way I did. It's strange—Levi and I never actually dated, but losing him felt like the biggest heartbreak of my life.

"Of course it will," says Levi, without missing a beat. "You're you. I can't imagine anyone meeting you and not wanting to get to know you."

I feel my face flush against the breeze. It means more coming from him than I can say, but it's not as simple as that. The truth is, it's almost impossible these days to meet people in a way that gives you time to be friends first, to feel each other out. Most people expect to know whether you're attracted to them on the first or second date. But it's never been like that for me. I've always had this strange feeling of not being able to keep up. I can't run headfirst toward something without knowing there's a solid foundation under my feet, and judging from all my friends' stories about the dating out in the wild, I worry there aren't a lot of people willing to wait for me to find it.

"We'll see," I joke, trying to brush his words off even when I know I'll be spinning them back and forth in my head tonight. "Anyway, all that's to say—I was right. Once I came back to Benson Beach to run Tea Tide and couldn't jet off with Griffin anymore, I could sense him getting restless. He said I wasn't the June he knew. That I wasn't *adventurous* anymore."

Levi lets out a derisive noise, but I just shake my head.

"The truth is, I was relieved. To have an excuse to stay here, I mean. It felt like—for a long time like he was leading, and I was following, and for the first time I finally had a solid reason not to follow." I take a breath, gearing myself up for what I say next. "What he did sucked, but I'm weirdly not upset with him. I'm upset with myself for not breaking things off much earlier. I would have come home sooner. Had more time with Annie. Avoided this whole mess."

Levi shakes his head. "I think—we don't have control over what happens. But we control how we react to it. And losing Annie changed us both."

"Or maybe it just reminded us who we actually are," I say quietly.

I can tell from the way Levi's brows loosen that the words catch him by surprise. That the words don't quite know how to settle in him. For me, I think it comes down to this—there was a person I was pretending to be when I was with Griffin. Someone who took too many risks and stayed too far from home. And losing Annie didn't just bring me back to Benson Beach. It made me appreciate that life is both too short and too long for being something you're not.

I can't speak for Levi, but this much I can say: "I know you're worried about how it affected things with Kelly, but—I'm really glad you're writing again."

Levi's lip quirks. "Well, for what it's worth, I'm glad you're home again. Partially so I don't have heart attacks hearing the stuff you were up to anymore."

I offer him half a smile, my eyes teasing. "Did you really check in on me?"

But Levi's eyes are suddenly solemn on mine. "June," he says, and hearing him say my name like that, low and urgent, tugs at something deep in my chest. "Of course I did. I asked Annie about you every time we talked. And sometimes it scared the shit out of me, knowing you were out in the world doing things that just seemed— dangerous. I worried all the time."

His gaze is holding me like a hook, the blue in his eyes dark enough to brew a storm. For a moment all I can do is stare back until I find my voice.

"I didn't know," I say, the words quivering.

I cast my eyes at my feet. I want to tell him that I worried about him, too, because I did. I don't think a day has gone by in my whole life that I haven't wondered about Levi.

But I didn't check in on him. The guilt of that churns in my stomach, especially knowing what I know now—that he was clearly lonely and out of his depth when he moved to New York. That he was dealing with his mom getting sick and the burden of keeping it secret, of taking it on himself to help with the debt. And I couldn't see past my own hurt to even ask how he was doing.

When I lift my head again to look at him, I realize there's a part of our conversation still weighing on my chest, one that I can't let sit.

"Levi—you shouldn't have to feel settled for someone to love you. I know it might not mean a lot coming from someone who spent most of their twenties decidedly unsettled, but I mean that," I tell him. "I don't think anyone ever gets to be settled in life. I think you just find people who weather it with you."

I don't know Kelly beyond what Levi's told me, but I know Griffin wasn't that person for me. That if it hadn't been losing Annie, something else would have shaken us down the line. I only hope that if Levi wants this, that he has that perspective, too.

And just like that, the storm clouds are gone from his eyes, and he's staring at me again so openly that I feel like I can see all the way down to the core of him. Further than I've ever seen. So far down that if I peer close enough, I'll have answers to the questions I can't bring myself to ask. Ones that have the power to hurt me more than I thought they ever would again.

"It means a lot coming from you," he says, his voice so quiet it almost gets swallowed by the wind.

I feel raw all of a sudden, standing under his gaze, realizing how much we've said. How much we've exposed. I glance back, feeling untethered, and see we've wandered far past the boardwalk and the crowds.

I seize on the only solid thing I can think of—an old pattern. A version of the two of us that's already set in stone.

"Well," I say, squaring my quaking shoulders, "if we're going to get back in time for the next rush, I think a race is in order."

It takes Levi a moment to process what I've said, still standing in place with his eyes on me. Only after I dig my heels into the sand does he shift to get next to me, easing his legs into a stretch.

"We don't have any scores to settle, do we?" he asks.

I tilt my chin toward the boardwalk. "Sure we do, pistachio."

We ran our flavor options for the sheet cake past Mateo and Dylan over text. Mateo responded with Either sounds good to me! and Dylan responded with a series of unhelpful thumbs-up and party emojis, so we still haven't given a final flavor to Cassie.

Levi's shaking his head at me with that same exasperated affection. "How do you solve problems with people you *can't* demand beach races from?"

"In boring ways," I say easily, priming myself to run. Levi settles next to me, resigned, as I say, "On your mark . . . get set . . ."

And Levi takes off.

"Hey!" I protest, springing to my feet.

He turns his head just enough to say, "You got a head start last time!"

And I can't argue with that, only because I can't afford to waste my breath. I pull myself forward with the kind of speed I didn't know I had in me, managing to catch up to him within a few seconds.

Then we run and we *run* and it feels less like we're racing each other but more like we're chasing off something else. I feel it slip away for a moment, the weight of everything lifted off my shoulders. The lingering hurt of everything that happened with Griffin and the realization that the years I spent with him were built on something flimsier than I ever knew. The constant ebb of guilt and panic about the state of Tea Tide. The uncertainty I've felt ever since Levi came back to town, wondering if I can trust him, wondering if I can trust myself.

The weight of all of it is gone, and without it, I feel like I'm flying. Untethered again, but in a way that doesn't scare me—in a way that leaves so much more room for a future I haven't let myself consider yet. One where I turn things at Tea Tide around. One where, after this whole Revenge Exes thing is over, I might be able to open my heart up to someone else again. One where Levi and I are finally settled in our friendship, and I can feel the kind of peace I think I've been waiting to feel since I was seventeen. It all seems as wide open and vast as the ocean beyond us, close enough to touch.

Levi gets ahead of me by half a foot, and another burst of power surges through my body. I pull forward, a lopsided grin stretching over my face, and yank off the sunglasses he had propped on top of his head.

"Hey!" he says, skidding to an indignant stop.

Then I do something I haven't done since we were kids at the end of one of our grueling cross-country runs—I pivot sharply and run straight for the ocean, clothes and all. I get in as far as my knees before I turn back to see Levi at the edge of the water, half incredulous, half impressed.

I dangle his sunglasses in the air before I secure them on my face. "If you want these, you better come get them," I taunt, diving straight into the next choppy wave.

The next moment, everything is the murky, deep green and blue of ocean floor and rushing water, the cold jolting my bones, electrifying me. I'm giddy by the time my head bobs back up over the surface. I shake the long, wet strands of hair out of my face and there's Levi, bobbing up a few feet away. He turns his head to the side, his wet curls plastered to his head, glinting dark gold against the sun.

"I demand a rematch," says Levi, breathless and grinning. "And my sunglasses."

"You're right," I say. "You'll need them to hide your shame when I kick your ass."

Levi shakes his head, his hair dripping salt water at the edges. "I'll need them to enjoy the view when I kick yours."

My grin sharpens. "Or you could enjoy *this* view."

I reach my arms out and plant them on his shoulders, pulling myself up to dunk him underwater. In an instant, his hands wrap around my waist, his fingers pressing against the sharp, gasping laugh in my ribs as he pulls me down with him.

For a few moments everything is still—just silence and weightlessness, just our hands anchoring each other against a quiet vacuum. It's just us. Nobody watching, nobody posting, nobody expecting. I open my eyes against the salt water and make out the blurry edges of Levi, and this moment feels like it has a strange kind of infinity to it. Like we can be whoever we want down here, and it won't count. But with my body half tangled in Levi's, my heart beating against his fingertips, his shoulders steady against my hands, all I want is to be myself.

A wave pushes us back to the surface, pressing our bodies together so close that my hair, freed from its ponytail, sticks to his arm. I can smell brine and sweet summer wind and Levi's still-distinct earthy sweat. His smile broad and contagious, his blue eyes studying my face like he's accounting for every freckle, every angle and curve. There's salt water slipping down his cheeks, catching on his lips, gleaming in the late afternoon light. We drink each other in, our ankles knocking into each other as we tread under the surface, but neither of us making any attempt to part.

He takes his hands off my waist but comes even closer, carefully untangling the strand of wet hair caught on his sunglasses and pulling them off my forehead. The current nudges us closer still, almost like it's got an agenda of its own—so close that our knees are grazing, that it feels like any moment, our noses will skim each other's, like we're both one small tilt of our heads away from something more than that.

Once the sunglasses are off, Levi searches my eyes, his own gleaming. "I think you're plenty adventurous," he says.

And right now, I feel it—electricity in my skin, vibrating in my body, humming in every place Levi and I have touched.

Chapter Twelve

"Well, if it isn't Benson Beach's most infamous celebs," says Gerry when Levi and I walk up to the entrance of the one and only tourist-free bar in town, unsubtly named the Bar. "I assume you're here to autograph everyone's cocktail napkins."

Gerry looks very much unchanged from high school, sporting the same close-cropped haircut and wearing the same plaid flannel with the same high-waisted jeans she probably owned back then. She gives me a teasing smile, then leans in to hug Levi and clap him on the back. She was in his year in high school and co-ran the Science Olympiad team with him, but is now otherwise occupied as the host of the Bar's open mic nights on weekdays, where her wry, understated sense of humor has everyone in stitches between sets.

By virtue of this talent, she's also in demand for all the queer weddings in and around the Benson Beach area. It started when she got ordained to officiate a wedding for two of our classmates a few years back who wanted a less traditional ceremony, considering one bride's parents were religious and the other bride's were anything but. Gerry seamlessly handled the whole thing, with both families happily crying and cackling throughout the ceremony in a display that Annie declared "absolute fucking magic, like watching high-stakes wedding Jenga." Ever since then, Gerry's been known not just for the jolt of fun she adds to weddings, but her ability to adapt to any kind of situation to make ceremonies all the more personal and meaningful.

Enough classmates have gotten married over the past few years that we've all seen her in action, so we planned on her officiating Dylan and Mateo's wedding before there was even a wedding to plan. When they approached her about an outdoor ceremony incorporating a few touches of the Catholic mass Mateo's parents wanted to keep with the overall party vibe that both families enthusiastically agreed on, Gerry immediately and delightedly rose to the challenge, Zooming with both sets of parents to make sure she got everything just right.

Mateo and Dylan have been meeting with her on and off for the past few weeks to plan out the ceremony, but still wanted to go over how their vows would fit into the ceremony, now that they've both written theirs. We figured we'd make a night of it, since we've been missing so many happy hours lately as it is. Then Dylan added Levi to the group chat to invite him along, which is why Levi is now stretching his long limbs out after being subjected to another drive in Bugaboo.

"Forget the cocktail napkins," says Levi to Gerry. "We figured we'd get some Sharpies and go for the front door."

Gerry laughs, then steps aside to let us in. "It's nice to see your face around town again, dude," she tells him before turning to me. "And yours too, June! Feel like it's been a hot minute. Where's the rest of the crew?"

"Sana's got deadlines, but Mateo and Dylan should be by soon," I tell her.

The thing is, I don't usually see much of Gerry or her girlfriend, Lane, since we come in on Thursdays, when there aren't any open mics. I feel a quick pang that we haven't been able to keep it up lately, especially knowing how much Dylan loves all our weekly traditions—everyone going around and sharing the weirdest part of their week, or splitting whatever '90s-themed snack the bar happens to have in its ever-running rotation of them. But at least we'll be able to catch up tonight.

"Oh, they're coming by tonight?" asks Gerry. I tilt my head because it's unlike Gerry to forget a meeting on the books, but she adds, "Sounds good. Can't wait to get emotionally compromised by their vows."

We head into the Bar with its familiar low lighting and framed Benson Beach memorabilia on the walls, nodding at people we know and people we know of, which makes up most of the people here. What the Bar lacks in name creativity, it makes up for by being one of the most fun spots in town—it's rare there's a night that doesn't come with some new story about a classmate cutting their own bangs in the bathroom or one of the town's older residents busting into a drunk karaoke medley. If you're going to let loose, this is the safest, most supportive place to get it out of your system. What happens in Benson Beach Bar stays at Benson Beach Bar, as the saying goes.

Just as we settle in to a table in one of the dimly lit corners of the Bar, Gerry takes the small elevated stage and adjusts the mic. "Good evening, one and all," she says, eyes scanning the crowd. "Before we start, a quick reminder that yes, our tater tots are delicious, but please enjoy them with a modicum of dignity. I've heard enough *When Harry Met Sally* reenactments tonight that even I'm blushing, and I'm pretty sure at least half this town has seen my tits."

"Thunder and Lightning!" Lane calls appreciatively from the audience.

Gerry settles a hand on her chest and says, "Forever honored you remember their names. The two of them will join me tonight in appreciating our very talented lineup for this evening, all of whom will be rewarded for their efforts with free throat lozenges they can claim up at the front. Without any further ado, let's welcome Hannah to the stage as our first performer for a night of good old-fashioned, wholesome scream poetry."

I blink. Levi goes very still.

"Please tell me she did not just say what I think she said," says Levi.

"Oh my god," I wheeze, putting a hand to my mouth. "Oh my *god*."

Levi's face is a cross of disbelieving amusement and mild horror. "You monster. You waited ten years to exact your revenge."

"I didn't know!" I say, nearly gasping from the effort not to laugh as the first performer walks up to the stage. "I swear! Tonight was supposed to be the night people shared excerpts from their original fiction." I know this for a fact because I was hoping it might inspire Levi to come back and share some of his own.

But Levi shakes his head. "No, no, I see clearly now. Everything leading up to this moment was in your hundred-step plan to trap me in this bar and—"

"AGING IS A SCAM."

We startle and there is Hannah, who cannot be any taller than five feet but apparently has the vocal cords of a lion, yelling into the mic. The *mic*. Because apparently what we were missing from the time Levi accidentally dragged us to scream poetry as teenagers was *more amplification*.

We may very well not survive this night.

"DO YOU THINK GOUDA GETS UPSET ABOUT GET-TING OLDER? NO. IT JUST GETS MORE EXPENSIVE AT TRADER JOE'S," Hannah bellows ferociously. "BE LIKE GOUDA! KNOW YOUR WORTH!"

"Scream it, girl!" someone calls from the audience.

"Goudadvice!" calls someone else.

Levi lifts a hand and says to the server, "We're going to need as many tater tots as you can legally give us."

The night only gets increasingly more chaotic from there. A retired teacher gets up and screams a rewrite of her wedding vows, ending with an "I WILL LOATHE AND DISHONOR YOU ALL THE DAYS OF MY LIFE!" so visceral that I'm sure wherever her ex is, he just shuddered without knowing why. One of the nail techs at Levi's mom's salon follows her up by screaming in multiple languages and finishing it off with an "IN CONCLUSION, FUCK YOU, SARAH, FOR WRECKING MY DUOLINGO STREAK." Another guy comes up to the mic and just yells, "AHHHHHH! AHHHHHHHHH!" over and over again, and then tips his hat with utter sincerity and says in a soft voice, "Thank you. I've been workshopping that one for a while now."

In between sets, I text Dylan: Where are you two??? You're missing some top-notch cheese puns and we're running out of tater tots.

Dylan's response is immediate: Are you at the bar? I thought we were meeting up tomorrow?

And then I realize with a guilty thunk in my chest—the reason we're here for scream poetry isn't because I mixed up which open mic was on which day. *It's because I mixed up the actual days.*

Oh crap. I'm sorry. Levi and I came tonight, I text. Any chance you can make it?

Dylan starts typing, then stops, then starts again.

"Shit," I murmur to myself.

"What's up?" Levi asks.

"I fucked up the dates," I admit. "We were supposed to meet them here tomorrow."

Levi raises his eyebrows. "Oh, so this wasn't you getting revenge. This was the universe avenging you."

More like me being a jerk. I should have paid more attention to the date. Not just for Dylan's sake, but because Levi's been looking forward to hanging out with us as a group again, too. I'm about to look up and apologize, but an incoming text from Dylan lights up my phone.

Nah we've got a Rainbow Eagles meetup tonight. Can you still make tomorrow?

I wince. I rearranged everything I had to do this week to make it here tonight as it was. If I go out a second time tomorrow, there's no way I'm going to be able to keep up with the chaos at Tea Tide.

Shit shit I can't. I'm sorry!!! I owe you a beer!!

The read receipt pops up immediately, but Dylan doesn't type back. I set the phone down and rest my head in my hand.

"Hey. Don't beat yourself up. There's a lot going on." Levi puts a hand on my shoulder, and the weight of it is so immediately, ridiculously comforting that I almost forget what he's talking about altogether. "And at least you didn't break anyone's Duolingo streak."

I smile despite myself. Levi squeezes my shoulder again before he lets it go, and I feel the warmth of it spread through me, loosening some of the tightness wound into my bones.

"All right folks, that's the end of our scheduled lineup, but the catharsis doesn't need to end," says Gerry from the stage. "Do I have any takers for the open mic?"

Her eyes settle on us with clear mischief and Levi immediately ducks his head, but it's too late. Half the bar has turned around and spotted us. The commotion is instant. I cannot for the life of me stop cackling when I look around and realize that one corner of the bar is occupied by half the staff of the salon where Levi's mom works, and another by a cluster of former Science Olympiad members who all light up at the sight of Levi like it's a surprise second Christmas.

"Seems to me like maybe two people here in particular might have some grievances to air," says Gerry with a smirk.

Levi's face is red enough to reheat our tater tots as he waves her off, but the rest of the Bar isn't having it.

"Let 'er rip, kiddo!" says one of the nail techs from the salon.

And then, to Levi's absolute mortification, one of his former teammates starts chanting "Levi, Levi, *Levi*" until the entire bar is chanting along with them, even people who clearly have no idea who he is.

"Aw, come on," I say. "Give the people what they want."

Levi looks over at me, his expression a mix of bafflement and panic. "What would we even say?"

I bite down a happy smile at the *we*—at the assumption I'm going up there with him, even though the crowd clearly has one very singular demand. That the two of us are in this together, for better or worse, the same way we have been since the first Revenge Ex tweet hit the internet.

At that particular thought, a grin starts curling on my face.

"Uh-oh," says Levi, before I've even spoken.

I lean in and grab his hand, snaking his fingers through mine. "Do you trust me?"

"Unfortunately," says Levi, without missing a beat.

I yank him up to his feet then, much to the delight of the entirety of the Bar, which is roaring with approval. On the way up to the mic, I pull up Twitter on my phone and type our names into the search bar. Within an instant it's pulled hundreds of tweets from strangers, ranging from supportive to confused to downright annoyed by our existence.

I tilt the screen so Levi can see it, too, and he lets out an amused breath of a laugh. I lean toward the mic first, staring at the crowd, and yell with all my might, "WHY DO PEOPLE CARE ABOUT LEVI AND JUNE SO MUCH? GO GET A HOBBY YOU BUNCH OF SEX-DEPRIVED NERDS."

The bar immediately erupts with laughter. Levi's trying not to grin and failing spectacularly when I hand him the phone. He lets out a surprised laugh at whatever he reads on it, then leans in close to the mic and yells, "GOD DAMMIT I WISH SOMEONE WOULD WRONG ME SO I COULD PULL A LEVI AND JUNE AND JOIN THE REVENGE EX MOVEMENT."

He looks at me with eyes so full of mirth that all at once I feel giddy, near electric, like the stress of the last few months is sliding off my shoulders and under the stage. I grin up at him as I nudge him out of the way of the mic and yell into it, "BOLD OF LEVI AND JUNE TO HAVE AN ORIGIN STORY SO ICONIC THAT THEY SINGLE-HANDEDLY DESTROYED EVERY DATING APP ON MY PHONE."

Levi grins back, nudging me in turn to yell, "LITERALLY A CRIME THAT DUNCAN HINES HASN'T SPONSORED LEVI AND JUNE AFTER THAT CAKE NONSENSE."

I let out another sharp cackle, then lean into the mic so close that I can feel Levi's breath against my cheek. There's a split second where I almost forget to speak, so overwhelmed by the tempting heat of him I only just barely manage to yell, "MY FUCKING KING-DOM FOR A MAN WHO LOOKS AT ME EVEN ONCE THE WAY LEVI SHAW LOOKS AT JUNE HART."

I glance over at Levi after I say it, anticipating the next tweet he's going to yell into the mic. But Levi isn't leaning in. He's staring at me with a fondness so unmistakable I feel the impact of every word in that tweet—that I feel a whole lot else on the heels of it, curling in my smile, fluttering just under my ribs.

I'm so swept up that I don't even notice the entire bar has gone quiet, staring at us as we stare at each other, until Gerry steps onto the stage.

"The Revenge Exes, everyone!" she says, clapping us both on the back.

We startle back into reality, which is somehow even louder than our yelling. Nobody is more effusive than Levi's high school buddies except for maybe his mom's friends, and the display has Levi looking so bashful that I feel a little cinch in my heart at the sight. I've wondered if maybe Levi's avoided some of his old crowds since he got here, worrying that he'd been gone too long to jump back into their new rhythms. But from the near-deafening applause and cheers, it's all too clear how happy everyone is to have him back, and how much it means to Levi that they are.

"Get the fuck over here, Levi!" one of his friends exclaims, the others clearly about to descend on him.

He looks to me, and before he can ask if I want to join, I give him a quick hug. "Go hang with your nerds," I say into his ear before I pull back. "I have a whole mountain of work to get back to at Tea Tide."

"You're sure?" Levi asks.

He looks almost boyish when he asks, a shade of the Levi he was when we were kids. I nod, reaching out to squeeze his elbow, and say, "Very sure."

Levi smiles appreciatively, then leans in close and says, "All right. But just know that in another ten years, you should be on your toes. Because I'm dragging you right back here to get revenge on your revenge."

I lean in farther and say, "I'd be disappointed if you did anything less."

I can feel Levi's smile before we pull apart enough for me to see it. His friends find him a moment later and even then, he still glances at me, giving me a quick, happy wave before he practically gets swallowed into their pack.

As I'm leaving, I cast a glance back at the inside of the Bar. At the performers all flushed and pleased with themselves, cheersing with a round of beers in the corner by the stage. At one of the walls teeming with half the beach's lifeguards finishing up their shift for the day. At Levi getting hugged and hair-ruffled and playfully shoved by his friends. At the way this place isn't just a bar, but a community. Another version of home.

My chest aches and warms at the same time. It's what I've wanted for Tea Tide from the start, but it's always been hard to fully envision it. All at once, that version of Tea Tide feels less like a hope and more like a possibility—like once all this mess is over and we're solidly back on our feet, I really could build a home like this of our own. Something soft and safe and welcome to everyone. Somewhere you don't just come to visit, but come to stay.

I tuck the feeling into my heart and step out into the sweet summer air. For the first time in a long time, I don't dread the mountain of work ahead of me. For the first time in a long time, I see what might be on the other side of it, and love every inch of the view.

Chapter Thirteen

I'm terrible at trivia and even worse at sports, but I'm *very* good at drinking Blue Moon—so even though I'll be out of my depth at Games on Games, the hybrid sports and trivia bar Levi and I are checking out for Mateo and Dylan's bachelor party, I'm raring to go.

Technically, we don't need to vet it. It has an absurd number of good Yelp reviews, and Sana's a regular, so she can vouch for them. But Sana decided it would make an excellent casual Revenge Ex date, so here I am, dressed in a black crop top and high-waisted ankle jeans with a pair of combat boots and my hair pulled into a messy French braid, waiting for Sana's outfit approval.

Except when Sana answers my FaceTime call, she's got on her "I mean business" blue light glasses she only wears when she's about to pull an all-nighter at her laptop.

"Oh. Cute," she says, tilting her head at me. "Where are you headed?"

I blink. "Did you forget?"

Sana winces. "Right. Shit. Sorry, I'm out."

I point a finger at her through the screen. "If you think you're going to fake us out and sneak pictures a *fourth* time—"

"No, seriously," she says, pulling the camera back so I can see she's not only in her Deadline Sweatpants (I suspect the only pair of sweatpants Sana owns), but she's got a can of Pringles propped on one leg and several empty cans of Red Bull leaning precariously on the other. "I'm on a roll right now."

"With what, an essay about testing the limits of your mortality?"

"My idea for *Fizzle*. I have to start writing it tonight while my brain's buzzing." She presses the phone to her lips, the screen going dark for a moment while she gives it a loud smack of a kiss. "Have fun. I'll see you on the other side."

"Bye," I say, but she's already hung up.

I stare at the phone with mild concern, because this is the most I've heard from Sana in the past two days. After I told her about that call I got from Griffin and she spent no fewer than ten minutes on a rant about why his next reality show stint should be on a ten-foot-wide island in the Bermuda Triangle, she suddenly went very quiet and said, "Oh. *Oh.*" Then she scooped up her laptop like it was the one thing she was grabbing in a fire and left so fast she almost knocked into the sprinkle shelf.

I'd have asked what was going on, but I got pulled under the current of Tea Tide so fast I've barely been able to come up for air since. After all the scrambling with inventory, event scheduling, and keeping up with the steady flow of customers, I still have a mountain of unanswered texts and next week's shift schedule to work out with the part-timers. That, and the end of the month is fast approaching. While I have a lot of loose ideas for ways to sustain Tea Tide after the chaos dies down, I haven't had any time to solidify them, to put them into motion.

But at least that time hasn't been wasted. At this rate, I'll definitely have enough money to front the first three months of rent. The rest I can get a handle on from there.

I feel a twinge of guilt when opening my texts, seeing one of them is from Dylan, asking when we want to reschedule drinks. I completely forgot to text him a day we could meet up. I know he and Mateo are getting fitted for their suits tonight, but I make a mental note to get back to him as I pull up my thread with Levi.

Sana's out for tonight. She won't be able to take any Revenge Ex pictures.

Levi's response is immediate: Oh no. It's almost like we'll have to hang out as plain old friends.

I grin. It's the answer I was hoping for. Besides, it's not like we're incapable of documenting it for ourselves. The universe gave Levi those long selfie-taking arms for a reason.

"Plain Old Friends"—not a bad scone name. Still want to leave at 8? I shoot back.

I'll be the one in the clown nose trying to shove myself into your clown car.

Only Levi isn't waiting for me when I walk to the lot behind Tea Tide. I wander over to his condo and see him out in front of it, talking low into his phone and nodding. There's something intimate in his posture, something so deeply personal that even though he's out in the open, I feel strange for catching him in it. His eyes sweep up to meet mine and he gives me a quick, indecipherable nod.

I step back, waiting another minute while he wraps up and heads over to me, apologetic.

"Everything all right?" I ask him.

Levi looks down at his phone like he's considering it. "Yeah. That was Kelly."

I stare at his phone right along with him, trying to school my face before I ask. Before I rip off the Band-Aid. "So it's settled, then? You're getting back together?"

"No." His voice is light. With surprise, maybe, or relief. His expression is dazed, so it's hard to tell. "But I think I'm just . . . done trying."

The words feel like a faulty firework shooting through me—like something I wasn't prepared to hear, and now that I have, I don't know what to make of them, or how I feel about them. Already I feel myself starting to recalibrate, but I can't do that unless I know what happened. What "done trying" really means.

"Did something change?"

Levi shakes his head. "She's been half in and half out with me and with Roman ever since this started. Telling me she's just stuck." He presses his lips together, like he's playing it back in his mind. "And the thing is—I think the Revenge Ex thing was working. The last few times she's been in touch, she's seemed upset by it. Asking me how serious it was. What I'd do if she left Roman."

"Oh, shit," I say before I can stop myself. I hadn't realized they were talking in terms quite that blunt.

He turns his eyes to me then, plain and direct, and shakes his head. "But talking to you the other day—it made me realize I don't want the idea of me being with someone else to be the reason she comes back. I don't want to force it." He reaches his hand out to nudge mine. "It's like you said about being settled. I think that's why she's waiting. She wants me to be something I'm just not right now."

My fingers curl into each other like they're looking for the warmth of his hand again. "I'm sorry," I offer quietly.

He reaches an arm up to rub the back of his neck. "Honestly . . . it's a relief not to try anymore."

The air between us seems fragile right now. This entire time he's been back, we've been working with a script, of sorts. June and Levi, former friends. June and Levi, the Revenge Exes. Now we're just June and Levi, and possibly have to figure out what that means for ourselves.

"Do you want to cancel?" I ask. Which is the closest I can come to asking, *Do you want to end our break-up pact?*

Because that was the deal, the only part that was really set in stone. We'd drop it the moment one of us said the word. Now Levi doesn't have anything to gain from this, and I suddenly feel like I have too much to lose. Not just with Tea Tide, but with all this time I've gotten to spend with Levi, too.

"No, no, I—I want to go. I need to get out of my own head." He smiles down at me, like he's coming back to himself, and says, "Besides, when have the two of us ever just been able to have a regular night out? It'll be fun."

The swell of relief in me is embarrassing, so much that I have to keep my own smile in check. I'm wary on the short drive over, knowing that Levi is probably in that weird adrenaline state that comes after making a big decision. That sense of relief you get at just being able to make it, before the weight of all its consequences settles in. But I take his cues, and we spend the drive talking about the loose ends we need to tie for the wedding, and by the time we arrive, Kelly feels like she's in the rearview mirror.

As it turns out, the place is quite literally split down the middle, with the actual bar smack in the center of it. On one side, the walls are deep navy and crowded with sports memorabilia and flat screen televisions pointed at every angle, and on the other, the walls are a deep maroon with a series of cozy booths and high-top tables where they're setting up trivia for the night.

There's a game starting, so we decide to scope out the sports section first. "Go grab those last two stools," I tell Levi. "I'll get the first round."

Levi raises his eyebrows at me when I come back with two Blue Moons—his with one orange slice and mine with no fewer than seven. In my defense, I very rarely abuse my dimples to wheedle things out of strangers. But when it comes to scamming free orange slices on a beer, I will throw any semblance of a moral compass I have out the window.

"Got enough vitamin C there?" Levi asks, and only then do I realize he hasn't witnessed this routine of mine before.

"Wait," I say. "Have we never actually had a legal drink out in public together?"

I slide onto the stool next to Levi's, the two of us pressed in so close that my knees graze his legs when I settle in.

Levi takes his beer from me with a nod of thanks. "The last time we shared a drink, it came out of a Franzia box in your cross-country duffel."

"The coach *did* tell us to stay hydrated," I point out.

Levi smirks. "The whole team still owes you a debt."

Just then, a commotion starts to ripple through our side of the bar. We both glance up to see the game on the screen is starting.

"What team are you rooting for?" I ask.

Levi squints. "Uh. The blue one?"

"Cool. Then I'll root for the green."

We cheers our drinks, take hearty sips, and promptly forget that sports exist by the time we set them back down on the bar. Levi asks me what Sana's up to, I ask him about his dad's auto shop, and it's like a rubber band that's been stretching through reality snaps comfortably into place. Suddenly we know the characters in each other's lives again. We aren't just talking about things that happened in the past, but things that are happening right now. Things that are going to happen. Making wisecracks and inside jokes that didn't exist between us a few weeks ago, the kind I didn't think we'd ever make again.

We're nearly at the bottom of our first drink, laughing at Dylan for commissioning two wedding-themed sweater-vests on Etsy to surprise Mateo, when I say, "I feel like we're in a parallel universe right now. One where we do this kind of thing all the time."

By now, the rest of the bar has gotten invested enough in the game that Levi and I have scooted our stools closer together, insulating ourselves against the noise. Our faces are so close that I don't miss the quick dim of his eyes before he glances at his beer and says, "We missed a lot."

"Do you ever wonder what it would have been like if we'd stayed in touch?" I ask.

Levi is careful for a moment, like he's worried answering the question will open an old wound. But I'm not asking to rehash the past. Levi's been back long enough for us to find this new rhythm together, one I thought we never would. A part of me is just genuinely curious how it would have evolved over all these years, if we'd had them.

"Yeah," he says. "I wondered that a lot."

The words fill me with a warmth that has nothing to do with the beer.

And then, to my surprise, he lets out a breathy laugh. "Like sometimes—I don't know. I'd be doing something that seemed objectively ridiculous. Like I'd be interviewing for a job all dressed up in my first suit, or I'd get roped into some fancy auction up in a high-rise looking out at the city where they'd serve wine that cost more than my rent, and I'd wonder what you would say about the whole thing." His eyes soften with the smile he gives me, the kind that's both self-conscious and sweet. "Anytime I felt out of place, I would think of you. Something funny you might say. And then I didn't feel so out of place anymore."

The warmth in my chest spreads out, equal parts comfort and ache. "I would have paid good money to see baby Levi in his first big finance interview."

Levi lets out another laugh. "Just imagine me with pit stains and mortal terror in my eyes, and you're halfway there."

I smile, skimming my finger over the brim of my glass, staring into the dregs at the bottom. Levi goes quiet, like he can sense the words I'm working myself up to say.

"It's funny. There were moments like that for me, too," I tell him. "Not necessarily when I felt out of place, but when I felt . . . scared of something I was doing. Or lonely, even." I feel the weight of his gaze on me, so compelling that I can't help but look back. When I do, his eyes are so open and steady that whatever lingering self-consciousness I had falls away, and I say, "You were the person I went to when I felt that way, and it just made sense to keep thinking of you."

Levi leans in, and there's the usual heat I feel between us, but there's something else just under it. Something protective, something solid in it that makes it less of a feeling and more of an intent.

"What kinds of moments?" he asks.

"Oh. I don't know." I catch a strand in my braid that keeps coming loose and tuck it behind my ear. I could tell him about a lot of times I was scared. About a rickety bridge over a waterfall I was sure we were going to fall through. About diving so far underwater I was terrified I'd lose sight of the surface. About a helicopter ride so choppy I was sore for days from tensing up.

But the fear was sharp, and then it was done. It was the ache of the loneliness that lingered that seems like the part worth telling.

Levi's still watching me patiently when I finally say, "It's weird to say I was lonely, I guess, because Griffin was there. But we didn't talk much one-on-one. We were always part of a group. And then we'd be alone at night most of the time, and there wasn't much to say." I swallow, feeling my throat bob with the effort. "And I just remembered thinking sometimes—Levi and I never run out of things to say. And even when we did, we'd just make up stories instead."

I'm smiling when I turn to him, but Levi's own smile has almost faded entirely. I knock my knee into his to bring it back. Then I like the feeling of it so much that I let my leg linger there and feel him shift his own leg to stay close to mine.

The loose strand falls out from behind my ear again. This time Levi is the one who reaches out, the tips of his fingers skimming my forehead, grazing my ear as he tucks the strand back. "You know you've always got me, right?" he says. "I know things weren't great between us, and I'll regret that forever. But if you ever need me. No matter what. You've always got me."

The words stun me with their intensity. With the way that ghost of a touch seems to make every one of them spread like electricity under my skin.

"I know," I tell him quietly, because I did. He was always there in the phone I didn't pick up to call, the gap I was too proud to bridge. It's why I thought of him in all those moments. Why it was so natural, so easy, to fall into him the day of Annie's funeral without saying a word. "I knew."

He nods. "Good," he says.

Then he turns himself from me, going very still, clutching his empty glass like it's anchoring him to the bar. Like he's doing the exact same thing I'm doing right now and letting the regret of the past few years settle in with a new kind of weight.

I reach out and put my hand over his, weave my fingers through it. His eyes sweep over to mine and I feel the pulse of it then, tight between our fingers, steady between our gazes. The unshakable part of us that somehow endured all these years of barely speaking. The part that always will.

"You know you've got me, too," I say.

And then that faded smile comes back, easing onto his face like the sun easing back out from behind a cloud. I squeeze his hand one more time before I let it go.

"I know you have to go back to the city and your real life at some point," I say. "But I hope we can still be like this. Hang out whenever one of us is around. Catch up, even, on all the things we missed."

Levi nods, then leans in conspiratorially. "You know," he says, "there's even a wild contraption called a phone. So even when we're not in the same city, we can still catch each other up on our lives. Like magic."

"We'll see if you'll ever have enough time for that, busy business guy," I say.

Levi says without missing a beat, "I'll make time."

My throat feels thick then, because I can tell he means it. I just don't know if he'll be able to follow through with it. It's all well and good to say we'll stay in touch, but this is just more uncharted territory for us. I don't want our friendship to get lost in it again.

Someone taps a mic from the other side of the bar. We break apart, glancing up to see the blue and green teams in a dead tie, the actual sports fans around us on the edges of their seats. We duck out toward trivia just as something happens with the football that makes half the room cheer and half of them groan and all of them chug their beers.

Levi tilts his head toward the other side for me to grab us a spot and says, "I'll get the next round."

He heads over to the bar, but when I scan the other side of the room, I come up empty of any free tables. I'm about to settle for hovering by the wall when a team in matching hot pink T-shirts that read TEAM FORTY WAYS TO FUNDAY waves me over to their table.

"Are you looking to join a team, darlin'?" asks a woman with a blond pixie cut and a sleeve of flower tattoos. "Because we have the space."

"I should probably warn you that I'm terrible at trivia," I tell her. The first and last night Mateo ever took me out with his team, my only helpful contribution was polishing off the nachos.

"You also don't seem to be in your forties, but we'll make allowances." She narrows her eyes at me, looking me up and down as I settle onto another stool. "Do we know each other?"

I actually got this a lot even before we went viral. Benson Beach is a small town, and most people in it have popped into the shop at least once or twice. "Have you ever been to Tea Tide?"

The name instantly sparks her recognition. "Oh! You're one of those . . ." She snaps her fingers. "Vengeance Exes, aren't you?"

We've never actually been recognized in public outside of Tea Tide and the boardwalk before, so I can't help but laugh. "Yeah, I'm June," I say.

She lets out a howling laugh of her own and pats me on the back hard enough to give Dylan a run for his money. "Pam," she introduces herself. "Now where's your other half?"

Right on cue, Levi arrives with two more Blue Moons in hand—his with one orange slice on the rim, mine with a whole party of them. He takes the slice off his glass, his eyes crinkling with mischief before he puts it directly in my mouth. I'm so caught off guard that my tongue accidentally grazes the tips of his fingers, and if I'm not mistaken, his cheeks go every bit as pink as mine. I wonder if he feels the same slight shiver up his spine in the aftermath of it, too.

"Well, shit," says Pam. I look up to find most of Forty Ways to Funday looking at Levi, like they alternately want to pinch his cheeks and pinch a whole lot of other places. "You two really are cute as a button."

I hope the goodwill of that cuteness is enough to make up for the fact that, as far as trivia team members go, Levi and I are dead weight. Between my nonstop traveling and working and Levi living in his little Ivy League–finance bro bubble, the two of us are so laughably unaware of broader pop culture that we might as well have been dropped here from Mars. It wouldn't be so bad if Forty Ways to Funday didn't have a group rule that for every question you personally get wrong, you have to take a drink—Levi and I have drained our beers in no time, the two of us both so mutually sheepish that we're practically caving in on each other, like we're protecting the rest of the bar from our failure.

"Aw, shit, Pam. The kids are dry," says one of our team members, picking up my empty glass and tilting it.

Levi shifts to get off his stool for another round, and I'm already disappointed at the loss of his leg pressed against mine when Pam puts a hand on Levi's shoulder to stop him.

"Other rule is if you've gotten enough wrong to drain your glass, you have to do a dare of the group's choosing," she tells us.

I laugh. We're two beers and a deep well of shame into the night, so I don't even bother asking where this rule came from. "I dare us to get an answer right."

"I dare us to stop trying to answer at all," says Levi.

"We'll be deciding that dare, kiddos," says Pam.

"Mercy," says Levi, turning to her with crinkling eyes. "Haven't we been through enough?"

Pam relents the way I'm pretty sure anyone in the world might under a full Levi smile. "Fine," she says. "Dare's simple. Give your gal a kiss and we'll call it even."

"Fair enough," says Levi. He moves in easily, and even though I anticipate the kiss on the cheek before it happens, it doesn't stop my breath from catching in my throat—his lips graze so close to my ear that I can feel the fine hair tingling from the warmth of him.

"Aw, come on," says another one of them. "That's no kiss."

"Yeah, Levi," I tease, leaning in close. "That's no kiss."

Something shifts between us then. That same air that felt fragile between us earlier tonight is suddenly charged. All at once there's no teasing glint in our eyes. There's a challenge in mine, and something else in his—a heat I've seen in them before that isn't just simmering, but burning.

"Do you want me to kiss you?" he asks, leaning in farther to meet me.

My tongue skims my lower lip, my eyes catching on his mouth and then meeting his again. He's not just asking for show. He's asking sincerely.

The way he's looking at me, I feel something warm curl low in my stomach, something equal parts dangerous and irresistible—a feeling that demands to be followed all the way down. It shifts me forward in my seat, never once breaking my gaze.

I've been walking at the edge of this line with Levi for so long, and if I don't take the chance to cross it now, I never will. He's going to leave for New York soon. Everything's going to fall back into its regular rhythms, and this entire Revenge Ex scheme will be nothing but a funny story we talk about one day. But right now—right now we're squarely in the in-between. Right now is just ours. And right now, I don't want to just pretend at this feeling, don't want to press up against the glass of it anymore. I want to feel it, all of it, just once before we have to let it go.

So I give him a sincere answer: "Yes, Levi. I want you to kiss me."

Levi braces his hand against the back of my neck, warm and steady. We lean into the kiss, and there is nothing slow or searching about it. Nothing close to the way I imagined it, in the times I let my heart get away from me. It is all heat, all impatience, somehow achingly sweet and reckless at the same time. It's so much, but not nearly enough—whatever satisfaction I feel right now has only doubled the demand for him, widened some cavern in me that wants as much of him as I can have.

I'm so lost in the rush of his mouth on mine, the heat of his lean arms taut against my fingers, that it feels like we've been plucked right out of the current of the world. There is no background noise, no past, no future. It's singular and undiluted and *Levi and June*, heady like its own drug.

We break the kiss only because breathing demands it. The world slams back into place like a boomerang, leaving us right where we started, but with something entirely new.

I'm so dizzy in the aftermath that the first thought that manages to crystallize in my brain is *Oh. That's what it's supposed to feel like.* Because not once in all the years I've been alive have I felt anything close.

I have no idea how many seconds have passed, but it's enough that everyone around us has moved on. Nobody is watching by the time Levi's fingers tighten around the hair at the base of my neck ever so slightly before pulling away; nobody is watching as I unwind my leg from Levi's stool and pull my hands out from where they wandered, unbidden, under his shirt sleeves. Nobody is watching as we stare deliriously at each other, breathing like we just finished another ridiculous beach race.

I should break the tension. But I'm too far gone to do anything but stare at his mouth, feeling the heat of it radiating through me like aftershocks, trying desperately not to let myself imagine other places he could put it. Other places I'd love to put mine.

Levi's expression is every bit as rapt as mine, and all at once, I understand that my little plan didn't work. The kiss didn't end anything. It opened up an entire world, one that stretches far beyond this place, past the parking lot and every road it will take to get us home. One with enough potential to spill into the ocean, into the night stars, and all of it hinges on what one of us says next.

Levi settles a hand on my thigh, squeezing over my jeans. Every muscle in my body quivers under that one touch, and the sound of his voice saying so low that only I can hear it, "Do you want to get out of here?"

I'm already halfway off the stool when I breathe out the word "Yes."

Chapter Fourteen

The earlier heat has been tamed by the darkness and a slight breeze, the parking lot all balmy and sweet with the kind of midsummer warmth that borders on magic. I close my eyes and breathe it in, a little lighter on my feet than I thought I'd be, enough that I almost lose my balance and end up grazing Levi's arm with my own.

I straighten up to play it off but can't quite wipe the stupid grin off my face, the aftermath of the kiss still humming in my lips. I can't remember the last time I felt this electric, buzzing with so much energy it feels like I am outside the edges of myself, soaking in everyone else's happiness right along with mine.

"Safe to say we can never show our faces at a single trivia night on the Eastern Seaboard again," says Levi.

"Yeah." This time I lean into him on purpose, and he seamlessly reaches his hand out and puts it in mine.

That potential is still thrumming between us, unspoken under the words we're actually saying, but so loud that I'm barely registering anything else. Levi's eyes catch mine again, and as he leans in, I feel a thrill that starts in my stomach and slides all the way up, arching in my back in anticipation of another kiss.

But instead he says quietly, "What if I didn't go back to New York?"

The thrill goes flat in me before the words can settle. I blink up at him.

"You mean . . . what if you stayed in Benson Beach?" I ask.

Earlier I'd been worried that Levi was taking this situation with Kelly too lightly, that at any moment the reality of it was going to come crashing down. Over the course of the night, of the reminiscing and the catching up and the kiss, I forgot to worry about it. Only now it feels like reality is settling in the wrong place. Somewhere in me, instead of in him.

I stop at the edge of the parking lot, searching his face. "That's a really big decision to make, Levi."

"I know," he says, tugging lightly on my arm. "That's why I want to know what you think about it."

"I . . ." Have no way of answering that without feeling like the most selfish person in the world. I glance down at the pavement, and then back up at him, and by then, I can see my uncertainty leaking right into him. "I think you might be getting ahead of yourself. Have you really thought through what that would mean?"

Levi presses his lips together, shifting his weight between his feet. "Do you not want me to be here?"

"Of course I do," I say quickly. "I just . . ." I carefully pull my hand out from his, and I don't miss the quick streak of hurt across his face. "You've lived in New York for a decade. We've been pretending to date for two weeks now so you could win back someone else. Someone you only decided to move on from a few hours ago. You've barely had any time to process it."

Levi shakes his head. "I feel like I've had too much time to process it. Years of it." He's more earnest than I've seen him in ages, but it's grounded in resolve. "I'm not nearly as happy there as I am right here, right now."

Everything about this is so tempting. I could fall into these words like warm sheets and tuck myself into them. Wrap myself up so tight that I can't see the world beyond them. But somebody has to, and I'm not sure if Levi is thinking straight.

"Exactly. You're happy right now, Levi," I say as patiently as I can. "You've come out of years of living this life you didn't plan to lead and you're just coming up for air."

He isn't shaking his head anymore. Just staring at me, the blue of his eyes striking in the dark, the openness of them so stirring that I forget where we are.

"I'm happy with *you*," he finally says. "I thought . . . I thought maybe you felt the same way."

The words reach in too deep and too fast, and something in me gives way. Something I've held around my heart for so many years that I feel raw, letting it fall at our feet. The last protective barrier between me and Levi—the truth.

"Of course I do. I always have. And that's just it, Levi—I can't risk it again." My throat is so tight that it's an effort to say it, even as it's tumbling out of me, even though the words have been waiting on the tip of my tongue, the back of my teeth, for years. "You cut yourself out of my life in high school over a crush. If you start telling me you're here for good, and you wake up in a few days or a week or whenever from now, and you change your mind? It's going to break me all over again."

I'm almost out of breath when I finish. The confession empties me out, makes me feel like a stray balloon that's going to go up and up and up if one of us doesn't reach out and grab it, and fast.

But Levi's just staring at me, stunned, every other emotion knocked right out of his face. "Wait—June, what do you mean about high school?"

I take a step away from him, coming back to myself. "Oh, come on, Levi. Everyone knew," I say, my skin flaring hot from my ears to my chest. "Hell, they still do. All everyone in town says about us is that it's 'about time.'"

"But you didn't like me," Levi says slowly. "You said so yourself. Loudly. To my face."

"If I recall, you said it first," I remind him.

The memory doesn't slam into me, because it's always been there. Like it lives somewhere deep under my skin, where it's been burrowing since the day it happened.

Of all clichés, it was just after prom. We'd gone as a group, Annie, Levi, me, and Mateo. Annie had peeled off pretty quickly to dance with some brooding guy in her English class. Mateo left early to meet up with Dylan for a sci-fi movie they'd wanted to see in theaters. And Levi and I, left to our own devices, spent the entire night dancing while our classmates snickered and pulled faces over our shoulders and we pretended not to notice.

It was a perfect night. Like Levi was a chorus to a song I'd known the words to my whole life, and we'd just reached the bridge. The melody was shifting, swelling, turning into something new.

I'd wanted to tell him how I felt since the start of my junior year, when suddenly Levi and I were holding each other's gazes a little too long, keeping each other a little too close. And standing there with my cheek pressed to his shoulder, in my lavender dress with my hair all carefully styled in the intricate, swirling updo Levi's mom had swooped it into just hours before, I almost did. But I knew Levi was going to Stanford with Annie. So I decided if our feelings really were mutual, I'd wait for him to say something. He was the one leaving, after all. I didn't want to feel like I was tying him down.

When he dropped me off at home that night, he kissed me on the cheek, and asked if I wanted to meet up the next day and go for a hike in the woods, just him and me. I was up for hours after that, so giddy that it felt like my heart was going to burst in my chest, that I woke up still wearing my dress with my heels kicked onto the floor.

That morning I was still daydreamy and dopey, walking down to the beach to run some of it out of my system, when I heard people arguing under the boardwalk. Levi and Annie.

I was just going to ignore it and start my run. Annie squabbled all the time. Whatever it was about, it would be forgotten by the time they knocked their sandy shoes off on the front porch and came in for breakfast.

But then I heard Annie saying my name, and when I shifted myself out of the way of the wind, I could hear her words, plain and distinct: "You're only doing this because of your big, stupid crush on June."

"What crush?"

Levi's question froze me in place like a rabbit listening for footfalls, but Annie's voice was what made me stay. It was clear she was crying.

"Oh, come *off* it, Levi. You two have been all over each other for months. You're flirting up enough of a storm that even your damn coaches think you're dating."

"She just flirts with me to be funny. You know how June is. It's all just a joke to her," said Levi, quick and placating. "She knows I don't like her like that."

The words felt like a clean slice right through my ribs, so sharp and so fast that I couldn't even feel the pain of them. Just the white-hot humiliation, the shock of disbelief. It felt worse than a rejection. It felt like a betrayal, or maybe something worse. Either he was lying to Annie and throwing me under the bus, or we'd so fundamentally misunderstood each other for the past year that it made every moment between us feel cheap.

I didn't hide. I marched under the boardwalk and confronted them both right on the spot. It was like I didn't have a choice—my body was moving before I could think, and then there they were, Annie red in the face and Levi looking more stricken at the sight of me than he would at the boardwalk collapsing.

Levi's voice pulls me out of the memory, the calm in it jarring me, bringing me back to the balmy night. "Did Annie ever tell you why we were fighting?"

I drop his gaze. "No."

He steps off the curb where we've been standing and I follow, settling in closer to the exterior of the bar, where fewer people can see us.

Levi worries his lip with a guilt that I know too well—a guilt for something that happened back then that only feels magnified now. The same way anything involving Annie does, now that she's gone.

"That morning I told Annie I was going to New York. I blind-sided her. She was furious, and I still don't blame her. We'd been talking about going out to the West Coast together for years, and then I was dropping this bomb on her." He runs a hand through his hair, and I can tell it takes a lot of effort to meet my eye as he says, "She said—she said I was only doing it because of you."

"Why would she think that?" I ask, not bothering to hide the bitterness in my voice.

"Because I was." Levi says it so plainly, so honestly, that it feels like that same slice in my ribs is opening again. Like I could look down right now and stare into my own beating heart. "Because I hadn't even left yet, and I already missed you so badly I couldn't stand it."

I shake my head. "That day on the beach. You said . . ."

Levi's voice is so steady that suddenly I'm the one who's gone wobbly, like we're just taking turns trying to steer this conversation before it can spin out from under us.

"I know what I said. And I was horrified you heard it. The truth is, I was just saying whatever I could to calm Annie down. I didn't want to fight, so I just—was a coward about it," he admits. "As soon as I realized you heard, I was going to take it back. But then you turned around and said you didn't like me, either."

Those words were a sharp line in the sand—a divider between the end of childhood and the start of something else. Levi avoided me the rest of that summer. Left for New York early to get his bearings and didn't do anything more than send short texts in response to mine for two solid years. When I finished up my freshman year of college and I realized he was still in touch with Annie and not with me, I gave up on him altogether.

He tried to come back, though. It's easy for me to push that aside, but he did. Around the time I graduated and took off with Griffin for the trip that turned into a few dozen more, he started texting every month or so. Called on my birthdays. Asked if I was ever coming into the city. But by then I was so angry with him that I wouldn't budge. I told myself it was the only choice I had, the only way to protect myself from the hurt—but now that I'm looking into Levi's eyes, I understand that it wasn't just that. I was looking to punish him. I wanted him to feel just as awful as I did, so I seized on my own silence like a weapon.

"It was all just a fluke, then," says Levi. "A misunderstanding."

But I shake my head. It wasn't a misunderstanding. Maybe it was in the heat of that moment, but the rest of it was on us. I was too stubborn, too proud to try to fix anything. And Levi—I think he was just scared. He'd always avoided any kind of conflict, always felt everything so deeply, so viscerally when we were kids. All I can think is that these plans he made, the molds he made himself fit into, were an easy way to push those feelings out.

An easy way to push *me* out. And once I was out, I was determined to stay gone.

"We had so much time to fix it," I murmur, more to myself than to him. It's almost worse, knowing his side of this story. Understanding we didn't waste all this time because of a mistake. We wasted all this time because of who we are as people. Who we are in our bones.

"We still have time," says Levi. "And we've been starting to fix it, haven't we?"

There's a smile tugging at my lips, but it's aching and sad. "We've been playing pretend."

"If I'm being honest, June, I wasn't playing at anything." Levi's throat bobs. "Those moments that made us go viral? Not one of them was staged. Maybe Sana told us to be there. But every single one of them was just us."

He's right. But it doesn't change the fact that we had to pretend to care about each other to even let ourselves care. This entire time, we've had a safety net under us. If it ever felt like we were coming too close or going too far, we always had the option of saying it was for the sake of our pact. What we're saying now is so outside of that safety net that if we stumble, we're going to freefall.

"I look at those pictures and I almost don't recognize myself," says Levi. "I haven't felt this happy in a long time."

"I'm glad for that. I really am. But I'm worried," I admit. "That this is all just—a vacation to you. That this is all happening really, really fast."

I stand by what I said—that I don't think anyone should have to be settled to be loved. But I know Levi. This isn't just his life in flux, the way it's been since Kelly cheated on him. This is Levi making a choice that seems bolder than any he's made in years. It feels reckless. It feels unlike him. And if I'm going to have Levi, I want *Levi*—not some temporary version of him I might lose when he comes to his senses. Not one that might be as easy to lose as he was all those years ago, when we let our pride and our fear get in the way.

"How about this, then." Levi takes a step closer to me, and it feels like it isn't just bridging the gap between us right now, but the careful, quiet one we've kept between us since he got back. "Let's take the whole . . . moving back thing off the table. We take all of it off the table, even," he says. "We just take it one step at a time. You and me."

I stay rooted in place, but my head tilts up to his like there's something magnetic in it, something that couldn't pull my eyes off his if I tried. "We don't even know what that looks like anymore," I say, still cautious.

"If that means we're friends, that means we're friends. But June . . ." He reaches out and holds the tips of my fingers with his hand, light and searching. "What I felt for you then? What I feel for you now? It never went away."

My fingers curl around his on instinct, pulling both of his hands into mine, pulling him closer to me.

"Me neither," I say quietly.

His hands squeeze mine, the question in them before he asks it. "What do you want to do?"

The word *want* snags in my chest like a hook and pulls. I want to go back and undo the past—not that day under the boardwalk, but all the days that came after it. I want to know what the future holds before I take too many steps into it. I want to rehash every-thing that's ever happened, I want to scorch the earth and start new, I want to be able to trust this wholly and completely without all the *what if*s and *what about*s still rattling in my head.

But there is one thing I want that's louder than all the others, crackling between us. One thing I want that I know I can have. One thing I've wanted for so long that it feels like it's grown roots in the marrow of my bones.

I lean in, my hips slowly closing the distance between us. "You mean right now?" I ask.

Levi's fingers loosen from my hands and settle so gently on my waist that, if it weren't for the warmth spreading out from under my ribs, they'd feel like an extension of me. Like the dip above my hips was meant for the shape of his hands. "Yeah," he says, his voice low, his eyes hungry and half-lidded in the shadow of the bar. "Right now."

"This," I tell him, and then I catch his lips with mine and sink into the heat of it, the sweet shock of it, the world slipping out from under me so fast that it feels like we're falling into a brand-new one, and it's just Levi and June all the way down.

Chapter Fifteen

By the time we reach my apartment, my fingers are trembling with the anticipation, fumbling with the keys like I've never seen the door before. Levi only makes matters worse when he presses his chest to my back, settling a hand on my stomach to pull me closer against him, grazing my ear, my neck, my shoulders with his lips.

That's it, then. The next headline about us. *Revenge Exes Fall Off Spiral Staircase to Their Horny, Unsuspecting Deaths.*

My eyes flutter shut, my knees near to the point of buckling, and I decide if the universe takes me out like this, it will be one hell of a way to go.

By some miracle that certainly doesn't have anything to do with me, the door opens, and we spill through it. Levi uses the hand on my waist to pivot me, uses his other to slam the door shut. He backs me into it, pulling away from my face to take a long, slow, satisfied look at me—it's the first time we've been truly alone all night, and in that one look I feel some last barrier burn out from under us, ignite the sparks between us into an open flame.

He settles his hand on the underside of my jaw, using his thumb to skim my cheek. He leans in just close enough for our foreheads to touch, but holds my face there, not letting me get close enough to kiss. Just drinking me in and taking his time.

"You," he says, his voice low, "are so beautiful."

I almost hold my breath so I don't laugh. He catches the quick, self-conscious quirk of my lips, and uses that same thumb to brush the bottom one. Whatever breath I was tempted to hold is knocked right out of me by the gentle way he parts my mouth, by the instinctive way my teeth graze against the pad of his thumb, my tongue skimming over his salt and earthy sweetness.

"I mean it, June. Everything about you."

He finally tilts my head up to kiss me again. I'm held in the sweet, aching pressure between Levi and the door, so rapt with the feeling of his lips on mine, with the hardness of him pressed against me, that I could go boneless with want right now. I don't recognize a single one of these demanding, searing impulses coursing through me. It's like my entire life, I've only ever had the taste of something described to me, and now I'm finally taking my first juicy, absurdly rich bite.

I reach my hand up to the back of his neck, digging my fingers into the heat of his scalp, tangling them in his curls. He lets out a shudder of pleasure and I feel it echo into me, landing square in my chest.

We come apart, catching our breath, and when I open my mouth to speak, I'm nowhere near as eloquent as he was. There's nothing in me except the raw, bare truth: "I want you so badly I might die."

His pupils are near blown out when he kisses me again with an entirely new urgency, leaning back from me just enough to hook his hands under my thighs and lift me onto him. With him so flush against me, I can feel his own want throbbing all over my body, so overwhelming that it feels like my blood is simmering just on the verge of a boil. He's pressing his lips into my neck, my shoulder, my collarbone, and then I'm being lowered onto my own bed, slow and gentle and easy, and I'm staring up at Levi and thinking to myself I could see every edge of the world a hundred times over and never see anything half as beautiful as him.

It isn't just that it's Levi. It's Levi with those curls of his mussed from my own hands. It's Levi with his lips red and raw from my mouth on his. It's Levi with his gaze roaming my body, settling his eyes on mine, tender and burning and dark with want. It's Levi undone, Levi unspooling, Levi who is giving me every part of him in this moment before I take the rest.

I ease myself up, taking in the full sight of him. He steps forward, settles the tips of his fingers at my hairline, running them through the remnants of my messy braid.

"You have no idea how many times I've thought about this," he tells me.

There's a boldness surging through me, and it's so solid and demanding that I ask, "Like when?"

He leans in, his knee coming down beside me to press into the mattress. "When we were dancing that night, and you were wearing that red dress, and all I could think about was . . ." As if to demonstrate, he uses his other hand to slowly take one of the straps of my crop top and slide it off my shoulder.

"I didn't realize you liked it so much," I tease.

"Oh, I hated it," he says. "Because every time you moved in it, all I could think about was getting you *out* of it."

My chest blooms with a slow, satisfied warmth as he traces the line of my collarbone with his knuckles.

"I thought about it that afternoon in the ocean," he says, coming closer. "How easy it would be to just—lean in. Kiss the salt water off your lips."

This time he does just that, a slow, aching kiss. One unlike the others that have come so far, exploratory and gentle. Just as we sink fully into it, he pulls away, grazing my lower lip with his teeth as he goes. Then he kneels between my legs, pressing his hands to my thighs.

"I thought about it when you were running toward us on the beach. Before all of this started," he says, kissing the sliver of skin between my top and my jeans. "You run like—like you were born to do it. Like you have your own gravity. Like you're flying."

I'm blushing, burning all over my body, the words seeping somewhere deep under my skin. I have so many words of my own, so many things I want to tell him. But I'm so overwhelmed that I can't put any of them in order. There's just Levi kneeling on my carpet, saying the kinds of words to me I stopped imagining him saying a long time ago, and my head is swimming trying to keep up.

I lift my hand and press it into the crook of his neck, leaning down to kiss his temple, his cheek, the soft shell of his ear. He shivers, and I tell him, "You shouldn't have told me about that dress. I'm going to use it against you."

He lifts his head to look at me and says plainly, "June. You could use anything against me."

And for some reason these are the words that hit home, that strike something in me so tender that I can't help myself from saying it. Suddenly, I need him to know.

"I've thought about this, too," I admit. "Dreamed about it, even."

He eases himself back up, sitting on the edge of the mattress beside me. "And what happens in those dreams?" he asks. He gently tugs at the hair tie at the end of my braid, starts coursing his fingers through it, unraveling it.

For the first time in the night, I feel self-conscious. For the first time in the night, I wonder if I'm a little bit out of my depth here. I know Levi inside out and backward, but the truth is, I'm not so sure I know *myself* that way.

The truth is—the truth Levi must know, even if neither of us will say it—I've only ever been with one other person. And only now that I'm more undone by the mere *start* of this with Levi than I ever was in my entire relationship with Griffin do I understand just how much I was missing out on. Just how many things I never thought I was capable of feeling, never even imagined were possible to feel.

And now I'm feeling them all at once, and it's so alternately overwhelming and freeing that it feels like all the years I missed out on are colliding in me at once, demanding a satisfaction I'm not even sure how to ask for.

"June," he says gently, stirring me back.

I tilt my head to look at him. "Those dreams . . . everything that happened in them was almost abstract," I confess. "I don't even necessarily know what we were doing in them. Just that you were there, and I was looking at you, and—and I could feel you. All of you." I swallow hard. "I never felt that way when it was actually happening."

Levi watches me, his hands still coursing through my hair. "You have all of me," he says. "However much you want."

And my throat aches almost as much as the rest of me then, because it's one thing to know it, but another thing to hear it. Sweeter than dreams, sharper than hope. I lean in and kiss him again, on his lips, the curve of his jaw, the plane of his cheek, anywhere I can reach.

"Good," I say. "Because I want every piece."

His teeth graze his lower lip as he stares at me, as his fingertips skim the hem of my top and then pull it off with a slow reverence.

He settles it on the edge of the bed, taking in the black bra underneath. Then he leans down and presses his lips to the top of my breast, and then to the other, making me shiver with the warmth of his mouth against my cool skin. He reaches for my right breast and kneads it slowly, deliberately, tucking his thumb beneath the underwire to stroke my nipple.

It's such a small touch. Such a subtle, little thing. But even that sends a tremor through me that feels like an earthquake in comparison to anything I've felt before.

Levi reaches to unclasp the back of my bra, and by then I'm aching for his hands on my breasts, for the fullness of his palms against them. But he's still moving with that tantalizing slowness, savoring me so openly that I forget my own nakedness, forget that this is a part of me few people have ever seen; forget to feel anything but the flush of satisfaction at the way he's staring at me right now.

He cups my breasts, and with him so close, the heat of him so compelling, I am all at once fixated on having more of his skin against mine. I find the hem of his shirt with my fingers and he leans back just enough to let me pull it up, lifting a hand to yank at the back of the neck and pull it over his head, and there he is. A torso I've seen plenty of times. He never lost that lankiness he had growing up, still all lean hardness and quick ease. I set a palm on his chest, trailing my fingers down to his stomach, feeling him tense under my touch.

"You know, when you run," I say, relishing every dip and plane of him against my fingers, "it's like you're made of something else entirely. Indestructible. Determined. I've always admired that."

I put my lips to his collarbone, sucking gently as my hand works my way down to the hem of his jeans, undoes the button.

He sucks in a sharp breath and says, "Is that why you were always so intent on kicking my ass?"

I smirk into his shoulder. "Someone had to keep you humble."

"Believe me, June," he says, his voice hoarse, "you'll never have to work to do that."

He abruptly hooks his hands under my arms, pulling the rest of me onto the bed, hiking me all the way up so I'm propped against the mountain of pillows. He eases himself up to meet me, lying beside me and angling his body into mine. I move in close enough that our noses touch, and we're just on the precipice of a kiss when I feel the tips of his fingers against the space between my breasts, and I let out a quick gasp. He undoes the button of my jeans, watching me carefully as his hand dips low into them, past the seam of my underwear, into the throbbing heat between my legs.

"Jesus," he murmurs low, and only then do I realize I'm achingly, desperately wet for him. That I wasn't exaggerating before. That if I don't have him tonight, *all* of him, it may very well be the end of me.

I'm wriggling out of the jeans, cursing the high-waisted trend for the first time I can remember as it takes the longest few seconds of my life to free myself of them. Levi's hand dips even lower, making sweet, slow circles with just enough pressure to drive an ache that spreads up and out, loosening my entire body. I lean forward, reaching for the waistband of his jeans again, desperate to return the favor, but Levi shifts closer.

"Let me," he says.

"I'm—" I put a hand to his forearm and he stills. "It's not going to—I mean, I—don't know if that's going to work."

Which is to say, the few times Griffin tried, it never did. It always took so long that we would either drop it or move on to something else.

"Do you like it?" he asks me.

I barrel past the question. "I don't want you to have to wait on it, or think it has anything to do with you if it doesn't work."

"Do you like it?" Levi asks, this time slower, closer to my ear.

"Yeah," I breathe.

And he picks up the pace again and says, "Then let me."

He slides a finger in and I'm already so wet that I barely feel it happening until he curls against me and my hips buck at the slight pressure, every part of me already aching for more. He settles his other hand on the back of my neck, bracing me, catching every tremor between his fingers. I lean in, desperate for any part of him I can taste—I breathe deeply into his neck, leaving a gentle, sucking kiss that makes him let out a low groan I can feel humming in my own lips. He slides in another finger and I gasp at the surge that follows, the *demand*, my body sinking into his hand as deep as it will go.

Every inch, every steady, rhythmic bend of his fingers feels so dizzying that I'm already breathless, like I've been sprinting for miles and never want to stop. It almost feels illegal to feel this good. Like I've accessed some part of the world I'm not supposed to know exists, because now that I do, there won't be any going back. There won't be any forgetting that I can come apart like this, that there are places all over my body I've never even thought could burn this bright.

"Levi," I say, and then I surprise myself: "I need you inside me."

It's the first time I've ever been so direct in bed. The first time I've ever actually said the word *need* and meant it. Everything before has felt so performative, like I've been going through the motions, but now everything else is moving *me*—like I'm in a tide that's pulling me along, dipping and rolling and cresting.

"You're sure?" Levi asks into my ear.

I press my hand against his jeans, feeling the hard length of him through the denim, relishing the quick gasp that leaves his throat. "I got screened after the breakup. So both my IUD and I are *very* sure," I tell him.

His lip quirks, something devilish in it. "I did, too. And good," he says, deliberately curling his fingers even deeper. "Because I could keep doing this all night."

I let out a keening noise, but I know what I want. I know myself. It's not that I'm worried this will take too long, or that Levi won't want to take his time. It's that I really, truly *need* it—it feels like some part of me is so open, so ready, that if it isn't full of him now, I'm going to burst.

"Please, Levi," I say.

He pulls his fingers out slowly, watching me the entire time, watching my mouth drop open at the loss of pressure. I ease myself up to work on the waistband of his jeans, trying to be like him— trying to take my time, trying to savor every moment of this. But I'm greedy. Almost desperate. Glad that Levi promised all of him, because anything less isn't going to be enough.

Once he's down to his boxer briefs, I press my lips just above them, threading the tip of one finger under the waistband and tracing the edges of it, feeling him shiver under my touch. I hook my finger and pull down slowly, releasing the length of him, and *oh*. My mouth is actually salivating, my heart thrumming with an anticipation so wild it doesn't know what to do with itself. My lips find the tip of it, licking softly, savoring the salty, bittersweet taste.

"Jesus," Levi murmurs.

He shifts so he can press his thumb between my legs again, continuing with those slow, tantalizing circles. I give another slow, exploratory lick up and down the length of him, digging my hands into his hips, anchoring myself as they sink lower.

"Okay, okay," says Levi, his voice barely more than a breath, "that feels—so good that you're going to have to—stop, if the two of us are going to . . ."

I take my mouth off him, using it to aim a wicked grin into his face. He responds to it in kind by pulling me farther up onto the bed again, then maneuvering himself until he's sitting upright and staring down at me, the blue of his eyes uncharacteristically dark as he roams every curve and dip like he's making a map of me.

My hips shift up in silent protest at the loss of his touch, and Levi only smiles softly and says, "Let me look at you."

There's too much colliding in me at once. This feeling of being *seen* without any other feeling accompanying it—without wondering if I deserve it, or if he really means it. Of letting myself enjoy this moment of being appreciated, of being cherished, and letting the feeling settle in my bones.

But my entire body feels like a live wire. If I can't touch Levi again, I'm going to implode.

"All right," I say, "you've looked."

And then I pull myself up and grab him by the shoulders, pushing him to the other side of the mattress, using the momentum to straddle him between my knees. Levi's pinned under me, all of him deliciously on display—the rise and fall of his chest, the planes of his torso, the open want glinting dark in his eyes. I push my fingers into his hair, pinning his head to the pillow, saying, "My turn."

It's a strange thing, to feel this present. This powerful in my own body. And this *used* to it, like this was in me the entire time, just waiting for the right person to bring it out.

And here he is—staring up at me, equal parts awe and appreciation, like he's never felt anything like this before, either. Like we've both been waiting to feel it for a long, long time.

I lean down, meeting his lips and deepening the kiss until we're chest to chest, skin to skin. I can feel the warm, pulsing length of him teasing my entrance, the first ripple of pleasure before a breaking storm. I sink farther down, easing him into me slowly, relishing the hum of his groan into my mouth, and then the sound of my name, "June, *June*," like it's something precious, something holy.

I take the full length of him and the feeling of it is so complete, so overwhelming that for a moment, I don't even breathe—for a moment, I'm not fully a person. Like basic biology doesn't apply to me anymore. There's just this feeling, this abstract feeling from a dream now made so sharply, beautifully *real* that already, I feel it knocking everything I thought I knew out of order. Already, I feel it burning the ground of all the lesser experiences I've had in its path.

I press my hands to his chest, steadying myself as I rock forward and back, adjusting to the fullness. To the sensation of wanting this to *last* and last and last, in a way I never thought I would. Levi murmurs my name as he cups my face, stroking my cheeks, my jaw, and when I pick up the pace, I let out a gasp, the two of us shuddering so in sync I can't tell whose body it began in or where it ended.

"I had no idea," I say out loud without meaning to. "I had *no idea* it could feel like this."

His hands are roaming farther down now, landing on my waist, following the rhythm of me as I ride him. I feel him hit that impossibly sweet spot in me and have to close my eyes, have to throw my head back for the way it stuns me, the delicious friction of it, the way it's building so steadily that for once, a resolution isn't an *if*, but a *when*.

The feeling is startling enough that I slow my pace, and Levi eases himself up and says, "Can I . . ."

The pressure of his fingers tightens around my waist and I nod, already shifting before he moves me, settling me down with my back bare on the mattress. There's an excruciating moment when he slides out of me and I am aching with the loss of it, but then he's on top of me, then he's sliding back home, and my back arches up to meet him with a new kind of shock. From this angle, he's hitting that sweet spot and then some. From this angle, I can feel the friction of him so thoroughly that it feels like he's reached into all of me, pulled me apart like something juicy and ripe.

He presses his finger just above my entrance again, and this time there's nothing light or teasing in the pressure; it's constant and relentless and perfect bliss. He picks up the pace and I stare up at him, and the sight of him in total and unmistakable rapture seizes in me, stirs every part of me, the feeling familiar but utterly foreign at the same time.

"I'm gonna—" My breath hitches, overcome with the heat pooling in my stomach, with the dizziness in my head, with the utter, bone-deep disbelief. "I'm gonna . . ."

Only a handful of times have I ever come from sex. Every true peak and valley I've ever felt has been self-given, in the minutes after sex or whenever I pleasured myself alone. I thought I knew what the buildup felt like—the mild disappointment and milder relief—but that . . . all that was nothing. A hiccup. A series of blips. *Nothing* compared to the heat coiling so deeply in me that it is awakening something that's never been touched, something that growls in me low and deep, both satisfied and *angry* to have been kept waiting so long.

I'm desperate to give in to it. Desperate to know what kind of bone-quaking, earth-shattering feeling might come on the other side, even knowing that I am going to lose myself in a way I have never been lost before.

Levi's next thrusts are slower, deeper. More deliberate. He presses himself into me, his teeth grazing my earlobe just before he says into my ear, "Tell me, June."

The way he says my name just then blazes straight through my body. The tenderness and the heat of it. The possessiveness and the freedom in it—the way I know deep down, further than any of this goes, that he is the only person I ever want to say my name like that.

That I could hear it a million more times in that tone of his and it would have the exact same searing, near-damning effect on me that it does right now.

"Oh, god," I say, my words coming out in a strangled gasp. "You're gonna make me come."

His face is burrowed in my neck, his mouth sucking ruthlessly against the sensitive skin, his fingers digging into my shoulders—all of it grounding me so thoroughly into this moment that I am more present than I've ever been in my own body, feeling every inch of myself at once, from my swimming head to my curling toes.

"Then come," he says, a low, gentle command.

Even the buildup doesn't prepare me for how fast it happens at the sound of his words, as if they cast a spell over me. I am undone, powerless against the shuddering ecstasy of it, the need to press myself closer, closer, *closer* to him as my breath stalls and I let out a cry of pleasure in a pitch so unfamiliar that I don't recognize it as my own even as it comes out of my own throat.

I'm senseless, weightless. There is only the pressure of Levi's hands roaming my body, the heat of my own clinging on to his back, the surge of mutual oblivion. I am somehow both lost and found, somehow outside of my own body but more myself than I've ever been. The peak of my pleasure shudders through my body with a force that borders on violence, a force that seems to command Levi in turn; he lets out a gasp and a groan of pleasure so intense that I don't just hear it but feel it vibrating in his chest against mine, feel it lingering in the air between us, a sound I seize and know I'm going to hold on to forever. A sound that is wholly and spectacularly mine.

I don't even realize I'm gasping his name over and over until he's murmuring mine back. By then, both of our eyes are wide open, staring into each other's, and we're breathing warm, stunned air in the few inches between us. I stare up into eyes that are somehow achingly familiar to me but startlingly new, like some new depth of them has been revealed, and I am finally seeing into the whole of him. As if he has been waiting to show it to me, or maybe I have been waiting to finally see it.

It's love and it's fear and it's everything in between. It's ancient with understanding and fresh with desire. It's everything I feel reflected back at me, anchoring me in this moment so surely, so steadily, that it feels every bit as shocking to my system as everything that came before it.

But this—it's a gentler kind of shock. A quiet, settling kind. Levi holds my face between his hands, using his thumbs to wipe away tears that somehow slid out of me in the heat of our pleasure, ones that are still streaming out of me even now.

"You're okay?" he says.

"I'm . . ." *Everything*, I want to say. I'm everything I've never been, everything I didn't even know to ask for, because I didn't know it existed. This feeling of completion. Of no longer knowing the beginning or the end of me, but not minding one bit, because at the borders of it there was still this: a person who knows me. Who looks at me like this. Who holds my face in his hands and stares at me with such unselfconscious, unselfish care that it suddenly feels absurd to me that I spent so much of my life without it. That I settled for the brief, cheap shine of any other kind of pleasure when Levi has brought me the sun.

"More than," I finally say, my eyes tearing up again. "Levi."

He smiles down at me, the kind of smile I've never seen on him before, easy and slow and dazed. *Mine.*

"June," he says right back.

He brushes the other tears from my cheeks, then slowly pulls himself out of me. We let out twin gasps at the loss of the pressure, aftershocks to the earthquake of us, but his gaze on me never wavers.

After we've cleaned ourselves up, we ease back on top of the tangle of sheets together, his eyes searching mine, two blue flames in the dark. "Do you want me to stay?"

"I want you to stay," I tell him. And I don't just mean tonight. I don't just mean my apartment. I mean *here*, in Benson Beach, in my heart, where he's never so far that I can't reach out and touch him like this again.

The new smile of his softens. He presses a kiss that starts at my temple, travels to the tip of my nose, to the edges of my lips. With steady hands he repositions us, shifting his body to the mattress so we're still side by side, still linked by his arms wrapped around me as he gently eases the front of his body to the back of mine. I am so warm with the reassuring heat of him that I forget to overthink the intimacy of it the way I always used to do, forget to feel the sound of my own heartbeat, forget to worry about what he's thinking of me, forget to worry about anything at all.

"Good," he murmurs into my ear. "Because there's nowhere else I'd rather be."

The words are a balm for my hammering heart. I press myself farther into him, taking the hand of the arm that's draped over my shoulder and weaving my fingers into his. He squeezes back the way I knew he would now that I'm leaning fully into this innate trust I have in him, the one I have wanted to let myself feel for longer than I can trace back.

I don't mean to close my eyes. I take in a breath to say something—to talk about what just happened. To tell Levi how much this means to me, in case he didn't already understand.

But I feel it in the weight of his arm around me. The understanding, and the calm in it. The way I don't have to be anybody but myself in this moment, because he understands my heart by touch alone.

For years, I waited and waited to fall asleep second so I could have a few moments on my own. Moments to finish myself off or collect myself, to rationalize the disconnect. But Levi pulls me in with his arms and wraps his leg around me, the weight of his upper thigh pressing against mine, and before I know it, my eyelids slide shut. There is nothing to question. Nothing to overthink. I am heavy, I am fulfilled, and for once, I am entirely still.

Chapter Sixteen

I wake up smiling. I wake up with my forehead pressed into Levi's shoulder, my nose grazing his collarbone, my ankles hooked between his feet. I wake up with Levi's chin resting on my head and the low, hoarse sound of him saying, "Good morning."

I breathe in deep, peeling my eyes open. Even then, the whole scene feels like something out of a dream. But there's no denying the sweetness of this reality—of the warmth of Levi wrapped around me, the sweet ache of last night still thrumming in my core. Flashes of his lips on mine and all over me, of his breath hot against my skin, of our bodies moving in tandem. Moments too bright, too visceral, for even an imagination as vivid as mine to make up.

Levi shifts and I tilt my head up to look at him. His eyes are all sleepy on the edges but bright in the early morning sun gleaming in through the window. I've always loved waking up with the sun on my face. I love waking up with it on Levi's even more. The way it's catching in his hair right now has turned every mussed tendril golden brown.

He kisses my forehead, and something about that simple gesture—the familiarity, the ease of it—pulses a current of absolute giddiness through me. The kind of moment where you realize you've gotten something you've wanted, and it's all you thought it would be and then some. I muffle a laugh, burying my head in his chest.

"Oh, now we're being shy?" he teases.

I can't help it. The smile I woke up with is now a full-on grin, the kind that's threatening to split open my face. I lift my head and aim that grin at him in full force, and he smiles back with that same slow smile from last night.

"I've had a lot—and I mean a *lot*," I emphasize, pressing myself closer to him, "of time to think about how good that would feel. And I didn't even come close."

Levi nods. "I'm pretty sure you broke my brain. I haven't slept in past six thirty in my entire life."

I glance at the clock on my nightstand, relieved to see it's only around eight. I have one of our full-timers open the shop on Fridays, so I don't need to be there for a few hours. When I look back over at Levi, my eye catches something that makes me entirely too smug.

"I gave you the biggest hickey," I tell him, tracing the red mark on his neck with my finger.

"Boy, do I have some news for you about the state of your own neck right now," he says, brushing the tangle of my loose hair off it to take a look at his handiwork.

"We're going to need a whole lot of foundation," I tell him. "Do you think we can get the Revenge Exes sponsored by CoverGirl?"

"We can have Sana look into it, right after . . ." He settles a knuckle under my chin, tilting my head up to kiss me. We're warm and morning-stale and everything about it is slow and easy and perfect. I pull away from him, basking in the simplicity of this, in the seamless way we've transitioned from the people we were to the ones we are right now.

I already feel the heat of last night coiling in me, the anticipation of another round of it. I pull away from him to ask if he has anywhere to be, and then something distracts me—Levi's phone screen lighting up on the nightstand behind him, flashing Kelly's name.

My stomach lurches. Somehow, conveniently, I'd forgotten she existed. Forgotten everything that led up to last night, all the tangled roads that led us here.

Levi follows my gaze to the phone. He shifts just far enough to flip it over, screen down.

"You're sure you don't need to get that?" I ask cautiously.

He leans in and kisses me again. "I'm sure. But I should charge it in case my dad wants a hand in the shop today. You mind?" he asks, holding up my cable.

For the first time, I actually regret taking over Tea Tide, because the idea of blowing everything off to sip iced tea and watch Levi fixing up a car in faded denim and a T-shirt is more appealing than anything else my brain can conjure.

"Go for it," I tell him.

He connects his phone, presses a kiss to my forehead, and says, "I'll be right back."

Even with the phone turned over on the nightstand, I can see it glowing again almost as soon as he closes my bathroom door. I watch it, transfixed. I can't help myself. It's the part of me that's been waiting for the other shoe to drop since Levi got to town, the part of me that wants to protect itself even now. I flip the phone back over.

Sixteen missed calls. *Sixteen missed calls.* All of them from Kelly.

His phone is on silent, so he must not have realized when we were tangled in each other, his back turned. Shit. It could be an actual emergency. My hands are shaking when I set the phone back down and call, "Hey, Levi?"

He can't hear me over the sound of the sink. I reach for my own phone and impulsively google Kelly's name, and boom. There's the headline. Not All Cinderella Stories Have Happy Endings—Inside Roman Steele and Kelly Carter's Split.

I click the link. It's an interview exclusive with Kelly. "He's just the loveliest man, through and through. Exactly what you hope he'd be," she's quoted as saying. "But I know my heart, and it belongs with someone else."

The electricity of last night starts to numb. I stare at that quote for so long that it brands itself into my eyes. Even after I skim to the bottom, see the photos of Kelly the publication embedded from her Instagram, see the other quotes she gave them about the charity work of Roman's she's going to continue with, all I see are those words. *I know my heart, and it belongs with someone else.*

That someone else walks out of the bathroom and sees me sitting on the bed with my knees hiked to my chest, staring with wide eyes at my phone, and immediately says, "What's wrong?"

I open my mouth. *Nothing*, I almost say, like I can sweep an entire interview from a nationally renowned publication under my bed, and all sixteen of Kelly's calls along with it. But he's crossed the distance between the bathroom door and my bed in an instant, and I'm handing him my phone, watching him scroll. Watching the concern furrowed in his brow lift to surprise, to bewilderment.

Before he can finish and look over at me, I say, "Kelly's been calling all morning."

As if on cue, his phone lights up on the nightstand again. Levi blinks at it. I press my forehead into my knees, bracing myself.

"I can deal with it later," he says.

And my heart cinches. Something in me is already starting to crack. I lift my head and say, "It's a lot of calls."

Only after this one ends and the 17 missed calls notification appears does he see what I mean. I don't know Kelly, but from what I've heard, she's a levelheaded, calm person. Someone like Levi. Someone who appreciates order and routines and a plan. Someone who doesn't call enough times to make a phone combust.

The phone rings with the eighteenth call right on its heels, but Levi doesn't look at the phone. He looks at me. Like I'm the one who has to make this decision, not him.

And for a split second, I feel it—a white-hot sliver of anger. The unfairness of this being put on me when I don't know this woman, don't know his history with her, and suddenly have no idea where I fit into any of it.

But I swallow it down, quick and brutal. Because if the bottom falls out from under us right now, well—we didn't make any promises to each other. We didn't stake any claims. We're in a limbo where the Revenge Exes technically never ended, and June and Levi technically never began.

And even if all of that weren't true, I don't want to be one more person in Levi's life who sets the terms for him. He followed Annie's plans. He followed Kelly's. I'm not going to try to tilt this in my favor by making one of my own.

So I give him a quick nod. He nods back. And then he picks up the phone.

"Hey, what's—"

She must start talking immediately, because Levi goes quiet. There's an intense focus in his eyes, which he aims at the floor, deliberately avoiding my gaze. Then his brow furrows, so sharp and so quick I feel my stomach drop.

"You're—you're coming *here*?" he asks.

I want to sink so far into the mattress that it swallows me whole. Levi's eyes flit to mine, half apology and half shock.

"Yeah, of course I know where—I can meet you there. But you should have called before you left," he says, abruptly turning his back to me. "No, I don't want to—okay. That's . . . fine. Text me when you're close."

She says something else into the phone, words I can't hear but recognize the rhythm of. Words I've ached to say to him, that I wish I had the courage to say even now.

But louder than any courage I can summon is the common sense. The reminder that Levi has a whole world he's built outside of me, outside this town. That I am one night in a sea of thousands of nights he spent with her. That I am a few weeks of fun against years of him building the foundation of an entire life that I'm not a part of, that I'll never fully understand.

He hangs up the phone and presses it down to the nightstand, keeping his hand on it.

"She's on the bus right now," he says.

I know exactly which bus he's talking about. In high school, we used to call it the Drunk Bus. The direct line between Benson Beach and New York, where underage high school and college kids would go back and forth in the hour and a half from the city.

The one time we took it together, Levi, me, Dylan, and Annie, we went to see a Broadway show. We stuffed our faces with dollar slices and snuck two six-packs onto the bus, chugging them before we got home. I rested my head on Levi's shoulder for the back half of the drive, already knowing he'd let me do it, a moment that felt stolen and earned at the same time.

And now I'm still stuck in between those feelings, unsure of where we stand. Unsure of what happens for us next.

"All right," I manage. "Well—good luck."

His brow furrows again, his eyes searching my face. "I don't want her to be here any more than you do."

"It's fine," I say tightly, and I try to make myself mean it. "You were with her for years. You and I were—last night was just a night."

Levi's mouth parts, and for a moment he doesn't make a sound. For a moment, we're both suspended in time, Levi stunned by my words and me determined to hold on to them, like they're the only armor I've got.

"It wasn't 'just' anything to me. You know that." Levi's tone can't settle, torn between insistence and hurt.

I stay very still, trying not to let it seep in. "I also know we said we were taking everything off the table. I just want you to know you can—do whatever it is you need to do."

"Whatever it is I need to do," he says, his voice dull. Prompting me to elaborate.

"We both said a lot of things last night is all," I say, my throat thick. "I don't want you to think I'm holding you to them."

"Well, that's just—" Levi lets out a strained laugh, running a hand through his hair, shaking his head against his fingers. "What do you want, June?"

It's close to the same question he asked me last night, one that I had an immediate answer for. One that I should have one for now. I want Levi. Of course I want Levi. But wanting Levi last night was simple; wanting Levi now that Kelly is back in the game comes with a risk I don't know if I can take.

"I want you to be happy," I say, which is the truth. But the truth under that is that if he's going to be happy with Kelly, I want to know now. I want it done. I want a clean break. And if pushing him toward Kelly is going to make the inevitable happen faster, it's better for us both.

His eyes soften then, like he's seeing it all play out on my face. "Being with you makes me happy," he says. "Tell me to just stay here, and I'll do it."

I can't. I'm not going to be the reason Levi makes his choice about Kelly. Whatever he decides to do, I want him to have full rein to decide it.

I tilt my head at the door and manage a small smile. "It's fine. She came all this way," I say, without any edge in it. "But it's up to you."

Levi considers me for a moment. Then he leans into the mattress, cupping the back of my neck with his hand, and pulls me in to kiss me on the forehead. We stay like that for a few long moments, Levi rooting his fingers into my hair, me leaning into the warmth of his lips.

"I'll meet her so we can talk. Let me know when you're finished up at Tea Tide," he says as he pulls away. "We still have to measure out our spot on the beach for the wedding chair rental company."

I nod. I'm only half-present when Levi pulls his clothes back on, when he slides his phone into his back pocket, when he leans in and says, "I'll see you later tonight." He's out the door and I'm still sitting on my mattress, the sheets bunched around me, feeling so much at once that I wish it could cancel itself out and let me feel nothing at all.

Instead, I throw on my clothes and wander to the building across the street from mine, then up another spiral staircase. I knock on Sana's apartment door. She's red-eyed, exhausted, but wide-awake when she opens it, her laptop propped against her hip. She takes one look at me and says, "Oh, shit. I hate saying I told you so. Don't you dare make me say I told you so."

I hold myself together just enough to say, "Fine. Then I'll say it. You told me so."

Sana drops the laptop on the table by the door and pulls me in for a hug so tight that it feels like she's keeping the pieces of me together.

"If it helps," she says into the crook of my neck, "I'm, like, sixty percent sure everything's going to work out just fine."

I bleat a laugh and she holds me tighter. The swell of gratitude for her is enough to bowl me over, but even then, I can't help the thought that comes unbidden, the one that will be on the edge of everything as long as I'm alive: *I wish Annie were here.* I wish she were here to tell me to buck up. To remind me who I am. To set me right in that fierce, uncompromisable way she always did.

Maybe that's the scariest thing about losing Annie. Moments like this, when I realize I may not have her anymore, but I still have what I need. Moments like this, when life goes on without her because there are other people I can depend on, other people who depend on me. Moments that I ache for both my sake and hers, because I never wanted to imagine a future where we weren't each other's first lines of defense.

"Come inside," says Sana, patting my head. "I have Pringles and Red Bull and Aiden's 'hardcore work jams' playlist to keep us company."

I pull away from her with a watery smile and a nod, letting her tug me inside. Maybe everything is, for lack of a better word, as *unsettled* as it can be. But at least there is a soft, over-caffeinated place to land.

Chapter Seventeen

"Mateo, *no*," Dylan says with a gasp, launching himself toward his fiancé heroically.

Mateo freezes, still holding the tiny ceramic baby he picked up from our parents' mantel. The usual person our parents have on call to clean between Airbnb bookers was busy this morning, leaving it to me and Dylan, plus one procrastinating Mateo, who has a stack of papers full of phone numbers and Instagram handles he has no interest in grading today.

"Is it fragile?" Mateo asks, eyes wide behind his glasses. He and my mom are so bonded by their love of history podcasts and flea markets that I'm pretty sure the idea of doing anything to upset her would cause him physical pain.

"I wish," says Dylan ruefully, keeping a wide berth between himself and the ceramic baby. "It's haunted is what it is. You could launch that thing straight into the sun and it would come out with its creepy grin intact on the other side."

Mateo stares down at it, puzzled. "It's an infant."

I roll my eyes, taking it from his careful hands and setting it back on the mantel. Technically, this cleanup is taking me away from the little free time I have to come up with better long-term ideas for Tea Tide. But given that my brain's resting state right now is "panic about Kelly stepping foot in Benson Beach," I probably wasn't going to get much done anyway. So I'm taking the advice Sana gave me on my way out of her apartment an hour ago. I'm not going to overthink it. In fact, I'm just not going to think about it at all.

Seeing as I've checked my phone approximately fifteen times in the last two minutes, that's easier said than done.

"Dylan had a nightmare about it coming to life when we were younger and tried to throw it away," I explain to Mateo.

Mateo's eyes soften, turning to my brother with that same lovesick look he's had ever since we were teenagers. "Aw. Little Dylan."

I snort. "He was fifteen. Also, say cheese."

Mateo turns just in time for me to tap the camera app on my phone and take a quick picture. "What for?"

"Your students let me into the 'Professor Díaz's SWEAT!!!er Vests' account on Instagram," I finally confess. "I don't think they've seen this one, so I'm earning my keep."

Mateo's mouth drops open. "For someone who's been dodging literal paparazzi right and left, I'd think you'd be a little more sensitive to the sanctity of my Friday vests."

Indeed, this one featured a subtle pattern of knit comets and dinosaurs in a deep navy and royal green he'd opted to pair with a short-sleeve button-down. It seemed like a waste for him to spend it here indoors all day, changing sheets and recounting Dylan's grudges against a Precious Moments knockoff.

Dylan leans in and puts a loose arm around Mateo's shoulders, mouth half-full of a granola bar he liberated from the pantry. "Leave my fiancé alone, you monster."

"He was my best friend before you realized you wanted to suck face with him," I remind Dylan with a pointed look.

"Hmmm." Mateo plants a quick kiss on Dylan's cheek and shoots me a placating look, but otherwise continues to rearrange the mantel. "It must have been nice to have autonomy outside the Hart family, but I can't seem to remember what it was like."

To be fair, Dylan has been absorbed into the Díazes every bit as aggressively as Mateo has been into us. Dylan first won their love with his bottomless appetite and appreciation for all of Mateo's family's cooking, secured it with the uncanny lifting abilities he's put to work at every Díaz wedding, quinceañera, and baby shower for the last decade, and immortalized it by proposing to Mateo in his parents' massive backyard so that the Díaz cousins could immediately descend on them with enough wine and cake that they probably could have just gotten married on the spot.

"Also, please tell me this irrational fear of ceramic babies isn't a manifestation of your *actual* fear of children," says Mateo. "Because as we've discussed, my mom is expecting no less than three."

Dylan looks offended. "Only three? That's not enough for our soccer team." The tenderness of the moment is slightly undercut by Dylan side-eyeing the ceramic piece and saying, "Plus I assume none of our kids will be possessed by Satan like this thing is."

Dylan uses the arm he still has slung around Mateo's narrow shoulders to squeeze him into his side, the gesture so innate and familiar that I feel an unexpected pang in my heart. I wonder where Levi is right now. I wonder what he and Kelly are saying to each other. I wonder enough to check my phone yet again, because I am nothing if not a sucker for an empty screen.

Except it isn't empty. There's a text from Griffin. Just checking in about that special! They could even squeeze us into the New York studio next Saturday—they'll book you a hotel and everything!

I roll my eyes and tuck the phone back into my pocket, getting back to work.

"Seems weird that strangers sleep in here, huh," says Dylan when we reach the one room we always come to last.

For the most part, Annie's room is exactly the way she left it—bubblegum-pink walls, massive seashell collection, ancient Sims CD-ROMs, and all. But the dressers were cleared out for guests, so everything worth saving is now kept in a locked cabinet in the walk-in closet.

"Yeah," I agree, my chest too tight to say much else.

"And strange that things just keep moving without her." Dylan reaches out and picks up one of her debate trophies, one of the many where they misspelled our last name as "Heart." Annie never corrected them. She liked it better that way. "Especially now. Me with Mateo. You with Levi."

I let out a breathy laugh. Dylan turns to me and says, "I bet that'd make Annie happy."

My throat feels thick with all the mounting guilt. I've been so wrapped up in my feelings for Levi that I've forgotten there are other people in our crossfire, too. That if we don't work out, Dylan might find out we lied the entire time. That if we do, it might not have made Annie happy at all. That years ago, Annie was so intent on me and Levi *not* happening that she got into a screaming match with Levi over it.

I haven't even had time to process that yet. It doesn't know how to settle in me. Maybe because I don't think Annie's anger had much to do with me at all—she just wanted Levi to be in California with her, and I was a factor standing in the way of it.

But I was also her sister. And I think that's why I can't peer at that argument too closely, can't follow it all the way down. I know she was only seventeen when she said it, but at one point her own plans with Levi were so important to her that she didn't care if I got hurt so she could keep them. She didn't care if Levi did, either.

"Yeah. Maybe," I say.

Dylan sets the trophy back down. There's nothing reverent or careful about it, which is its own kind of respect, I've come to realize. I always tiptoe around everything, but he treats the idea of Annie the same way he treated her when she was here.

"Gotta say, though," says Dylan. "As fucked up as it is, what happened to you and Levi—it's . . . nice."

"Nice?" I say, raising my eyebrows at him.

"I mean—nice having everyone around again."

I fluff one of the pillows on Annie's bed. "You missed your buddy Levi, huh?" I tease him.

For once, Dylan isn't ready with that easy smile. "I've missed you, too, sis."

I lean my knees against the edge of the mattress, feeling suddenly uncertain. "But I've been home a long time now."

Mateo knocks softly on the doorframe. "Hey, Cassie says we can swing by and take a look at some mock-ups for the cake, if we want to meet her at the bakery."

"I can finish up here," I offer.

Dylan tilts his head at me. "We've barely had a chance to catch up. You're sure you don't want to come with?"

There's a moment I almost say yes. Cassie is still checking in with me periodically about meeting to talk about expanding, or at least other ways we could tweak Tea Tide. Maybe it's just the way everything in my life has shaken up lately, but the idea doesn't put the same pit in my stomach it has for the past two years.

Then my eyes sweep past a framed photo—me and Annie in poofy princess dresses at my sixth birthday party, both of us drinking apple juice out of fancy teacups, our hair tangled in our crowns from running around in the backyard.

I'm angry with her, I realize. For what she said to Levi that day. For what it set into motion. But more than that, for the years afterward when she still had him as a friend, and I didn't.

I know that part was my fault and not hers. But I'm angry about it anyway, and guilty for being angry, and so tangled in all of it that I can't even let myself think about doing anything drastic with Tea Tide right now. It would almost feel like it was out of retaliation, if I did it with this anger in my heart.

"I should stick around here today," I tell Dylan.

He lingers for a moment, long enough to prompt me to look up. But by then, he's already headed toward the door, leaving me alone in Annie's room. I settle on the edge of her bed, breathing deep, trying to let the anger go. Trying to fill the space it takes up with the good, because we had more than our fair share, and Tea Tide will always be at the heart of it.

I can't pinpoint a moment we decided to open a tea shop in town; I just remember that it was a thread that followed us our whole lives. We were all early risers, and my mom would make a massive pot of tea every morning and make it last the whole day, letting us sneak sips when we were little and have our own cups when it was decaf. We had these giant seafoam-green mugs my dad got my mom for her birthday, and I remember clutching mine with hands all sticky from Eggo waffles or coffee cake on weekend mornings, sitting in a too-big chair on the porch, listening to the ocean and watching the neighbors go to and from the beach.

My mom always used to say how nice it would be to have a tea shop by the sea. How it was a shame that the closest place with decent tea service and good scones was in the city. It made those annual Christmas trips to the city special—we always went to the

Russian Tea Room for their holiday service while Dylan and my dad went off on their own—but it was one of those ideas we all daydreamed about, turning it back and forth like a lazy wave in our minds until eventually it stopped turning and just sank in: we could do it ourselves.

I had no intention of holding Annie to it—Stanford opened her up to such a massive world of opportunity that I wouldn't have done anything to limit it. But she persisted in talking about it her whole time there. Planning color schemes, dreaming up menus, keeping an eye on prime Benson Beach locations. She wanted a quiet, pretty place where she could write. She wanted to leave her mark on the place we called home.

"I'm just going to do it," she said to me over the phone one day. I was somewhere at the top of Norway, staring at fjords in bright daylight at midnight. She was freshly graduated and back in Benson Beach. "It'll be here waiting for you whenever you get back."

It was our dream, but it was also my safety net. An assurance that I could go as far as I thought I needed to go and still have a life waiting for me. A job. A sister. A home.

I understand now that it was less Annie assuring me that there was a place for me and more Annie asking me to come back and take it.

The little girls in the photo are still watching me. I turn away from them and toward Annie's closet, now empty of all the things I borrowed that never found their way back. Without consciously deciding to, I pull the key out from under the nightstand and walk over to the drawers full of her things.

Dylan put them all in here in the days after the funeral, so I'm not sure what to expect. Mostly it's old toys of hers from when we were kids. Her baby blanket. A few art projects from when she was younger. A finisher's medal from the local 5K Dylan convinced her to do when she was a senior and he was a sophomore, after which she wheezed at him very pointedly, "Never. Again."

The next drawer is more of the same, plus the graduation program listing her as the salutatorian, where she gave a two-minute speech about how she wasn't qualified to dispense any knowledge, just goodwill—a speech that infamously ended with the words, "Good luck out there, everyone. The only real advice I can offer you? Just try not to fuck up."

I smile at the memory of the absolutely scandalized look on the principal's face as my parents tried to muffle their laughter from the audience. It was a phrase she uttered often and with relish, but certainly not one anyone ever expected her to blurt with dozens of camera phones trained on her. But that was Annie for you—she said what needed saying, whether you wanted to hear it or not.

I set the program on top of a pile of loose papers, but not before I see Levi's name on one of them. I know precisely what the papers are before I decide to lift them out of the drawer. It's the missing pages from when Levi started *The Sky Seekers*. Annie must have printed them out when we were all still in high school, and she and Levi were constantly swapping their pages back and forth to critique.

What's funny is I've spent the last two weeks trying to plow through Levi's new manuscript about New York, and I've only managed to get about halfway through. But this—I sit on the carpet and gulp it all down in one go. It makes me startle at old memories. Makes me delight in all the little details, at the cheeky dialogue between the characters, at the unique ways Levi has of looking at the world and the way we interact with it.

But it also makes me ache. It isn't finished. It's just the potential of something—a story that, with the right care and focus, could be crafted into something iconic. A story that wouldn't just be a testament to Levi's writing talent, but his ability to see into people's hearts.

Maybe it's a story Levi will never write, but it's one he deserves to remember. So when I stack the pages back together, I don't set them back in the drawer. I tuck them under my arm, glancing at the picture as I back my way out of the room, at the two cheesing girls in their princess dresses.

"He needs these," I tell little Annie, and I have to think older Annie knows that, too.

Chapter Eighteen

$\mathcal{B}$y the time I roll into Tea Tide, I have at least seven fires to put out, the main one being that thanks to a late supply delivery, we're fresh out of Revenge Ex scones. And the customers who came in specifically to get one are *not* taking it lightly. After a brief panic brainstorm, I send out one of our part-timers to the corner store with the instruction to buy a box of just about any cookie she can find. We break them into chunks in the back, bake them into scones, and dub them "the Levi."

In other words, a giant cookie pretending to be a scone.

I figure he'll be in at some point today, and it'll be a cheeky way to cut through the tension of this morning. And although hours pass without Levi showing up, the Levi sells so dangerously fast that the owner of the corner store moseys in to ask what on earth we're doing with our multiple raids of her entire stock of Oreos, Chips Ahoys, and Nutter Butters.

"Something unholy," I inform her, giving her a giant, Frankensteinian scone on the house.

Sana comes in and delights at it—"It looks so ugly and so delicious!"—immediately taking a picture for Tea Tide's Instagram account. Even that doesn't summon Levi, but it does bring in an unexpected influx of late afternoon customers. We're moving so fast that I barely come up for air, and I'm glad for it. With the day whipping by, I don't have a single second to spare worrying about Levi and Kelly.

That is, until Kelly is directly in front of me, standing at the register with a warm smile on her face.

"You must be June," she says, holding out her hand.

I open my mouth to say something back, but my brain is still too busy processing her to get to the next step. She's beautiful. I knew that, of course, from all the photos of her and Roman Steele plastered all over the internet, but knowing it is entirely different from seeing it in person. Her honey-brown hair is in loose waves at her shoulders, her skin practically poreless, her green eyes wide but keen. She's wearing this breezy white dress and a pair of gladiator sandals, more polished than anyone in here by far but looking right at home.

Her smile widens just slightly, and shit. I want her to like me. No wonder she's so good at selling real estate. There's another world where she might be able to sweet-talk me into handing over the keys to Tea Tide right now.

"Hi, yes," I say, taking her hand. "And you're Kelly."

And you're in my store. Staring at my scones. Talking to me. Without Levi anywhere in sight.

There's something objectively aggressive about the whole thing, but she doesn't come off that way. More curious than anything. Less like she's sizing me up and more like she genuinely wants to meet me.

"I thought I'd come in and grab a bite while Levi's helping his dad in the shop," she tells me. "Plus I've heard so much about you."

"Likewise," I say, still too thrown off to say much more. I have this weird out-of-body feeling, like we're on our own reality show right now.

She leans in to peer at the display case. "Ooh, what's the Levi?"

"Oh, that's . . ." I watch a little pucker in her brow as she registers the cookie edges poking out of it. "More of a joke," I explain.

She nods, that warm smile still in place when she meets my eye again. "Makes sense. I'll never understand that man's aversion to a good dessert," she says. Her tone is somehow both conspiratorial and possessive. Like she's acknowledging that we both know him deeply, but that she's also not threatened by me in the slightest.

In fact, I'm starting to think that might be the entire point of this casual drop-in.

"Well, if it's named after Levi, I'll have to bring him one," she says brightly.

I feel a dip of disappointment in my stomach. Half the point of the scone was to get to watch his reaction to it.

"And let a perfectly good scone go to waste?" I joke weakly, hoping to change her mind.

She winks at me. Literally winks, so effortlessly it puts every cute girl who's ever starred in a toothpaste commercial to shame. Then she says, "Oh, trust me. I'm used to finishing off Levi's desserts by now."

My eyes go wide and hers just stay trained on mine, unyielding. She pulls out her clutch to pay.

"Oh, don't worry about it," I say. As I bag up the scone, something in me rises to meet her, turning to steel. "Levi's already our best customer."

This may be true only in the sense that he's here more often than not, but her smile goes static. "Well, thanks on his behalf," she says, taking the bag from my hand. "I'd let you know what we think of it, but I'm not planning on staying in town long."

Her unspoken words are almost louder than the spoken ones—
she thinks she's going to make quick work of getting Levi back to
New York. And now that I've been subject to her combination of
stunning beauty and uncompromising resolve, I'm not entirely sure
she won't.

My stomach is churning by the time I close the shop for the
night. I haven't heard a single word from Levi. I check my phone
screen for quite possibly the bajillionth time and realize it's not just
because of the dread. It's from plain old missing him. We've gotten
into such a rhythm of chatting back and forth at Tea Tide, of texting each other quick updates and jokes, that the day feels entirely
off-kilter without it.

I take a deep breath. Last night didn't just change things between us. It solidified them. It bound us in a way we've never been
before. Part of me just wants to trust it the way I did so easily when
we woke up this morning. But a louder part of me is terrified because suddenly, there is so much more to lose.

But right now, I don't have any control over the situation. What
I do have control over is getting the measurements of the beach
space outside of Tea Tide so I can figure out the chair rental situation before it's due tomorrow. I pull the measuring tape out of the
office drawer and trudge down to the beach.

It's hard to wrangle without a second person, but not impossible. I'm just under the boardwalk finishing the last stretch of it
when I hear a laugh carry over the soft breeze. I lift my head and
see the outline of two people at the water's edge against the fading
light. Even from this distance, I recognize Levi in an instant—the
curve of his slight slouch, the lean lines of his frame. Kelly's beside
him, the outline of her so indistinct that she can only be leaning
into him.

And Levi's letting her. Levi's walking arm to arm with her, making her laugh, soaking in the sunset with her. Levi's looking like one half of a picture-perfect couple, like I could take a photo right now and sell it as a postcard, as a whole life. There isn't a single person in the world who would look at them right now and not want a piece of whatever it is they have.

I blink away, my eyes stinging. It's not just that they're so close, not just that they fit so well. It's that they're so lost in each other that Levi must not even realize he's right outside of Tea Tide.

I stand under the boardwalk long after they pass, utterly still. I wait for it to come crashing down. The hurt. The humiliation. The first crack of a heart about to break.

But I'm just hollowed out. Like last night I opened myself up and made so much room for everything—the feelings I dismissed, the ache I was determined to ignore, the hope that felt too fragile to touch—and I don't know how to be empty of it, now that I've let it in.

It's over, I realize. Maybe not me and Levi, but this little charade of ours. The Revenge Exes existed so Levi could get Kelly back, so I could bolster Tea Tide. Now Kelly's here, and Tea Tide is close to making the money we need to front the three months' rent.

Close, but not entirely there. As far as I know, I'm out of party tricks—at least any that will work in the short-term. I can't make another viral moment fall into my lap to get us through the final stretch.

And then I realize that's not entirely true. In fact, this is a problem with a concrete solution. This is a problem I can solve.

I pull out my phone and bring up my text thread with Griffin. I can do the special next Saturday. What time?

His answer is immediate. AWESOME. I'll send you details as soon as I get them. Is it okay if it's live?

If anything, that's a selling point. The faster we can get a last push of customers through the door, the better. I figure even if Levi and I have fake broken up by then, just being on the show will help me get people in the door.

Sure, I text back.

Thank you thank you thank you, June. Seriously. I owe you one!!!

I lean my forehead against a beam under the boardwalk, letting loose a long breath. I thought maybe I'd feel better, committing to this. Fixing something that could be fixed. But then that hollow part of me fills itself up again, my heart throbbing, my chest raw with ache. I hope it isn't really over. I hope this whole day was just a silly, overblown blip. I hope it so recklessly that there isn't any other feeling left, and then I hold on to it like a balloon, trying my best not to squeeze it so tight that it bursts.

Chapter Nineteen

I wake up the next morning with a pounding headache from tossing and turning all night, plus several texts from Levi.

I'm so sorry. I lost track of time. Thank you for sending the measurements, says the first one. He must have seen me mark it as resolved on our shared document for the wedding.

I'm expecting the next text to be some kind of reassurance or explanation about Kelly, about his "losing track of time," but instead it says, Do you still want to go through the pictures for the rehearsal slideshow today?

I blink at the screen, the words stirring me awake faster than my alarm did. Gathering our half of the photos for the surprise slideshow the families are making for Mateo and Dylan is a task we've both been putting off for reasons neither of us has to say out loud. So many of our group's best memories, so many of the photo-worthy moments we've got, have Annie right at the heart of them. But the next Airbnb renters are coming tomorrow, so if we don't go tonight, we won't be able to get in for a week.

Also—"The Levi"? August Hart. You have some explaining to do.

My lips tug upward, but the satisfaction is fleeting. There are no other texts, and suddenly the silence about the Kelly situation is screaming between my ears. I should just ask what's going on, but I can't bring myself to do it. It feels too needy. Like this is some sort of test in our trust, and if I'm the one who bends right now and asks, it means I'm the one who's questioning it. It means I'm the one who doesn't have faith.

And then I realize whatever I'm feeling right now—it's not just the dread of the situation. I'm angry with him. He spent years shutting me out, and this feels like a quiet version of it. The last thing I want to do right now is go through old pictures with him. The last thing I want to do is rehash the last time we were on the verge of something, and he pulled away.

I groggily type back a text with a joke to break the tension, hoping it might prompt him to explain, but I'm too upset to finish it. Instead, I send a curt, No worries. I can handle the pics.

Levi starts to type back immediately. What time are you heading over?

I set the phone down. Still no explanation about Kelly. Not even an explanation about where he is right now. Which must mean she's still in town, possibly even staying in his condo. My stomach churns. She's possibly even in his bed.

I sit upright, the thought of it sending another angry charge through me. I know Levi. I know that isn't what's happening right now. But I'm also furious that I'm so in the dark about all of this that he's leaving me to imagine it. Maybe I didn't have a right to know what was going on between him and Kelly when we were just playing at a relationship, but after everything we said to each other, after everything we did, this feels almost cruel.

I know he doesn't mean for it to be. I hear the word in my

head—*unsettled*—and I remember that's what he is right now. That's what our entire lives are right now. And I can make space for that. I just didn't count on what might happen if he were unsettled about me.

He doesn't show at Tea Tide that day, but he's waiting for me outside my parents' house when I walk over. My brows lift in surprise, and only then do I realize I was scowling the entire way. He's leaning against a beam on the front porch, his head tilted down. His eyes sweep up to meet mine. There's an apology in them, and something else. A quiet caution that makes me want to stay rooted to the sidewalk and not let him say a single word.

"How long have you been standing out here?" I ask.

He holds my gaze. "I don't want you to have to go through those photos alone."

I nod, and for a moment, the rest of it fades. The reality of the task in front of us sinks in, and as I feel the weight of it settle between us, I'm glad that I don't have to shoulder it alone.

But once we walk inside, it suddenly feels like we're in a play. The stage directions are telling us to walk down to the dusty basement, to pull out the photos my mom has categorized by year in the back closet. They're telling us to sit on the couch and start spreading them out neatly on the coffee table. They're just not giving us any lines until I finally work up the nerve to say, "Is Kelly still here?"

"No, she went home a few hours ago," he says evenly.

The word *home* strikes a dissonant chord. I can't tell if he means her home or theirs.

He shifts on the couch, angling himself toward me. "I'm sorry she showed up like that," he says. "That was—I mean, you know how unexpected that was. And the timing was just—absolutely awful."

I can tell he's going to say more, but I can't spend one more second wondering. "Are you two getting back together?" I blurt.

His eyebrows rise, his face so immediately stricken by the question that I realize it never even occurred to him I'd ask it. "No. June. I'm sorry," he says, not just with the sincerity of before, but genuine earnestness. He turns and looks at me, really *looks* at me for the first time since we walked into the house, and he must see it then—the uncertainty, the dread, the frustration. "Oh, June."

He reaches out and wraps an arm around my shoulders, and I press my forehead into his collarbone. The relief is so staggering that I can feel the slightest quiver in my voice when I say, "I didn't hear from you all day. I wasn't sure what to think."

"I just was—yesterday really threw me for a loop," he says, using the hand wrapped around me to squeeze my shoulder. "There were a lot of things she wanted to say, and—things I needed to say, too. We were together for a long time."

"I know," I say, but it doesn't come out as understanding as I want it to. There's an edge in my voice, an edge I've been teetering on ever since he answered her call.

"June," he says, pressing the words into my hair. "I meant everything I said that night."

I linger there for a moment, my eyes closed, trying to let the words sink in. But I'm too uneasy. Too on guard. I pull away from him slowly, meeting his worried eyes.

"But it's like you said," I say carefully. "You were together a long time. And until a few days ago, you were trying to make it work. And then she's here, just like you wanted, asking for you to get back together—that is why she was here, right?"

Levi nods, his eyes sweeping down. Then he gathers up the hands in my lap and holds them in his, his touch featherlight. "I told her I've moved on. And I have, June. Kelly and I have been drifting apart for a long time now. I think I was just so jarred by everything else in my life shifting that I was holding on to the idea of us. I'm pretty sure that's why she came here, too. Just out of fear of everything changing." He squeezes my hands gently, like he's pressing the words into me. "But I don't feel that way anymore. Things between me and Kelly—they're over."

"But," I supply. Because I know there's a but. I might believe every word he's saying, but I saw it in his eyes at the front door. I heard it in the silence of this past day.

Levi's grip softens. "I'm going back to New York for a little while. Just to square things up."

I go as still as he is, like I'm seeing something flash out of the corner of my eye and bracing for potential impact. "Like what?"

"The apartment. My job." Levi looks away from me again, toward the small pile of photos we've been poring through. "And . . . to be honest, to finish the draft. It's due soon, and I haven't made much progress."

I slowly pull my hands out of his, settling them back in my lap. Levi just leaves his own resting on my thighs, like he's waiting for them to come back.

"I guess our little pact didn't help matters," I say, trying to keep my tone light.

Levi turns back to me, shaking his head vehemently. "June. Every second of the Revenge Exes has been more ridiculous than the last, but you have to know I wouldn't have traded a single one of them for the world."

The knot of dread in my chest loosens slightly, enough that I feel a reluctant smile twitch at my lips. Levi seems relieved to see it.

"What I mean is—every time I try to write that manuscript, the tone is just all wrong. Like being here instead of where it's set is throwing me off," he explains.

The twitch of a smile disappears, my brow furrowing in concern.

"So basically, being here where you're happy instead of there where you're not?"

There's that same expression he was making at the door when I arrived, the one with the apology in it. Like he doesn't want it to be true any more than I do. It makes me ache for him—both the Levi in front of me and the Levi who wrote that first manuscript. The one who was so determined to face everything alone.

"Where are you staying?" I ask.

"There's a spare room in the apartment we were using for an office, so I'm going to stay there." And then, off my worried expression, he adds, "Kelly works long hours. I'm barely going to see her."

But I'm not worried about Levi being around Kelly. It's the fact that he's choosing to be around her. That after everything we just said to each other, all the unspoken promises I thought we made the other night, he's choosing to be somewhere I'm not.

"How long will you be gone for?" I ask, my throat dry.

"Two weeks—three at the most, depending on what arrangements I make for the move." He says the words quickly, like he's been rehearsing them in his head since he decided. "We'll just be an hour and a half apart. We'll still be able see each other. And then I'll be back."

"So you're leaving soon," I realize.

He hesitates for a moment and then says, "I'm leaving tomorrow."

This stings with more force that I'm expecting it to, enough that I'm blinking like I just got bowled into by a sharp gust of wind. I press myself farther into the couch, farther from him.

And then I almost laugh. "I guess I'll see you next weekend," I say.

"Yeah?" Levi asks, a lift in his voice.

"I'm doing that special with Griffin." I give him a tight-lipped smile and say, "You don't mind if I use the whole Revenge Exes thing to blow up our spot one last time?"

Now it's Levi whose eyes are cloudy with worry. "Of course not," he says anyway. He lets out a breath of a laugh. "Aren't we technically still Revenge Exes?"

We are, but suddenly I don't want us to be. I want us to just be June and Levi, the way we should have been from the start. I want to have enough of a foundation together that Levi wouldn't have things to settle in New York, and I wouldn't have all the doubts swirling in my head.

"Yeah," I say. "Guess so."

Levi leans in, close enough that I'm aching for him to be closer even as I feel like I have to hold some part of myself away. "What made you decide to do the special?" he asks.

"Part of it is to get a last surge of traffic for Tea Tide. But the other is just . . . for closure." Only now that I've said it out loud do I realize how much I want it. A firm ending of my "Griffin era." A clean slate so I can start out fresh with whatever's coming next, whether Levi is part of it or not. "It's like you said about Kelly. We were together a long time. This will be a clean break." I tilt my head at him. "Or at least, one where I'm not crying a geyser into a hot mic."

He nods stiffly, accepting but clearly wary. I can hear the reluctance in his voice when he settles on saying, "Just—be careful."

I tap my palm on his knee, light and quick. "You too."

We search each other's faces then, and I see it—the unwavering trust. The mutual understanding. The way we know each other too well to feel anything but. Maybe it will be enough to get us through this and maybe it won't. It's the first time in my life I've ever been scared at the feeling of hope, knowing just how much possibility is on the other side of it, but I cling to it just the same.

We set to work on the photos then. The first few boxes are easy to search through—squishy versions of Annie and me and Dylan, our parents parading us around Benson Beach with cheeks shiny from sunscreen and Cheerios tangled in our hair. It seems wild to me that at one point, my parents were wrangling three kids under four years old when they weren't much older than I am now.

We set aside a few cute shots of baby Dylan for the slideshow—a particular favorite of mine has Dylan propped on Annie's lap, with me sitting next to her and staring down at Dylan like he's an alien—and move past the baby pictures. Levi starts showing up in them not long after that, first in shots with just Annie, then in shots with the rest of the Harts as we quietly absorbed him into our chaos.

Levi stops at one and holds it off the table. It's Annie and Levi in their kindergarten class together, dressed up as Raggedy Ann and Spider-Man and holding matching candy bags. Annie's got a frilly sleeved arm wrapped around Levi's shoulders, and his toothy grin is so wide under his mask I can practically hear the little-kid laugh about to bubble out of him.

"You two were so close," I say quietly.

Levi's own voice is hoarse as he stares at the picture like he's both in that memory and a hundred others at once. "Yeah."

"We have doubles of that one. You should keep it."

Levi nods and sets the photo aside from the others before carrying on, notably slower now. We work like this in relative quiet—a respectful, shared thing, like we're trying to avoid walking on two different graves. Levi's memories of Annie, and mine.

It feels like the present is suspended, like we're dipping in and out of years gone by. The elementary school years full of face paint and field days, the town Fourth of July parade and long beach days in the summer, sandy limbs and wet, tangled hair. The preteen years full of braces and middle school dances, Annie in her debate club T-shirt, Levi carting around the AlphaSmart keyboard he used to type on before he could buy a cheap laptop, me and Dylan on the bleachers at our first track meets. Fewer shots of high school—mostly ones of family vacations and graduations, because by then we were starting to save everything online.

The last box is a mess, but a delightful one. It's stuffed to the brim with Polaroids from Dylan's old camera taken in overexposed sunlight, all of us at a theme park the summer before I turned seventeen—a perfect summer. The summer before I started crushing on Levi, and we were all just happily coexisting in each other's orbits the way we had as kids, but with the freedom of teenagers who had access to a car. I cackle at a particularly prophetic image Annie must have taken of a tiny, pre–growth spurt Mateo staring moony-eyed at an oblivious Dylan, who was busy plucking a nacho fry out of a platter in Levi's hands.

"I can't believe it took them until college to get together." I laugh, pulling the photo aside for the slideshow, fully aware that Mateo will make me rue the day. "Mateo had it *bad*."

"Don't know if it would have done him any good to figure it out earlier. Dylan just didn't seem interested in dating until college." Levi smirks at the next picture, all of us exhausted and sweaty on a bench, Mateo yet *again* sneaking a glance at Dylan. "But yeah. He had it bad."

Our laughter tapers off at the next picture. Me and Mateo asleep in the back seat. Mateo's head is propped on the window, but mine is resting on Levi's shoulder, and Levi's eyes are on me.

"I remember that day," says Levi with an unmistakable fondness.

"Me too." I tap a finger on my sleeping face and say, "Someday you and that boy are going to have a strangely passionate internet fanbase by the throats."

Levi hums. "Someday you're going to do a *whole* lot more than that."

His hand has wandered to my thigh, the pressure of his fingers searching, cautious. I lean into him, and it's so tempting to give in to the warmth uncoiling in my chest right now, in to the sweet hum just under my skin that starts exactly where his hand is resting.

But louder than that is the ache of everything that feels unresolved right now. The fear that Levi will go back to New York, come to his senses, and change his mind. The fear that this is just going to be an encore of the last time we broke each other's hearts.

"Someday you're going to have a whole lot of regrets," I say to the picture.

"Hey," says Levi, grazing his nose against my temple. He stays close, his breath warm against my cheek. "We're going to be okay. These weeks will fly by. I'll be back, and things at Tea Tide will settle, and we'll throw Mateo and Dylan the best damn wedding Benson Beach has ever seen and make total fools of ourselves on the dance floor."

I turn my face toward him, and Levi kisses me slow and deep. Levi kisses me like it's an apology and a promise. I kiss him back, terrified, because I can't help but kiss him like it might be goodbye.

It's Levi's own words I'm remembering as I stamp this moment into my heart, trying to take hold of something even as I'm preparing to let it go: *Let's take the whole moving back thing off the table. We take all of it off the table, even. We just take it one step at a time. You and me.*

Those steps suddenly feel like we're taking them on a tightrope, and I'm the only one of us willing to look down.

We pull away, but Levi's hand stays steady against my jaw. I lean into it, savoring the feeling even as I ask him something that might damn us.

"If you stay here, what are you going to do?" I ask. "I mean—are you going to write like you planned?"

"That's what I'm hoping," he says.

I ease myself away from him, then root through my bag at my feet. My fingers stop on the papers I carefully put into a thick folder yesterday, that I've had stashed away since. It feels less like I'm giving him an old manuscript and more like I'm surrendering the very last piece of my heart.

"I found this in Annie's things," I tell him, handing him the early scenes of *The Sky Seekers*.

I see the recognition dawn as he flips through it. The recognition and something else—a longing. A nostalgia. They streak across his face so quickly that it would be easy to miss it if I hadn't felt all of it myself.

"Anything you write is going to be a hit. I know that," I tell him firmly, sincerely. "But I thought you should have it. Not just for the sake of your writing. But because it's yours."

He thumbs through it, taking it all in—both the typed words and the scrawled notes in the margins. Some of them his and some of them Annie's. Not just a story, but a capturing of a moment in time.

When he looks up, he gives me a watery, grateful smile. The kind that cinches in my chest.

"Thank you," he tells me. He sets the pages next to the photo of Annie with the same kind of reverence. "I've been remembering pieces of it lately, but—this is so much more than I ever thought I'd have back." He lets out a self-conscious laugh. "And it's nice to know I had other ideas once. I've been so focused on getting this manuscript done that I'm not even sure what to start on the other side of it."

"Well, if you ever want to revisit an old idea, you know I've got even more than that stashed in my brain," I say, tapping my temple.

"I'd like that," he says warmly. "Even if I don't go back to it. But I'd like to think someday I will."

There's a wistfulness that settles between us then, one that makes us both go quiet, lost in our own thoughts. I wonder if we're in the same place right now—wandering through our old woods, the sunlight streaming through the trees, the cicadas humming under our feet, the world an infinite, sprawling thing ready for us to create anything we wanted.

After a few moments of quiet, I nudge him with my elbow and say, "Maybe someday you'll even write me into something, huh?"

I mean for it to be a cheeky way of letting him know I still recognize all his characters. Annie did, too. It's right there on the first page in her purple ink: *You planning on asking me and Dylan for our life rights orrrrr??*

But Levi's expression dims. His eyes linger on mine, the guilt in them so acute that it's almost like his trail of thought has woven its way right into my own head. Flicked on a light and exposed something I probably should have noticed a while back.

"Oh," I manage.

Because it feels like a cosmic joke. I was so focused on wondering why I wasn't in *The Sky Seekers* to even think to look for myself anywhere else.

"The girlfriend the main character is so tortured about in your New York book. The one he loves but feels like he has to leave behind, to break up with for her own good." I close my eyes, feeling a rueful smile bloom on my face. "That's me, isn't it?"

When I open my eyes again, Levi's own smile is just as sad. "I was just—processing, in my own way," he says. "I missed you so badly. You have no idea."

But of course I do. I spent the same years missing him, every version of him I could imagine. The Levi who was my best friend. The Levi I fell for in high school. The Levi he is right now, because there is no iteration of Levi I haven't pined for, haven't wanted at my side. When you love someone the way I love Levi, it becomes every bit as much a feeling as it is a part of your own soul. Something inevitable. Something permanent. Something that never quite had a clear beginning and will never end.

It should be an earth-shattering moment, letting myself acknowledge that I'm in love with Levi. But it isn't. It's quiet and gentle and sure. It has been a part of me for so long that it doesn't know any other way to be.

No, it isn't the love that scares me. It's what might happen to it. I pull in a quick, shaky breath and say, "I'm going to go ahead and guess they don't have a happy ending."

He does just what I'm hoping he'll do. He leans in to wrap his arms around me, to hold me so firmly that I sink into the warmth of it, breathing him in like I can keep the feeling of this in my chest after we come apart.

"It's only a story, June," he says. "We get to make our own endings."

I nod into his chest, but that's just it. I don't want an ending. I want a beginning. And right now—with Levi leaving in the morning, with the doubt swimming in my heart, with so much unresolved between us and the pasts we're leaving behind—I feel like I'm still holding my breath, waiting for the story to start.

Chapter Twenty

It turns out there are some perks to having your ex-boyfriend humiliate you and make you a national laughingstock, because months after the fact, you might get a plate of free mini croissants and little strawberries cut into cute shapes next to a folded note that says *Welcome to New York, June!!* That, and a sweeping, ridiculous view of downtown Manhattan from one of the top floors of a very swanky hotel, paid for courtesy of the same reality show producers who zoomed in on you wiping snot off your face with your own sleeve in HD.

There's a strange kind of calm in me as I stand by the window and take in the sea of buildings cutting across the sunny skyline. In a few minutes, a car will come and take me to the studio. In a few hours, the interview will be finished. And not long after that, the Griffin chapter of my life will be sealed shut. I may not be entirely certain what's on the next page, but right now, that's comfort enough.

This much I do know—Levi and I are going to meet up afterward and get a celebratory drink in the hotel bar, then do some decidedly steamier celebrating up in the room. Tomorrow we'll go on a run in Central Park and catch a matinee and grab a quick dollar slice before I get on the bus to go home. But what I'm hoping is that I won't go right back to doing what I've been doing ever since Levi left a week ago, which is mostly feel like I'm stuck in limbo, half with Levi and half not.

It's not as if we haven't kept in touch this week. We call each other in the morning and after Tea Tide closes. We text each other links to funny memes and TikToks about the Revenge Exes still floating around. We've started an email thread of the Gallery Game where we just send each other random pictures of framed museum art with a bed emoji and a question mark and the other either responds with a check mark or a giant *X*.

We're fully in the present with each other, but that's just it—we're only in the present. Neither of us has said anything about the future. I have no idea when Levi's coming back or where he's planning to live, no sense of whether I can ask him to a concert happening in Benson Beach a few months from now, no real picture of what we're going to look like moving forward. The wedding is in a month, and beyond that, there's just a murky, unplanned gray.

But these are all conversations that will be much easier to have face-to-face. I just have to get through the interview without doing anything vaguely meme-able, and we'll have all the time in the world to talk it out.

"Well, don't you look stunning?"

Griffin greets me at the midtown studio with a big, boisterous grin, his dark hair subtly gelled, his camera makeup already in place. They've put him in a well-tailored navy suit with a white button-down, matching the navy trim on the dark green floral dress someone from wardrobe thrust into my hands the moment the town car they sent deposited me here. I blink at him from behind the two makeup artists making quick work of my face—"Don't worry, dear, the mascara's waterproof," one of them said to me with a wink—and offer Griffin a flat "Thanks."

He hovers there for a moment like I'm going to return the compliment. When I don't, he shifts his weight for an uneasy second and then says, "Hey, thanks again for doing this. You're a real pal."

The word "pal" sounds so ridiculous coming out of his mouth after the literal decade we spent together that I'd let out a snort if someone weren't actively setting powder on my face right now. But with that aborted snort is a strange kind of relief. Griffin's here, in the same room that I'm in for the first time since he broke up with me, and I feel . . . nothing. Not nostalgia, not hurt, not even anger. Not anything but the urge to laugh.

A quiet surge of confidence flows through me, an invisible armor. Whatever lingering nerves I had about the interview, about facing Griffin one last time, all fade somewhere underneath it.

"Sure thing," I say breezily. "It'll be nice to give the audience some closure."

Something flickers and dims in Griffin's practiced smile. A quick surprise followed by an unmistakable disappointment. I bite down another urge to laugh—it's clear he thought he was going to find an entirely different June. Or maybe not a different June at all. Maybe he thought he was going to find the old June, the version of me that compromised too easily, who placated and gave in because I'd rather him push me into things than pull away from me.

But that June is long gone. He knew that before he broke up with me. I moved back to Benson Beach, and suddenly I wasn't Griffin's June anymore, but the June who was learning to run Tea

Tide, who said no to his whims, who was growing and changing without him. He knew he couldn't handle me trying to reach my best, so he dumped me in a way where he could put me at my worst.

But I'm still here. Stronger than ever. And with one look at his uneasy face, I can tell it's driving him up the wall.

"Let me know if you need anything," he finally settles on saying, the smile back in place.

I give him a tight smile of my own. "I'm good, but thanks."

Watching him slink away is so satisfying that it feels like its own kind of closure. Now whatever happens in this interview will just be icing on the cake.

A half hour later, I'm perched on the plush velvet chair they put me in, delicately crossing my ankles, sitting at the exact casual-but-confident posture that Sana's been drilling me on all week. She's still neck-deep in whatever she's trying to write for *Fizzle*, but she got me in touch with a friend who has media training, and between the two of them, we worked out a script for pretty much any scenario *Business Savvy* might throw at me.

One that I need right off the top when Archie, the severely chipper host of *Business Savvy*, slides into a chair a few feet away from where Griffin and I are seated and theatrically winces at a sound coming through the speakers.

"Oh, dear," says Archie with a glance toward the screen behind us. He turns back to the camera and says cheekily, "How on earth did that end up there?"

It's me, of course. Crying Girl. Bawling my eyes out on my couch and hiccuping out "I just—I just—" like they're the only two words I know, my face so blotchy and mascara-streaked that I look like the world's most tragic tomato.

But I was ready for this. Sana made me watch the clip ten times a night like it was exposure therapy. I might as well be watching a video of paint drying.

"Don't do that to her, Archie, come on," says Griffin, all at once making a show of being protective and serious. "That's uncalled for."

I settle deeper into my chair and smirk. This was clearly a setup to rattle me and make Griffin look all chivalrous for defending me. One that I derail when Griffin turns to me with a put-upon sympathetic expression and realizes I'm not only unfazed, but amused.

He opens his mouth to say something else he must have rehearsed, but I cut him off, leaning toward Archie.

"No, no, Archie, keep it rolling," I say gamely. "I'm trying to get a Kleenex sponsorship over here."

Archie lets out a surprised laugh. "That's the spirit!"

The clip fades out and Griffin clears his throat. "Gosh, June," he says, pressing his hands together and sitting on the edge of his seat to better face me. "I know we've talked about how sorry I am about that day, but I really am. I'm going to feel awful about doing that to you my entire life."

I can see the camera zooming in on his apologetic face from the corner of my eye, another one panning in to catch my own. I smile easily, feeling less like I'm in an interview and more like I'm in a mildly amusing puppet show, watching Griffin try not to tangle his strings.

"Aw, don't worry, pal," I say pointedly, enjoying the way it makes his eyes flash in irritation. "Thanks to you, I always get to story-top at parties."

He settles his expression, composing himself into the picture of apology again. "I'm just so upset at the idea of hurting you after everything we've been through."

"Right," says Archie. "You two were an item for . . . how long?"

Griffin blows out a breath and shakes his head, like the years somehow flew out from under him. "Wow. It's hard to say, since we go so far back as friends. We've just always been around."

Ten years, I could easily supply. We dated for ten entire years. And even though it would be briefly satisfying to drop that bomb on Griffin on live television, I don't particularly want to cop to it, either.

"I'm sure it is. And as I understand it, the two of you were drifting apart before the show started," says Archie, with an authority that leaves no room for protest. "But you're both good friends still, right?"

Sana warned me that in all likelihood, they were going to have an entire narrative of their own crafted to tilt in Griffin's favor, but this feels low even for him. In hindsight, we should never have been together in the first place. But us drifting apart didn't make it any more okay for him to go off and cheat.

"Sure," I say, turning to Griffin with a steely-eyed smile. "We're friendly."

A vein in Griffin's temple twitches, like I'm toeing a line. I hold his gaze steady. A warning that if he pushes any of this too far, I'm more than willing to cross it.

"But despite that, you dated a mutual friend of yours—Levi Shaw—to get back at Griffin," says Archie, leaning back and raising his eyebrows in amusement.

I let out a sharp, stunned laugh. "There are a whole lot of reasons I'm dating Levi, but I can promise you none of them are to get back at Griffin."

"No. No, of course not," says Griffin, with a little too much ease. "That was all just in good fun, right, June?"

I know that syrupy tone. It's Griffin in his element, Griffin at his most *Griffin*. It's the same tone he used countless times when he was asking me for things without really asking, knowing full well he was going to get his way.

Which means whatever he's going to say next, he's planning to do just that.

Griffin turns to the host, and it almost feels like slow motion, the way he leans in, the way the calculating smile curls on his lips.

"I mean, get this—Levi and June have only been pretending to date."

I feel my entire body go stiff before the words even have a chance to sink in. For all the scenarios Sana ran me through, we never once anticipated this. Hell, even as it's happening, I can't wrap my head around it. Like if I just will it away hard enough, I can make Griffin take it back, make him swallow whatever it is he's gearing himself up to say next.

Archie raises his eyebrows with such comic surprise that there's no way this wasn't staged. "Is that so?"

"Yeah. I grew up with them, so I knew right away," says Griffin, with that same charming smile that looks waxier than a Ken doll's.

The adrenaline is buoying me now. Griffin's expecting me to get flustered the way I did last time, but last time I came into a sneak attack. This time I came prepared. Maybe not for *this*, but prepared enough to handle it.

I say in a wry, even tone, "Well, shoot. That's all news to me. Someone better tell Levi while we're at it."

"Aw, come on, June," Griffin says playfully, turning to me. "It's okay. Now everyone knows there really aren't any hard feelings. We're all friends."

Archie leans in toward us, eyes gleaming at me. "So this entire Revenge Exes thing—was it a lie or not?"

"Well, first of all, we were never the ones who called it that," I start, but Griffin doesn't let me get any further.

"Oh, I have it on good authority that it is," he says. "June and I come from a small town, after all."

"You know what they say about secrets in a small town," says Archie, with a nod toward the camera.

Griffin turns to me with what he probably thinks is an affable look. "And it's not like people weren't going to find out eventually," he says. "Especially since Levi moved back in with Kelly and all. You guys had a fun time, and now it's water under the bridge. I'm just glad we all got to have a laugh out of it in the end."

I suck in a breath to let Griffin have it, but Archie interrupts me with the seamless authority of someone who's watched a fair amount of people lose their shit on live television. "Well, folks, things are certainly getting wild over here—let's see what else we can dig up on the Revenge Exes when we get back."

I'm frozen in my seat, blinking at Griffin. The fury in me is so white hot that I feel like I could burn out every one of the studio lights aimed at us right now. I'm trying to decide who I'm angrier at, Griffin for throwing me under another bus or myself for being stupid enough to let him, when someone starts removing my mic.

"What—the interview's not done," I say.

"We're finished with your portion," says the producer firmly.

I shake my head, pulling away. "But I have more to say—"

"We're finished with your portion," she says again, her eyes flashing a warning. I understand right then that this is a fight I'm going to lose. Even if they let me stay on, there's no way they don't have a contingency plan to make me look even worse.

"Right," I say.

Griffin has already stepped away. The moment my mic is off I'm hot on his heels, but I don't need to be. He's standing off to the side, his eyes finding mine so fast that it's clear he wants a confrontation. And he's going to get one.

"That was uncalled for," I tell him. "And a down-and-out lie."

"June, don't bullshit me," he says, all the fake warmth out of his voice. It's almost a relief to hear it—at least now we can cut the crap and have a real conversation. "Kelly told me the whole thing."

I let out terse laugh. "Kelly? When on earth would you have talked to Kelly?"

Griffin is both furious and smug, and neither suits him. "She got in touch with me last week. We got dinner. She spilled the beans on your little scheme to make me look bad before we'd even ordered drinks."

I can't even process the bit about Kelly, stuck on Griffin's accusation.

"Oh my god." I laugh in earnest now, stepping back, incredulous. "You really think everything is about you, don't you?"

Griffin's face goes beet red. "Why else would you do it then, June? You didn't talk to Levi for *years*, and then suddenly you're all lovey-dovey?"

"And how exactly does that make *you* look bad, Griffin?" I ask, but the moment the words are out of my mouth it clicks. The last of the laughter tapers out of me. "It doesn't. You know full well you did that all on your own. It's just that you hate him. You dumped me, but you don't want me to be happy with a guy you hate."

Griffin shakes his head sharply. "I don't want you to pull one over on me with a guy you hate."

Now that I'm seeing him like this, stripped of all his niceties, his put-on charm, I'm almost terrified I didn't see the extent of it earlier. That there might be some universe where I was willing to keep ignoring it, where I'd still be stuck trying to be the girlfriend I was never quite going to measure up to no matter how hard I tried.

It doesn't matter. In this universe, I don't have a single second left for him to waste.

"Let me be clear—this was never about you. And no matter how or why it started, Levi and I are together now." I lean in just close enough to make the words stick. "I'd tell you to get over it, but I don't plan on ever seeing you again."

Only then does Griffin start to lose some of his bravado. Only then does it become clear that he's been waiting all this time for me to bend the way I used to, even break the way I did when we broke up. Now I'm immovable, and Griffin doesn't know how to interact with something he can't move.

"I don't see why you're all bent out of shape about this," says Griffin. "The way I see it, you and Levi played us, and now we've played you right back."

There's a hand on my shoulder. "Miss Hart, your car is here."

On the quick drive to the hotel, I figure out the extent to which Griffin "played" us. A story about the Revenge Exes being fake has already hit the internet; the producers of *Business Savvy* must have had it planted for at least a week. There are photos of Levi going in and out of the apartment building, one where he has two cups of coffee in hand, another with Kelly smiling at his side. There are quotes from two different outlets confirming they got photos of us from the same source. And the rest of the special was spent essentially breaking down all that evidence for the live audience after they came back from commercial.

I'm numb to it all as I scroll, my phone blowing up with people calling one after the other—Levi, my parents, Dylan, Levi again, numbers I don't even know. A text from Sana pops up, the only notification I bother opening: I got you a ticket for the 6pm bus back if you can make it.

I hope Sana is prepared for me to kiss her on the damn mouth the instant that bus turns in to Benson Beach.

I scramble for the backpack and the duffel bag I packed, desperate not to be in the city for even a second longer. Only when I spill out of the elevator into the massive lobby, I stop short.

There is Levi, his back turned to me, in a heated conversation with the concierge. The sight of him feels like turbulence, a wild current that can't decide how to take shape. There's the staggering relief. The innate part of me that sees Levi and instantly feels at ease. But then there's something else pushing just under it. The something that made me dismiss his calls in the car, that made me so willing to seize that bus ticket Sana bought without giving him so much as a heads-up. Something that started as anger, maybe, but might be something deeper. Might be something worse.

When we made this break-up pact, the only thing we promised was to be honest with each other. And Levi wasn't. I don't mind that he told Kelly. I don't even really care that she ratted us out. But Levi didn't tell me that he told her, which means it could only have been motivated by one thing. He wasn't telling her for the sake of clearing the air. He was telling her because there was a part of him, however slight, that still didn't want what he had with Kelly to be over. And he didn't tell me because he felt ashamed.

Maybe I'm wrong. I want so desperately to be wrong. But no matter what I am, I know I can't have this conversation with him right now. It's too fresh, too raw. If we talk about it now, it feels like so much else is going to get pulled up from the depths with it. Things I'd rather stay buried, because I'm terrified if we say them out loud, we'll be over just as soon as we've begun.

The best thing I can do right now is go home. That's what I tell myself, at least, when I turn to leave the hotel lobby and hear Levi's voice from behind me: "June."

One of my steps falters, but I keep walking.

"June, wait," Levi calls.

I raise my hand for a taxi and one stops with astonishing speed.

I pull the door open just as Levi catches up with me, his eyes brewing with worry, with regret.

"June," he says one last time, and I shake my head—consider apologizing—but no. If I say one word to him, a whole lot more of them are going to follow, and I can't have that conversation right now. I close the taxi door behind me, tell the driver the intersection for the bus stop, and watch Levi's stricken face disappear.

Chapter Twenty-one

When I was younger, I had a very aggressive tree-climbing phase. There was one thick tree smack-dab in the middle of our woods with a tangle of branches that went up and up and up, so high that once you reached the top, you could see to the edges of our whole town—the little nucleus of Benson Beach's main square that led out to the boardwalk, which wove into the narrow streets full of mismatched homes beyond it. The strip of the beach against the bright, staggering blue of the ocean spanning the bluer sky. I'd get to the top and feel the wind on my face, flooded with both a strange kind of terror and thrill—the fear of the height I'd climbed, but the satisfaction of having climbed it. The fear of the world being so much bigger than I thought it was, and the anticipation of everything it had in store. The fear of knowing I'd have to climb back down, and the comfort of knowing no matter how long it took, Levi would always be waiting patiently for me at the bottom.

I've thought about that tree-climbing phase a lot over the years.

I'd use it to justify a lot of the reckless things Griffin talked me into. *I used to do things that scared me all the time*, I'd think to myself. *I climbed that tree even when it terrified me. How is this any different?*

I understand now just why it was different. It was my choice. My tree to climb, my fear to decide to feel, my limits to test the edges of without anyone pushing or pulling them.

I'm thinking of that tree when the sun comes up the morning after the interview and I open the door to my apartment to catch Levi already sitting eagle-eyed on his porch, clearly waiting for me to come down.

He meets me halfway between Tea Tide and the condo, eyes red from lack of sleep, looking every bit as spent as I feel. His expression is another shade of the one he made before the taxi pulled away—streaked with a sincere regret and a restlessness just under it, soft in his eyes but tight in his jaw.

I wonder what I must look like to him. Guarded, probably. Exhausted. Confused.

But more than anything, relieved that he's here. That when we're close enough to see everything brewing in each other's eyes, for a moment, we see down to the bottom of it. The part that's just us without the noise of the rest of the world. I lean into him, pressing my head into his shoulder, and his arms wrap around me so steadily that I close my eyes, tempted to stand here forever. To pretend that yesterday didn't happen, that I'm not already worried about what comes after today.

"I'm sorry, June," he says, his voice low in my ear. "If I had any idea Kelly would say anything, I never would have told her."

Then why did you?

I know I have to ask, but I can't make myself do it. Not yet. I shake my head against his chest, raising my own arms to press my hands into his back, to sink further into the steadiness of him. I just want this right now. I don't want the storm on the horizon. I want to stay here, right in the eye of it, for as long as we can.

"It doesn't matter," I say. "At least not in the grand scheme of things."

Levi pulls back from me, keeping his hands settled on my waist. "Of course it matters. It's my fault Griffin sprung that on you."

I shake my head. "It was my fault for being there in the first place. I thought I was one step ahead of him, but it turns out he'd taken one *hell* of a leap."

I try for a slight smile, but Levi doesn't return it. "I wanted to talk to you after, but you just . . . took off," he says.

I take a slow step back, prying us apart. As far as shutting this conversation down goes, so far, I am not doing a very good job. "Sorry. I just had to get out of there."

"You know I would've gone with you," he insists.

I nod. I knew it then, but I especially know it now—he must have taken the late bus in last night, the one that lived up to the Drunk Bus name. "It's really okay, Levi. We're okay," I tell him, because maybe it's best if we don't examine this too closely. If I don't ask him why he told her, then he doesn't have to give me a reason that might shake us.

He doesn't acknowledge it with a nod or a follow-up. He just takes a breath like he's steeling himself and says, "What are you up to right now?"

I look down at my sneakers, barely even remembering that I must have laced them up. I woke up so tangled in texts and calls and links to articles about us that it was the only move left that made sense.

"I was going to go for a run," I say.

He nods. "All right." And then he starts following me down to the beach without so much as putting on his shoes.

As we reach the part where the loose sand gives way to the damp, hard sand under our feet, I can tell he's working his way into breaking the silence. I break it before he can.

"How about this," I say. "We race to the next pier. And if I win, we never talk about what happened yesterday again."

I try for another smile, my eyes glancing at his bare feet. Even at full speed, there's no way he'll beat me without sneakers. I dig my toes into the sand gamely, feeling the relief of the run before it even starts. The relief of this conversation being over before it even has to begin.

But then Levi reaches out and settles his hand around my wrist, gentle but firm. "I want to talk about what happened."

I keep the smile as intact on my face as I can. "And I'm saying there's nothing to talk about," I say lightly.

Levi doesn't let me go. Just traces the pad of his thumb on the soft skin of my inner wrist, stepping in closer. "We've been running away from a lot of things, June. I don't want to run anymore."

He's right. Even if I can't accept it in my heart, I feel it in my body. I'm exhausted in a way that goes deeper than muscle, deeper than bone. I've been running from my feelings since this whole thing began. *Literally* running any time Levi and I had a conversation that felt like it went too deep, that gave away too much— challenging Levi to a race when a conversation got too real has been in the June playbook since we were kids.

I pull my wrist out of his grasp and start walking down the beach slowly until he falls into step beside me. It's quiet this morning, the way it always is toward the end of the summer. A settled kind of heat that's waiting to break.

"What do you want me to say? That I'm embarrassed?" I tilt my head at him. "It already happened to us before. We'll get over it."

Levi is quiet for a few paces. Thoughtful. The wait feels like wobbling that tightrope again, wondering if our next words will tilt me over or set me right.

"At the beginning of this we said the only real rule is that we'd be honest with each other," says Levi. "And that means about everything, June. You're upset. I know you are because you just keep shutting me out. Pushing me away." He shakes his head. "I don't want us to sweep things under the rug. If you're mad, be mad. Talk to me."

I stare at our feet, our mismatched rhythms finding the same pace, and feel it brewing beneath us. The storm I've been avoiding. The one that was on the horizon a whole lot earlier than the interview yesterday; the one that's been gathering speed since Levi came back to town.

I can't avoid it anymore. I come to a stop on the beach and turn to face Levi.

"Why did you tell Kelly about the pact?" I ask.

Levi nods like he was expecting this question, like he's glad that I asked it. "I wanted the chance to talk to her about it. To someone who understood the whole situation, and understood me," he says.

I close my eyes for a moment because it's not the full answer I'm looking for. "But you didn't tell me that you told her. I want us to be honest too, Levi. And I think there's a reason you didn't tell me. I think—part of you still wanted that door with her to stay open."

I'm hoping he'll deny it. I'm hoping he'll get riled and start listing off all the reasons I'm wrong, and even though I won't quite believe it, at least some of the sharpness of the hurt will go away.

Instead, he lets out a resigned breath. "Maybe for a moment," he admits. "I was scared. I didn't know how you felt after that night at your place."

The words feel like a cold current running through me, icing my bones. An armor against the immediate heat of panic, of the words hissing under my skin: *You were right.*

"I told you how I felt," I say with an eerie calm. "I told you in that parking lot how I felt. It never went away."

"But you still pushed me away the next morning." His tone isn't accusatory, just quiet and a little sad. "The same way you are right now."

I don't deny it. For the first time, I lean all the way into it. I glance up at him, into his tired, aching eyes, and I step off the tightrope.

"I know you had no control over Kelly being here, but when she was, you didn't send me a single text." It doesn't feel like falling yet. My voice is steady, composed—this part, I've had a lot of time to think about. "I had no idea what was going on between you two, or what that silence meant. Then right on the heels of that you tell me you're going back to New York, where you're living with her all over again. And that—we talked about all of that. I know you have things to settle. I get that."

His eyes are pained, like he wants so badly to interject, to explain. But he already gave me explanations. What I need now is for him to understand where they left me and why I can't help but fixate on them now.

"But this whole week we haven't even said a word about anything beyond it," I say, and then I feel it—that swooping pit of dread. The worry that once I say these fears out loud, I'm going to make them true. "Not when you're coming back, or where you'll live, or what you'll do. Not what we're even going to look like. And to me, that's you pulling away. That's you coming to your senses. And if me pushing makes you come to them faster, then it's better for us both."

I feel almost empty without the words locked up in me anymore. Like all this time they've been keeping me balanced, keeping me upright so none of this would be able to knock me down. Without them, I'm hollowed out again, like I've given some part of myself up and Levi can choose to fill the space however he wants.

"You're right," he says, his eyes sweeping to the sand. "I probably have been avoiding talking about the future. I got back to New York, and I just . . . I kind of shut down. I was overwhelmed. I think it just hit me then—how much time had passed. How quickly things were shifting all at once. That I really have no idea what I'm going to do next, because I haven't had to think about writing anything beyond this manuscript in so long that I don't even know if I have any other ideas. It was easier to try to focus on the day-to-day of wrapping things up than what came next."

"Because you're still not sure," I say, and the words are almost pleading. Like I need him to understand that about himself so I don't have to be the one who is constantly on guard for it.

Levi shakes his head. "I'm just trying to adjust. It's like you said yourself—it's happening fast."

"Exactly," I say, and then I feel it starting to bubble up again—the simmering panic, the heat. The frustration. "I knew that. I still know that. You told me back then you were sure, that it didn't matter how fast it was moving, but clearly it *did*."

"It mattered in the sense that—that yeah, there are some things that are going to take time for me to wrap my head around," says Levi. "But that doesn't change what I want, June. What I've known I want, what I still want."

And there it is again, the word *want*, the double-edged sword. Because wanting something isn't the same as committing to it. To understanding the reality of it. And I'm terrified that Levi still doesn't.

This time, I aim the words not just to push him, but to push him too far. Maybe even to hurt. It's the bottom of everything I've been trying not to peer into, every fear I've been trying to keep from coming to the surface, but now I'm yanking them up by the ugly roots.

"You don't know what you want, Levi," I say, my jaw so tight that it feels like my entire body is aching with it. I gesture outward down the beach with my arm. "You've just lived half your life on everyone else's terms. You started writing that New York manuscript because some college kids made fun of you. You stayed in a relationship for years to stick to Kelly's plan. You let Annie scare you out of *looking* at me when we were kids. Don't stand there and tell me what you want, because I don't think you have a clue."

Levi's face is so stricken that I know I've hit my mark and then some. I've finally done it, then. I've finally gotten to the core of the hurtful truth that was just going to stay unspoken until it eventually destroyed us. I've hit the self-destruct button, made us into a fast explosion instead of a slow decay.

He looks down for a moment, his throat bobbing. I feel the thick, rotten tension of the words between us, but I don't do anything to pull them back. I wait. I stand in the awful aftermath and wait.

When Levi lifts his head, I still see the hurt streaked through his eyes, the gray flecks stark against blue. But his hurt isn't like mine. It isn't jagged and angry. It's soft and it's sad. I feel myself deflating before he even speaks, before he even hands me a truth of his own.

"I think you're scared, too," he says quietly. "You're scared of things changing. You're scared to do anything different with Tea Tide. You're scared to do things that make you happy now that Annie's gone."

The sound of Annie's name punctures the last of the anger in me, pulling it out of me until it feels like I don't have anything to hold on to. There's just the bare truth of his words. The way I've been able to avoid that truth even when I've worn it like a second skin since the moment I found out Annie was gone. The way Levi knows exactly how to speak it out loud, because he feels it, too. The guilt that isn't just moving on without Annie, but the guilt of outgrowing her. The guilt of being older and having revelations and experiences she'll never be around to have herself.

And now the guilt of so much of it being with Levi, when we both know there was a time she didn't want us to be together. And the hurt of knowing that we'll never be able to tell the version of her who would.

Levi takes a step toward me, just close enough that I could so easily lean my head into his shoulder again, that I could lean the rest of myself with it. But I'm still too at odds with myself to be a part of him. Torn between facing the truth of his words and wanting to run from them.

"You're scared of this. I know I'm partially to blame for that, because you're right—I have a lot of things to figure out. And if I haven't been great about talking about them, if I've made you feel like I'm pulling away—some of that is because I can't work out the past without feeling ashamed of it." He lowers his voice, tilting his head to better meet my eye. "Particularly in how long it took me to fix things with you."

It seems so strange to me now that only a few weeks ago, we were barely on speaking terms. That I managed to live for so long on a few texts back and forth every year when right now he has more of me than I've ever given anyone, than I ever imagined I could. That now I'm here, stuck between this awe of experiencing love in a way I never have before, right alongside the terror of knowing I could lose it.

"But this is more than fixing the past. This is a whole future." I feel the heat of what I'm saying rise in my cheeks, but there's no other way to say it. Levi and I were never going to cross this line halfway. It's part of why it's so overwhelming to cross it. "One day you might change your mind."

"You think I'm not scared that one day you'll wake up and do the same thing?" Levi asks. "That everyone isn't? You and I both know nothing in life is guaranteed." He holds himself up straighter, squaring himself when he says, "And you're right. I have lived my life on other people's terms. And that's what really scares me, June. All of the time that went by scares me. The idea of losing more of it scares me, especially more of it without you."

"And I'm scared you're going to regret this," I blurt. Before he can protest, I add the quiet, selfish fear that's brimming just under it: "And I'm scared of it being my fault."

Levi shakes his head, but there's a patience in it. A steadiness. "Why would it be your fault?"

I take a breath that feels like it shakes all the way up. "The thing is, I lived my life on someone else's terms, too. I only just got closure from that last night," I tell him. "So I know exactly how you're feeling right now. And you're making all these changes so fast that I'm scared I could become like Griffin was to me, or Kelly was to you, and decide things for you."

The worst part is I know I have it in me. I've nudged him toward *The Sky Seekers* a few times, and I've been supportive of his other manuscript, but I know how easily I could have justified pushing harder. I've asked over and over if he really wants to be here, knowing that if it came down to it, I don't think I could ever move to New York for him. After all these years of compromising too much for Griffin, I hate the idea of Levi compromising too much for me.

But Levi just shakes his head again, and this time he isn't just steady, but firm. "You're not deciding anything for me. I knew before I even got back to New York that I don't belong there anymore. I spent a week trying to write that miserable manuscript anyway, and I still hated every second of it." His eyes burn with a gentle kind of heat, so compelling that I'm drawn closer to them, that I can't look away. "All I wanted was to be *home*," he says, his voice almost catching on the word. "I wanted to be running on this beach. I wanted to be close to my parents. And most of all, I wanted to be with you, eating cold pizza on your couch, getting smushed in your car to go on another ridiculous date, working side by side in the back of Tea Tide all day."

My breath feels caught in my throat. It feels like another version of the future I saw for us, the one I only let myself imagine for a few moments before I let it go. But this one is present. A solid foundation. Something that can ground us if we land in the right place.

"I want that, too," I say. "But the way everything's still moving right now—we're not there yet."

He's quiet for a moment, searching my face. I stay very still, watching him take in every part of me, watching a quiet decision settle in him.

"How about this, then," he finally says. "This time we leave everything on the table."

My lip quirks, and I'm on the verge of a breathy, almost exasperated laugh when Levi's hands settle on my waist. There's a firmness, an urgency in his touch. It thrums through my body, settling me like an anchor, pulsing in me like a demand. When my eyes find his, I don't just see the ocean blue of them. I see a small kind of infinity. Like being on the top of that tree all over again, staring out at the endless expanse of blue, awestruck and yearning and scared.

He leans in so our foreheads are pressing together. I'm breathless, my eyes wide open into his, feeling the words before he says them. Like hearing it out loud is just a tidal wave of a current I've felt my whole life.

"I love you, June." He says it plainly, sincerely, but with more depth in his voice than I've ever heard before. Like he's pulling it out from the blood in his veins, the marrow of his bones. Something that is every bit as much a part of him as the pieces that keep him alive. "It's the only thing I'm certain about. The only thing I always will be."

He holds my gaze, and in those words, I see so much beyond these next few weeks, beyond manuscripts and morning rushes and this wedding. I see a life. I see lazy weekend mornings on a porch with mugs clutched between our hands. I see Levi typing in a corner booth at Tea Tide, exchanging quick smiles with me from the register during the lunch rush. I see beach runs and Blue Moons, books and giant cookies pretending to be scones, laughter and hurt and understanding. I see a home with extra rooms that we'll fill one by one, see indistinct shapes of kids with bright eyes and curly hair, part Levi and part me. I see sunrises and sunsets spilling in and out of the same horizon that watched us grow up, only to watch us grow old.

I close my eyes and let it settle in me. It's warmth without a burn. Electricity without the sting. It's a part of me already, too, but now it's waking up and trying to stretch its way into this new reality, trying to breathe on its own when I'm still struggling for air myself.

Levi doesn't wait for me to say it back, not even when I open my eyes again. He leaves one hand on my waist and uses the other to cup my jaw, his thumb grazing my cheek.

"Once I'm finished wrapping things up in the city, I'm staying in Benson Beach," he says. "I will be here, and I will love you, no matter what we are going to be to each other. And if you need time, I can give that to you, June."

Only then do my eyes start to sting. It's the way he is saying exactly what I need to hear. It's the way he understands me so deeply in this moment that it means more than those three words ever

could on their own. It's the way I need that time more than anything right now, not to be certain about Levi, but certain in myself.
That I'm going to be able to love him the way he loves me, without
doubting him, without pushing him away. Without hurting him
for the sake of protecting myself.

I nod, and I tilt my head up, pressing a kiss to his jawline. I
linger for a moment, soaking in the heat of him, the reassurance
of him. He squeezes a little pulse at my waist, against my cheek,
and then pulls away, walking back up to the boardwalk the way we
came. I glance down the length of the beach, toward the row of
piers and out to the woods beyond it. I don't lift my feet to run. I
stay right where I am, settling into the sand and tucking my knees
to my chest, facing the tide.

Chapter Twenty-two

I may be having one of the most tumultuous twenty-four-hour spans of my life, but the internet is having a damn field day. Yesterday the Revenge Exes were social media darlings, and now we're getting unceremoniously tossed into the meme fire to burn.

There's now a Twitter trend indicating I'm no longer Crying Girl, but newly dubbed Lying Girl. A TikTok from the same body language expert from before, pointing out all the "evidence" that Levi and I secretly hate each other, one of which was him scratching his nose. An article with a menacing headline—What Else Are the Revenge Exes Hiding? People from Their Past Reveal All!—that actually doesn't have much to it, considering nobody in Benson Beach would actually shit talk either of us beyond one quote saying Levi seemed "standoffish" in high school and that my "scones tasted dry." (Honestly, more offensive than whoever commented what's all the fuss over this dumb bitch about anyway??? by far.)

I know it's a whole lot worse than that, but I'd only been back from the beach for a few minutes before Sana essentially busted down my door and took my phone and computer away from me before I could get any further.

"I can take it," I say, burrowing into the couch. "I'm fine."

"No, you're not." She jerks her thumb back toward her own apartment. "I have a lovely ocean view from my window, you know. With free front seats to whatever break-up show you and Levi were putting on by the shore this morning."

I wince. "We're not broken up."

"Oh. Well, that was one hell of an emotional display for two people talking about the weather."

She starts rooting through my fridge and immediately locates the pizza box and pulls it out with two Blue Moons.

"It is eight in the morning," I remind her flatly.

She cracks open the two beers like she can't hear me.

"Sana, I have to get down to Tea Tide in, like, ten minutes."

"Oh, sweet summer June. You are not going anywhere near that cesspool of internet gremlins right now. There's already a blob of them waiting outside. Not a line, mind you. A full blob."

I sit up so straight the couch springs squawk under me in protest. "Well, then I *really* need to get down there. We've only got four people on staff."

"Mateo and Dylan are on it."

"Shit," I mutter, running a hand over the top of my ponytail.

I've barely spoken with either of them. I just sent them both texts on the way back from New York letting them know I was all right and I was coming home. I haven't even had a chance to explain the situation to them, and at this point, I'm not even sure how. "We were pretending to date and then we were kind of dating and then got publicly outed and now are in a self-inflicted limbo" doesn't sound quite as snappy as "the Revenge Exes" did. Especially since both of those just boil down to the same thing, which is: *I lied*.

"Hey. You basically organized their entire wedding this month," Sana points out. "They can handle a few unruly tea drinkers for a day while some of this blows over."

Instead of handing me the slice of pizza like a normal human, she slides it into my mouth like I'm an ATM. I bite into it as I take it from her, scowling, and she sets an open Blue Moon on the coffee table in front of me, taking a swig from her own.

"Oh. Wow. That felt . . . collegiate," she says, blinking.

I surrender, taking a cautionary sip of mine. My brain doesn't know what to make of it except to give in to the complete and utter anarchy. I take another sip, heartier this time, and immediately regret it. It aches all the way down, the taste of it sending me back to that night Levi and I spent at the bar a week ago. That night we spent tangled in the sheets of the bed I can see from my open bedroom door. Even the stupid pizza makes me think of him burrowed on this couch, and suddenly it feels like everything in the world goes straight back to Levi, Levi, Levi.

I set the pizza and the beer down, steadying myself. Sana nudges my knee with her foot.

"Tell me what happened."

So I do. I start with the interview ("That absolute fucknut," Sana mutters), get into my great escape ("The Drunk Bus never once let a girl down," says Sana, holding her beer up in the air), and then dive into the details of the entire conversation with Levi, down to the part where he told me he loved me, and I was still too terrified to say it back.

When I'm finished, Sana takes a sip of Blue Moon, staring at the coffee table in thought. When she looks back at me, I'm expecting her to tell me I'm being ridiculous. To go down and fix things with Levi right now, before it's too late. But she just nods and says, "I think you're both right. You need some time."

I nod, picking at the label on my bottle. "Yeah?"

"I mean, I ship it harder than anyone, don't get me wrong. But yeah. He's moving fast. You're moving slow. You've both got good reasons to do it. But I think some time is the only way you can meet in the middle on that."

"Thank you," I say. It doesn't make me feel any better, but right now it's the only thing stopping me from feeling any worse.

She narrows her eyes at me. "You are being remarkably cavalier about this whole thing."

I raise my eyebrows at her. "You forget this isn't my first public humiliation rodeo."

"I mean about this whole mess with Levi."

I turn away, because the more we talk about it, the less "cavalier" I feel. Like now that the shock of the conversation is over and the weight of it is settling in, I'm suddenly restless. Uneasy. Picking apart everything we said, the words each taking on their own weight, shifting against me like uneven stones.

In those few moments of quiet, my throat is already so tight that I know it's just a matter of time before it hits—the humiliation of last night, the ache of this morning, the anger I have for so many parts of it. I feel it looming like a shadow, a wave about to crash into me from behind.

I swallow hard, wondering if it's going to hit before or after Sana leaves. I'm hoping I can keep it together until then. As much as her comfort means to me right now, whatever is gathering inside me feels like something I need to ride out alone.

"Which, by the way, I have thoughts about," Sana continues. "An entire thesis, if you will."

But before Sana can get into it, there's a knock at the door. We exchange wary looks. Everyone we know who has the emotional clearance to knock without texting first is helping at Tea Tide right now. I get up to my feet slowly, squinting through the peephole, and mouth the word "*Shit*."

"Just a sec!" I call through the door, then turn to Sana and hiss, "It's *Nancy*."

"Well, now this really feels collegiate," she says, diving across the coffee table to hide the beers.

I glance at myself in the mirror—still in my running clothes, hair yanked into a ponytail, decidedly sleep-deprived—and discern that I look just enough on the human side of zombie. I plop a piece of gum in my mouth for good measure, turning to make sure Sana has erased the evidence of our early morning frat party when I swing open the door.

"Hey," she says, looking far more put together than I am in one of her rotation of loud dresses, her bangles glinting against her wrist in the sun. My eyes reach her face and I feel that uneasiness in me start to stir with something fresh. Whatever this is, it's not a casual drop-in. "Do you have a minute, Junebug?"

"Yeah," I say, clearing my throat. "Yeah, of course."

I glance back at Sana apologetically, and she gives us both a salute and heads out. I let Nancy inside, feeling clumsy as I shut the door too hard behind her.

"Can I get you some tea?" I ask.

Nancy is standing in the kitchen area, her eyes trained on me. "No, I'm fine. I'm actually—this is a quick visit."

I still have a week left in August for the rent, but I say anyway, "I'm so sure we're going to hit the three months today. I mean, you saw the people outside, right? We're so close. I can get the check to you tomorrow."

If the words spill out of me too fast, the silence that follows them is entirely too slow. I feel it stretch between us like it's part of my own body getting pulled with it. I don't know exactly what she's going to say, but I can feel the wrongness of it in the air before she says it.

"You don't need to do that," she tells me. "That's actually what I'm here to talk to you about."

"Oh?" is all I can manage.

Nancy breathes in deep. "You know I respect the hell out of how hard you've been working. And I know it hasn't exactly been easy, these last few weeks, with all this . . . internet stuff going on," she says, making a vague gesture at the air in front of her. "And it's smart that you've been using it to your advantage. But June, we talked about this. And I just don't see any signs that this is going to work as a business model for Tea Tide in the long-term."

My throat is suddenly so dry that it feels like all the moisture has been sucked out of the beach air. "Right. But I, um—I've been working on some ideas. Sending out some feelers for more community-based events." My heart is hammering in my ears. "And you—you saw the new scones, right? Like you were saying, we're revamping things again, getting people excited."

She nods carefully. I'm so used to Nancy being loud and brash that it unsettles me even more, seeing that she clearly hates having this conversation as much as I do.

"Getting strangers excited," she corrects me. "People who are coming to town for a show and aren't coming back. It doesn't fix the problem right here at home, June. All of this hullabaloo is making even your regulars feel unwelcome. The place is so packed that I haven't been able to wait in line for a scone for weeks."

I feel the pizza churn in my stomach. Come to think of it, I haven't seen much of Nancy at all this month. Or any of my parents' friends who usually come in for scones and loud gossip, or any of my own high school and college friends who come in for scones and even louder gossip.

"But it'll die down soon. Yesterday was kind of the big—finale, I think," I say, wincing at the word my brain settled on. "Everything's going to calm down."

Her expression is sympathetic, but her voice is firm. "I remember us having a very similar conversation the last time Tea Tide had a big surge like this. That you were going to address it once everything calmed down."

For the first time in ages, I feel like a kid again. Like I've slipped into an old June and I'm just a bundle of unfinished bones and Nancy isn't just my landlord, but one of a sea of grown-ups in charge of me.

"But we said three months' rent, and I've got it," I say, my voice pathetic in my own ears.

"You offered the three months' rent, but I said a clear plan to make Tea Tide more sustainable. I don't care about the money half as much as I care about the businesses on this boardwalk having long-term, beneficial impacts on our community—not just during the peak of tourist season, or blips like this, but all year round."

She pauses momentarily for me to absorb it, but I can't. I seize on the silence instead, asking, "What can I do?"

Because it can't be too late. It can't all just end like this—not after the whiplash of learning how to run Tea Tide on my own, not after the years of struggling to keep it above water, not after this entire summer of letting the internet tear my personal life to shreds just to try to save it. Not after the silent promises I made to Annie to keep it safe, to keep it the way she left it, like it meant I could keep a piece of her here, too.

"You have a few options," Nancy says cautiously, like she wasn't expecting the conversation to get this far. "You could consider closing shop. Maybe trying something new."

I have to stop breathing for a moment so my eyes don't fill up with tears.

"Or moving Tea Tide somewhere else," she says. "If you're open to the idea, I can give you some contacts."

Her words sound like a distant humming in my ear because none of them are the ones I want to hear. None of them are going to keep the original Tea Tide intact, our vision of a tea shop by the shore, the dream Annie built and I let slip through my fingers like the sand beneath it.

She reaches out and puts a hand on my shoulder, squeezing it, a phantom of her usual boisterous hugs. I don't blame her. I probably look one good hug away from falling apart.

"I'll let you think it over," she says. "Don't be a stranger. I'm happy to help in whatever way I can."

I nod numbly. She lets herself out, and I want to be furious with her. I want a concrete urge, like to throw a pillow or yell at my reflection in the mirror or hit the beach and run for miles and miles. I want to be able to break down and bawl out a river the way I did when I was Crying Girl, a quick, brutal, ugly kind of relief.

But the ache settling deep isn't a loud one. It's guilt and it's grief and it's so, so quiet that all I can do is stand there and let it seep into me, one awful drop at a time. It's understanding that there's nothing to get angry at because there's only one person to blame, and no amount of throwing or yelling or running is going to separate me from myself.

I settle back on the couch, listening to the distant sounds of Tea Tide opening below. I close my eyes and try to memorize the rhythm of it, try to hold it while it's still here. But I don't recognize the voices. I can't follow any pattern in the constant, almost violent jangling of the front door bells. If I went down there right now, I wouldn't know a single face. And slowly, dimly, I understand why it isn't crashing down on me all at once. I may have lost Tea Tide this morning, but the truth is, the Tea Tide I was trying to hold on to was already gone.

Chapter Twenty-three

*P*acking up Tea Tide feels like its own kind of funeral, one that moves in stops and starts over the course of two excruciating days. I let the staff know first, in a meeting and over a few phone calls that I manage to stay composed for even though I feel like I'm rotting from the inside out. I call all our local suppliers to stop deliveries. I set up a storage unit on the edge of Benson Beach to hold the tables and chairs and stools, the baking equipment and the metal prep tables and our giant mixer, the teacups and the plates and the itty-bitty spoons. In a particularly grim moment, I even imagine a Death to Tea Tide scone—just throwing together every cast-off ingredient we have left in the back into a batter so it won't go to waste and walking away.

For now, though, I'm in a strange limbo in between the ending and the end. I'm packing the boxes up little by little each night on my own, but nothing has been collected yet. I haven't said a word to anyone about it. I'm gutting the place from the inside out, but technically we're still open for another few days, baking scones on a sinking ship.

Around midnight on day three of packing up what I can without disrupting too much of the flow, I accidentally drop a teacup. I stare at the shattered pieces of it on the pale pink linoleum floors Annie must have sent me a hundred near identical colors for before settling on. I crouch, leaning on one of the seafoam-green chairs she and I painted flowers on one Christmas when I was home. And I look at this teacup—a nothing-special teacup; just one of the dozens of identical pink floral ones hanging from the wall—and the instant my fingers graze the broken handle, I start to cry.

They aren't the big, gulping tears I was bracing for. They aren't even the wretched, guilt-fueled tears that have been stinging the backs of my eyes since Nancy delivered the news. The tears are quiet and insular and the kind that are only meant for me and for Annie. For two little girls who had big ideas and thought they had all the time in the world to see them through.

I've been trying to avoid thinking of Annie all through this process. I can't stop myself from thinking how disappointed she'd be, how angry. But I think maybe the truth is worse—she wouldn't be. She'd know how hard I tried. She knew how much this place meant to me, too. I'm not upset because I've let Annie down; I'm upset because Annie isn't around to let down at all.

I ease myself all the way to the floor, just sitting for a moment in the silence, holding on to the broken handle. In my mind these past few years, Annie has stayed static. The way she was is the way she always will be. And the more time that passes, the harder it is to reconcile that I'm still changing. That I always will be. And that with every single one of those changes, there's going to be a part of me that wants to turn over my shoulder and ask Annie what she thinks of it. A part of me that ghosts a thumb over my phone, that still thinks of her as the *first call* when something happens to rock my world.

Back then it felt like I needed her before I made any decisions. Not necessarily for her approval, even. I just felt better about my world when Annie knew the edges of it. It's what I'm itching for now, in the growing pains of everything changing so fast. I want so badly to know what she would think about everything that happened with Levi. I want to know what she'd do next with Tea Tide, if she were in my shoes.

But when I ask those questions now, there isn't any version of Annie who could answer them. Not seventeen-year-old Annie who had her sights set on Stanford with Levi. Not twenty-three-year-old Annie who started Tea Tide from the ground up. Not the twenty-nine-year-old Annie she'd be, one I've never met, one who might surprise me every bit as much as I've surprised myself.

I'm not stalling because I'm scared of asking Annie. I'm stalling because I'm scared of moving forward myself.

I set the handle next to the other broken pieces and ease myself back up, taking a moment to look around the space in one of its final, untouched moments. In the quiet, I finally feel it. Under the grief, under the guilt, there is a soft kind of sadness in me. One that started as a yearning and is now ending as an ache. One that has nothing to do with Annie and everything to do with me.

There were so many things I wanted to do with this place. I wanted to make it a community meeting ground locals could rely on and tourists could explore. I wanted to test out wacky, ridiculous scones and watch people's reactions to them in real time instead of hearing about them from thousands of miles away. I wanted to establish a presence here so firm that I felt confident recreating it in other places, giving them all their own personal quirks and touches. I wanted Tea Tide to have its own distinct kind of magic.

The magic isn't gone. I can still feel it humming under my feet like it was just waiting for me to seize it, for me to remember it was there at all. But I've been so busy trying to hold on to the past that I lost sight of the present, and now it feels like it's all falling out from under me, making the future hazier than it's ever been.

I take a breath then, and I push them out of me one by one—all the questions I've wanted to ask Annie. I let them slip back into the magic beneath me, dip under the boardwalk, slide into the sea. I wait to feel like there's something missing in me, but she's still there, the same way she always will be. The love doesn't leave. Just the parts I'm still demanding from it, when all it's wanted in these past two years is to settle in me. To accept that Annie's gone.

To accept that I have to make my own choices now. To accept that I have to live with them. To accept that I *get* to live, and I'd better start doing it on my own terms if I want it to count.

I drift back to the office as the questions start blooming out of the floor again, taking a new shape. This time, they aren't asking Annie. They're asking me.

What do you want to do?

I close my eyes and stand in the haze of the future. It's thrilling and it's scary how fast it can take shape and change and take shape again. How this ending can give way to so many little new beginnings. How I get to be the one to choose.

I pull my phone out of my pocket and find Cassie's email, and when the shapes change again, I feel a kind of peace wash over me that I haven't felt in a long, long time.

Chapter Twenty-four

"Uh, June? I'm pretty sure that pillow started its life as a scone."

I jolt up so fast that the swivel chair would go out from under me if Dylan didn't reach out and stop it abruptly with his hand. When I look up into Dylan's frowning eyes and see the way the light has shifted in the windows, I realize I must have conked out somewhere between reading Cassie's very prompt late-night reply to my email, boxing up the last of the serving platters, and searching for every commercial kitchen in a ten-mile radius.

Dylan gingerly lifts the smushed half of stale scone from the desk I was sleeping on top of and says, "Okay. You need a real nap."

I shake my head, rubbing my palms over my eyes. Several incriminating crumbs fall into my lap. "I've got too much to do."

"Yeah, I figured. Because I had to learn Tea Tide was shutting down from Mateo, who found out from another professor, who found out from one of his students, who found out from I don't even know where," says Dylan in a rare display of what might almost be passive-aggression.

I run a hand through my alarmingly tangled hair. Word travels fast in Benson Beach, but it seems to travel faster every day. "Shit."

The plan always was to tell everyone this morning, but then that plan got slammed into sideways by the *new* plan, which is in such a state of flux that I figured I'd just wait until it was taken care of before I said anything. That, or maybe I just started snoring into a pile of carbs before I could get so far as to consider anyone else.

"Yeah. Sana's pissed, by the way, so watch out for that," says Dylan candidly.

He reaches into his backpack and produces one of the endless protein bars he has on hand at all times. I'm hungry enough to eat the backpack.

Dylan leans against the desk, nudging the swivel chair with his foot. "Why didn't you say anything? You were just going to pack up all of this and haul it yourself?" He gestures at his chest, clad in a shirt Mateo got for him that says LIFT OR LIFT NOT, THERE IS NO TRY.

I rip off a piece of bar with my back teeth, priming my body for the confusion of something with a nutrient in it. "I was, I just— wanted to get the ball rolling."

"Or you were avoiding us."

I blink, awake enough to recognize that this is the second time in a minute that Dylan has called me out. He has every right to, but I'm so unused to it that it feels like watching a puppy learn to bark.

"Or that," I admit. I let loose a breath. "I'm sorry. Everything just kind of exploded. I already felt terrible about lying to you and Mateo about everything with Levi, and we hadn't even gotten to that yet."

Dylan starts fiddling with the desk drawer, unable to keep still to save his own life. "June, no offense to you guys or your delicious Revenge Ex scone, but neither of us care about you guys lying about dating."

I search his face. "You seemed really excited about the idea of it is all," I say, the words sounding silly now that I'm actually articulating them. Maybe it wasn't that I didn't want Dylan to know that we were lying. Maybe even then some part of me was hoping it wasn't a lie, and Dylan believing in it made it feel true.

"Yeah, of course I was," says Dylan. "I've missed the hell out of you both."

We both go still at that. I glance down at my crumb-filled lap, feeling the shame tinge my cheeks.

"I'm sorry," I say quietly. "It's partially my fault Levi stayed away for so long."

Dylan waves a hand at that, and I wonder for the first time how much he knew about the situation. Growing up, I always felt like a buffer between Annie and Dylan—it was often me and Annie or me and Dylan or all three of us, but never just the two of them. It occurs to me how much that might have shifted, with me gone for all that time. I feel a sharp guilt that I've never really asked.

"I'm not worried about Levi. It's just that—I've really, really missed you." He stares at his sneakers, his jaw tense in a way I rarely see it. Dylan may be a blunt guy, but he doesn't often go this deep. "I know you've been back. And I know we hang out once a week. But even then, it's like—sometimes you get so wrapped up in trying to do everything on your own that you forget that I'm right here."

I hear the words he's not quite saying, the ones that would strike deeper than Dylan's willing to go—that I've been so wrapped up in trying to get along without Annie that I've taken Dylan for granted. Dylan, who is still right here. Dylan, who is the only person who lost exactly what I lost, whose grief is the closest shape to mine.

It's been nearly two years since I've been back, and I'm realizing this is one of the first sit-down, serious conversations we've had to-gether. Maybe it isn't that Dylan is suddenly someone who doesn't mind calling me out. Maybe it's that Dylan's been changing, too, and I've just been so distracted by things in the periphery that I missed it happening right in front of my eyes.

"I mean, this whole thing with you and Levi planning the wedding—I was really hoping it would be a chance for all of us to hang out more," says Dylan. "And I know we've all been busy, so that's my fault, too. But what I'm saying is I want us to be able to be a part of everything in each other's lives. The messy stuff, too. Like Tea Tide. Or whatever the heck is going on between you and Levi."

I reach out and put a hand on his knee. It's strange. My whole life, Dylan was my little brother, and that made me and Annie his keepers. But in the same way a lot of things have been shifting lately, I feel something else move out from under us. The dynamic between us isn't little brother and older sister so much anymore. It's grown-up siblings who can depend on each other equally. Be each other's keepers.

"I like the idea of that," I say with a soft smile.

Dylan smiles back and nods, a little misty-eyed. He shakes it off just as fast, with the relief of someone who did what they came to do and is satisfied with the results.

"Speaking of Levi, have you heard from him at all?" he asks.

I glance at my phone. "Yeah. We're texting back and forth while he takes care of the move."

"Yeah, us too," says Dylan. He frowns. "Although the other day all he sent me was a random picture of some painting of the city he and Kelly were deciding who should keep, with a bed emoji and a question mark."

I try and fail to hold in a snort. "That sounds about right."

He nudges my chair with his foot again. "I haven't really asked him, but is everything okay between you guys?"

I nod. "There are just a lot of balls up in the air right now," I say.

"But nobody's going to have another ten-year stalemate of silence, if that's what you're asking."

Dylan grins. "Mostly just wanted to know if you're going to be able pose for the cameras without one of you tripping the other on my wedding day."

I tilt my chin, leveling him with my eyes. "Dylan Hart, I promise you that your wedding day is going to be the best damn party Benson Beach has ever seen. Hell, if we play our cards right, Levi and I might very well have a future in a joint wedding planning company."

Dylan's grin softens. "I already know the day's going to go well. All the people I love are going to be there."

My eyes well with tears. "You are a big sap, little bro."

He perks up. "A big sap with big muscles," he reminds me, gesturing at the half-full boxes strewn around the back. "Let me help with this."

For so long, Tea Tide has felt like my responsibility alone that it only seems natural to try to wave him off. But it's becoming clear to me that the issues with Tea Tide weren't just that it was at a standstill. I also didn't make much of an effort to ask anyone for help. Not just my family, but people like Cassie or Nancy, who might have connected me to other small business owners in the area. I've been treating Tea Tide like an island, but it is quite literally on a very crowded shore. One that's full of people who are on my team.

"Okay," I say. "But the thing is—Tea Tide is only sort of shutting down."

Dylan tilts his head. "So Nancy's only . . . sort of kicking you out?"

"Oh, no, I'm fully getting the boot," I confirm. "All of this still has to get carted out of here fast."

Dylan jumps up off the desk like he's going to start lifting boxes right then and there, a known destination for them be damned.

"But first, uh—a question," I say, putting up a hand to pause him. "You've driven the track team bus a few times back and forth from meets, right?"

"Sure, yeah. Why?"

I tilt my head at him. "How would you feel about driving a massive food truck?"

Dylan's eyes light up. "Are you going to turn Tea Tide into a sconemobile?"

It feels surreal to say it out loud for the first time, like I'm breathing the idea of it into the world. "I'm going to try," I say. "Just to see if we can make something work. That way I can keep the full-timers on and keep the business running while we look for another location."

It's not a permanent solution and far from what I envisioned for Tea Tide. But it's an ember of it, one I'm certain I can fan into a flame, if I get the chance. One that really is all my own this time, because I'm starting it with my own hands from scratch. I'm doing what Annie did all those years ago and building this place back up, one step at a time.

"Okay," says Dylan, pulling out his phone. "I can assemble the troops. What all do we need to do?"

Within the next hour, I have a somewhat cohesive to-do list, and the four of us plan to spread out over Benson Beach like Tea Tide Avengers. Dylan is going to stay here and help pack up more of the back. I'm going to meet up with Cassie to check out the food truck she only uses for weekend wedding events, and then a commercial kitchen not too far off where I can rent space to bake scones. Sana is going to adapt our logo into signs that can go on the truck and start making fliers announcing the new truck and how to follow its location on Tea Tide's website—a strategy we're putting in place so we don't get mobbed by the last of the Revenge Ex onlookers by posting on Instagram. Mateo is going to look into the university and community schedules to see if there are optimal places we can ask for permits to park the truck during events.

By noon, my brain is practically spinning with the magnitude of everything there is to get done, but there's an electricity in it, a pulsing demand. I'm almost startled at the intensity of it. Even when Tea Tide was stable, I always felt like I was struggling too much to really enjoy it. Now that I'm finally letting myself play with it, now that all the old rules are being thrown out the window, I feel the same kind of visceral excitement I did back when Annie and I dreamed it up as kids.

"Have you told Levi about any of this?" Dylan asks on my way out of Tea Tide. "I'm sure he'd want to help."

"He's got a whole move of his own right now. And I'm sure he's putting finishing touches on his draft," I say. "Besides, everything will be squared away by the time he gets back. I'll tell him then."

Dylan just lets out a quiet "Hmmm."

And even though he technically hasn't said anything, I know that he's right.

I close the office door when I call. Levi picks up on the first ring, and the sound of his voice unravels something in my chest, like I can feel the familiar vibrations of it against my heart. I almost forget why I'm calling. I just want to hear his voice again.

"June?"

"Hey. Hi," I say. "Okay, I just want to start with—everything's fine."

"She said, ominously," Levi quips, but I can hear the worry in his voice just the same.

"Okay. Everything's—well. It's going to be. I just wanted to let you know that Tea Tide's lease isn't getting renewed. But it's okay," I say quickly, before Levi can interject. "I've got a whole plan. We're going to find a new location. Everything here is under control. I just wanted to let you know, so you didn't come back to find some coffee shop and thought I'd sold my soul to the devil or something."

Levi's response is so swift it knocks around the air in my chest. "I can get on the next bus."

I close my eyes and let myself feel the comfort of his words, even if I'm not going to take him up on them. "It's really all just logistics from here," I tell him.

"I don't just mean for the logistics, June," he says quietly. "I mean for you. Do you want me to come? Because if you do, I will."

I do want him here. Just the sound of his voice makes me ache for him, like I can reach across the miles and pull him into me right now out of sheer will.

But underneath that want, there's a steadiness I never felt when I thought I was in love before. The trust in Levi that whether he comes back now or comes back later, he is coming back. The trust in myself that I can be a whole person without Levi and make all these decisions with a confidence all my own.

I spent most of my adult life chasing after that kind of trust, and only now that I feel the depth of it between us do I realize it isn't something you catch. It's something that you build.

"I want you to finish things up there," I say firmly. "Same as I will over here. This whole thing with Tea Tide is like you rewriting your manuscript—this is my rewrite."

There's a quiet beat, and then Levi says, "If you change your mind, I'm on the next bus."

I feel another kind of trust right then. A trust Levi has in me not just to know what I need right now, but to tell him the truth. And the respect he'll have for that decision either way.

I press the phone closer to my ear. "I know," I say quietly.

He must sense that I have to go, because he says, "Good luck."

"You too," I say. "And by the way—I don't care what hideous painting you hang over your bed. You still get a pass from me."

A lot of things are about to change, but the satisfaction I get from making Levi laugh will never get old.

I start searching through the dusty metal cabinets in the back of the office then, digging in deep for the first time since I took over. Somewhere in one of these drawers I know Annie kept a big binder full of all the recipes she created for the scone ideas I'd sent her. I still want to make new ones, but now that we're starting fresh— now that we're starting on my terms—I don't feel the same ache I felt at the idea of bringing back the old ones. I want to infuse the past with the future. A mix of what it was and what it will be.

The binder only takes a few minutes to find. Underneath it is a whole mess of loose papers that I'm planning on ignoring, except I recognize that neat, tidy handwriting, and my eyes catch and don't let go.

It's Levi's. I pull the papers out, all beaten up and creased at the edges, and skim them. It's a slew of ideas for stories. Some of them just a few words, some of them fleshed out with several paragraphs. Some with character names and settings, some just with a feeling. The kind of thing he probably did in a class one day and passed over to Annie to see if anything stuck out to her.

Maybe none of the story ideas will be helpful to Levi down the line, but the reminder will be. He was brimming with story ideas once. If he opens himself up to them, he could be again. And if he wants someone to talk them out with, the way he did when we were kids, I'm here to soak in every word.

I tuck the pages into the binder, his old magic with mine. Then I flip the pages and start looking through the scone recipes one by one, each more ridiculous than the last. I pluck a few of them out to start, the ones closest to my heart—the rosewater-flavored Oopsy, Not A Daisy scone inspired by the time I picked flowers surrounded by poison ivy and ended up itching a rash the whole time I was visiting Annie at Stanford. The ham, egg, and gruyère cheese Wakey Fakey scone from the time I ate a croque madame after taking a red-eye flight to Paris and apparently had an entire, deeply expensive conversation with Annie about it that I still can't remember to this day. The pretzel and peanut butter Flight Risk scone from when Annie joined me on a trip to Amsterdam and we had to sprint through the airport like we were in an action movie. A map of places we've been and memories we scored into our hearts. A roundabout way of coming home again.

I soak them in, only balking for a moment when I realize how much work Annie put into all these concoctions I made up. But as soon as I think it, I hear her words clear as day, like she was waiting for this moment when I was already steady on my own two feet to say them: *Just try not to fuck up.*

Chapter Twenty-five

O ver the course of the past few weeks, I've discovered that there are very few scenarios where I can look at Levi without my thoughts straying in a less-than-PG direction. But even that does nothing to prepare me for what might be the sexiest thing my eyes have ever beheld: Levi Shaw kneading scone dough, his sleeves rolled up to his forearms, his hands and shirt covered in flour, so deep in concentration that his teeth are grazing his lower lip.

I've been anticipating seeing Levi again for two weeks, imagining what we might say or do when the moment came. But I wasn't expecting to find him here, and suddenly all the imagining is out the window, replaced by a firm mental reminder that there are probably laws against doing most things I want to do to Levi right now in a shared commercial kitchen space.

"Hi," I say.

Levi looks up, flour streaked on his nose, his eyes bright in the early morning sun starting to slip in through the windows. "Hey, you," he says, matching a smile I realize has already bloomed on my face.

I cross the room slowly, feeling that pull between us grow taut with demand. "How did you get here?" I ask.

The phone call I made to him about Tea Tide seemed to break some invisible barrier that had kept us only texting since our conversation on the beach. Since then, we've been talking on the phone with each other every night, keeping each other company as we packed and baked and got ourselves in order. Last night he said he'd meet me at the food truck once his bus got in, so the last thing I'm expecting to see is Levi here, a mere fraction away from producing his own soft-core scone porn.

"I took the early morning bus. Dylan said you guys were taking the day to catch up on making the dough, so." He gestures at the open recipe binder, which now has a rotating scone calendar attached to the front. "I figured I'd give us a head start."

I walk over, staring at the perfectly portioned scone dough ready for baking or freezing for later this week.

"Where on earth did you learn to do this?"

"I was in the back of Tea Tide pretending to write for weeks. I picked up a few tricks." His cheeks tinge pink. "Or maybe I just liked watching you bake."

I continue to stare up at him, torn between a tenderness and a sudden, demanding heat pooling low in me. Before I can decide what to do with it, Levi pulls me in and holds me tight to him. I breathe in warmth and brown sugar and Levi and feel a tightness in my chest finally start to loosen even as my heart quickens against my ribs, fluttering so fast that that beat of it spreads all over my body.

"I missed you," I say into his shoulder.

He presses his fingers into my back. "I'm glad to be home."

The word *home* hums under my skin, spreads another, softer warmth through me. I know his things are in storage. That he's still staying in the rented condo until he finds something more permanent. So he doesn't mean home like a place; he means the home right here in each other's arms.

It washes over me then, a calm, cool tide. He came back. I knew he would. But it's one thing to know it; it's another one entirely to have him here pressed against me, solid and steady and whole, and understand without another word that he's here to stay.

We pull apart, our arms still wrapped around each other, and I tilt my head to better look at his face. This face that I've memorized every curve and angle of, every smile and twitch and quirk, enough to know the expressions that are for me and me alone. Like the one he's settled into right now—a deep and solid kind of contentment in the curve of his lips, a steady burn behind his blue eyes. Satisfaction and desire and so much love that I'd be overcome by the magnitude of it if I didn't feel it myself.

I know we still have a lot to talk about, a lot to work through. But I trust us to figure it out. More importantly, I trust myself to try. If these past few weeks have shown me anything, it's just how much of my life has opened up now that I'm looking ahead instead of trying to hold on to what I've left behind. Now that I'm living for myself and my passion and for the people I love, and not just to get by.

So I don't worry about the words or the work or what's next. For a moment, there's only us—two people who have weathered a storm and come out together on the other side. Two people built to withstand more of them, when they come our way. Two people built to last.

I arch up and press my lips to Levi's, sinking into a deep, roaming kiss, the kind that really does feel like coming home. He presses me into the metal table until I slide back onto it. My legs straddle him as he closes the distance between us, holding a hand to the back of my neck to steady me as the kiss intensifies, two weeks' worth of ache and yearning pent up and spilling out of us at once. I'm half aware of where I am, and half dizzy with the need to touch every part of him I can possibly grab hold of, account for every piece I've been missing while he's been away.

Somewhere outside, a car door slams, followed by the telltale *beep beep* of someone locking it up. We pull away, both breathless, both searching each other's faces. Both seeing the heat of our own desire, and what's shifting into place under it. The understanding. The trust. All of it stronger now than it was even two weeks ago, fortified not just by a shared history, but a shared future.

Levi keeps his hand on the back of my neck for another moment, his eyes blazing with all of it at once. "I don't ever want to go that long without kissing you ever again," he says lowly.

I slide off the table, pressing another kiss to his lips, setting that clock back again. "That sounds like a good deal to me."

Levi's eyes soften on mine, the two of us suspended in the quiet promise of the words.

A few moments later, the door opens, and another baker comes in from the parking lot with a merry wave. Levi and I are both blushing faintly, the deeper conversation we still want to have hovering between us, a bookmark slid in it for later.

Later. That same calm washes over me again, now that I know we have time. The time Levi gave me, and the time stretching out in front of us farther than we can even see.

Levi works on his batch as I start pulling out ingredients, the two of us spending the next minute catching each other's eye and trying not to laugh like kids who almost got caught making out in the hallway. I'm about to ask Levi how the last of the move went when he preempts me by asking, "How was the football game last night?"

I set down a giant carton of eggs. "I can safely say I still know nothing about sports, but I *do* know that warm carbs are the only thing that can bring two rival teams together," I tell him. We sold out of our entire supply of Flight Risk scones before the end of the second half, and enough kids took a picture of the QR code Sana taped to the bus that I'm pretty sure we finally got our Gen Z "in."

Levi passes behind me to grab another pan, ghosting his hand on the small of my back. "What a wholesome, family-friendly sports movie you've just inspired. Did anyone burst into song?"

"Maybe next time. We've already been invited back for every game this season."

Levi's eyes are unabashedly proud. "Look at you, taking Benson Beach by storm."

It's hasn't even been two full weeks since we started using what Dylan dubbed the "Tea Tide Mobile" around town, but we've already made quite a name for ourselves. On weekdays we'll plant ourselves in places with foot traffic where we managed to get quick permits— close to the town square or in the parking lot of the boardwalk or outside the university. In the evening sometimes we'll head over to community events like football games and the big art show that the Benson Beach Museum of Arts hosted. Heck, one night we asked Games on Games if we could try our luck in the parking lot during trivia night and sold so many Wakey Fakeys that the owner joked about ditching the bar scene and opening a scone shop of his own.

It's literally chaos on wheels, but I love every second of it. I love the days when I'm manning the truck and get to talk to familiar faces and new ones. I love taking moments to explore at all these games and events and feeling like I'm part of the currents rippling through Benson Beach again. I love when someone pokes their head in and asks a question I haven't heard in a long time, one that makes something under me hum with pride: "What are the specials for today?"

And most of all, I love that it's been a team effort every step of the way. That there are already memories of people I love in every corner of the truck. The little scone doodle with stick legs and arms Mateo drew as a joke that we ended up putting on all the fliers people can grab with their order. The driver's seat of the truck that now permanently smells like Dylan's aftershave. The window where I got a truly iconic picture of Sana leaning down to plant a kiss on her now-boyfriend Aiden while handing him a scone.

And now Levi, here and making scones with his own hands, part of this new world of mine that's been opening up by the day. One that feels wider and more full of potential than it ever did, even when I was seeing more of the world than anyone I knew. One that makes me feel more like myself than I have in years. My life is more unsettled than it's ever been, but I've never felt more settled in it.

"Oh, hey. Now that you're here—I wanted to show you something I found." I pull the binder open to the folder in the back, where I tucked away Levi's notes. "These are super old, but Annie had them in the back of Tea Tide."

Levi blinks at them in confusion. "I don't even remember writing these." He thumbs through them slowly, his eyes catching on a few of the ideas in confusion or amusement. He shakes his head, and when he looks back at me, there's a bright energy in the blue of his eyes. "This is wild. I think I wrote these all down in the same day."

I tap the pages. "And just goes to show you how bottomless that brain of yours is," I say. "I know you were worried about having other ideas after you wrapped up this manuscript, but that's just it. You're brimming with them."

"It's been a long time," says Levi, with a trace of doubt in his voice.

"It's also been a long time since you've let yourself be in this mindset," I say. "You just need to let yourself have time to ease into it is all."

Levi's eyes linger on the pages, and I feel my words sinking in, even if it takes him a moment to speak. "Or maybe I just need to get cracking on whatever this . . ." Levi squints at his own handwriting. "'*You've Got Mail*, but ghosts' plot was supposed to be."

I stand on my tiptoes to get a better look at the page because I missed that one. "The only thing spicier than rivals in love are undead rivals in love," I say.

Levi's lip quirks. It's not the almost-smile anymore, though. Just a soft and genuine one. It occurs to me that I haven't seen the almost-smile in weeks.

"Thank you, June. Not for saving these, uh . . . banner ideas from teenage me," he says, not without a bit of sheepishness. He lowers his voice. "But for reminding me. And for believing in me."

I feel the warmth of it twofold—not just the belief I have in Levi, but knowing how much it means to him.

"Of course," I say. "The faster we expand out the Levi literary universe, the better. Speaking of, I meant to ask—has that editor gotten back to you yet?"

"Oh." Levi sets the pages back down on top of the binder, scratching the back of his neck. "So—I didn't submit it."

I blink. "But you finished it."

"I did, but then . . ."

He shakes his head, letting out a breathy laugh.

"When I first wrote it, I had this sense there was something wrong with it. I thought that's why it needed rewriting. But I realized the problem wasn't with the writing, it was just—it wasn't me." He looks right at me then, and says, "Or at least, it's not anymore."

"So you're just going to leave it be?"

He considers his answer carefully. "The way I see it—if that book sells, and I have to commit to writing more books like it . . . I'm not going to have a very long career, because I'm going to be miserable for every second of writing those, too."

Levi tilts his head at me with a teasing expression, like he's waiting for an "I told you so." And I won't lie—there's a part of me that is more than a little relieved at this turn of events. But there's a much louder part of me that's worried about where this leaves Levi.

"Well," I settle on saying, "I'm glad that it isn't you anymore. Because it seemed like a lonely way to be."

Levi nods. "It was. I'm glad I had it to cope at the time. But I think that's all it really was—just a way to get through it by trying to pull myself outside of it." He tilts his chin down to level with me. "I don't want to pull myself out of my life anymore."

"So how are you feeling now?" I ask. "I mean, writing-wise."

And now Levi's teasing expression shifts into a full-on smirk. "You're about to be a very smug woman."

"Have you tasted my scones? I'm already a very smug woman."

Levi leans in, setting his palms on the metal table to steady himself, a quiet electricity in his eyes that already feels like it's humming in me, too.

"I read the notes you found on *The Sky Seekers*. And then after I finished the other manuscript, I sat down and read them again. And then I opened up my laptop and I just—" He shakes his head, laughing to himself. "It was like the words were bleeding onto the page. I couldn't type them fast enough."

A grin cracks my face so quickly it might split it in half. "I'm not going to be smug. I'm going to be insufferable."

He smiles right back, but raises his hands up and says quickly, "Don't get excited yet. I'm moving slower now. There are a lot of things I can't remember. And things that I definitely need to retool." He pauses for a moment, considering. "But it's not like being stuck with the other manuscript. It's a nice kind of stuck. Like before it felt like there was only one road I could go down, and it was a mess.

But now it's like—there are too many to choose from. It's a nice change of pace."

I nod, the grin on my face softening into a close-lipped smile. Whatever it is that's crackling in the back of his eyes right now, I feel it, too. I've been feeling it ever since the truck hit the road and I started getting a front-row seat to people's reactions to the old scone specials.

"It's funny," I say, "because weirdly, that's how I feel about coming up with new ideas for scones. Like there are all these new ways I could go with them, but there's so much going on I could draw from that I don't even know where to start."

Levi presses in close enough that we're shoulder to shoulder and gives me a slight nudge. "Maybe we brainstorm, then. Help each other out."

I'm quiet for a moment. Then I say carefully, "Maybe we do it back in our woods, the way we used to."

Levi blinks, and abruptly our tone shifts from teasing to sincere. "Do you have any time today?" he asks.

My flutter of anticipation is so absurd that it feels like I stole something back from childhood. "We'll probably drive the truck back to the lot around three."

"Text me," says Levi. "I'll come meet you."

As if on cue, Sana waltzes into the kitchen, hair pulled into her topknot, rocking the new apron she embroidered for herself that says SCONE DADDY on the front pocket. She halts the moment she sees Levi.

"Oh, he's not allowed to be here." She gestures at Levi with an open palm. "This is objectively too hot, and we don't have time to shoot a scone-baking calendar right now. Out."

"That's not a terrible idea," I say, looking Levi up and down. "Maybe he could borrow your apron."

"Not on your life, September," he says, the tips of his ears going red.

Sana jerks a thumb toward the parking lot. "But actually, you should jet. Dylan's out front to give you a ride back to your place."

Levi winces. "Next order of business—getting myself a car." He looks at me pointedly. "Preferably one that doesn't belong in a LEGO house."

"Your disrespect for Bugaboo knows no bounds," I say.

He leans in and presses a quick kiss to my temple. "See you this afternoon."

Sana wiggles her eyebrows and hardly waits for the front door to close behind Levi before she says, "Um? Details, immediately? Also—and I cannot emphasize this enough—how dare he. There's only room for one scone daddy in your life and that position's taken."

"Don't you worry, I think you're safe. Also, what brings you here bright and early?" I ask.

"I wanted to help. And also scam a free scone. But mostly run the draft of the piece I'm submitting for *Fizzle* past you," she says, with an uncharacteristic self-consciousness.

My eyes widen. "It's finally ready?"

She lifts a hand up with a so-so gesture. "It's getting there."

Just then, my phone lights up on the table where I left it, Griffin's name popping up on the screen. I make a gagging face and am just about to send it to voice mail when Sana reaches out and stills my hand.

"Wait. Answer it," says Sana. "I want to hear what he has to say."

I tilt my head at her. "Why?"

"Research purposes for the article." Sana pulls out her phone and starts recording a voice memo, then shoots me a quick, apologetic smirk. "Humor me."

I shrug, swiping to answer the phone and pressing the speaker button. Griffin doesn't even wait a beat before launching into what appears to be a very prepared spiel. "I know you're angry with me right now, but you know I did that special for *you*, right? For Tea Tide. So you could keep getting more business."

"Oh?" I say, turning to Sana, both of our eyebrows rising immediately.

"If you'd just let me explain instead of running off like that, you'd know I was doing it for your own good," says Griffin. "They want you to be on the next season of the show, you know."

Sana has to shove her face into the crook of her elbow to muffle her laugh. I keep talking, if only so Sana's curiosity is sated. Considering all the help she's put into Tea Tide, I owe her a lot more than that.

"I've had such a lovely time on it, how tempting," I say.

"Look—you can believe me or not." Griffin lets out a performative breath. "But I care about you, June. More than Levi with his stupid fake dating thing, dragging you along the *exact* same way he did in high school."

I know he's digging at the bottom of the barrel now, because never once in our relationship did he acknowledge the clear crushes Levi and I had on each other in high school. He must really be willing to throw his pride into the wringer if he's copping to it now.

"And we had a good thing going, June," Griffin persists. "We still do, if . . . I mean. If you're open to it."

Sana mouths words that I suspect are *The audacity! Of this man!!!* as I lean toward the phone and say mildly, "And this sudden change of heart has nothing to do with the fact that the internet hates you for dragging me through the mud again?"

I didn't bother checking myself, but Sana has gleefully filled my inbox with tweets and articles over the past two weeks. After the initial shock of the interview, the narrative shifted out from under Griffin pretty fast—my favorite commentary ranged from literally why can't he leave crying girl alone?? let her fake date that hot piece of ass in peace????? to pretty sure griffin would step on god's face to get more attention. It didn't stop me and Levi from getting heat, but watching Griffin's plan backfire made it a little easier to swallow, that's for sure.

Griffin waits a moment to answer, and I can practically hear his teeth grinding through the phone. "Let them hate me. You're the only one whose opinion matters."

"Well, that's unfortunate," I say easily, "because I think you're a joke."

"June, I'm trying to tell you I *love* you," says Griffin adamantly. "I always have, and I always will."

It should sting that this is actually the first time Griffin's ever said those words to me out loud, but all I want to do is laugh. Except then the realization clicks into place, and I'm not laughing—I'm straight up cackling.

"Oh my god," I wheeze. "Oh my *god*. Lisel dumped you."

There's a telling beat of silence, and then Griffin says tightly, "We're broken up."

I look to Sana, who nods at me. Whatever she wanted out of this call, she must have gotten it.

I feel a strange kind of buoyancy then, knowing the next words I say to Griffin are going to be the last. "I'm hanging up now," I tell him. "Good luck with your life."

The instant the phone disconnects, Sana and I both burst into hysterics, falling into each other and laughing so hard that every head in the commercial kitchen swivels around to look at us.

"That was priceless," says Sana, tapping the button on her phone to stop the recording.

"And will live forever in infamy now," I say as she saves the file. "Are you going to sell that to the highest bidder?"

"God, the temptation. We could buy so much Taco Bell with that money. But no." She shifts on her stool. "Honesty hour. This piece I'm trying to write and pitch for *Fizzle*—it's about gaslighting in millennial relationships, using Griffin as the peg. I've been interviewing psychologists and looking at the dynamics of other internet-adjacent couples in public breakups and how the media coverage shifted public opinion. It's a whole deep dive."

"Holy shit," I manage, both surprised and impressed. "That is precisely the kind of article you'd kill at. And *Fizzle* would kill for."

"Right?" says Sana, her eyes getting that hungry gleam in them when she's right on the verge of cracking a good story. It's been a long time since I've seen it. "It's getting a little more personal, though, so I want to check in with you before I submit it. Now that the Revenge Ex thing got blown up anyway, I was thinking of getting more specific about how you and Levi started just for context for the article."

I smirk. "It also makes a great peg. Very clickable."

Sana elbows me in the arm. "You can take the girl outta digital media . . ."

"Oh, trust me. The digital media is fully out of the girl. There are only scones in here now," I say, gesturing at myself. If I never see another headline about Griffin or Kelly or the whole mess of this summer, it'll be too soon. "But to be clear, you have my blessing. I'd just run it past Levi, but I'm sure he'll be fine with it, too."

Sana leans in, eyes on the door Levi walked out of earlier. "Speaking of, that situation seems . . . resolved?" she says. "Judging by the kissing and the scone-making and the 'see you this afternoon' of it all."

I smile down at the scone batter I've been neglecting. "We still haven't talked."

"Talking's overrated," says Sana, taking over Levi's batch where he left off.

"Says the woman interviewing psychologists."

"And what for?" says Sana. "When I clearly should just quit writing and become a matchmaker full-time."

"I thought you were our handler."

She hip-checks me. "And I *handled* getting you two alone so you'd eventually get your heads out of your asses and fall for each other for real."

I raise my eyebrows at her. "What if we hadn't, hmm? What if we became mortal enemies and terrorized Benson Beach with our mutual hatred the rest of our days?"

I'm joking, but abruptly, Sana is not. She gets in close, raising her eyebrows right back. "June. I saw the way you two looked at each other the literal first moment he got back into town, and I knew the two of you had it bad," she says. "Also you take for granted that I have pretty much stalked the two of you every step of the way. You and Levi—you're perfect for each other."

The words are so blunt that they take me by surprise, but just as quickly, I feel the warmth of them spreading in me, taking deep roots. "Yeah?"

"Yeah." Sana slows her scone work down to a stop, and really looks at me then. "You know what it is? Other than the absurd chemistry of two hot people being mutually attracted to each other, of course."

I resist the temptation to roll my eyes, knowing from the look she's leveling at me that she's about to get serious.

"It's that both of you were a little bit lost a few weeks ago. But neither of you pushed. Nudged, occasionally. But mostly just encouraged each other. Tried to make things easier, when you could." Sana's expression is far away for a moment, almost dreamy, like she's here and not. "Neither of you wants to change the other one or tell the other what to do. You just want each other to be happy. And that's what love is supposed to look like."

My throat goes tight. For a moment, I'm there again—the June I was a few weeks ago, getting to know the Levi he was then. We were more than a little lost, I know, but Sana's words give me a new perspective I hadn't fully understood yet. Levi and I spent most of our adult lives with people who pushed us. Who amplified qualities that were already there, but to serve their own purposes. Kelly took advantage of the part of Levi that wanted everything settled and planned, and Griffin took advantage of the part of me that loved exploring new things. They didn't just push us, but pushed us too far.

And we fell into those patterns because we thought they made sense for us. We held on to them for dear life because we thought that because they understood us, it was meant to be. But the truth is, we'd never known what it was like not to just be understood, but supported. Believed in. Cared about for more than what we could offer, but what we already were, what we wanted to be.

Or maybe I did already know that feeling. I think about Levi when we were kids, always waiting for me at the bottom of those absurdly high trees. Never telling me not to go up or when to come down. Just steadily being there if I needed him, the way he still is today.

It's always been there between us, I realize. We were just waiting to remember how it felt.

"That . . ." I have to take another breath to steady my voice. "Thank you for saying that. That's a really beautiful way of putting it."

Sana reaches out and gives the hand I have on the table a quick squeeze. "Well, like you said," she says cheekily. "I *have* been interviewing psychologists the whole week."

"You might be a great matchmaker, Sana," I say, "but you're also a fucking great best friend."

Sana grins widely, slapping her hand down on the scone dough. "And don't you forget it."

Chapter Twenty-six

As kids, it was easy for us to imagine that our woods had magic in them simply because it was ours. The beach where we spent most of our time was an open stage where we saw everyone and everything, where we were always seen in turn. Like the expanse of the ocean promised a certain kind of freedom that the beach could never quite deliver because there was never anywhere to hide.

But the woods were insular, the paths tangled, and everywhere you turned there were tall, ancient trees that would keep your secrets. That would hide your edges and hold your stories, blot out the too-bright sun and muffle the too-loud world. It was our first real taste of independence, of existing in a world where we governed ourselves. We would lose ourselves in it, sometimes together, sometimes splitting off in pairs or on our own, and always reenter the world in a kind of haze, like we'd gone somewhere much farther than the edge of town. And the way Levi would spin stories through these trees, weave them through the twisting paths, it sometimes felt like I'd come back from an entirely different world.

Walking through these woods now, seeing them with these fresh eyes so much higher from the ground, I still feel the rustle of that old magic in the low, late-summer breeze. I smell it in the distinct, briny sea salt against the fresh pine. I feel it in Levi's warm hand wrapped around mine, the hand he took a few minutes ago when we reached the mouth of the trail and walked back into this place together for the first time in years.

Levi squeezes my hand and I look up at him and see a reflection of that magic in his eyes, too. Something lost but never fully forgotten, something that is changing its shape to adjust to the new shapes of us.

"Tell me where you left off in the story," I say to Levi.

And he does. A lot of it is still easy for me to follow because I read the same notes Levi was working from. But once he starts digging in deeper, there are moments of thoughtful quiet between us that are punctuated by one of us lighting up with a memory or a new idea. Some of the pieces come back quickly, and others seem to stretch, like they're taking their time waking up. We reminisce and remind and rebuild, breathing life into the old story even as Levi starts to shift some of the pieces and make them new. Like we're not just walking down a path back to the stories we used to share, but a bridge between the past that built us and the future we're building.

We reach the top of one of the highest of the small peaks on the trail, and it feels like a good settling point for now. Like if we get any further, there will be too much for Levi to have to remember to write down later. Not that it will matter—I already feel all the ideas pressing into me the way they did when I was a kid, and I carried them around with me for weeks. Some of them tightly enough that I still have them with me after all these years.

Levi settles his gaze on me, and there's a quiet intensity in it that stirs deep in my chest. He steps in closer, shadows and light from the trees casting golden afternoon sun on his face, and I think for a moment he's going to kiss me. I lean in with anticipation, but when my eyes are firmly set on his, he stays rooted in place.

"I know you think I didn't put you in the story," says Levi, his voice low and steady, "but that's just it. You are the story. I started it for you. Before I wanted to be a writer. Before I wanted anything much at all. I just wanted to watch that look on your face whenever I told it."

I smile up at him. "So you wrote me a story about the people I love," I say. There's an entirely different magic in understanding this; one that will never be written explicitly on the page but felt in the space between every word.

He couldn't have known then that it wouldn't be just a story, but a remembrance. Another way of keeping Annie's love in our lives, of capturing that fire of hers that we can still feel the warmth of even now. I feel the same ache for her I'll always feel, but the grief is shifting again in that way it has since I lost her—I don't feel the guilt of it anymore. It makes so much more room for the love.

Levi's voice is hoarse when he speaks again. "I want to keep making stories with you, June. Stories that are all our own."

I nod, the words feeling like they're sealing something between us. "Me too."

He takes my hands again, weaving his fingers through mine. "I know I said I'd give you time. And I mean it. But I want you to know that everything's settled now. I left my job. I squared everything away with the old apartment and finalized my lease here. I'm not asking for anything from you. I'm hoping. I'm—" He swallows hard. "You know how I feel. I know it doesn't undo the past. But I'm still hoping for the future."

I squeeze his fingers with mine, a smile curling at my lips. "Levi, nothing's settled," I say. "We're two big messes right now, you and me. But I don't need settled. And I don't need any more time. I just needed—I needed to be sure of something in myself, before I let myself be sure of this. I needed to let myself move on. And right now I need . . ."

I search his eyes, and then trail my gaze down to his lips. I tilt my head just as he leans in, and the kiss feels like a final floodgate opening, like a swollen sky has split and finally let out a swell of perfect, warm rain to wash our hearts clean. Like we're finally coming together with our whole selves, every certainty and messy, unformed part of us, every piece we've held back and pieces we haven't even formed yet to give.

It sweeps up again under our feet, in the loose pines shaken by the wind, in the promise of a new season just as the one you're holding on to gets chased away: magic. We've felt it before. Spent years trying to feel it again. One quiet promise, one soul-stirring kiss, and it all spills back and leaves this impossible happiness in its wake.

We stand at that peak for a long time, holding each other, sealing ourselves up tight. We talk about things of great and little importance, things present and yet to come. We talk about the wedding and talk further into the future—to Sana's birthday and the long list of songs she has lined up for karaoke, to Dylan and Mateo's one-year anniversary and the cake flavor they still haven't decided on for the top tier, to what my parents are going to do with the house long-term. We talk like the future is a given. We talk long enough that the sun starts to dip low in the sky, nudging us back down the trail. He gathers my hand up in his again, and we start to make our way back home.

"We forgot to brainstorm scones," says Levi before we reach the trail opening.

For the first time in my life, I might actually be too dazed to think about baked goods. "Right," I say. "Well, we have a whole lot of misadventures to draw from."

"I personally would not object to an Uptown Funk scone," Levi suggests.

I raise my eyebrows at him, impressed that he came in with a snappy idea ready to go. "Ooh," I say, remembering our shared cold pizza on the couch. "Pepperoni and sun-dried tomato with a mozzarella cheese crust."

"Now *that* is a scone I'd enjoy," says Levi.

"Domino's, but make it bougie." I twist my lip to the side, thinking. "Maybe a Gallery Game scone?"

"Carrot cake–flavored," says Levi solemnly, "as an homage to those terrifying cartoon carrots."

I give him a surprised once-over. "Wow. For someone who hates desserts, you're an excellent partner-in-scones."

Levi slows his pace then until we both ease to a stop. "I've got another idea, too." He looks almost bashful when he adds, "Actually, I went ahead and took the liberty of making a test batch."

Levi shrugs off the small drawstring backpack he brought with him, opening it up to reveal a Tea Tide scone sleeve. I can smell it before I can fully see it—the bright burst of orange and the headiness of milk chocolate. It's heaven in a scone.

"I figured if you were going to make a Levi scone, I'd make you a June one," he says, handing it to me.

I hold it up, taking in the flecks of orange zest and hunks of chocolate, the scone perfectly crisped. Levi wasn't kidding. He really was paying attention to the scone-making in the back. And to me, with my old love for milk chocolate and new obsession with citrus. A scone that's part old June and part new.

"Aw. I feel bad," I say, on the verge of a laugh. "The Levi scone was a punch line. You actually made me a dream scone."

"I heard your punch line is selling out when it rotates in on Tuesdays and Fridays, so I'll take it on the chin." Levi nods at the scone, and when he meets my eye, I see a quick glint of mischief in his. "Go on. Try it."

I hold his gaze as I take a bite. He really outdid himself. The scone has a perfect, satisfying crunch on the outside and just the right density on the inside, the zesty orange flavor balanced perfectly with the richness of the chocolate. Just as I'm about to ask him how the heck he mastered the delicate art of scone-making just by watching, I feel it—a telltale *crackle, pop, pop*, tiny fireworks on my tongue, between my teeth.

"You did *not*," I cackle as the Pop Rocks start to go off in earnest, loud enough that I'm sure Levi can hear it, too.

He finally breaks out in a smile he's clearly been trying to hold back. "You set yourself up for this."

"And you set yourself up for *this*," I say, reaching up to wrap my fingers through the soft curls on the back of his head, pulling him in for a kiss. Soon enough, there are Pop Rocks going off in both of our mouths, and we're laughing through the kiss, the vibrations of it pulsing through each other's bodies.

We're breathless by the time our lips part, our foreheads still pressed together, leaning against each other like we'll fall over laughing if we don't. Our eyes meet, and I feel our own kind of crackle in them—the instant recognition, the unmatched understanding. The way we have always been able to see deep into the cores of each other, to feel the depths of the other's hurts and triumphs and everything in between. A thread between us that kept its pull even after all these years apart, too steady to break, too strong to unravel.

"I love you," I say, the words easier than any I've ever spoken out loud. They've been a part of me for so long that it feels like they were beating in my heart long before they left my lips.

Levi's smile softens. His eyes, which had been brimming with laughter, now brim with something else. He holds my gaze, and I feel the love between us like a lifeline. Like the thread is tightening, holding us closer than we've ever been.

My own eyes are starting to tear up at the sight of his. Levi kisses me again, slow and deep. When we break apart, he says quietly into my ear, "I love you, too."

It's only the second time I've heard him say it, but I already know that it won't matter how many times I hear it. I'll still feel the warm tingle of it spread through me every time.

"And to think," Levi quips, "all it took was a scone."

I laugh, wet and muffled. Levi thumbs a stray tear away, and I look up at him and say, "Yeah. We could have saved a whole lot of time with all our fake dates, huh?"

"Oh, yeah. What a drag those were," says Levi, pulling me in closer. "What a task it was finally getting to hold your hand in that museum," he says, wrapping his fingers through mine. "What a bummer seeing you move in that ridiculously sexy dress," he adds, using his other hand to skim my hip and reach back to lightly squeeze my ass. He draws in even closer and says into my ear, "What a shame to know the exact face you make when you . . ." He lets the words hover, warm and teasing. "Take a really good bite of a scone."

The blush might start in my cheeks, but by the time he's finished speaking, it's spread all over my body, a relentless, crackling flame. "Thank goodness you survived," I say wryly, my own hands wandering to his back, pulling him flush against me.

Levi's breath hitches just slightly, and I can feel the exact reason why pressed against my hip. "Yeah," he says, swallowing thickly. "Thank goodness."

I'm already straying far beyond this spot where we're standing, like the heat of my desire was just waiting for me to fan it, to burn up all the other thoughts. I only separate myself from Levi and start walking because there is a long list of things I'd like to do with those flames, and none of them can happen here.

"I guess we should finally, officially end our pact," I manage to say, despite the breathlessness.

Levi's hand has already eased back into mine. "We can make it a promise, instead."

I nod slowly, letting the satisfaction of this moment sink in. Pressing it to my heart so I'll always remember the feeling, even if I won't be able to recall the words.

"I like the sound of that."

"Good." Levi's eyes glint again as he adds, "We'll get Sana to draw up the terms."

It only takes a few more steps for us to reach the edge of the woods and slowly make our way out of the trail. Only it doesn't feel like it did when we were kids, like trading one world for another. The magic follows us back out this time. It's still pressed between our fingers, steady in every step. It's old and it's new, unchanged and changing, but always, always ours.

Epilogue

One Year Later

$\mathcal{D}$ ylan pokes at the little cake on its stand. "I think it's ready."

I swat his hand. "It's going to be full of holes if you keep that up."

In true form, Dylan can bench press 250 pounds, run a marathon, and climb precariously steep trails like a mountain goat, but somehow cannot manage enough self-control to let the top tier of his wedding cake defrost for his and Mateo's first anniversary.

"Besides, Sana's not here with the champagne yet," I remind him.

"She couldn't just grab something from the wine shop down the street?"

"Dylan. This is our 'Jam-four-ee,'" I say, parroting the nickname that he gave this night himself, since we are celebrating four distinct occasions at once. "You think Sana wasn't going to seize on the opportunity to get one of those gigantic, toddler-size champagne bottles at the liquor store?"

His eyes light up. "Is she really?"

"Yes. And you're in charge of opening it. What else was all this lifting for, if not leading up to this specific task?"

The lights brighten around us then, illuminating the front of the shop—illuminating the brand-new Tea Tide. I glance around the familiar space with its unfamiliar new shades, and for a moment I feel a swell of pride so intense it nearly bowls me over. It took a solid year of hustling out of the commercial kitchen, driving the food truck all over Benson Beach, but little by little, we carved out enough of a space for ourselves in town that we were able to bring Tea Tide back to its original location, where everything began.

This isn't the Tea Tide it used to be, though. We've swapped out the vintage teacups for cozy mugs. The dainty florals and pastels are now a little bit bigger and brighter. The tables and chairs are lighter, easier to move around the space for events and rotating weekly themed nights. There's art from local artists hanging on the walls for sale, in collaboration with the museum. It's louder and looser and Benson Beach down to its core, a "no shoes, no problem" kind of vibe, somewhere you can kick back after a long day at the beach or relax with a book. Somewhere you can walk inside and get a sense not just of Tea Tide, but of the whole town it calls home.

Nancy had been subletting the old space for the year we were gone, but after seeing the strides we were making, she offered us the space back to bring that same energy into a fresh, new Tea Tide—one we both knew I could handle, now that we'd ingrained ourselves so deeply in the community. And as overwhelming as it might have been to make another big shift back into the space, the transition was almost seamless, like collecting all these threads we'd been weaving over the last year and finally twisting them into something whole.

With the new décor and vibe, it may seem like a total revamp, but after a year like this, it isn't, really. We've been at the heart of so many local events and gatherings with the Tea Tide Mobile that it was just a matter of collecting parts of Benson Beach along the way. Now we have a bartender from Games on Games who is leading game nights on Tuesdays, a bunch of university students who are leading an open mic on Wednesdays, Levi himself spearheading writer nights on Thursdays, and a local band we'd park next to when they performed in the park doing live music on Sundays. It's been a slow and steady change, one that has had its fair share of growing pains, but one we've grown into just the same.

Tonight, we're setting the stage, but tomorrow—our official reopening—we'll get to see it all come to life. I'm so excited, it will be a miracle if I sleep a wink.

"Were you guys just going to celebrate in the dark?" asks Levi, coming in from the back with his hand on the light switch, the other hand occupied with holding several champagne glasses.

In my defense, I've been so busy with last-minute touches to Jam-four-ee and keeping Dylan away from his own cake that I didn't realize the sun was starting to set.

"We were just waiting for you, the light of our lives," I tease, walking over to kiss him hello. It's been five hours max since we took a lunch break together at the condo we're now both living in, but with all the flurry of preparing for tonight's celebration and tomorrow's opening, it feels like we've been *go, go, go* all week.

Levi sets the glasses on the table, then leans in to deepen the kiss, settling his hands on my waist. I feel the last lingering stress of the day ease out of me as I sink into the familiar warmth of him, breathing in that earthy-sweet smell.

"Happy Tea Tide Eve," Levi says, eyes bright when he pulls away.

Mateo pointedly clears his throat to get past us, plates and napkins in hand to set on the little table at the center of Tea Tide where we've propped the cake and a little shrine to all the things we're celebrating, including some new scones. Levi and I pull apart, his hands still on my waist, as Mateo takes in the display.

"Dare I even ask what this one is?" asks Mateo, pointing at a plate of scones.

"A *Fizzle* scone," I say, beaming. "A Red Bull base with a baked Pringles crust."

Of the four celebrations tonight, one is marking the one-year anniversary of Sana's job at *Fizzle*, which they offered her almost immediately after her article, "Griffin Hapler: A Study in Modern Millennial Gaslighting," went so viral that everyone from college students to stay-at-home parents to pop stars was retweeting it. It only further blew up when Lisel not only shared it on Instagram but went way further into detail in a video about Griffin's manipulative personality than anyone was anticipating. (Griffin is now relishing a pseudo-career as the "villain" in *Business Savvy* spin-offs, which suits everyone just fine.)

Safe to say, Sana has been kicking ass right and left with hard-hitting cultural commentary pieces ever since. If we made a new scone every time one of her pieces went viral, we'd probably need to add another floor to Tea Tide.

"Hell yeah," says Dylan, visibly restraining himself from taking a bite of one.

"I'm scared of the inside of your brain," says Levi, not without affection.

"And this one?" Mateo asks.

"The Sky Seekers scone. Blueberry and sriracha." Off Mateo's curious look, I shrug. "It's the closest thing I could think of for a 'water and fire' theme like the main characters' powers."

Levi smiles over my head, because it's also one of the few scones he'll actually eat since it isn't a "giant cookie." And also because he is sheepish that we're celebrating *The Sky Seekers* at all when he insists there's nothing to celebrate over yet. But a few months ago, when he finished the first version of the manuscript, the editor interested in his New York book put him in touch with an agent who specialized in young adult novels. The agent loved it, and now that the two of them have gone back and forth perfecting the draft these past few weeks, they're finally going to start submitting the finalized version to editors, starting tomorrow. Plenty to celebrate, in my opinion.

Mateo doesn't have to ask about the third plate of scones—the Revenge Ex, which we only whip out on special occasions these days. It seems like coming full circle on Tea Tide opening again counts as the perfect one.

"Oh, phew," says Sana, walking in with a champagne bottle large enough to hold half the Atlantic. "I was just texting Aiden to make bets over whether Dylan would wait for me before he wolfed down the cake."

"I wouldn't dream of it," says Dylan, taking the bottle from her. And then, after a beat: "But if we don't pop that bottle soon, I *am* going to start eating it with my bare hands."

We make quick work of our "cheers" then, raising our glasses to Sana's eloquent toast: "To all of us being stupidly in love and kicking ass at life." A minute later, we're cutting into the defrosted cake—a pistachio cake with lemon zest and lemon frosting, two flavors that do, in fact, pair perfectly together—and lounging on the cozy bench with mismatched pillows I put right up in the front, where there's a picturesque view of the ocean. We spend the evening recounting funny moments from Dylan and Mateo's wedding ("I didn't know June could scream like that until 'Uptown Funk' came on," says Mateo, haunted), Sana's favorite articles ("I still can't believe I made a former cast member of *The Office* cry!"), our upcoming plans for the still-operational Tea Tide Mobile, and the ideas Levi is tentatively outlining before he decides on what to write next.

Once the night winds down and we've finished picking up after ourselves, I feel a thrill of anticipation and excitement jolt through me. They're those nervous first-day-of-school jitters I haven't felt in so long that I'm relishing them even as I take a breath and try to push them down.

Levi takes my hand in his, the gesture so instantly grounding that I feel myself relaxing even before he says, "Want to take a quick walk on the beach?"

I nod, squeezing his hand. We lock up the shop and I revel in the satisfaction of it, of having an entire place to open and close again, four solid walls that are distinctly, perfectly Tea Tide. Maybe not the Tea Tide we envisioned as kids, maybe not the Tea Tide Annie was striving for, but the Tea Tide that feels like home. The Tea Tide that feels like sitting on the porch with our mom, bare feet dangling from the chairs, little hands reaching for the decaf tea she poured out of the pot. The Tea Tide that feels like looking over at Annie from the brims of our mugs, a shared spark between sisters, a happy, hopeful, messy moment in time that feels more preserved in this version of Tea Tide than it ever was.

The warm breeze lifts Levi's curls and ghosts up my thin Tea Tide shirt as we wander down, still hand in hand, walking to the faint glow of the lamps on the boardwalk beyond us. It's a quiet night, the beach mostly empty, the waves sounding like little whispers against the sand.

"Hey," says Levi. "You want to race to the pier?"

I raise my eyebrows. We haven't done this in a while.

"What are we racing for?" I ask, turning to look up at Levi.

Only it's not the Levi I'm expecting to see, with that new, easy smile I've gotten used to or the old mischief in his eyes. They're both still there, but under something that's brimming, something that's hopeful and nervous and so sincere that it feels like the breeze has dipped low in my stomach before I even know what he's going to say.

His throat bobs, his eyes so earnest on mine that my heart starts fluttering in my chest like it's trying to fly out of it.

"If you win," he says, his voice quiet and steady, "you marry me."

All at once my eyes are welling up, a smile blooming on my face.

"And if you win?" I manage to ask through the tide already swelling in me, threatening to tip me over right into the sand.

"If I win, you marry me," he says, with a watery smile of his own.

I twist my lip, trying not to laugh, trying not to cry, but the way he's looking at me right now—with so much love that it puts the infinite expanse of the ocean to shame—it's proving a near impossible feat.

"Those are some pretty high stakes," I say, my throat tight with happiness.

Levi nods and says, "We'll have to give it our all."

"All right," I say, drawing a starting line in the sand. The first one I've ever drawn knowing that it doesn't have a finish. "On your mark—get set—*go.*"

And then we're off, feet flying, wind whipping around us, breathing in salt and sand, past and future, heartache and hope as we run our last race, the endless one, the only one that counts. The one that stretches beyond the pier, beyond the view I used to stare at from the top of my old tree, beyond the two of us, pulling us forward even as we push ourselves toward it. Already I can feel these moments becoming a part of our history; already I can feel the magic of them crystallizing in my heart, a steady certainty against wild joy. The beginning of something that isn't the end of anything else, that doesn't have an end of its own.

I know what's going to happen before Levi's arm wraps around my waist, before he swoops me up again the way he did a year ago, just before the photo of us in the sand dune went viral. I let out a giddy, half-shrieking laugh just the same as we cross the pier together and Levi angles us back into the dune, the two of us rolling in a heap until we come to a breathless stop, backs against the sand and eyes staring up at the stars. I turn my head toward his and find his eyes already on mine.

"Dead tie," he observes, shifting himself up to offer me his hand.

I take it, easing back onto my feet. "So what now?" I ask, lightly teasing as he pulls me in tight.

His voice is low, almost hoarse with feeling, as he gives me a quick squeeze before he lets me go. "It seems I'm just going to have to ask the old-fashioned way."

Levi's hand dips into his pocket, producing a small velvet box. He gets down on one knee in the sand, and I know he's probably had this planned for weeks—probably expected this to go a certain way—but suddenly I can't stand to have him that far from me, so I'm sinking to my knees too, facing Levi as his lip quirks through the beginning of happy tears.

"June Hart." His eyes have the same spark in them that I feel igniting in me, like we're passing back and forth a shared flame. "I'm already the luckiest person I know—lucky for every single day I've spent with you, from the time we were kids to the life we have now to all the days we have ahead."

He leans in close and opens the ring box, but I don't look down. I'm staring into the blue of his eyes and seeing that endless ocean from the top of the world again, a lifetime of possibility, a bright, wide-open future that's all ours.

"Will you marry me?"

I lean in to kiss him because he already knows my answer. Because we've known what we are to each other since the end of the very first race we ran, and every one we've run since—the two of us side by side in a constant tie. Same as we always have been, same as we always will be. Wherever it is we're going, we'll be together, every step of the way.

Acknowledgments

I would like to first and foremost thank the wild raccoon that snuck up on me and put its little paw on my keyboard while I was writing the first draft of this in Central Park. Your input was not necessarily welcome, but appreciated; if you want to discuss plot details on future novels any further, you (unfortunately) know where to find me.

My sincerest thank-yous as always go to Alex and Janna. Alex, your heart and your patience and joy for this genre are woven into every page of the books we've worked on together, but none as much as this one. I am so grateful for your guidance that if I tried to measure it on a scale against a thousand of our favorite desserts, the gratitude would still win out. Janna, so much of the happiness in my life is because you took a chance on baby me after that first phone call where you were like, "What genres do you like to write?" And I was like, ". . . What are the genres?" I have no idea what alternate universe I'd be existing in now without your support and understanding and tireless effort on my behalf, and I am deeply thankful I'll never find out.

Thank you to everyone at St. Martin's Press for helping pull this book out of the ether and turn it into a book-shaped thing. The labors of love that go into it are NO JOKE, and I am extremely in awe of everything that gets done behind the scenes.

In lieu of listing all my friends' names, this time I'm going to just put a sweeping "I love you" to all of you. I can't believe how lucky I am to have so many excellent humans holding my heartstrings; it has been the joy of my life to watch us all evolve and grow and become absolute unhinged gremlins at Taylor Swift concerts.

My biggest thank-you as always goes to my family. If I close my eyes and picture a perfect day from childhood, it starts with one of those weekend mornings we spent making scones and scamming chocolate chips from the bag, and ends any number of happy ways, because there are too many to count. What a lucky, delicious, good life.

About the Author

Clinton B. Photography

Emma Lord (she/her) is a digital media editor and writer living in New York City, where she spends whatever time she isn't writing either running or belting show tunes in community theater. She graduated from the University of Virginia with a major in psychology and a minor in how to tilt your computer screen so nobody will notice you updating your fan fiction from the back row. She was raised on glitter, a whole lot of love, and copious amounts of grilled cheese. Her books include *Tweet Cute, You Have a Match, When You Get the Chance,* and *Begin Again.*